BETTYANNE TWIGG & ALBERT
MARSOLAIS

Skyehag

First published by Marsolais & Twigg Publishing 2022

First edition

This book was professionally typeset on Reedsy.
Find out more at reedsy.com

This work of fiction is dedicated to those many who were unjustly persecuted as witches in Scotland of old.

Contents

Preface

This is a fictional story about Norman MacLeod (b. 1685, d. 1706), 20th Chief of Clan MacLeod as told by his friends, Elspeth MacLeod and Malcolm Forrester.

Chapter 1: Elspeth

On the road between Edinburgh and Glasgow, Scotland; July 1705

There was no pain, just a feeling of having been struck. The arrow that fixed my upper left arm to the back of the stagecoach seat quivered slightly as the vehicle's wheels lurched over the rutted road. A streak of blood had already discolored the stuff of my sleeve. I was held as surely as a pinned insect. Was someone hunting this close to the road to Glasgow, or was it a highwayman bold or desperate enough to brave daylight? I considered the package from Robert Bruce, a goldsmith in Edinburgh, which lay in one of my trunks. 'Twas nothing grand enough to warrant chancing this, only a dozen knives and forks, salts, a thimble, and two snuffboxes, and we are yet scarce out of Edinburgh! The only other possessions of value were my books. The small trunk containing the ones I was taking to Skye was under my seat. Concealed in its false bottom was a priceless ancient grimoire that not even Janet knew about. I had brought it back from Italy. It was on the list of forbidden books, but surely no one in Scotland realized I had it. All this blazed through my mind as I fought to make sense of what had just happened.

There had been a shout then the coach slowed, followed by a stamping of feet overhead from passengers riding on the roof. And after hours of being jostled about, Scathach, my hugely pregnant mastiff, had vomited the remains of some tiny creature onto my feet and the floor, and I had bent down to twitch the hem of my skirt out of harm's way. That movement saved my life.

Cawdie placed his strapping bulk between me and the window and pulled the leather curtain across the opening. Dark auburn hair clubbed at the nape framed his face and revealed blue eyes filled with concern and a nose that might have been noble had it not been broken too many times. Things blurred for a moment. Janet reached for me, but I shook my head. I was pinioned at an awkward angle and the dog was still vomiting wet warmth on my ankle and shoe. I finally found my voice. "Janet, cut away the cloth. I need to see."

Janet nodded in her composed way, pulled up her skirts, removed the *sgian dubh* dagger from its sheath on her calf, and quickly cut around my sleeve above the arrow. Slitting the fabric over the shaft, she pulled the bottom half down and off. The arrowhead was solidly embedded in the wood of the coach. It had passed through the fleshy part of my upper arm and the thinly padded seat back. The shaft was so near the surface that the ridge of skin stretched tightly over it was defined clearly. Not dangerous then, just a flesh wound. I considered it as dispassionately as I could manage. I could have Janet slit the skin over the raised ridge or I could just pull my arm from the arrow in a reverse of the *per expulsionem* method I had learned while at medical school in Italy. I chose the latter. No need to enlarge the injury. "We will need cloths from my bag. When I pull away, it will be messy. Cawdie, you will have to break the fletch off," I said serenely, my voice trembling only a little.

Cawdie was Janet's betrothed. He had been appointed my guard when I left Skye to study medicine. Janet Ross was my handmaiden, though she was but eleven years older than me. Her parents were killed during a raid by the MacDonalds on the day my mother died giving me birth. My father saw me as the cause of her death, and naught but a useless lass at that. I was told he simply walked away and took the King's shilling. The Chief of Clan MacLeod, weary from fighting, and having no time nor patience for drama, thrust me, still bloody and wailing, into Janet's thin arms. My screams stopped her tears, and she has cared for me for twenty-two years. Cawdie has been in love with her for half that time. He protects us with his life.

Cawdie bent to me, grasped the shaft firmly between his right hand and the finger and thumb of his left, then snapped the feathered end off about two inches from where it entered my arm. Janet placed a towel loosely around my arm below the arrow. I inhaled deeply and tugged my arm forward off the broken remains. The feel of wood sliding through raw flesh left me nauseated. Blood flooded from both entry and exit wounds into the towel. I let it, as it would cleanse the wounds. After a moment, Janet pulled the towel up over both holes and secured it firmly with strips of linen. I tried to smile my gratitude to the woman who was my mother in all but birthing. She and Cawdie exchanged unspoken words with their eyes, in that infuriating way that people who care about you communicate. Cawdie looked down thoughtfully at the fletch, pulled the rest of the bloody shaft from the seat, rolled both pieces in a scrap of cloth, and placed them somewhere in the folds of his plaid. My arm began to hurt.

The stagecoach had stopped. Sounds of hoofbeats and shouting could be heard from without. Cawdie opened the coach door and jumped down lightly. I could not resist putting my head out a bit to see, though Janet pulled imploringly at my uninjured arm. One of the outriders sent as protection lay motionless on the track behind us, his horse prancing nervously nearby, reins trailing. An arrow jutted from the man's back. Two of the remaining outriders circled nearby, guarding the coach, while a third galloped away in pursuit of the lone attacker who had vanished into a nearby copse. The outside passengers noisily scrambled down from the top and basket of the stagecoach, adding to the tumult. Cawdie ran to the downed outrider, knelt, and turned him carefully on his side. The highwayman's aim had been true. The outrider was dead.

Cawdie closed the sightless eyes gently, stood and returned to the two outriders. The third came back as they spoke. It seemed our assailant had escaped into the trees and used the shallow waters along the banks of the burn to hide his direction. Our coachman had leapt to the ground after settling the horses and was attending to the frantic complaints of those outside. Some were already demanding to know how long we would be delayed. The driver and Cawdie conferred and then the driver told them they would have to wait until some arrangements could be made to take the outrider's body back to his home in Torrport. The dead man deserved that much consideration at least. Janet helped me from the stagecoach, and I looked around to see where we were. Scathach followed, her distended belly slowing her.

A large stone castle flung itself skyward some distance from the road. It was surrounded by a strong curtain wall with towers at the angles and a moat fed by lochs on both sides. A heavy wooden door, studded and hinged with oiled iron, was centered on one wall. The building seemed familiar, and I realized we were little more than three miles west of Edinburgh, at Corstorphine Castle. It was impressive and beautiful. I had passed it before while traveling between Glasgow and Edinburgh. And when I worked in Torrport, I discovered that it was once Malcolm Forrester's ancestral home. But the Forresters no longer owned it.

I smiled to myself. Malcolm would find interesting this tale of my being forced to ask for help from the owners of his former family home. I wondered how he was faring. In truth, I missed him more than I cared to admit. He was the brother I never had and tended to restrain me when I became too caught up in events. We were Doctors of Medicine, taught in Europe, but in Scotland he was permitted to practice as a physician, and I was not. Being female, I was denied the right to do so; although in Italy, I was fully qualified and accepted. It was a bitter thing to endure, and I had long decided that one day and somehow, I would be recognized as a physician in my own country.

But for now, I was required to go home to Dunvegan, Skye, and defend myself against malicious charges of witchcraft, simply because I had been taught how to stop arterial bleeding with my hands and had done so before a jealous village healer who insisted that such a thing could only be done by a witch. That is how I found myself bound for Skye with an arrow wound and a sick dog. I looked down at Scathach, who was determined to lumber after me as we walked down a well-kept lane toward Corstorphine Castle. The great central door in the wall opened before we were halfway there, releasing a tiny gnome of a man who capered toward us. A flurry of multicolored ribbons fluttered from his clothing and his bald pate glossed wet pink in the sun.

"Lady, what need you?" He craned his scrawny neck to peer around us, trying to see what was causing the muddle, but took a hasty step back when he smelled the vomit on my travel skirts and shoe. He clucked when he saw my bloody, bandaged arm.

"We need to send a message and arrange transportation for a body to the town of Torrport. One of our outriders has been killed. I wish his master to know of this as soon as may be," said I, worrying that Sir Ross Campbell, who had ordered the outriders to accompany us to Glasgow, would be displeased with any delay or mistreatment.

"Yes, yes, my lady. I beg you, come this way. I will fetch my mistress." He cast an anxious eye on the ruin of my gown and the reddened cloths on my arm, bobbed his head, and scampered back up the path to open the huge gate for us and guide us to the castle doors. I motioned for Scathach to remain outside. She sank heavily into a cool shadow, eyes following the wee man. The flagged ground floor of the entrance was cleanly kept, and the ceiling vaulted. An elegant woman of uncertain age, who wore her years well, walked quietly toward us. A young maid fidgeted beside her; face flushed with barely controlled excitement. The wee man spoke rapidly. The lady listened attentively, then nodded and murmured instructions that sent the girl scurrying for warm water and linens and the gnome in search of stools and the stable master.

Within moments I found myself sitting, soiled bandages stripped away, my arm being washed with mint-scented water, my hem and foot sponged to remove the vomit, and the stable master dispatched to deal with the body. Meanwhile, the lady serenely issued orders to her staff, questioned us gently, defined our place in her world, and made certain of the direction of the corpse. A most formidable woman, indeed. I was impressed. She paused when she lifted my hand to clean it and saw the golden ring with the carnelian intaglio of Fortuna I always wore. Then she smiled, looked in my eyes and introduced herself as Lady Myreton. And when I told her that my name and that I was returning home to my family in Skye, her hands stilled again, then resumed their task. She lifted one elegantly winged eyebrow and inspected me intently. "Ah ... So, you are the *cailleach chneasta*, the white witch?"

Beside me, Janet gasped audibly.

"I know your Aunt Mairi," Lady Myreton continued, watching my face as she spoke. Talk of my alleged witchcraft had evidently spread well beyond Skye. Before I could answer, a tall, well-made young man dressed for riding, strolled unhurriedly into the hall. Disordered dark curls clustered damply about a pleasing face. Lady Myreton presented him as her stepson, Robert. He observed the busy scene with apparent indifference through half-closed eyes that hid their color, then asked languidly if he might be of service. When told that the situation was taken care of, he made his bow gracefully, assured us that he was our obedient servant, and left, trailing a faint odor of sweat, cloves, and horse.

Lady Myreton seemed to have forgotten her questions and had become interested in the salve of beeswax, honey, and powdered lichen that Janet use on my wounds. I gave her a spare jar of it after explaining its use and make. She, in turn, told me of a few new concoctions she was composing in her own stillroom. When she had tied the fresh bandages to her satisfaction, Janet and I thanked her profusely for her kindness and hospitality.

Redressed and composed, we bade farewell and left as quickly as we had come, concerned that our trip had been delayed too long. As we walked, I admired the well-ordered gardens, large stables, tack house, and a tidy stone bothy near a stream edged with cresses.

Back at our overburdened conveyance, we found the other passengers much happier for having been soothed with ale served by Lady Myreton's servants. When the passengers saw us, they returned with alacrity to their seats, ready to be on their way. Scathach reluctantly maneuvered herself onto the wooden coach floor which had been cleaned, and we settled ourselves to continue our journey. I ate seed cake and drank warm ale Janet gave me. She and Cawdie went unusually silent. My arm throbbed painfully now, and quite suddenly I was extremely tired. The coach began to move again. A feeling of lethargy overtook me, and I suspected that Janet had added something to the ale. Just before I fell asleep, I noticed that the outriders had changed to a rotation about the coach so that three of them could guard it.

When I awoke, my head was cushioned on Janet's lap, the ends of her woolen *arisaid,* tucked warmly around me. The pain in my arm had settled to a dull ache. I sat up quickly and looked out the window. The road had narrowed and become congested. We shared it with a sturdy gray Highland pony pulling a cart whose wheels were fastened to the axletree, making them turn together. The cart carried more peat than five wheelbarrows could manage, and two scruffy boys marched beside it. Behind the peat cart was a tired-looking muddy brown horse with a hooked yoke supporting wooden panniers filled with bundles wrapped in tan sacking. A girl carrying a switch walked beside the old horse, her hand laid lovingly on the animal's hide, occasionally patting it softly. A stylishly dressed woman riding side-saddle passed my window next, accompanied by her servants. She controlled her skittish mount with graceful ease, looking about with interest and carefully avoiding those walking.

The not-quite-musical sound of the driver's horn announced that we were approaching a posting inn, signaling to the innkeeper that the driver would be changing the horses and needing food and ale for passengers. Such stops were usually about a quarter-hour long, not for the comfort of the humans but for that of the animals. It was barely enough time to use the privy and find something to drink. I did not bother looking at the food. Unscrupulous innkeepers often took payment from the harried and hurried travelers, laid out a meal, and before the food could be eaten the warning that the stage was leaving would sound. If you were late, you were left behind. The same food was presented to the next group of unwary passengers, with a bit of gravy or mash hiding the place where someone might have managed to grab a mouthful. We had our own food and drink and offered to share it with our outriders. They were polite but took little, eyes constantly moving, alert to any threat. How could they have been caught unaware at Corstorphine? Sir Ross's men were superbly trained and intensely loyal. To others he might appear to take the death of one of his men with equanimity, but I knew he would seek his own peculiar method of revenge. I shuddered slightly, closed my mind to all thought, and fell into a fitful sleep.

* * *

The horn jerked me awake again at the toll gate on Gallowgate Road approaching Glasgow. The way was less rutted now. Gallowgate was the fruit and vegetable market of the city, and as we drew closer to the center, many of the houses we passed dressed themselves as shops, offering colorful produce in wooden stalls and bins before their doors. After the last terrible fire, the old wooden buildings had been rebuilt of stone with slate or tile roofs, giving the city a neat and prosperous face. The streets were crowded with people of every description engaged in doing whatever their lives imposed.

My nose stung. The smell of Glasgow began here: a unique mixture of fresh flowers, rotting flesh, vegetables, and excrement. By law, citizens were forbidden to leave piles of dung outside their homes, yet the smell of human, horse, and cattle waste mingled with that of half-hidden urine storage pots was strong. The contents of the urine pots were aged, then used for cleaning and dyeing, as well as for flavoring in some ale recipes. Although I have tasted urine to test for *diabetes mellitus,* the idea of adding it to ale did not appeal.

The stagecoach continued into the city, finally stopping at the market cross on High Street, where Gallowgate meets Trongate, the center of Glasgow. The square teemed with wool and linen merchants, bright bloomy Indian muslins vying with softly colored wools. The grain market was located conveniently near the horse market further up High Street, and the salt market meandered in the opposite direction, toward the river. Errant winds reeked of the meat market just north of Trongate and the fish market at Westport. Other odors fouled the rancid layers of air in this part of the city. An elderly cousin of mine from St. Kilda, both amazed and appalled by the smells and sights of the city, once said that he wished only that his village could be "blessed with the ale, brandy, tobacco, and iron that Glasgow had, but without its reek." Glasgow is my favorite city in Scotland.

Cawdie and Scathach left the coach first. The sea wind was fresh, so I donned my woolen cloak and stepped down gingerly, watching where I put my feet as Cawdie called to a man offering a cart. He and Janet piled our baskets and bags on it, and we walked while it trundled slowly over the rutted cobblestones on High Street, toward my cousin's home.

A bawdy song praising "these sugared plenties" drifted from an alehouse, inviting unchaste thoughts to benefit the whores selling their "plenties" inside. Merchants and vendors hawked their wares in oddly pleasing melodic voices. I looked around, making note of the shops selling commodities. Tomorrow I would seek the items my Aunt Mairi requested in her last letter: greenfish, two lights, a frying pan, a fire shovel, and sixteen ells of red linen.

My uncle's house was notable for its cleanliness. The street before it had been swept, the door freshly painted. A brass knocker gleamed rosy gold in the long light from the now molten sun sinking behind the houses at our backs. Cawdie applied the knocker to the door's striker, and it opened almost immediately revealing a woman encased in a tower of starched white linen topped by a round, pleasant face sweetly surrounded by a white cap.

"My Lady Elspeth!" she exclaimed.

"'Tis me, indeed, Olene. Is Uncle Angus home? We have come for a visit, and I bring word from his son...and letters."

Her face dimpled into a smile. "Sir Angus will be verra pleased for both, my lady, as will we all. He has sorely missed Sir John and troubled by the work he was about in Edinburgh. But here I stand like a looby. Come in, come in, and be welcome, indeed." Her eyes went to Janet and Cawdie. "Lady Janet, a sight ye be for these old eyes. Have ye brought this great lummox to heel yet?"

"And how might I best do that, when he pines only for you and your apple tart?" Janet retorted.

Cawdie laughed, picked up the rotund woman, and crushed her perfectly ironed linen apron into tiny pleats with a bearlike squeeze. The commotion brought my uncle, a master at the University of Glasgow. His passion was botany, and the building of a small physick garden at the school had consumed him of late. He was thinner than I remembered or liked, but his face lit when he saw us laughing, knowing at once that we carried no evil news. I raised my skirts and ran to him, feeling his too-slender body shake as we embraced. I looked up and smiled. "Your son, John, sends his love, and a wee packet for you, uncle."

He looked beyond me to the others. "Cawdie, Janet," he said. "'Tis blessed we are for your coming...and bringing Elspeth. Olene, we have family. Open their rooms!"

We adjourned to the warmly paneled library, where flames burned hot in the carved wooden fireplace, and did all those things people do who have been apart too long: examined each other surreptitiously for change, poured out half-done thoughts, and drank Olene's excellent ale a bit too quickly. Uncle Angus's clothing was sober but fashionable, albeit a little loose. His son, my cousin John Beaton, a physician in Edinburgh and good friend of Malcolm Forrester, would probably look the same at his age: strong and erect, with the sharply defined Roman beak that gave the Beaton men a distinctive look despite their tendency to look angelic.

I gave Uncle Angus the letters, one from John with a packet containing seeds for the new physick garden. He looked down at them, then at me. "He is well?" I understood exactly what he asked and spent an hour giving him news of his son. He knew I had been ordered home and why and was concerned but said little because Janet had come to say that my room was ready. The day had taken its toll, and I needed refresh and rest.

My arm was stiff and painful the next morning but healing nicely. Uncle Angus was at table, somber in his dark clothing. A black academic robe lay on a nearby chair. His face had gained color overnight and his empty plate declared his appetite was sound. He smiled. "Good morning, Elspeth. Would you like to see the physick garden? 'Tis in progress, of course, but of interest. There are a few things you might wish to take home, and I have questions for you." He looked at me eagerly. "You have seen the physick garden of Mattheus Silvaticus at the School of Salerno. You can tell me where we are lacking in mine." His tone was too casual, and I wondered what he was seeking from me.

"I would like that above all things." I looked up as Olene bustled in carrying a tray of hot chocolate, butter, and bread. "Ah, Olene, you remember! I thank you." She blushed and smiled, plump, rosy, and reassuring as always. I had told no one of my injury thus far. It was not evident, and I wanted no fuss. I ate quickly, then we left, my uncle donning the round flat hat that protected his thinning pate.

* * *

Glasgow University was nearby, the stone High Street frontage an imposing taste of what lay behind. We passed the broad steps leading up to the church and entered a passageway through the next building leading to the Great Yard behind the college. Going through the walkway, I heard a scrabbling from overhead and a furry shape dropped to the flagstones before me, lurched a few steps, and lay still. It was a black rat. A man dressed in the trappings of a ratcatcher hurried in, stooped, and scooped up the creature. He deposited the limp corpse among several others in a cage fastened atop his stick. A wee boy looking improbably like the ratcatcher shadowed him, clutching a wooden chest in his thin arms.

I had seen the man's ilk many times. 'Tis said that people tend to take on the look of what they know best. The man resembled a rat. His long nose and mustache twitched. Slightly too small clever eyes darted from me to my uncle. Square-toed shoes tied with soiled pink silk laces supported skinny legs and rounded belly. His clothing was a deep mottled brown that served to diminish the unimaginable stains of his craft, the whole topped with a short black cape. Greasy hanks of gray hair stringed from beneath a wide-brimmed, and two sheathed blades dangled from his wide belt.

"And a good day to ye, Sir Beaton," said the ratcatcher. "Ye see me hard at work." He gestured at the rats, some still stirring in his cage. "'Tis glad I am to meet ye. I be wanting a few wee things from yer garden as agreed, in payment fer me services as usual." His breath, fetid with decay, flavored his words. I was hard put not to step back. He bowed to me as gracefully as any courtier, his mien servile, his rat eyes bold.

My uncle replied, "Aye. Come to me later. My niece has but a brief time here and I wish to show her the gardens before she leaves for Skye."

The ratcatcher's eyes flicked toward me, something quickly hidden in their depths. Was it surprise? 'Tis much appreciated, sir. Tis seeing ye later, I be. I wish ye both well." With one last speculative glance at me, he faded into the darkness of the passageway, the lad scarcely visible behind him.

We continued along the wide gravel path. Before us, stately rows of fruit trees and beds of herbs and vegetables, all well tended by their individual lease or tack-holders, flourished in meticulous order. Pippins, pears, cherries, and apricot trees stood free or clung to walls. The whole had been modeled after the old medieval monastery gardens, partitioned into carefully measured plots. On our left, gardeners were cutting turf and turning the soil for new beds. Willow baskets and flats filled with seedlings waited nearby to be transplanted. My uncle inhaled a deep breath as he viewed the scene before us. "Is it not wonderful? The college has given us a part to grow our medicinal herbs." He begged a small empty basket from one of the gardeners and gave it to me. "In case you see anything you would like to take to Skye."

We walked along the neat rows, discussing uses for the herbs. Common and rare grew together in healthy profusion. I saw colewort, beets, asparagus, spinach, sorrel, lovage, marigolds, parsley, thyme, mints, and more. Gourd vines tumbled over fruit-espaliered walls.

Valerian and hollyhocks speared upward, the mixed odors and colors intoxicating.

We veered to the right and came to the reason for our visit. Last year a piece called the "Little Yard" had been set aside for a new garden. Much was ado. Rock walls were being constructed to enclose the space and two gardeners were turning the earth. The new sun-catching stone walls would warm the area on two sides. Stout wooden poles shielded young hedges of briars and whitethorn on the other two, and small palings protected a completed corner.

"What is in that one, uncle?"

"The one I most wish you to see. It contains plants that are difficult to grow, and in some measure dangerous. Many are rare and should not be easily accessible." He was quiet a moment, then said, "Mairi has written to me of the problems in Skye. I would have you take a letter and package to her." He opened the narrow wooden gate and we entered. Well-ordered rows of hemlock, nightshade, henbane, monkshood, and foxglove patterned the ground. "'Tis a poison garden, is it not?"

He nodded. "We furnish such things to the ratcatcher and those who use them to purge their homes and lands of certain vermin." His expression was troubled. He pointed to the trees, which bore carroty red fruits that reminded me of oranges. "We have requests for the seeds of this one." He turned to me. "Do you know of it and its use?"

"I do. 'Tis a two-edged sword that can both kill and cure, as are most of these. Many think *nux vomica* is used in the poison known as Aqua Tofana...sometimes called inheritance powder," I added wryly.

"All things are poisonous. 'Tis the dosage that determines it," he replied, parroting Paracelsus.

I was careful in touching the plants in the enclosure but added a few seedlings to those in my basket for the garden at Skye. He questioned me about the plants in the Salerno gardens and for a goodly time exchanged opinions about treatments and remedies. We strolled back to the only door that entered the college from the Great Yard. I asked to see the famed lion and unicorn staircase in the inner close. As we stepped inside, boisterous voices erupted from a clot of red-robed students in one corner. "That great woolly crown! Will yer red rag nae lie still? Keep that tongue quiet!" It was Cawdie's voice.

Chapter 2: Elspeth

Why was Cawdie here in the inner close of the college? I set my basket down and started toward the disturbance. Cawdie emerged laughing with a slender young man whose orange-red hair clashed cruelly with his crimson robe. He stopped when he saw me. "Done, are ye?" he grumbled. Cawdie was guarding me even here! A complicit look passed between him and my uncle, and I decided acceptance was best and contented myself with observing the lion and unicorn steps created by William Riddell. The knot of red academic robes dissolved into a group of young men who bowed politely and forbore flirting with me in the presence of a master. There was whispered mention of a nearby bowling green now used to replace the one taken by the new garden, crude challenges, a jostle or two, a half-promise, then Cawdie nodded at my uncle, and we left.

On our way back to the house I purchased a few things from my shopping list, punished Cawdie by making him help choose ribbon colors at the drapers, and burdened him with packages of woolens and linens. He just smiled, bought bright blue silk ribbons for Janet, and chose the rope needed by the laird. I ordered barrels of olive oil, refined sugar, and spices, and planned a visit to the port apothecary who offered rare and exotic wares not often seen elsewhere. The smell of tallow from the chandlers and soap manufactories was noxious when the wind shifted, reminding me to get scented French and Italian soap to take to Skye as well. Unexpectedly, a searching tendril teased the edge of my thoughts. I turned quickly and sought to follow it, but the street was filled with people, and it was lost.

We were closer to home, and it had begun. I sighed and closed myself away securely. It would be a while before we left for Skye, and I wanted to enjoy Glasgow.

* * *

Passage to Skye for us and our rapidly accumulating goods had been arranged by the Chief of Clan MacLeod, known locally as the MacLeod or Laird MacLeod. The river Clyde was mostly shallow for the fifteen miles to the Port of Glasgow, and draft boats were needed to take us to the larger ships. John Mouse, Master under God of our ship, the *Dougall of Oban,* sent a shallop for us. The flat-bottomed boat sat high in the water, even though it was piled with cargo and people bound for landings along the coasts. I settled on a soft bale and pulled my cloak around me, watching the activity. Scathach sniffed the air and curled up at my feet. I patted her great furry head in commiseration. She was beginning to waddle. I cannot imagine the discomfort of having several pups wriggling about in my belly.

Cawdie and Janet stood at the railing, speaking quietly. He was standing astride a chest, one foot against its side, an old traveling trick. The shallop pushed away from shore and headed toward the Port of Glasgow, and the *Dougall of Oban,* a Scottish birlinn, designed primarily for loads of cargo. Minutes later, we boarded and found our cabin, then left with the tide after a brief delay for two tardy passengers. It would take two or three days to sail to Skye, depending on the winds and weather.

I kept the plants from the college with me to make certain they were kept safe and moist. Next to them was a wooden box Uncle Angus had presented to me as we left. It was filled with packets of seeds, instructions for their care and a fine drawing of a knot garden. The contents would be a valuable addition to the gardens at Dunvegan Castle, our destination. I sat on the narrow bunk, unfolded the letter I had received from Aunt Rhona while I was yet in Torrport, and read it again. Aunt Rhona is my great-aunt and sister to Aunt Mairi, the current leader of the white witches and most experienced healer of Clan MacLeod.

The words in the message had not changed. I was to come home at once. She had reason to believe that Laird MacLeod was in danger, and yet stranger, that my sister Erika might be alive. How could that be? Erika had died of smallpox before I left to study medicine in Italy. The memory of that terrible evening was vivid. Her once beautiful face, so covered with smallpox pustules that in places it looked like one yawning raw eruption was still fresh in my mind. Ranuff, the youth we had both loved, stood impassive on the other side of the bed. I could hear his breathing, feel his anger and pain. He had chosen her. They were betrothed and he was losing her. I had placed my hand on her burning skin and tried to will my strength into her. And failed.

The next morning, I was told that Erika had died during the night. The old laird, weary of the chaos of unceasing death, had permitted Ranuff to take her body to the keep at Talisker which Ranuff held for him. Her burial was without thought for our feelings. There was no funeral and no farewell. I would never forgive Ranuff for taking her before I could say goodbye. That was four years ago, and I still missed her.

But Aunt Rhona was not given to fancy. There had to be sound reasons for her to write such things to me unless it was simple dotage. I folded the letter and returned it to the bag. With her letter and the laird's command to return home, there was no choice. Whatever might be awaiting me there I would discover soon enough. And it would be of interest to see what had changed in my absence.

* * *

Our first stop when we reached the Isle of Skye was Rubh' an Dùnain. The *Dougall* carried supplies for the shipyard at Loch na h-Airde, where Clan MacAskill repaired ships and built fishing boats. They were the hereditary *comes litores* or coast watchers for the MacLeods. King James had outlawed private navies in 1609, and the MacAskills had suffered a great loss of income from war shipbuilding. But they kept their allegiance to the MacLeods and guarded the southern part of Skye, both inland and on the sea.

Many of our fellow travelers went ashore, most carrying bundles. The village of Dùnain sat at the end of a shallow valley. That day, it was wreathed in silver white fog, and I turned toward it. Dark grey smoke rose from holes in the thatched roofs of the stone and turf dwellings. The insides of the huts typically were dark and oily with soot from the continuously burning peat fires built in the center of the rooms. The MacAskill house was notable for being constructed of dressed stone, with a chimney and gable on one end instead of a smoke hole. The opposite end was rounded and had been built at an earlier time. All the buildings and walled enclosures were neat and well kept. Every bit of precious arable soil had been planted in softly undulating lazy rows by the tacksmen who leased the strips of land.

Aunt Mairi had lived in the village while training a healer. And as a child I had visited several times, and I loved exploring the ruins left by the old ones. Playing at the shipyard on the freshwater loch, connected by a canal to the sea, was my favorite of all. There on the docks, an old seaman might trade a tale or two for the wide-eyed attention of a wee lass and teach her as well how use a gauge to make a fishing net.

Cawdie and Janet were nowhere to be seen, so Scathach and I followed the exodus to the peninsula while the ship was offloading cargo. Solid ground rocked beneath my feet then righted itself as I regained my land legs. The path to the village led past the canal that had existed beyond memory. The air seemed suddenly cold and heavy, and I shivered. Someone was watching us. Scathach growled, raised her head, and leaned against me, staring at the ancient stones of the dun on the headland. I saw nothing, then a wisp of the fog lifted and dispersed, revealing the form of a petite woman dressed in soft sea green and grey. She carried a covered basket. A long-haired black dog stood at her side; head cocked. Strands of hair escaped the woman's thick braids and blew around her pale face. She smiled at me and moved to intercept us, for I was unable to move, my feet suddenly rooted in the earth. Scathach's fur bristled. The woman glanced at her, said something in a gentle mellifluous voice, then continued walking toward us. She held out the basket, then unexpectedly stopped as though she had encountered an unseen wall. She looked wildly around, and then back at me, her dark eyes flaring.

"Ah, ye did not come alone! Clever girl." She smiled as sweetly as a young maiden, turned, and walked gracefully away, her silvery green skirts swaying as they faded into the lichen-covered rock walls of the dun, her dog following. Then they were both gone, and I could move again. Scathach started after them, but I put a restraining hand on her. I had no idea who the woman was or what she meant. But for some reason Malcolm's face appeared in my mind and I wished he were here. Abruptly, I craved the ship.

* * *

The next day we arrived at Dunvegan. Cargo and passengers were disgorged into a crowd waiting to help us at the stone quay. We began the laborious task of getting everything up to the castle bailey. There is only one entrance into Dunvegan Castle, through the sea gate. About halfway up the side of the massive basalt rock the castle stands atop, an iron portcullis bars the way. It opens into an upwardly sloped and stepped path just wide enough to admit a single person. Easy to defend, difficult to portage. By the time I reached the bailey, I was ready to put down my bags and bundles, my injured arm well-aggravated.

Our ship had been sighted long before by the locals, as it slowly sailed into Loch Dunvegan, and the bailey was filled with the usual taciturn clansmen and chattering women. It was good to be home. My cousin and chieftain, Norman MacLeod, the MacLeod of MacLeod, stood just outside the entrance to the castle building. A woman faced him; one hand laid possessively on his arm. He looked up, saw me, and shook her hand away. She turned to see what had drawn him. Flawless ivory skin lay tight against the perfection of her face. She might have posed for a statue of Isis I once saw in Italy. Her blue eyes were heavy-lidded beneath slightly arched brows, and a straight nose poised proudly over a bowed red mouth and rounded chin. Curly dark chestnut hair clustered on her brow. She was Ysabell Talisker, the healer who had accused me of witchcraft. Faint unease unfolded inside me. She measured my unimpressive self, lifted her dark brows at the sight of Scathach swollen with pups, grimaced, and stepped back, losing herself behind the people surging toward our group. Many of the faces were familiar, but one, as usual, was painfully absent: my father's.

Our welcome was warm. Cawdie and Janet were soon the center of a laughing circle of people hugging, slapping, and making rude and bawdy comments about their forthcoming nuptials. The young laird greeted me politely and asked that I see my Aunt Rhona and his wife Anne as soon as might be. Norman looked thinner. He must have lost a stone since last I saw him at Torrport this June past. His dark hair was tousled, and his blue eyes limned with red. He motioned for one of his *lucktaeh* guards to take my things. Cawdie had been one of that elite group of the laird's personal guards before becoming my protector. They were highly trained fighters, dancers, and seamen. Cawdie had been the old laird's *galloglach*, the warrior who stood with his laird both day and night. He had transferred that loyalty to me.

The laird did not bother to speak further, just led me purposefully down the hallway to my room, a clansman in tow with my bags. We were near in age, and Norman had been as quiet when the four of us were children. Erika and Ysabell gave him little choice. Especially Ysabell. She had a wicked tongue and constantly vied with Erika for leadership, while keeping Norman tied tightly to her side. I had observed the war between them but had no desire to take part.

I have not trusted Ysabell since the day she invited me to her cottage in the village when I was young. I liked her mother, the village healer who always smelled of warm peppermint, so I went. When we were alone, Ysabell wove me a sorrowful tale of how she was no longer friends with Norman because of terrible things he told her about me. When I did not respond at once, she commiserated and asked if I did not hate him for telling lies? Was he not an evil person and dishonest? I was less than six years old at the time, but something seemed wrong. So, I lowered my eyes and piously replied that "God said we should not hate anyone."

There was a muffled snort and Norman crawled from beneath the bed, brushed himself off, and faced Ysabell. "I win," he declared. "I told you she would not say dreadful things about anyone."

That taught me something I remember to this day: mind your words to others. And do not trust Ysabell, ever.

We stopped before the familiar door and Norman patted my shoulder awkwardly then hurried to retreat. Even the laird feared Aunt Rhona. I knocked, then entered. The smell was the same. When I was a little girl Aunt Rhona was already past her fortieth year. I thought she smelled a bit like a mouse. Now that I am grown, I can identify her odour as a combination of long hair, starched linen, lavender, and the grassy sweet smell of urine that becomes stronger with age. The clansman put my belongings inside the door, nodded stiffly, and left.

We would be sharing the bed chamber with my aunt again. The room had not changed since I was a child, except it seemed to have grown smaller. Aunt Mairi had occupied it with Aunt Rhona while she lived here, and then my sister Erika, me, and Janet, after mother died. Janet slept on the trundle bed stored beneath ours. It was still there. Cabinets, a fireplace, and crowded but artfully arranged shelves obscured the remaining walls. Aunt Rhona lay pale and motionless, breath rasping through her open mouth and surprisingly perfect teeth. I went to the bed and touched the blue-veined wrist of the wrinkled and gnarled hand that lay on the coverlet. It was hot and dry. Pale gray eyes opened at once. Aunt Rhona is one of those women with young faces and old hands. Despite her age, her face was only slightly lined.

"Ye have come, child. Praise be to the gods! Ye must go at once to the laird's keep in Talisker, before 'tis too late. Ranuff holds it for the laird and is using it to hold them. You must go to them ere 'tis too late!" She clutched my hand and tried to sit up. "Swear!"

"I swear, aunt. I swear! I am here. Please be calm. Tell me why you think Erika yet lives? And who is *them*?" I spoke soothingly, leaning in to comfort her, rubbing her cold hands, and willing to humor her folly to comfort her.

"The sacred stone...Erika wrote to me. Told me I must hide it. So, I did. I...I thought it lost, but she told me where it was. Now I have it, but you must take it. I cannot keep it. I am not fit enough and 'tis dangerous...I am too weak...and done. 'Tis you who must go on. Find her...and the child... before 'tis too late. Beware, and keep guard. They fear you, want you dead. Mairi will help but she needs your strength. We have grown old, child... " She was having trouble speaking. I put my arms beneath her and lifted her insubstantial body up to a better sitting position to help her breathe more easily, plumping pillows behind her for support.

She gasped, then said clearly, "Take my knitting. Take it at once! You must complete the pattern." Then she lay back, spent.

There was a light tap and the door opened. Janet came in, followed by Cawdie with the rest of our baggage. I tucked the blankets closer around Aunt Rhona and decided to say nothing about her words until I had time to think and speak with her more, but I did take note of the basket of knitting that stood on a table nearby. We unpacked and settled in.

* * *

A sharp rap, and the door opened. Aunt Mairi stood there, leaning into a walking staff taller than she. She glanced at Aunt Rhona's sleeping form and came toward us, seeming to float rather than walk. I met her halfway and pulled her slight form into my arms. We were of a height, mayhap I was a bit taller. I kissed her soft creased cheek and leaned back to look at her. Her arisaid was white with small stripes of green, blue, and yellow. A leather belt with a curiously engraved silver buckle was clasped beneath her breasts, a huge moonstone encircled with ancient gems glowing from its center. The belt ended with a silver rectangle about eight inches long and three in breadth, also engraved and adorned with fine stones. She wore blue sleeves closed at the wrist with fine buttons, and a white linen kerchief tight about her head and hanging down her back. I felt her wrap me in home.

Janet slipped away to sit across the room by Aunt Rhona. Aunt Mairi reached for my arm, touched the wound hidden under the dark cloth, and made a small sound, dismissing it. "You have spoken to Rhona?" she whispered.

"I have. She thinks Erika lives, but I do not understand why she would believe such a thing." Tears tried to form but I refused to let them.

"Erika is one of us, child. We would know if the circle was broken. Somewhere she lives, but we must find her soon. The laird no longer listens to me, and he is ill unto death. Did you not feel it?"

I had. "He looks ill, but it could be many things. He told me in Torrport that his son is sickly. You wrote that Lady Anne is great with child and tired, frightened, and fretful. The laird has much to concern him. What do you think is wrong? I have not been home long enough to understand what is happening."

"I sense evil, child." Aunt Mairi twisted her staff between her hands thoughtfully. "Perhaps poison. There are things that could be used to resemble illness. It would require an outside source...and someone who has access to more than we have here. Mayhap a traveler? Someone who comes and goes often from Dunvegan? You know Ysabell hates you still for being able to stop her patient from bleeding to death. And she is jealous of Lady Anne too. Ysabell is ever with Niall Morrison when he is here. That lad is pleasant and bonnie enough but fancies himself a better laird than Norman."

"Niall?" I felt myself flush. When I saw him last, I had been intrigued, even though I was in love with Ranuff. A few times I had attempted to make Ranuff jealous by flirting with Niall. It had not worked. "He wants to be laird?"

"Aye, and there are those who agree, since our laird is weak with illness."

This was worse than I thought. "You must tell me how I can help, then."

She moved one hand up and clasped it around the top of her staff. "I wish for you to take my place, child, as the clan healer and *Cailleach*. I have reached the fullness of my years and it is time."

* * *

Lady Anne was embroidering half heartedly, shifting restlessly under her swollen belly when I sought her out next morning. Her young son slept quietly in his crib, watched over by a wizened maid. Lady Anne's eyes seemed large in her small face, purple crescents curving beneath them. A glass of dark liquid sat within reach on a nearby chest. Anne was but a child herself, having been but ten-and-four to the laird's ten-and-eight when they were wed a few years past.

Lady Anne knew why I had come and readily answered questions and offered comment. She listed the usual plaints of being with child. She had not been sleeping well and was always weary, and her head ached. Some days blood spotted her chemise and she feared losing the babe. She was thirsty. She urinated too often. Her ankles were swollen. She was fat and ugly. The baby kicked constantly. And she was frightened. Lady Anne was not happily pregnant.

"Tell me my lady, have you seen the midwife about your bleeding and swollen ankles? What says she?"

There was a pause. She toyed with a ribbon on her sleeve before she answered. "I…have. 'Tis Lady Ysabell. She has been most kind." Lady Anne touched the cup beside her. "She gave me this, but I find it not to my taste." She looked up, like a child caught disobeying, and hastened to add, "But I have been drinking it as she wished."

"I will ask her about it. Until then, you need nothing but rest and plain water. Mayhap a barley tisane with honey, as well. I will prepare it for you." She looked relieved, and after we exchanged a few more words, I left taking Lady Anne's cup with me.

I knew Ysabell had instigated the charges of witchcraft that had brought me home, and I found it very odd that no one had yet said anything to me about it. I would have to speak with the laird when he was feeling better. I wanted the inquiry over and done so I could get on with my life. In the meantime, there was a growing list of matters to which I must attend. I sighed and walked a little faster.

* * *

The laird gave me a set of keys to the stillroom to make a new batch of salve. I inspected the room's contents and made a list of what might be needed or added. It was well kept and stocked, although some of the things in the high locked cabinet were dubious: unicorn horn and dragon's teeth among them. Medicine and myth were often intermingled.

I had smelled and tasted the bitter wine Ysabell had given Lady Anne. It tasted of laudanum and something else, a slightly unusual smell. I supposed the laudanum was to make her rest. Thomas Sydenham extolled its virtues and determined its dosages, but in Salerno there had been growing concerns about its addictive qualities. Thus, I used it sparingly. Still curious, I used my nose. Avicenna's use of the sense of smell had been part of my studies in Italy, but the strange odor in the contents of the cup eluded me.

I had just begun a batch of lichen and honey salve for my arm wound when the subject of my musing, Ysabell, opened the door abruptly. I wondered if she hoped to catch me doing something forbidden, since it took so little to prompt suspicion. "And what might our wee…healer be making?" she asked, malice flavoring her voice.

"A salve for cuts that do not heal properly." I kept my tone even. She inspected the containers in front of me. I pounded the strands of lichen in the mortar, releasing the powder covering them, and measured it into a jar. The remaining strings of white fiber, shorn of their dry covering, went into a clean bag. They were used to staunch bleeding. Ysabell pretended to gather herbs but watched every step closely. I heated the beeswax just enough to melt it, added precise measures of the powdered lichen and liquid honey, stirred the concoction smooth and poured the mixture into three clean gallipots to cool. It congealed quickly.

"Would you like one of these, Ysabell? If you wish I will give you the recipe, too."

She turned in surprise and looked at me uncertainly. "Ye would share with me?"

"Of course. We are healers, are we not? I assessed the consistency of the unguent, tied a circle of soft leather over the flared rim of one of the little pots, and held it out to her. She looked at me baffled, but took it, holding the still-warm vessel before her as though it were some unknown and dangerous threat, then left the room. A tall man I could not see well enough to identify joined her in the hallway before she vanished around a corner.

* * *

The herbs I brought from the new physick garden in Glasgow needed planting. I picked up a battered trowel and carried it with the herbs to the bailey and on the way obtained a pitcher to fill with water from the well. The herb garden in the castle was small, but well tended. I planted and watered the slips and seedlings, then stood and considered the bailey. Cawdie and Janet's wedding feast might be held here. I was mentally placing tables and tents when I felt Ranuff's presence. It had always been so. Without turning I said formally, "I greet thee, Ranuff Talisker."

"And I, thee, Elspeth MacLeod. Welcome home." His voice was the same.

Turning slowly, I looked at him. But he did not *look* the same as I remembered. Slender had become gaunt. His face was the color of old ivory, the lips I had ached to kiss were now a thin line beneath deeply sunken cheeks. He glanced about. Two women were laying laundry on the grass to dry. No one else was nearby.

"You look well. How was your sojourn to Italy?" There was a hidden sneer in the words. Anger seemed to boil from him in waves. He hated me for surviving smallpox when Erika had died of it. When he had taken my sister's body and vanished in the night without a word to anyone but the old laird, there had been no proper closure.

I had grown older too, and well over my girlish passion for him. I wasted no time being civil. "What do you want, Ranuff?"

"Why," his face twisted into what was supposed to be a smile, "I came but to ask if you would like to visit to Erika's resting place. I will escort you myself."

"I would like to see her grave. But I cannot yet leave. The laird has given me patients to care for. Aunt Rhona, Lady Anne…and others. Cawdie and Janet's wedding is soon…perhaps after that."

He frowned. "As you will, then. Tell me when you wish to go." He was not best pleased but accepted it and left after a lingering inspection that left me feeling diminished.

* * *

Cawdie and Janet were to make their vows in St. Mary's, the Duirinish parish kirk. The first banns had been called last Sabbath. Cawdie had a small cottage in Dunvegan village which he and Janet could use for privacy whenever they wished, and they had begun cleaning and repairing it like two children playing house. Both assured me that they would not be leaving me, although how they would manage that was beyond my comprehension. I suppose we would adapt as needed, but I no longer needed a handmaid.

Life assumed a shape. I cared for Aunt Rhona, who began to return slowly to her usual acerbic self. The clan women became accustomed to me, and I had enough patients to keep me occupied with two pregnancies besides Lady Anne's and the daily quota of accidents, abscesses, and a slash or two to enliven my days.

* * *

The laird appeared at the stillroom door one day. He had been reluctant to let me examine him, but after I found him short of breath during sword practice, he consented. He strode in, pulling off a pair of scented leather gloves then tucking them carefully into his belt. It was obvious he was losing weight, and Lady Anne said he was not eating well and had night sweats. I took his hand and touched his wrist to feel his pulse. It was too rapid, his skin dry and hot. "How long have you had shortness of breath, my laird?"

He squirmed uncomfortably before answering, "Several months, but not badly. Dr. Bethune gave me a syrup." He attempted a deep breath, coughed, and looked at me sheepishly. Herold Bethune is the family physician, but he is old and not interested in the latest ideas and treatments. The laird saw my look and quickly added, "All right. I have pain in my chest, and I tire easily. My sword has grown heavier." He smiled ruefully.

I had seen the tell-tale spots of fresh blood on his handkerchiefs and feared he had consumption, as it was often called, though I could not rule out other causes completely. I had read the book *Opera Medica* by the German physician Sylvius who speculated that consumption might be spread from one person to another, so I was concerned about Lady Anne and the children. But at this point, there was little I could do except hope they would not get it too. I reminded myself to ask Dr. Bethune what he put in the syrup. Mayhap I could add something for pain and fever. "Try to eat more and rest. You must stay well for your people and your bairns." He grumbled some impolite response but agreed.

After he left, I poured water into a basin to wash but realized my right hand had traces of powder clinging to it. Lifting it, I sniffed. *Must be from the laird's hand,* I thought. The scent of rosemary and roses assailed my nostrils, mixed with sweat and something else. This was the second time my nose had tried to tell me something I was missing. I shook my head and plunged my hands into the basin. I scrubbed them hard.

Chapter 3: Elspeth

Cawdie was creeled last night. He had to carry the traditional large creel or basket of stones from one end of Dunvegan village to the other until his beloved came out and hand-kissed him. He made it only twice around the village before Janet relented and rescued him with a buss. Such short shrift caused much hooting and laughter. Several of the clansmen made lewd comments on how his apparent lack of stamina bode ill for the marriage bed, then offering bawdy suggestions and volunteering their services to help. Cawdie growled, cuffed a few of them, then they all went for new ale and whisky at the tavern, where the broom hung welcome over the door. With the laird leading the way, they would drink until insensible and had to be carried one-by-one to their homes in a barrow. The last man standing was proclaimed the victor. Men are very strange.

The tavern belonged to Teresa MacKilliam. Her man went fishing one day four years ago and never returned. Teresa was a buxom, pretty woman with heavy waves of rich red hair, cobalt blue eyes, and rosy cheeks. She is much admired and sought after by every available male, and some not-so-available. Although kind to them all, she prefers four-legged strays of every persuasion, including a cadaverous old half-greyhound lurcher and an enormous ginger one-eyed tomcat who hisses at anyone who comes near. She also makes quite certain her customers get home safely after too much drink, and for that the women thank her.

* * *

I was not sure if Cawdie had been the last man standing last night, but this morning he was waiting for us, a haggard, handsome, and anxious bridegroom. He was wearing an obviously new saffron-colored linen shirt, his belted plaid carefully arranged over it and held in place with a massive silver brooch. His brightly colored stockings were tied with red garters, and soft leather shoes and an elaborately embellished sporran completed his attire. He straightened with relief as we joined him. Janet was beside me looking bride-beautiful in her new arisaid, with the jeweled silver brooch Cawdie had given her. Aunt Mairi stood quietly nearby, leaning on the arm of the laird who looked as pale as Cawdie, but for other reasons. Aunt Mairi had gifted me with an antique pendant of *lapis hecticus,* or white hectic stone, said to have strong healing properties. The stone was cleverly fixed within three hinged silver arms that opened to release it when needed. Sun fire flashed within, and it felt warm through my shift.

My arisaid was recent as well, purchased for the wedding. I left my hair loose and it fell below my waist in a wavy mass confined at my forehead by a crown of meadow flowers. It made me feel pretty. Some of my kinsmen eyed me with new interest. Even Ysabell flicked an assessing look, although compared with her I was plain. I realized I was happy to be here despite everything. Skye was home and would always hold my heart.

The pipes began to wail, and the piper began the procession toward the kirk. The path followed the creases between the soft heathery hills surrounding Dunvegan. Most everyone from the castle and village followed. Many brought baskets of food and small kegs of drink, a custom left over from the old penny weddings where each guest was required to pay a penny for attending. It was a way to gift the couple and share what they could afford. When we arrived at the kirk, Cawdie and Janet stopped outside the entrance, drew a circle on the ground around themselves, and exchanged vows, thereby honoring the old ways.

Cawdie gave Janet a beautiful dirk he had designed for her, and she presented him with the customary length of fine cloth woven by her own hands. Patterns for the various clan plaids were inscribed on pieces of wood bearing the number of every thread and the colors of the stripes, and she had followed his traditional clan's pattern. He would never part with the cloth. Cawdie touched her cheek gently, then they entered the kirk for the ritual ceremony and blessing of the offered fare for the *ceilidh*.

The ringing sound of the thirteen silver coins Cawdie had given the minister hit the offering plate, and it was over. Bagpipes shrilled. The kirk was far too small for everyone and when we came out into the sun, there was a roar from the awaiting crowd. The wildflower-strewn meadow nearby was spotted with wooden tables groaning beneath the now-sanctified food. Stools, tartans, and blankets patchworked the green for sitting, with a few chairs here and there for the elderly. The celebration had begun. Malcolm would have loved it.

The new bridegroom pulled Janet into the laughing crowd of people to begin the time-honored first dance as husband and wife. They linked hands and moved clockwise, stopping to dance the setting steps before the guests merged into the circle. The laird and Lady Anne joined them despite her belly. A shadow fell on my skirts. "Will you join me in the dance?" Ranuff stood before me, bowing.

I could not well refuse without insult, so I smiled back at him brightly and let him lead me into the set. His hand was cold on mine, and I shivered. He must have taken it for beguilement, for his smile widened. He danced well, performing the moves of the reel gracefully. We had begun the second one when a disturbance further down the line caused the dancers to falter and stop. The laird had stumbled and was kneeling, gasping for breath. Lady Anne was trying to pull him up. I left Ranuff and ran to him, almost colliding with Ysabell who arrived at the same moment. The MacLeod waved us both away and wiped his mouth. I stepped in front of him, my skirts shielding him from the crowd. By then Cawdie was there and helped him stand. Ranuff followed, and I saw him speak quietly to Ysabell before they offered to help the laird and Lady Anne back to the castle.

Aunt Mairi arrived, wielding her long staff imperiously, pushing the gathering people out of the way. She ordered Cawdie to get back to his new wife and let Ranuff help the laird. She and I would see to Lady Anne. Janet gave me an almost imperceptible nod, took Cawdie's arm, waved, smiled, and began to reform the circle of dancers. Ranuff helped the laird steady himself, and we started walking slowly back to Dunvegan Castle.

The laird regained some color, but Lady Anne fretted over him and by the time we were back at the castle, she was as exhausted and pallid as he. I noticed she was rubbing her middle. Aunt Mairi saw it too. She took Anne away to rest and told me to take care of the laird. Ysabell trailed along, insisting it was her place to attend them both. I sent for my bag and ignored her, discarding my flower crown, and hastily re-braiding my hair to keep it out of the way.

The laird balked at being ordered to bed, but fatigue prevailed, and he finally consented to lie down, closing his eyes at once. His skin was burning, stretched tightly over his bones, and bright flags of crimson flew in his cheeks. He was wearing his great kilt and a pair of scented gloves from Perth, in the latest style. The Glovers and Dyers Guilds influence had stretched to Skye and the laird's fine pair were colored to blend with his plaid. I removed both gloves, noticing again they were scented with white powder which left a thin coating on his hands. All physicians know of "inheritance powders" and other poisons used to clear one's path of human obstacles. Gloves were well-known carriers. I was chary of touching them and placed each carefully in an empty water bucket nearby.

"Ysabell, if you wish to help, get a basin of clean water and wash the laird's hands and face with lye soap," I said.

She made a small sound, as I turned. Her face was ashen, and her hands shook as she lifted the pitcher to pour water into the bowl. "Are you, all right?" I asked her. She nodded her head, found soap and a cloth, and came to the bed. We looked down at the laird. He seemed absurdly young lying there in his sweat-soaked shirt. His eyes were closed, his pale face. Suddenly Ysabell made a retching sound, put the basin down, and without a word, fled. I moved the basin closer, scrubbed his hands, poured clean water over them, and mine, and emptied the contents of the basin out the window, watching the filmy liquid splash against the lichen covered walls as it fell. I wondered if the residual contents would harm the plants below.

Aunt Mairi arrived as I finished. She told me that Lady Anne was not well and had been put to bed. She also had given her a tisane and instructed the handmaid to keep everyone away. I longed to tell Aunt Mairi what I was beginning to fear but decided to forego it for now and insisted she herself rest. She left, the retreating sound of her staff tapping the stones echoing sharply off the walls.

I stood looking down at the laird. He opened his eyes and turned toward me, reaching for my hand. "Elspeth, I have a confession. I brought you home under false pretenses. The charges of witchcraft were made, yes… and I am taking care of that. I will protect you with my life. If my life lasts," he said wryly. "Something is happening that I do not understand, but it is evil. Aunt Mairi wanted you to come home, your Aunt Rhona, too, but for other purposes. And I…I have my own selfish reasons. We are all in need of your skills. Someone is trying to kill me and my family. You have been trained in the finest school in Europe," he continued. "I did not lie… charges have been laid against you, but…they are of no import. I can take care of that. What I cannot do is defend my wife and family from these devious enemies!"

He gripped my hand painfully. I placed my own over his. "I am here," I assured him, "and here I will stay as long as required."

He sighed and closed his eyes again, his hold on me gradually lessening as he fell into a deep sleep. When I left, his personal guard was in place by the door. I was beginning to be frightened. The problems were multiplying, and beyond a few women I was not certain who could be trusted. I needed an ally with a detached mind, medical skills, and strong leadership. I would write to Malcolm and ask him to come to Dunvegan.

* * *

Aunt Rhona was sleeping fitfully when I returned to our room. My flower crown looked wilted and sad, but I sprinkled it with cool water and again loosed my hair. I needed to return to the ceilidh, at least for a while. Ranuff was waiting by the castle door, and we walked back to the kirk grounds together. Ysabell was nowhere to be seen.

Ale flowed freely amid increasingly boisterous claims to the title of finest brewster or brewstress. Ranuff brought me a cup of ale. I drank it slowly, watching the proceedings, but it was yet too early for seriously broken heads. I danced and smiled and renewed old friendships and got into a wee scuffle with an amorous young lad filled with too much drink. The sun and ale made me drowsy. Janet and Cawdie were surrounded by well-wishers, so I slipped unobtrusively away, returning to the castle so I may look in on the laird and Lady Anne. The way seemed much longer going back. I stopped beneath the ancient rowan tree where I had played as a child and touched its wide bole. The words Aunt Mairi taught me to say came back clearly:

Hear me, Saint Brighid, I ask in thy name
That my hands be filled always with thy healing flame.
I ask thee to make me courageous and wise,
To protect me from hatred and malevolent eyes.
I ask for the blessing of your presence in me.
As I ask it now, so mote it be.

I murmured the words aloud and touched the paired feather-shaped leaves on one arching branch. I felt better immediately, smiled at myself, and stroked the smooth grey bark. Into the thick trunk I breathed: "May I beg a small branch from you?" One must always ask permission of the rowan tree before taking any part of it. They are considered sacred and may not be harmed lest you bring bad luck to yourself and family. The wind soughed through the branches and a small one touched my face lightly. I gently removed the proffered twig, placed it carefully in my arisaid and went home to look for a piece of red ribbon to tie around it.

* * *

Two days later, Aunt Mairi found me in the garden working on the small space allowed for herbs. As usual I had not heard her footsteps. She motioned for me to continue and stood there fingering the carving in her staff, looking around, turning her face to the sun. The diffuse light washed away her wrinkles and just below the surface I could see the girl she had been. She spoke just loudly enough for me to hear. "This morning Ysabell came to the laird and told him that his wife was bleeding because you took away the potion she made. She also accused you of casting a spell over one of the village lads."

I sat back. "I took the simple, aye. Lady Anne needs neither laudanum nor anything else. As for the lad, he was as drunk as David's sow, and tried to pull me behind a gorse bush and paw me. He was fortunate I only kicked him in the shins and not the part he was using to think. His wife came upon us and screeched that it was all my fault, and that I had bewitched her man with my devil's hair. Then she dragged him off by his ear."

Aunt Mairi laughed, but then said seriously, "I told the laird as much, but you should know that he is beguiled by Ysabell. Anne is unattractive with the babe, and ill-tempered too. Ysabell makes clever use of that and is always there to soothe the laird and cast Anne as a fractious child. Should something befall Anne, Ysabell would be well placed to be his next wife. Aye, she is older, but not enough to matter to a besotted male."

I frowned. "Then mayhap the laudanum was not well meant."

"You have been away, child…people alter. Are you no longer sensing others?"

I flushed guiltily. I could not tell her I was deliberately blocking my feelings. "Not so much, Aunt Mairi. It saps my strength." The truth is that it hurt. I remembered the resentment I felt from my father, then his indifference. I had not seen him for years before I left for university and had not asked of him since I returned. It was easier to feel nothing. Yet I remembered the laird's words about needing my help, and guilt began to build inside me. I had deliberately rejected my gift because I believed it had hurt me and wanted nothing to do with it.

Aunt Mairi thumped her staff on the ground. "'Tis a gift from the lady. Do not waste it." She turned and glided away as softly as a dandelion seedling on the wind. In truth, I was a coward. I feared the pain, but I had been given a command. I would have to try harder.

I retrieved my basket and was strolling toward the castle door when I heard the sweet sound of a lute coming from inside the ruins of the old castle-keep. I turned toward it. The roof had long since fallen in, and the honey-colored light of afternoon poured over the stones, warming them. I had loved playing there as a child, hiding from Janet in the small caves created by rotting floors and walls, inaccessible to all but children and animals. The sound came from the farthest corner. The performer, hidden behind a screen of broken stones, was playing with such raw despair that I was unable to move. The music stopped unexpectedly and the player, garbed in his habitual black, stood. Impossibly, it was Sir Ross Campbell's manservant, Gregor Volkof. He put the lute down carefully and bowed, donning the blank face he wore like a cloak till no trace of the man who had been baring his soul with music remained.

"You play the lute?" I said stupidly.

* * *

"My lady." Sir Ross Campbell turned and made a graceful leg as Gregor, and I walked into the laird's library. It was a spacious room warmed by a substantial stone fireplace flanked by wooden bookcases. Tapestries and paintings covered the walls, evidence of Lady Anne's dowry. Two heavily carved chairs faced the flames, a table between them, on which Sir Ross hastily placed his cup as he stood. I hardly recognised him. He was richly clad and laced in the latest fashion, the red-gold velvet of his jacket only a shade darker than his sandy hair. But his beard was gone, revealing a strong jaw and a wide, well-defined mouth in a face that now verged on gaunt. I wondered if he had been ill, but the loss of weight and beard had rendered him quite attractive. His blue eyes regarded me with amusement. I had the uncomfortable feeling he could read my thoughts and felt the blood rising to my cheeks as he said, "I bring you gifts and tidings from your friends at Torrport."

"Sir!" I smiled at him with true pleasure. "When did you arrive? I am delighted beyond measure to see you. What could possibly bring you all the way to Dunvegan?" I looked from him to the laird, questioning.

"My Lady Elspeth, is not your charming self enough to bring me? And do you not remember that I have kin nearby?" He bowed low over my hand, speaking quietly so that only I could hear: "We must talk. I bring a warning. Your laird is in grave danger." I almost jerked my fingers free in shock but caught myself in time and simply bowed my head and tried to simper. It must have been effective enough. The laird seemed not to notice anything amiss, although something akin to glee flickered in the black depths of Gregor's eyes at my posturing. Heat suffused my face.

The laird offered me and Gregor a dram, but I declined. Gregor was still carrying his instrument, and deliberately engaged the laird in a discussion of the relative merits of the oboe and the lute, allowing Sir Ross to speak privately with me. It seems Laird MacDuff of Torrport was concerned about the health of the MacLeod and his family. They had bonded at the meeting in Torrport this summer past, and MacDuff was disturbed by rumors of poison and witchcraft at Dunvegan. When one of Sir Ross's informants repeated the tales, Laird MacDuff decided the MacLeod should be warned. Sir Ross said he would tell me more later. He looked at me for a moment, then said quietly, "And I fear for you as well, my lady. Never forget we are yours to command should you need us. I have business on Skye, so we shall be nearby." He bowed and returned to the laird.

His words shook me. I was certain that all this was more than I wanted to manage alone. Cawdie and Janet were lost in the world of being newly wed and I could not let my problems be a burden to them. I would cease procrastinating and write to Malcolm tonight, asking him to come help us. I trusted him as well as anyone, and lest he think I was having one of my feminine starts, I would send my Fortuna ring. He knows I would never part with it unless things were dire. Fortuna would protect and guide him on his journey as well. Till he arrived, I could look after myself. It never once occurred to me that Malcolm might not come. I simply knew I needed him, and he would be here.

* * *

Janet found me treating a neck boil on one of the kitchen maids. It had finally come to a head after being covered with a piece of fat bound to it overnight. She watched me silently as I used the tip of a scalpel to split the hot yellow center of the eruption, then pressed gently with my fingers to bring the core just above the surface. I twisted a length of thread into the congealed pus and pulled slowly upwards. The core slipped out followed by a spurt of blood and smelly matter. After washing it away I applied a honey, garlic, and sage salve. A clean bandage on the wound, a small jar of the salve for the lass, and it was finished. I washed my hands and looked at Janet. "Aye?"

"Lady Anne has begun her birthing and the babe is unnaturally placed."

We found Lady Anne sitting in a chair covered with linen pads and surrounded by her women. Her head was thrown back as she groaned and arched in agony. They moved as we entered, except for one who nodded and continued wiping Anne's face with lavender water. Ysabell stood quietly nearby, wiping her fingers on a crumpled linen towel. I ran my hand over Lady Anne's distended belly. The shoulder and head of the babe were palpably up. "Has her water broken?"

"Nay, Mistress," answered a toothpick of a woman, her brow furrowed with worry.

"Good!" It would be easier to turn the child while it was enclosed in the liquid. I rubbed Anne's stomach soothingly, noting the time between contractions, and reached into my bag for a bottle of oil of sage. I poured it into both my hands and on the skin of her belly. Closing my eyes, I found the babe by touch, fit my palms around the tiny shoulder and head, and firmly pushed them clockwise. Anne shouted some words I had not suspected her of knowing. The pliant bones of the babe resisted, then the wee body suddenly flipped and dropped into place. The water broke and her labour quickened.

Two hours later, Lady Anne gave birth to a mewling son. The after-burden soon followed, intact. There were no rips nor tears, so I cleaned her secrets with scented oil, put several clouts between her legs to absorb the sluggish bleeding, and we were through. Mother and bairn were bathed, put into clean linens, and fell immediately into a deep healing sleep ere the laird could be summoned from his bed.

Chapter 4: Malcolm

S*omewhere off the south coast of Skye, Scotland; September 1705.*

The squall pounced as we were nearing Skye, shredding the sail as men struggled to tie everything down and keep her upright. Captain Wilson held her into the wind, spindrift flying with each plunge into cold-dark waves. She was a birlinn merchant ship with a single sail and oars, well suited for these waters but not a storm like this.

One of the men lashing the sail pointed up to the yardarm and shouted something about gulls. Others were visibly startled when they saw them there in a neat row, malevolent eyes locked on us. More birds joined until a dozen or so perched, unruffled as if the storm were naught. It was a queer sight, but we had better things to do than gawk, and the captain was bellowing at us to work harder and bail faster. I was beside him in the stern, bailing and wondering about the seabirds and our fate, when he grabbed my arm. "Ignore them...a foolish superstition is all!" he shouted, white knuckling the rudder. I was not so sure. What people believe; they do. I had seen it too many times, and these men looked very alarmed.

I shook my fist at the gulls and cried, "In the name of God, be off!" Not sure why I did that, perhaps an instinct bubbling up from some terrifying ancestral memory. The birds cried back angrily, shaking their heads as if in disbelief, then they seemed to jeer as each one flew off their frightful line, one after the other. The men raised a cheer, as though by some miracle we had been saved. But our bailing was not enough and the birlinn started coming apart at the seams as rivets popped, like muffled gunshots punctuating the groans of loosing wood.

Within the hour we knew we could not hold on much longer, so the captain gave orders to ready ourselves to run her aground. He had turned the birlinn head-on to the beach and we roped ourselves to her and prayed she did not capsize. In those last yards, she bucked and rolled like an enraged animal trying to rid us from her back; then, on the crest of one mighty wave, she surged forward and smashed herself on the stony beach, sending us tumbling forward, submerged in roiling surf. We untangled ourselves and fought our way ashore as best we could, battling fear and chaos as much as the elements. Miraculously, no one was lost.

* * *

We had survived, but just, and now all we could do was wait for the inevitable attack, crouched in the stem of our broken birlinn. It was but a few hours after the wreck and the captain had spotted them first, men coming over the hills toward us, armed and huddling in groups beyond the range of our guns. They were not here to rescue us.

"It may be best for you to make your escape now, Sir Malcolm," the captain advised.

"I'll stay," I answered. "Don't much like wandering around in the gloom, anyway." I grinned at him, and in the twilight, I could see him nod from under a plaid pulled over his head. He was a man of middle years with a swarthy face, lined from alcoholic abuse and years at sea.

"As you wish," the captain responded with that look one gives a fool, then he glanced back at the men. "Could start anytime now, lads. *Ready weapons*."

They would come at first dark. They knew the land, we did not, and they saw we were pinned on that rocky beach like many others they had plundered. I had only my flintlock pistol, cutlass, and dagger, and needed to make the first shot count before they got too close. It takes a steady hand, and many men cannot shoot straight under duress. That would not be me. I have killed before. A shameful thing to admit if you are a physician, but sometimes circumstances required it. Well at least that is how I rationalized it.

We had twelve men of various ages, a few with damp muskets, plus the captain and me against God knows how many locals. In these parts they are of the MacDonald Clan, although their laird would disavow them if confronted. Plundering is an old and very illegal sport along these coasts. Many here would say it is their due, the harvest from *their* coast and as proper as any made by crofter or fisher. Others beg to differ.

We could hear them murmuring beyond the shrubs past the beach. It was unnerving and no doubt part of their plan. One of them shouted in a gravelly voice, "Walk away and you'll be unharmed. 'Tis nae ye we wish, guid sirs." He was speaking in a Highland Scots dialect, a mongrel tongue, part Gaelic and English.

I looked at our captain. It was a hard choice: our lives or his ruin. A few of our men whispered as the captain weighed his options. He had owned this wee ship, such as she was, only a few years before it was due to be scrapped. He told me he had saved over twenty years to buy her. Got her for a decent price, he had said proudly. I doubted that, seeing how easily her hull had caved on the rocks. If he walked away, he would never captain again, and experience a life of poverty till he died of grief and starvation in the Glasgow slums. It was all too easy to fall to ruin these days. "Watch your step, laddie," my father oft times counseled me.

"Shall we save ourselves, sir?" the captain asked, gripping the gunwale, the surf rocking us none too gently.

I leaned close. "Aye, we shall save ourselves, but only by fighting. I don't believe they will let us go free to testify to their crimes. There is only one way out of this." I tapped my pistol in case he missed my intent.

He extended his free hand. "If we live, it will be my honor to serve you in future, sir." I shook his hand warmly as a brother-in-arms. The bond of conflict does that to men. Then he crawled along the tilted deck and greeted each of his men with a handclasp and encouraging words. A few minutes later, standing tall on the foredeck, he bellowed to our opponents, "Come if you must! Your blood will wash our decks clean of the stench of this foul land, and when we are home, tales of your villainy will be told throughout Scotland."

He was taunting them. It was done. No attempt to bargain or cajole. I knew he had decided the right thing. Any sign of weakness would only have invited attack. Perhaps now they would leave. But it was not to be. Moments later we had our response.

"They're coming!" He did not have to tell us. We could hear them scrambling though the shrubs. It was almost dark, the last of the colour had drained from the evening sky, replaced by palpable fear under a vault of stars. "Don't shoot till they are clear on the beach," Captain Wilson ordered, then took position up front with his weathered musket.

The minutes before a battle feel overly long and have us wishing an end. Should we not savour this blessed time lived without pain and remorse? Instead, we wish them over and run headlong to death. Humans are a perverse species.

My pistol was ready and resting on the gunwale, eyes searching the shrubs. I took a few deep breaths to calm the nerves. We knew not what we faced. We could be overwhelmed in seconds, or not. It was in the hands of whoever decides the outcomes of battles.

There was movement on the right. "Wait," whispered the captain. "No firing till I say."

Then a shot was fired on our left, then a whoop, and one of our young lads fired back. Our captain cursed him. Then it was quiet again. I could hear my breathing and the men behind me settling on the deck. Looking up at the stars I remembered the letter from Elspeth and felt the well-worn Roman ring on my finger that had accompanied it. She was why I was here on the shore of this god-forsaken coast. Sir Malcolm, renowned physician, and son of Lord William Forrester.

I chuckled and thought I must thank Elspeth one day, provided I lived to see her again. She owed me a good meat pie and pint of ale, at the very least. We had worked together in Torrport till she was called back by her laird to face allegations of witchcraft. She is no witch, but her medical skills as a healer might be thought so by the ignorant. It had taken a month to find a *locum* physician to serve in my stead at Torrport, as I could not leave my patients without care. That delay put me into September and uncertain weather, and now I was paying the price.

More movement from the shrubs, then banging on the hull. They must be throwing rocks, trying to spook us, to make our boys waste more ammunition, or to gauge our strength and discipline. Then another whoop and clanging weapons like they were charging. We watched. Nothing happened and this time no one on our side fired. They did this on and off through most of the night, keeping us awake and on edge.

* * *

It was the bottom of night, perhaps around three or four o'clock, when bodies crave sleep, and the senses are disoriented. We were wrapped in plaids and skins, the chill from the sea relentlessly absorbing our body heat. Hours ago, we were ready to fight, nerves up, and now torpor was the rule. But it must be as bad for them. They knew we had muskets, but not how many. In truth we only had a few, enough to thin their ranks at best, provided our lads did not waste their chance. In battle, it is all about controlling nerves, and I was not certain we had the discipline.

The mind tends to notice changes more than routine, and that is why I heard something in the water, aft along my side of the ship, a noise like that of a seal or fish surfacing but not quite. Something had changed. I could sense it. A frisson of nerves tickled my spine. Leaning forward, I patted the captain on the shoulder and tilted my head in the direction of the sound. "I heard it too," his voice wavering from stress and fatigue.

"I'll go," I replied, then moved as quietly as I could over half-asleep men. No one was aft of the mast; all of us were in the fore, facing the enemy. The birlinn is a small craft much like a Viking ship, but shorter and with a rudder instead of steering oars. It could be rowed or sailed, and there were many variations and sizes plying these waters. Ours was about forty feet long, with a single mast and a crude serpent figure carved into the raised prow. The aft was floating freely, the fore caught on the beach. I wondered how likely it would be for a Highlander to be able to swim through freezing water to attack us from the stern. No doubt the captain thought it unlikely, so he placed all our men in the fore. I was not so sure. The captain was going with the odds; few Highlanders could swim well, and it would take mere minutes in that water to render a man unconscious. I peered over the side. Nothing but starlight flickering in the water. I pointed my pistol down, slowed my breath, and looked again. Still nothing. Was the sound just amplified nature, and nerves overreacting?

I sat back and thought of Elspeth's letter again. She believed someone was trying to harm and overthrow her laird and seize the MacLeod Clan of Skye. My father wanted me to investigate, "for the sake of Scotland," he had said. I could not refuse them. Amid these thoughts in the still air came a feeling, a sense of something malicious close by. I looked behind and there it was over me, a dark mass obscuring the stars. I tried to raise my pistol, but it was on me fast, its weight smothering me in fur. It was biting or clawing my face. I punched it hard, to negligible effect. It growled and clawed again. I tried to push it off, one hand on its hairy face, the other trying to grip the wet fur of its body. It seemed the size of a small bear—far too strong for me. I punched it again, but it was undeterred, so I covered my face with my arms as best I could as it continued its attack.

The creature roared in my ear, then I heard gunfire and metal clashing nearby. I cried out for help, but the cries of the other men drowned out my pitiful voice. I knew then I could not expect help, so I stopped struggling, hoping it would lose interest or assume I was dead. Its face came close to mine, fur pressed to my stubble, and it was reeking of that distinctive smell of onion and whisky—and at once I knew it was no animal! Seconds later, he rose and struck at me, the blow glancing ineffectually off my shoulder. He turned away and I could see his dark form crawling toward our men.

I yelled, "Behind you!" but no one noticed. My pistol was a yard away when I found it. I pulled my cutlass and crept toward him. Ahead, I could see bodies on the deck and men fighting furiously, grunts and shouts covering the sound of our approach. The man-creature was close to them, ready to spring. This was my chance, while he focused on his next victim. I was only a few feet away and if he turned on me, it was over. My pistol felt made of lead as I raised it. *Steady now, Malcolm. Make it count.* One deep breath as Father had taught me, then I squeezed off the shot. He lurched as my bullet found its mark, I backed away, just in case, and raised my cutlass. Two more heaves of his chest and he slumped. Everyone had heard my pistol shot. They looked back. The man-creature was a dark lump on the deck with me behind, cutlass raised.

"They got Rory!" one of the MacDonald men said. Then they began retreating, clambering over the gunwale, and running back through the shrubs. It was over quickly, at least for now, leaving us wondering what had happened.

We had a few injured, the worst a young lad with a nasty slash on his chest. I took charge and we quickly had torches, a makeshift bed, my medical bag, and of course the compulsory horn of whisky for him. He was grimacing as I pressed a cloth on the gash to stop the bleeding. "Looks like a nice clean incision of only four or five inches. You'll live." I chuckled to make light of it.

He took another slug of whisky. His body gave an involuntary shudder. "Thank you, emm…doctor?"

"Aye, my name is Malcolm Forrester and I'm a physician, from Torrport, near Edinburgh."

"We are lucky to have had you aboard, doctor," the captain said as he knelt beside me, concerned about the lad's health, and wanting to help. I asked him to hold the bandage in place while I fetched my surgery kit.

"It's a simple wound," I told the lad. "You'll have a scar to impress the lasses and prove you were in a battle." He giggled. Does not take much to change the mood sometimes. "Looks like the bleeding has stopped. I'm going to put in a few stitches. Have another swig of that whisky before I start. Could sting a little." I did not have to suggest it twice. He downed another large gulp.

I leaned closer to the captain. "Have two of your men hold him down. I'll stitch, and you wipe excess blood. Understand?" He nodded and waved over a few men and quietly told them. They knew what to do.

"It'll be over in a few minutes, son. Brave it out." His eyes were dilated, and a sheen of sweat glistened his smooth face. It is not that painful to be stitched up, but the mind can convince otherwise. I was using a curved surgical needle with silk thread, all new and purchased in Edinburgh before I left. The captain could see I was ready and when I nodded, he lifted the bandage. I wiped the incision with a whisky-soaked rag and flushed it with more. The boy's eyes opened wide, and his body bucked. The wound was oozing blood slowly, a good sign that nothing major had been severed. I worked quickly, pinching the skin with one hand while sliding the needle through with the other in a continuous looping pattern. The first few are the worst for the patient, even with the numbing of the whisky.

"Breathe, lad," I said calmly. "Only a few more." Of course, there were more than a few but the men held him securely and the captain wiped his face tenderly. It did not take long to finish. Afterwards they wrapped him in his wool plaid and soon he was asleep. There were a few other minor injuries, including my claw wounds that I treated before I slept.

* * *

Our attackers did not come back that night. We discovered at dawn that the man-creature was a hulking bearded Highlander dressed in a sealskin suit and wearing a cleverly made claw mitt fashioned from leather and sharpened bits of cow horn. By light of day, the world made perfect sense. We had lost one, throat slashed, when they had boarded our ship. The MacDonalds left four dead on the beach and the man-creature on our boat. We had done well, considering. But had the creature's attack from the rear worked? Cunning of them, between that and their other tricks.

Our dead seaman was Daniel Walker, one of the regulars on this ship, married and from Glasgow. I recorded his death, and at the next opportunity would lay responsibility for it at the feet of the MacDonald chieftain. Walker's widow deserved something.

* * *

"'Tis best to follow the drove road to Dunvegan." Captain Wilson had one knee on a patch of sand where he had drawn a crude map of Skye with his finger. "A few miles north along the coast is Kylerhea, where the cattle cross to the mainland." His finger made a hole on the east coast, then drew a line to the northwest. "You'll pass Broadford here, then go north to Kinloch Ainort on the east coast. From there go north and west to Sligachan, then across over and north again to Dunvegan." He made more marks and looked up at me to make sure I understood.

I was not certain I wanted to walk the last part of my trip, but the captain thought it best. We had been on alert all last night again, waiting for them to come back and have another go at us, but there had been nothing but night sounds, intensified by fear.

"How far is it from Kylerhea to Dunvegan?" I asked, hoping it was not as far as it looked.

"I'd hazard fifty miles, more with the ups and downs." The captain had the look of a man whose resilience was near an end. "Should take no more than a week, even if you dawdle and see the sights."

I was dubious. This is rough country, and one could get lost for weeks in the endless glens and mountains. "Are the drove roads marked?"

"Nay, beyond the lack of vegetation. But there is a river of cattle coming across Skye this time of year on the way to the Tryst at Crieff. Just ask the drovers you meet. Most are good men."

"And those who aren't?"

"Sir Malcolm, I am sorry, but I cannot guarantee your safety. We will try to repair my boat. We have the supplies, but it could take weeks, and who knows what the MacDonalds have in mind?" He looked tired and discouraged, kneeling on the sand like that. "Then there is revenge for killing their men. By custom, they have six days to kill us, but they must do it openly. It is without legal recourse—not that there is much out here in any case. Now is your chance to escape. I would take it if I were you. One of my men will accompany you to Kylerhea, then make his way home to Glasgow. He has a young wife and children and no stomach for this. As for me—" He stopped mid-sentence, perhaps not wanting to say aloud what we all felt.

He was right, of course. This could devolve into a bloody massacre. Men lose all sense of reason when it comes to honour and greed. "Then I shall take your advice." I reached down to help him up, my guts detesting the idea of leaving these men, but I knew others needed me more. Life is defined by these hard choices, and I hoped I would not regret this one.

He brushed the sand off his salt-stained clothes and said, "Then leave tonight so you can go undetected."

* * *

We spent that day assessing damage to the birlinn and unloading her. It would take a few days of work before the repairs could be made, made more difficult by having to carry everything through waist-high chop. The captain assured the crew that deep in the hold were wood, rivets, and caulking, enough to complete the repairs. By mid-afternoon we were exhausted and bone-chilled and decided to make a fire in the shelter of the stacks of crates and bales. The cargo was manufactured goods from the south, quite valuable to the right people.

To add insult, it had decided to rain heavily as we worked close to the fire to regain lost warmth. One of the sailors was busy boiling oats as others gathered driftwood to burn. I was sorting through my soggy bags looking for the basics and for medical supplies needed to keep me alive during my trip.

"This is Jamie," Captain Wilson said, tugging on the sleeve of a gaunt sandy-haired lad. "He will accompany you to Kylerhea."

I nodded. "Do you have a pack? It's a long walk back to Glasgow."

He looked at the captain, who said on his behalf, "Just a plaid and some oats. He's a tough one, aren't you, laddie?" The boy with the wife and children looked unsure.

"I'll be ready at sunset, Jamie," I said.

The boy was silent, but the captain bent close to me and whispered, "A word, if you please." He took my elbow and guided me away from the others. "I will do my best to deliver your goods to Dunvegan. You have my promise."

"And..." I said, waiting for the rest.

"And I need a favor."

"Of course." I smiled but inwardly sighed. They always need a favour.

"I have these letters. Two are *especially important*." He opened a small satchel on his belt. There were several papers, as well as a pipe and tobacco. He flipped through them till he found the two. They were folded and sealed with wax. "This one is for the innkeeper in Sligachan, the other for a gentleman in Dunvegan. It is *crucial* these letters be delivered, and my situation—"

"Aye, I understand, but I may not make it either."

The MacDonalds had not attacked the previous night; but they knew the ship was being unloaded. They had more options now. They could just wait and hope the ship could not be repaired. In that case, the captain would have no choice but to abandon her and the cargo. But if he could make the repairs, they could still sabotage her before the cargo was reloaded. The captain was in an exceedingly risky situation.

He pushed the letters at me desperately. "Just get past these wreckers tonight. Tell all you meet on the drove road you are a doctor, give them aid and they will help you."

"I'll do my best, but like you, I can offer no assurances."

"Then may God protect us," said he while looking to the sky and making the sign of the cross.

"I pray so," I muttered without much conviction, taking his letters, and quickly stuffing them in my cloak.

"I've given Jamie a letter for my wife, and one for Daniel Walker's," he said, "in case I should not return. You might wish to give him a letter for your family."

"I will."

"Now ask the cook for some oats and onions for your trip, and Godspeed."

"Good luck to you as well."

It was too wet to write, so I sat beside Jamie and had him memorize my father's name and address and told him he would be well rewarded. Then I finished packing and made a sling to carry my few supplies. The oats were ready, and we ate like condemned men at our last meal. My belly full, I leaned back against the crates and pulled a rain-soaked plaid around me. It was a depressing sight, our grim little band of castaways, dashed on the rocks like human refuse for the MacDonalds to scavenge. It would be a quite a feat if they could repair the ship and get out of here alive. I truly wished them well.

* * *

The last thing the captain said to us was, "Stay low and close to the water." Jamie was muttering prayers, eyes cast to the heavens. I was adjusting my sling. The captain turned away with a curt nod and told his men to assume defensive positions, this time with half the cargo on the beach to defend as well.

Jamie was rooted to the spot, and I had to tug on his shirt to get him moving. "This way, Jamie," said I, with an encouraging smile. We had only a few miles to the cattle crossing at Kylerhea, but the coast is rugged, strewn with rocks and seaweed, hard enough to manage in daylight, never mind at night without a torch. At least it was still raining, that and the sound of the surf masking the noise we made sloshing.

Time is deceptive at night, and in our heightened state of awareness, the hike seemed to take hours till we rounded the point and could see what we assumed was Glenelg on the right and Kylerhea ahead and to our left. We had made it! I sat on a rock, relief flushing away fatigue and stress; but then I thought I heard something behind us. I looked around, saw nothing, but just in case slid to the ground behind the rock, pulling Jamie down with me. I held my finger to my lips. He nodded. Then out of the murk came a tiny glow and the murmur of men. They, too, were following the shoreline and coming our way. We held our breath as they came close. The one in front was sucking his pipe, crouch-walking with something in his right hand. Another was several feet behind, cursing as he stumbled.

"Shut yer trap, John," the one in front hissed.

I could not count on Jamie for much in a fight, so if they found us, we would have to surrender. That was not an option I wanted to consider seriously, so I pointed to the water and tugged on Jamie to follow. We were only a few feet from water's edge, and it was easy enough to slither on our bellies into the low surf. I could hear Jamie moan as the chill shock bit home. We lay there wedged in a jumble of soggy wood, holding each other, listening, hoping they would not stop. My first thought was that I was glad I had wrapped those letters in oilskin. Funny, the absurd things one thinks to avoid present reality.

"Don't see 'em," one of them whispered as they stood on the shore a few feet away.

"Let's get back then," the other responded. "Could use a break from this shite."

I knew we had only minutes before the deadly chill set in, and I could feel my heart pumping hard to keep me alive. Jamie already was shivering. I had to get us out of here soon or it would be too late.

One of the men onshore took a drink from a horn, then passed it to the other. *Leave, for God's sake!* I thought, trying to hold on. I could feel Jamie pulling on my hand to rise out of the water. I forced him back under, but I knew I could not for much longer. My shivers had begun too, and I knew that once the shivering stopped, it was all but over. In the end, one does not care as the mind is enveloped in the lethargy that precedes unconsciousness. I remembered it well, hanging on to Captain Mackmain underwater as we tried to kill each other at Leith. *I hate freezing water!*

I lost focus on the two men for a time as thoughts internalized around agony, but it looked like they'd gone, so I released my grip on Jamie and tentatively rose out of the sea, hoping my eyes hadn't been fooled. "Jamie, let's go." It was all I could do to get those words past the shivers. He seemed stuck, or had not heard, so I dragged him up and we splashed ashore. "We need to keep moving," I urged. "Head to those fires over there," I pointed. He seemed aware now, muttering more prayers. I hoped he would be fine once we got moving.

It was raining hard, but it did not matter. We were as wet as we were going to be as we scrambled over rocks and debris as fast as we could, only a mile or so from safety. I had pushed Jamie in front, so I would not lose him, my heart buoyed by a fantasy of drying by a fire and warming my innards with oatmeal and whisky. Then there was a shout from behind, and a muffled gunshot. I glanced back. Two men, fifty yards away and closing fast. "Run, Jamie!" I yelled. I heard another shot. Did not look back this time. Jamie stumbled. I yanked him up. We kept going. I was at my limit, lungs aching. Then a scream from behind and some cursing. I wished them ill and grinned as I smelled the cattle for the first time.

Steamy heat from our bovine brethren welcomed us, accompanied by the less friendly sounds of dogs barking and drovers shouting. I pulled Jamie down behind one of the cows, scooting close and feeling her lovely warmth, trying to be silent while lungs heaved. Our cow shifted, looked back at us, nostrils flaring, sucking in our scent, no doubt wondering if we were a threat. I patted her gently, then peeked back and could no longer see our pursuers. Now we just had to deal with the drovers. "We'll stay here for a bit," I whispered to Jamie. "See what happens." He moaned in response.

I did not much like the idea of confronting the drovers in the dark. They could mistake us for thieves, and we did not need more trouble. I spoke soothingly to our hairy hostess. She settled, but the dogs did not, and it was but a few minutes before they found us there huddled in the muck.

"Get up, ye bastards!" The drover behind the dogs snarled menacingly, waving what looked like a pistol.

"Good sir … don't shoot! We are *not* here to steal." I got to my feet carefully, my hands in the air, so he could see. "Get up, Jamie!" I hissed.

"Ah see nae other reason a man would be here this night but tae thieve," the drover with the pistol said.

"I swear, good sir, we were shipwrecked and only seek hospitality. In the light, you will see that I am a gentleman accompanied by a boy who is on his way home to Glasgow."

"Billy and Bobby, heel," he said calmly to the dogs, and they immediately returned to his side. "And why should ah help ye?"

There was silence for a moment, then I remembered the captain's advice. "I am a physician. If you need one, I can trade for such as you can offer."

He grunted. "Ye sound like a damned Lowlander. If ye are as ye say, we can use ye, but nae tricks, mind ye."

I sighed with relief. "There will be none from me. Now if you can share that warm fire, we will be appreciative."

And so it was that we were cautiously welcomed to the drovers' camp. It was there I discovered that Jamie had been shot.

* * *

Jamie had been hit in the *latissimus dorsi* muscle just under his armpit. The bullet had sliced a neat gouge from back to front across his torso. We laid him down on some heather they had piled as a makeshift bed. There were two drovers and four dogs. The drover who had caught us was older, heavily bearded, with that sinewy look of a man who had lived rough most of his life. The other was much younger, with a scruffy beard and a crossed eye that made him look confused.

"Can you spare some whisky for the lad?" I asked the drovers.

Jamie is one of those taciturn types who says little and complains less. He lay there, his breathing ragged, enduring pain as though it were an expected part of life. The bullet had gone through his cloak and shirt, and both were soaked in blood and seawater. I had to work quickly. "Stay with me, Jamie, we'll get you home." I rolled up his soaked shirt and pressed it into the wound.

"Can one of you hold this in place while I find my surgery tools?" I said this as a command and the young drover instantly knelt to help. "I can use more light here too." The older man grumbled but pulled a few pieces of burning driftwood from the fire and laid them on the other side of us. There was no whisky forthcoming, so I removed Jamie's belt and had him bite on the end. "This will be quick, Jamie." I looked in his eyes to gauge his response. He gave a curt nod.

There was not much to it. I flushed the wound with my meager supply of alcohol, then let it bleed for a bit. There seemed to be no major arteries involved so I decided to cauterize and bandage. Even the drovers looked away as I pressed the hot metal rod home while Jamie screamed. It was all I could do for him. God and good fortune would have to take care of the rest.

* * *

The rain had stopped overnight. I awoke miserably cold and hungry, feeling Jamie beside me, warm and alive. At least there was that. The drovers were already up stoking the fire and cooking more of those dreadful oats. I had only been traveling several days and already missed my morning coffee with bread and jam while reading the newspaper. But my mind needed more useful thoughts.

It turned out we were camped on a slight rise, like an island floating in a sea of shaggy black cattle, hundreds of them being readied to swim the mile across to the mainland. Our drovers were not the only ones here. Several others were farther north, busy readying small boats used to guide the cattle. Our drovers said it would take all day to shuttle theirs across, tied nose to tail, five at a time, with a rowboat in the lead. Cattle are surprisingly capable swimmers, but even so the strong current and eddies were a challenge.

"Have some porridge, sir." The young drover offered a steaming bowl after I returned from relieving myself.

"It smells delicious," I mocked. That made the lad grin.

"Would you care for some fresh cow's blood as well?" he asked, obviously wittier than he looked. I chuckled and politely declined his kind offer.

Jamie was slow to rise. He was awake and alert, but the pain must have been tremendous. "Here, lie back on my pack. Have some oatmeal while I look at your wound." I pulled up his darkly stained shirt and he lifted his elbow while ravenously shoveling in my oatmeal. *At least he has a good appetite,* I thought. But the wound was inflamed. "This needs further treatment," I mumbled, searching my medical bag for that elusive blue bottle of Arquebusade herbal water, a secret and expensive formulation used for gunshot wounds. It was found near the bottom of my bag, of course. "I'm going to dab some of this on your wound. It'll sting." I noticed he'd finished my oatmeal, so in revenge I made sure his wound was well soaked with the Arquebusade. His eyes bulged, but to his credit he said nothing. "Jamie, keep it clean and when you come upon a farm, beg for some honey to put on it. It might help with the inflammation; and for God's sake take it easy with that arm, you don't want to reopen that wound." I hoped he was paying attention.

* * *

It did not take long for word to get around that there was a doctor available, so I spent the day treating minor complaints. The Highland drovers are a healthy lot when they are not killing each other. They come in all ages, from teenage boys to old men. Most are crofters trying to add some extra coin to the family coffers. I soon discovered they are a glib bunch too, once the barriers of suspicion are lifted.

An older man with constipation said his family was a sept of Clan Donald. He tried to tell me his life story, as much as he could fit in the minutes it took me to diagnose and treat him with a dose of an electuary made of bearberry leaves, prunes, and orange peel. He paid me with an onion, which I gratefully added to my supply. But there was one thing he said that stuck. He asked where I was going, and as soon as I told him, he snorted in derision. "There be naught you can do ta save that lad."

"Meaning?" I asked.

"He's one foot in the grave," the old drover chortled, "and the other being sliced away by his enemies."

"To whom are you referring?"

"The Laird Macleod, a course! 'Tis *well known* he's a weak one. They're calling for doctors to come save him and his wee one."

"It's *well known,* is it?" I repeated, imagining the carrion eaters circling.

* * *

By mid-afternoon, most of the cattle had made the crossing and my bag of oats and onions was full. There was but one incident that day, a humorous mishap that involved much yelling as the lead cow in a group broke free and pulled the rest with her back to Skye. Even the dogs had a challenging time convincing her to turn around. Perhaps she knew instinctively where she was headed.

Meanwhile, Jamie tried to make himself useful despite my admonitions. He could still walk, he insisted, and the cold ground was not so comfortable, even with the heather. So, he spent the day helping guide cattle into the frigid water. Turns out he made a wise choice, as by afternoon he was on joking terms with many of the drovers.

By dusk the drover groups had split. Some were camped on the mainland at Glenelg, while the rest were with us on Skye guarding the remaining cattle. We joined a group settling in for the night that included the old drover who had captured us. It was an evening I shall not soon forget.

* * *

The festivities started and ended with porridge and onions, this time cooked with liberal amounts of cow's blood and a lump of suet which turned it into a rich black pudding. It was quite good despite the ingredients, and we were well sated by the time one of the men brought out a small keg of whisky. It was fine drink, and we filled our cups often that night; and then someone unrolled bagpipes, and whisky-lowered inhibitions soon had us singing and dancing with wild abandon round the fire, boots thumping, kilts twirling, like a frolic of inebriated fairies. It was a time to celebrate. For many this would be their last night on Skye till spring, for others a time to say goodbye and head home for the winter. Whatever the case, all of us knew the days ahead would be arduous and often cruel. It was the life of a Highland drover, and for these few hours we would laugh, sing, dance, and pretend life was grand. But it never lasts, does it? Soon the whisky barrel was empty. Soon we slumped on heaps of heather, and soon we grew quiet, feeling the misty rain, hearing the cattle lowing, seeing dogs curl close to the remnants of the fire.

Then one of the drovers said, "And where are you from, sir?"

I was not sure who he meant. I had been daydreaming of that time last spring when we had begun our smallpox experiment, so full of idealism and resolve. We *would* find a cure, wouldn't we? I pushed that memory back to wherever it lives when he asked again. This time I knew he meant me, he the piper, eyes glinting from beyond the fire. "I'm from Torrport, born in Corstorphine, on my way to Dunvegan to see a patient."

"Thought you must be a *Lowlander*." I could hardly see his face, but that last part came across sounding like it was accompanied by a sneer.

"Are you from Skye, then? Handsome country, isn't it?" I offered him a smile that he likely did not see in the dark.

"Ah be from Skye, and if ye lived here ye would know it may look bonnie but 'tis treacherous as well, like many women." Everyone chuckled but me.

"I have not had that experience with women. Perhaps you have been unlucky."

"Ah have been unlucky to find myself here with ye, sir."

That jibe was not so subtle, and I was not sure of his intent, so I chose my words carefully. "We've had a fine celebration, have we not? I for one am glad of your company." I was half drunk and tired. It was the best I could do. Some men become belligerent when drunk, and cajole and avoid as you may, violence oft times puts the stopper on nights like these. I was the odd man here, and perhaps he saw an easy victim. Jamie lay asleep beside me. I gave him a nudge. He woke with a cough.

The piper continued, "Heard there were troubles. Men attacked and killed while fishing."

I sat upright, heart rate climbing, muscles tensing, my mind considering options. "If you mean the shipwreck, aye, a few were killed trying to plunder her. I was there, and *no one* was fishing."

Jamie must have missed the first part because he blurted, "And Sir Malcolm killed that ugly Highlander that was dressed as a seal!" He laughed, still drunk. I instantly regretted waking him. No one else laughed. Instead, all eyes swiveled to the rude piper, giving me a moment to glare menacingly at Jamie. He appeared stunned, then wisely decided to say nothing further.

"That was *me* Cousin Rory," the piper said solemnly, then looked down. At this point, I fully expected him to jump me or pull a pistol, but instead he shook his head and said, "He was an *idiot*, but his mother will miss him."

Even idiots have loving mothers. I had no remorse for killing him. He deserved it if anyone did that night. But empathy for his mother suddenly filled my heart, so I offered to help if I could. The drovers laughed uproariously, like I was a fool. Then they told me that his mother was the leader of the wreckers and likely her idea to dress her son as an animal to attack us from the sea. Truth often inserts its wisdom at unexpected times.

The piper chuckled and shook his head. I was relieved. Had I whisky I would have bought a round, but as it was, all I could offer were my services and thanks for hospitality. I was inundated with requests. The men of Skye knew my route to Dunvegan, of course, so it was, "Please visit my aunt in Broadford..." from one, "My mother has back pains..." from another, "You are going right by his cottage at Drynoch..." from a third, and on and on, till they'd filled my days to the brim with doctoring and I was beginning to wonder when I would have time to walk to Dunvegan before the winter snows. But overall, the day ended well, considering what further evil could have befallen us. I settled into sleep, thankful.

Chapter 5: Malcolm

I was expecting an exploding head with all I had drunk at our impromptu ceilidh, but this time whisky truly seemed the *water of life* and I felt better than I had in weeks. It was a good thing too because I had an exceedingly long trip ahead. Jamie was up as well, and I had a last look at his wound before he prepared to help the drovers ferry the last of the cattle.

"Repeat it." I waited for another recitation of my father's name and address as I pressed some coins into his palm. He sighed and said it one more time. I hoped he would make it home alive, for his sake and mine. "And *remember* the honey...the coin is for that and any further medical attention. The drovers will feed you, provided you work."

"Sorry about—" he was about to apologize again for what he'd said last night, but I shushed him with an "All's well." He was my tenuous link to home, a lad with an infected wound and many miles to walk, but he was young and savvy enough to be useful. He might make it.

I hoisted my pack and gazed up the mountain defile I was about to climb. The day was fresh, with a blustering wind and clouds fighting for space in the blue. The Western Isles of Scotland are as different from the Lowlands as from another continent. Edinburgh is surrounded by dense forests and lush rolling farmland, very prosperous when tended, an intimate land which makes one feel rooted. But then there is the barren Isle of Skye, painted in browns and greens with patches of purple heather and copses of stunted trees huddling in gullies. And those stunning vistas that stretched the eyes. One felt like gulping in miles of air and singing at the top of one's voice. It was that kind of place, a bounty for the spirit but a worrisome paucity for the body.

In a few miles I crested the coastal mountains and could see the hills undulating down toward the north-west and the village of Broadford. It had been a vigorous hike and the fresh air buoyed my spirits, but it did not take long to realize my attire was wholly unsuitable. My tricorn hat was useless, as it continually tried to fly back to Torrport. I stowed it quickly, then had nothing for my head but a mess of hair tied in back. But that was the least of my problems. The only good map I had was the one I had copied from the sand, but even in the first miles it was unclear which way to go beyond following the trail of dung.

To make matter worse, there were numerous streams to ford and the best spots were well-manured through use. First attempts were a disaster as my boots filled and breeches soaked with offal brew. And in these well-used places where a goodly number of people were about, I was forced to strip my lower clothing to wade across, to the sniggers of female onlookers. The locals merely had to remove their soft leather slippers and wool socks, then hike up their kilts, all done quickly and with a modicum of modesty. And many were barefoot, so even less bother. I resolved to buy one of those practical belted plaids at first opportunity.

The inhabitants used the drove roads to haul woven baskets of butter, and bags filled with crowdie cheese roped to the backs of short-legged ponies on their way to the market at Broadford. Some, mainly women and children, carried handicrafts such as woolens and leather goods to be traded for manufactured products from the south. It was that time of the year when crofters were moving from their primitive stone shielings in the high pastures where they grazed cattle to the lower meadows that afforded shelter from the fierce winter winds. Through the summer, they had stored their butter and cheese in the peat bogs found throughout the hills and now it was time to bring it all to market, and to shop and celebrate.

The hike surprisingly was full of interest, with the river of cattle going south-east to Kylerhea and the countercurrent of loaded ponies and walkers plodding to Broadford. In these parts, it is considered bad manners to pass a fellow traveler without stopping for conversation, however brief. The first I met were drovers pushing their herds down the steep road to the flats at the crossing. They were focused on their task and had little to offer but a nod and a "Guid day tae ye." My ears were accustomed to the local dialect now and my mind soon translated it all to more familiar forms, though the droll originals often set me to chuckling as I played over the words after such a meeting.

* * *

"Are you lost, captain?" said a tiny but not frail redhead of indeterminate age, wearing a fastidiously clean blue green arisaid with a white linen blouse frilled at cuffs and collar. I had felt a light touch on the back of my hand when she appeared beside me carrying a large bundle on her head and trailing a wee boy and a long-haired black dog, both eyeing me suspiciously.

"I might be," I chuckled.

"I'm on my way to the market at Broadford to sell my cloths." She squinted up at me while pointing down the valley trail.

"I am going there as well but not to market. Have some people to see and hope to find an inn, then eventually on to Dunvegan." My well-used introduction spilled out effortlessly.

"I wish you well, Captain Forrester, but others may not."

Her use of my surname startled me. "Do I know you?" I asked, thinking I had misheard.

"Aye, long-ago, mayhap. 'Tis good you invoked the name of God this time."

I had no recollection of this woman nor understanding of what she meant. It was unsettling. I sought firmer ground. "My name is Malcolm Forrester, and I am no captain, but a physician from Torrport."

"You are a physician now, Malcolm...but then..." She smiled in a way that suggested teasing, or something a tad malicious.

"I'm sorry, I don't remember." This conversation was making me feel unbalanced. Was it the altitude or Skye, or her loosing my bonds of reality? I felt light-headed. I had to leave and fast.

She seemed to notice my discomfiture and grabbed the boy, who looked much older now than he had seemed at first. She said to him, "Let's rest a while, shall we?" The pack slid off her bony shoulders and she descended gracefully onto a flat rock at the side of the trail. "Captain, you can stay at the cottage of my friend Gormal in Broadford. Ask the locals, everyone knows her. Tell her Doideag sent you." She pulled the boy close as one might a lover and whispered something in his ear which made him laugh.

"I...I must go," I said, willing mind and body back to mission.

She flipped her hand as one would dismiss a lackey. "Farewell, Captain Forrester."

"Emm...aye...farewell...Doideag."

With that perplexing encounter I decided not to linger on my way to Broadford, where I would most certainly *not* stay with someone named Gormal. But as it turned out, the powers who direct our steps had other plans.

* * *

It was early evening and already dark, with thick clouds and surly gusts spattering rain. I stood there in trepidation, observing the low stone hut that looked like it had grown organically from the rocky terrain. There was but one wooden door of about five feet in height, and no windows I could see. The roof was a thickness of ferns, dead and alive, with a whiff of peat smoke filtering through. It was Gormal's home.

It had been hours since I had met Doideag, yet the lightness and nausea remained. The trail had been rough in some spots and pleasant in others, mostly following winding glens that descended from the mountains. They led to Broadford, pleasantly situated beside a shallow curving bay with a road running parallel, lined with shops and homes. And it was herring season, the village cheerfully burgeoning as coins traded owners and months of lonely vigil in the mountains were being relieved with raucous parties. It would have cheered but for the lack of accommodation and threatening storms.

By the time I reached the western limits of the village I had run out of options. There was nowhere to stay. I could park myself on the ground beside the road or accept the hospitality of Gormal. So, I found a comfortable patch of heather and dropped my pack just in time to regret the decision as a gust of wind brought the first wave of rain. I scrunched down, pulling my cloak around like a tent. However, I could not sleep like that, and I was very tired. So, muscles aching, and already sick of my diet of onions and oats, I surrendered and entered the tavern seeking directions to the home of Gormal.

I should have bribed the tavern keeper to let me sleep on the floor once I saw his response to her name, how he blanched then took a step back and stuttered. But I did not, and that is how I found myself standing in front of Gormal's cottage that night. I was almost ready to walk away when the small door opened a crack, and a rotund, grandmotherly figure with honey hair and dark blue eyes bade me enter. I felt pulled in, not against my will, but out of longing. It was the light and warmth, and the smells of cooking that drew me, and something else, too.

"Set ye down by the fire, captain," said she.

I cast my eyes around her tiny cottage. It was but one room of no more than eight by ten feet and arranged like a perfect tableau of welcome. The fire on the floor in the middle of the room was surrounded by stones and low stools. A pallet piled high with heather and wool plaids was on the far side. A spinning wheel and loom were by the door along with bolts of cloth and bags of wool. All suggested comfort and well-being. I squatted on the low stool by the fire and watched her checking the simmering pot set on a flat stone.

"You have arrived precisely on time, Malcolm," she said, taking some bowls and a ladle from a carved wooden cabinet near her bed.

"You know I met Doideag?"

She was scooping stew into a bowl and arranging it with a round of bread and a mound of butter on a wooden platter. "Of course, her boy told me while you were wandering around Broadford today. We knew there would be nowhere to stay but here. 'Tis market day and herring season both, and we arranged this dreadful weather." She laughed gently while placing the tray on my lap, her voice disarmingly feminine.

I suppose I should have been suspicious, but I was hungry and cold, and she was offering what I needed, so good judgement found a place on the shelf of abeyance. She sat on the stool beside me, watching me eat, studying my face and saying nothing. I watched her too and wondered. Her unadorned green kirtle suggested modesty or lack of care; her amorphous grandmotherly face I could perceive indistinctly. It was one I would forget in an instant even if I studied it carefully. She was more a presence than a substance, although I knew she was real. The stew and bread were delicious, the best I had in many weeks. She poured some freshly made ale, then asked, "Why are you here, captain?" The peat flames flickered in her dark eyes.

"Doideag should have told you I am no captain, but a physician on the way to Dunvegan to help with the treatment of a patient." I was becoming slightly annoyed by these women and their silly assertions.

I thought she smiled, then said, "Aye, so you say. Have more ale."

She sat quietly, exuding nurturing warmth while staring at my face.

"More to the point, Gormal, what is it *you* want?" I finished the ale. It was oddly sour but full-bodied and quite satisfying. I leaned closer, trying to see her more clearly.

Her arm jerked suddenly and pointed at my hand. "You have the ring!" For a split-second her face came into focus, and I could see the anger and fear of an old woman as her breath froze. "My thoughts cannot enter!" Her body pulled back as though threatened.

I glanced down and realized I had been gripping Elspeth's ring tightly as though afraid to lose it. When I looked up again, she was gone. Moments later, I heard her voice emanating from the corner behind the bags of wool. "Do not come near," she pleaded.

"I'm not here to harm you, Gormal. I told you the truth. I've come to treat patients." It was not precisely the truth, but close enough since I was not sure Elspeth's fears concerning her laird were justified. "Come and sit with me. Perhaps we can help each other."

"That lass is clever," her voice tinged with malice.

"Aye, Elspeth is very clever. Underestimate her at your peril. But there is no reason we cannot be friends." I smiled warmly, sensing her shape gliding closer. "Bring another ale. And for a start, you can tell me about this ring."

* * *

That evening I learned that the ring was Roman gold with a carnelian intaglio of the goddess Fortuna. Gormal said it was from the hoard hidden by the MacLeod chieftain after the defeat of the Vikings by the Scots at the Battle of Largs in 1263. Thereafter, the Scots took control of the Western Isles. The MacLeods were Vikings and on the losing side in that battle, and it was a time of great trouble. As she spoke, I wondered how she knew all this and her connection to it.

"She gave you that ring for protection...from the likes of me, I assume," she said, "but I and my friends only wish to protect our people."

I was becoming drowsy, more than that, I had a feeling of languorous disconnection. It had been a long and arduous day and the ale was helping soften the pain. "I...am here to...help...not harm," I repeated.

"You should sleep, captain."

The light from the peat fire was dying and her image seemed to flicker with the last of it. I took a few deep breaths to clear my mind.

"Not yet," I said. "You have more, don't you? Why do you call me captain when you know I am not?"

"I am not certain you are not," she responded quickly. "Your ring has blocked me, as you well know."

"You speak in riddles."

"Then I will explain, since you seem ignorant of your past."

"Go on, then."

She began with a brief incantation in Gaelic which sounded like a blessing or a curse, then began telling me of a time after the ships of the Spanish Armada had wrecked on the Western Isles. "The king of Spain had a beautiful daughter. She dreamt of a handsome young man who filled her heart with love. And so, she left on a quest to find him, searching many countries till finally she came to the Isle of Mull, south of Skye. There she met the Chief of Clan MacLean and her heart leapt with joy. It was him! The chief was blinded by her beauty and promptly forgot he was already married. But soon his wife discovered his disloyalty and devised a plan to kill the Princess of Spain. This she did by blowing up her ship and all therein." Gormal stopped. "Is this of interest?"

Her story seemed to take days in its telling, and I was becoming impatient and heard myself say, "I see not how this has to do with me."

"You will soon enough understand," said she, with that charming laugh. "Of course, when the King of Spain found out, he wanted revenge and sought out his most capable captains. One was a mercenary, your ancestor Captain Forrester. He was skilful in sailing and fighting, and as we found out, he had a profound knowledge of *draiocht* or magic."

I suddenly snapped out of my hypnotic stupor. "Forrester...what of him?"

I thought I could feel her smiling at my response. "Captain Forrester arrived at Tobermory Bay on the Isle of Mull in a great three-mast ship and with orders to fill her hold with the limbs of all the Scots on Mull. The Chief of Clan MacLean and his people were very afraid because they believed no one could defeat such a powerful ship commanded by this man. So, the MacLean gathered all those in Mull with knowledge of magic passed down from the ancient Druids. He told them of the dire threat and asked for their help. One of those, the leader, was my friend Doideag."

I stopped her right there. "Gormal, you are saying this happened after the time of the Spanish Armada?"

"Aye, 'twas soon after, since you are asking, and I know it was more than one hundred years ago."

"May I remind you that I am a man of science, and your story has veered into the implausible."

"So, say you. May I finish, and you can decide?"

In the darkness, I began to sense others had joined us, as wavering forms, shadows becoming real. And stories came to mind, stories told by my family servants of magical creatures, and I recalled Father warning us. But I decided to hear her out. It was after all, her home. "I will be delighted to hear the end of this," I said touching the hilt of my sword and silently beseeching God and Fortuna.

Her voice now seemed to emanate from within me and the tale enveloped us in a weave of memories and emotions. I was no longer hearing but re-living it with her. I found myself flying high above a ship and could see the women as white and grey gulls gathering on the yardarm, and a furious tempest rising, trees uprooting and rocks splintering. On the deck was the captain of the ship. It was Captain Forrester. In a sudden whoosh, I entered his body. My breath caught as I felt his immense power, standing there with braided beard, his gnarled hands on the ship's wheel.

He was stronger than the women-gulls and the ship stood fast until the eighteenth and greatest of them arrived, the Gormal of Moy. She said to him, "Do you this with God's help?"

Captain Forrester laughed and shook his hatchet high. "I fear not you, and even without God's help will have your limbs in my hold before the day is out!"

Gormal shouted, "Without God's help, you have lost!"

And the women-gulls tried to lift the Great Quern Stone that grinds the fates of men, up and over the ship while the seas roared. But with even greater magic, Captain Forrester held the stone down. Then Gormal called Black Donald the Strong to help lift the Quern, and eventually the powers of all the women and Black Donald overcame, and Captain Forrester knew he must flee before the ship was sunk. So, he ordered the ropes holding her cut. But before it could be done, the Great Quern Stone fell, and all the ship's men were crushed into the sea. And from above, Gormal was heard to cry, "Aha, Captain Forrester, thou didst boast at desolate Mull's coast, but now thy ship is lost!"

Then lungs burst with foul water, and we were dark and dead.

Much later, perhaps years or decades, from the mud of the depths, Captain Forrester's decayed body rose and floated free as flotsam, and I awoke again in the body of Malcolm.

* * *

Gormal's letter, written carefully on a small sheet of vellum, was succinct. *Your belted plaid is on the chest. I will return tonight. G.*

Her hut was less appealing by the light of morning filtering through the cracks, with smells of burnt peat, mold, and stale food combining badly. There was a crude lean-to outside with a bucket of water, wash tub, and piled peat logs. I availed myself and it was a relief to feel clean and rid of the evidence of my trials; but the memories of my encounter with Gormal were disturbing and I grew angry because I knew she must have drugged me. At least I was alive and intact, but with a headache and muscle cramps which made me curse. I would deal with that woman later, but for now I had patients to see and little time.

Back inside, I stirred the embers and added some fresh peat logs, then found the belted plaid. It was a muted green and red checked wool, like the hunting tartan worn by many here, the same as she was weaving on her frame. She also included a white linen shirt, coated with tallow for waterproofing, and a pair of untanned turn-shoes with leather laces. I quickly stripped and slid the shirt over my head, then found the end of the plaid with the inside loops and set it on the ground in pleats. Then I laid on it and tied it around my waist with the twisted rush cord. It was a simple matter then to flip the remaining length of the plaid over my shoulder crossways and fasten it in place with the leather belt. I discovered she had thoughtfully included matching wool socks held up with garters, and a stylish wide bonnet of the same tartan. I was pleased as I strutted about the hut adjusting my new outfit, and despite my aching body and feelings of betrayal, I decided I would not kill her after all.

* * *

Broadford was not so much a cattle market as an assembly yard where crofters could bring cattle by the ones and twos and arrange with drovers to take them to the Tryst at Crieff on the mainland. This was done with a handshake and mental notes by both parties. The drovers, many of whom were crofters by summer, would gather a hundred or so beasts for the trip with the hopes of returning before the snows fell. It was a risky business, as profits were slim and losses high if even a few cattle did not make it. But it could be a good supplement if all went well. The crofters handing their cattle over to the drovers would use the profits returned, if any, to buy barley and oats and pay rent, continuing the cycle of poverty.

On this day, Broadford was full to bursting with animals vying for space with merchants, packs of children, beggars, and villagers eager for coin and sport. And the docks were worse. Dozens of boats were readying for the day's work and men were hauling sacks of salt to the grey sheds where women would gut, salt, and box the herring. The smells of the fish, cattle and humanity made a veritable banquet for the nostrils, contrasting with the crisp clean air wafting from the sea. I was humming a happy tune as I entered the tavern, once more seeking directions.

The tavern keeper did not recognize me till I spoke, then nodded approvingly as he inspected my new outfit. I looked like a Highland Scot now in proper dress and sporting a two-week beard. The tavernkeeper introduced himself as Arthur MacMorran and I told him that I could see patients today if he would rent me a room. After some haggling, and my reminding him of the benefits of increased traffic and goodwill, he agreed to provide a spacious room with ample water, soap, and towels in exchange for one quarter of my earnings. I was well pleased and tipped the girl who brought my morning porridge, milk, and apple.

I had promised a drover at Kylerhea to see a patient here, a boy with a strange twitch. So, I sent a note to his family and waited while the cleaning girl readied my room. Word to got out fast, and by the time I had organized myself and the room, there was a line-up from the stairs to the tavern door. I shall not relate the routine complaints that make up the bulk of a doctor's work. Suffice to say there were many that morning, from boils to backaches as we say, and it was past noon when the boy arrived with a woman, both huddled under a dark-hooded cloak. His arm holding the cloak was twitching and he was dragging one foot, and the prematurely aged face of the woman reached out to me with unspoken words of anguish.

"What is your name?" I asked, gesturing for them to sit on the bed.

"His name is David...David Love, and I am his mother, Ann Love."

She pushed him to the bed, and I said to him, "Nice to meet you. My name is Malcolm. What is your name again, lad?"

I watched his reaction. His hands were fidgeting, and he gave a lop-sided grimace before saying forcefully, "David, like Mother said." I smiled at that. He was feisty, a good sign.

"David, I am a doctor and I think I can help. Please, take off your cloak and shirt so I can examine you."

He looked at his mother for approval. She nodded and whispered to him, "Do as he says."

He was gaunt but otherwise normal looking, but for the almost constant movement of his limbs and face. *It must be very tiring*, I thought.

I asked the mother his age and when the problem had started. "Eleven," she responded, "and I first noticed him limping about five months ago."

"Was there anything of note that happened to him before that...an injury or illness, perhaps?" I took a cup, half-filled it with water, and handed it to him. "Have a sip, David."

His mother said, "Nothing I remember. But...he had the fever, but that was months before."

I was listening to her while watching the boy closely. He could hardly get the cup to his mouth, his hand jerking so, till finally he caught it with his lips and took a gulp.

"A fever, you say...hmm, and is this getting worse, the same, or better?"

"No different, I think...but some say he is bewitched, or the Devil has him, and he cannot go to school for they tease him so and he gets in fights." Her voice was quavering as she said that, and her face wore the look of a mother's grief. I took the cup from David's trembling hand.

"Mrs. Love, this is not the work of any devil or enchantment, I assure you."

"I am a good Christian, and my David is a fine boy." She hugged him as tears flowed down to her chin. David stiffened and tried to stop twitching by clasping one hand over the other.

"David, look at me. You have an illness of the nerves. You are not a bad person. This can happen to anyone. Understand?" He did not really, but I hoped my words were a comfort. I was wishing at this point that I had been able to bring my medical books, since all I had to rely on was the memory of that class in medical school at Leiden several years ago. "You have what is known as *Chorea minor.* It's a condition of the nerves that afflicts children your age." I was speaking directly to David because I sensed his determination and I wanted to empower his cure. "Chorea minor also is called Saint Vitus' Dance. It was more common years ago. The good news is that it should go away on its own in several months." I stopped and looked at them both. There was silence but for the murmuring of the crowd outside the door and muted laughter from the tavern.

"Oh, David!" She wept and hugged him again.

"Wait!" I held up my hand dramatically. "There is unwelcome news."

They both stared at me, holding their breath. "David must take some medication and treatments."

We laughed together, in relief, and I told them that he should bathe daily in cold seawater, followed immediately by warming by a fire and a brisk rub-down with a towel. They agreed. I continued. "I don't have the proper medicine with me, but you can make some yourself. It is called *Martis limatura praeparata*. You can make a crude version of it now, and order some from the apothecary at Fort William. To make your own, find some rusted iron from an old anchor or such, and scrape a goodly amount of rust off it, about half a teaspoon into a cup of apple cider vinegar. Start with half a dram a day of this solution and increase gradually up to two drams a day if he can tolerate it. Do you think you can do this?"

"I will try, doctor," she said, snuffling tears. David sat stoically but I thought I could see the grimacing spasms lessening and a wee smile form.

What I did not tell them was that I was not certain of this diagnosis and that it could be one of several other diseases, much worse, and that his life already could be a ruin. But for now, they must be brave and hope for the best outcome. It was all I could offer, but for one thing.

I took David's trembling hand and said, "Do you remember your Bible, the story of David and Goliath?" He looked up and nodded. "Then be fearless like your namesake. Let's go." With his mother in tow, I opened the door to the landing, and holding David by my side, faced the crowd lining the stairs. Conversation became silence when they saw us. And in my most authoritative voice, I said, "David Love has a medical condition of his nerves. I am treating him and expect a full recovery. He is *not* bewitched, *nor* in league with the Devil. *Leave him the hell alone!* Tell everyone you know. He is a good boy—one of yours—and he needs your kindness."

David was trying to be still. I could feel his tension, my hand on his shoulder steadying him. And I saw Elspeth's ring, Fortuna flashing golden in a mid-day beam of light. I raised Fortuna, or she raised my hand, and I slid her into his unruly dark hair. I imagined her kissing the top of his head and wished him good luck because if anyone needed it, he did. I ruffled his hair and gave a reassuring smile and returned to the room to wash and ready for the next patient.

* * *

The day was very satisfying and profitable, but for my bouts of nausea due to whatever that damned Gormal had fed me. It was late afternoon and I headed to the market to supplement my supply of oats and onions. Along the way, I imagined life as a vagabond medic going from village to village healing the sick and having adventures. I chuckled, thinking how long that would last. I had too much lust for the good things in life. But it is odd how one often wants what one should not have.

It was the harvest season and the market overflowed with tempting products, most too heavy to carry or difficult to prepare on the trail, so I settled on oat bannocks and salt-dried herring, plus a chunk of delicious cheese and a large horn of whisky to buoy my spirits. I returned to the tavern in time for a hearty supper of slow-roasted mutton served with heaps of neeps and tatties, rich with butter and milk and seasoned with late chives. A bountiful maid with tawny hair served me ale to wash it down. I was distracted by her quick smile and lusty laugh, but pleasant thoughts soon gave way to brooding over Gormal and I vowed I would see her that night and exact my revenge.

* * *

The moonlight touched the bay turning it a glittering silver; but the stars were blinking out one by one as clouds pressed in from the north, likely to be accompanied by more wind and rain. It was that time of year: the grasses dying, the trees bronze and golden, and the coming winter inexorable. I crouched in the black willows near Gormal's hut. It was near midnight, and I had slept well after supper. But now thoughts were dark as the night. She had bested me with poison, and I hated that, especially since she was just an old woman. I had come to her as a gentleman seeking hospitality and willing to pay, and she had abused me as though my life mattered naught. I could have continued on my way; but I had a sense I needed her, and then there was my damaged pride. So that is why I was waiting for the light in her hut to dim and I would enter unbidden.

It was time. The wind was rustling the crisp grass and a dog barked nearby. I put my shoulder to her door and drove it in, smashing the latch and tearing the leather hinges. And there she was crouched on the floor grinding herbs in a clay pot. She gasped and turned. I snarled, "We meet again, Gormal."

The next minutes were a flurry of scrambling grunts and screams as I caught her and tried to pin her on the filthy floor. She was ready with a dirk and tried to slash me. She almost succeeded but I smacked it from her hand and grabbed her flailing arms. She went limp and began to sob as my weight and strength secured her. I could see little in the gloom, but I could smell unwashed skin and feel her rotund softness beneath. I held her steady without speaking, letting the shock ebb.

"We need to talk," I said.

"Please, captain," she burbled between sobs.

"Will you behave if I release you?"

"Aye, aye. I will. Please don't hurt me."

"I should throttle and burn you, as you deserve, *witch*." I was angry and annoyed she had tried to cut me, and I wanted her to experience a reminder of what could be.

"I am *no* witch…a village healer is all," she said between wheezy gasps. I let go of her wrists to see what she would do. She lay passively, dark eyes dilated.

"No tricks or you will suffer, understand?"

"No tricks," she repeated, lolling her head.

"Stoke the fire, then." I got off her and watched as she unsteadily recovered from the humiliation. She carefully brushed the dirt from her kirtle then retrieved a few logs of peat stacked by the door. I could tell this was not easy for her, to be so threatened in her own home. I wanted her to fear and respect me, but I had to be careful. I did not want fear becoming hate accompanied by irrational behaviour.

"You must stop calling me captain," I said more gently.

"I am sorry…we were worried…and afraid."

"Let us start at the beginning. Who is Doideag and why do you care what I do?"

She started hesitantly. Slowly the story came out. They had been friends since youth, both the descendants of the women who had saved Mull from Captain Forrester. "My mother and hers taught us the healing arts, and we are friends of Mairi MacLeod, the oldest and most respected of us."

"How did Doideag know I was on that trail?" That part had been bothering me. My eyes locked on hers, looking for the telltale signs of lying.

"She didn't. Oh, where do I start? That is why I told you that story… and—"

"You make no sense, and my patience is short. Tell me the truth, all of it!"

And she did, and it turned out that meeting Doideag was an accident, but Mairi had asked all the healers to watch for me.

"Look for an arrogant young Lowlander, Mairi had written, *well-dressed and out of place."*

"Doideag's hut was nearby, and she was bringing clothes to market and saw you...and assumed," she shrugged. "You see, Elspeth sent for you, but she had been away from Skye for years and we needed to know you could be trusted, and when we heard your name...well, you can imagine the reaction."

"And that story of Captain Forrester," I interrupted. "Was there at least some truth in it?"

She smiled for the first time. "Aye, as it was told by our ancestors. 'Tis well-known in these parts and your name infamous...and you are a Lowlander too."

"I see." I was beginning to understand their caution, but then there was the poison. I nodded toward the almost empty tub of ale by the cabinet. "Have some ale," I said maliciously.

Her eyes widened as she glanced at the tub. "It was the ring...I could not see into your mind...I had to!"

"Nonsense! Speak sensibly!"

"*'Tis true!"* she protested. "The ring is known by many, and it is frightening...that she gave it to you of all people!"

I had to keep her focused. "What was the poison?"

"Just henbane ale...and you may have drunk too much." She shrugged as though my health was of little concern.

"Henbane is poison! Do you know the penalty for poisoning?" She had the look of an animal in a trap, but I was angered at what she had done and her lack of concern for my well-being. "You would be boiled alive. My father is a lord and judge, and you would have no chance. I should kill you now to save everyone the bother." I touched the hilt of my cutlass.

She screamed, "Please, no! What do you want of me? I shall give it."

"I want to know all." I set my jaw and scowled at her.

It must have worked because she told me more: of the weakness of the MacLeod laird and of those wishing his demise. "I was able to experience it with you and feel your spirit as we traveled together," she mumbled while staring in the smoky red fire. I was skeptical, of course, but told her to continue. "I sensed your goodness, but also that other part of you, the one you inherited from the captain, and it frightened me to feel it." She sighed then looked up at me. "And I could see your future, your suffering...for the laird and his family, and Elspeth...and I wept." She stopped and snuffled on her sleeve. "I am sorry we gave you henbane and Doideag's oil on your hand, but we had to be sure. We are of those protecting the laird and Clan MacLeod...Mairi and her friends, as our ancestors protected Mull from Captain Forrester."

The touch on my hand! Of course. I should have suspected then when it all started. "I am *not* Captain Forrester!" I reminded her sternly.

"You are a bit of him right now."

I did not feel sorry for her. She was a poisoner and received much less punishment than she deserved. If I fault myself, it is often for being too forgiving. "Witches with powers do not exist but in the minds of the deluded, nor do I think you can enter my mind. It is nonsense used to control the foolish."

"You are right," she said meekly, perhaps not wanting to antagonize me the more.

"Gormal, I told you the truth from the beginning. I am here at the request of my friend and colleague to help treat patients, and I will not abuse you further unless you deserve it." I sat back, hoping to lessen the tensions.

She nodded imperceptibly. "Then if you truly wish to help, I can tell you how."

"Do so."

She crossed to the cabinet and retrieved a painted wooden box covered with images of the early saints. In the box was a white cloth and wrapped in the cloth a stone of irregular shape, the size of a spear point. It looked unremarkable.

"This is the Brightstone." She lifted it to her brow while mumbling in

Gaelic.

"So?"

"So," she repeated, "so it has been passed from healer to healer for countless generations."

She waited for my response, but I had none. I am not impressed by relics and stones and all the other bogus nonsense that mesmerizes the simple.

She cleared her throat and held it out to me. "This...this will cure the laird of his illness."

"That is your medicine?" I scoffed. "I am a man of science, not magic and buffoonery."

She lowered her arms holding the box while keeping her eyes on the stone. "You may not believe but he and most here do."

We sat in silence listening to the wind ruffling the thatch, and I understood from experience that something like a simple stone could indeed heal, if the patent believed. It was the ancient way before science, and at times it worked. "Then tell me what I must do."

She wrapped the stone with loving reverence and closed the lid. "I cannot. Take it to Mairi, and if she decides, she will tell you." She bowed her head to the box, then with a look of fierce defiance said clearly, "If you abuse this stone, even Fortuna cannot save you!"

I took the box with a nod of acknowledgement then paid her overly much for the belted plaid and gave her my old outfit and suggested she sell it and use the proceeds to help the poor.

"God speed, Malcolm," was all she said in response, her formless face giving nothing away.

I left through the low door. Reflected from the firelight, I could see facing me many golden eyes and half as many hooked yellow beaks with red spots that looked like dripping blood. They were crouched on the rocks and grass staring at me, and for a moment I imagined them a flock of demons. It seized my breath. Thankfully, reality prevailed, and I saw that they were herring gulls bedding for the night. I muttered, "In the name of God, be off!" and touched Fortuna's ring for luck. They parted just enough to let me pass. My blatant hypocrisy struck me along with the first spatters of rain. I looked back as the door behind me was closing and caught a glimpse of Gormal smirking.

Chapter 6: Malcolm

There was a constant itch at the back of my neck as I trudged head down into the brisk north-west wind. It had been raining all night and I had stayed at the tavern and pursued carnal pleasures with that tawny-haired girl and drunk more ale than wise. So, this day was for penance as rain drove relentlessly into every seam and fiber of my plaid. "Keep the sea on your right," they said, "till you come to Loch Ainort, then go north through the glen to Loch Sligachan. The inn you seek is at the head of the loch." The directions were straightforward enough, complementing the obvious river of cattle and dung. It would take two days to walk to Sligachan, with a camp overnight at Loch Ainort.

It was just me and herds of cattle, dogs, and surly Highlanders. Some men stopped to talk, others merely nodded or made a gruff comment about the weather. The first part of the trail was flat, flanked on the right with seagrass and on the left with low hills. The cattle had eaten much of the grass, and close to the sea had churned the remains to mud. I was forced to walk a bit inland through the grassy hillocks. It was not easy going and after a few miles of ups and downs and many stumbles, my legs were tired, and I needed a rest. On a small hill with some shrubs in the lee of the wind, I set my pack down and enjoyed a well-deserved stretch, all the while thinking of my encounter with Gormal. I knew she had poisoned me with henbane, and that accounted for at least part of what I had experienced, but there was more, a sense of truth mingled with hallucinations. But I could not be sure and hoped that once I met-up with Elspeth, all would be explained and made clear.

Intruding in my introspection was what sounded like crying. I could not locate the source, so I reluctantly rose and climbed the little hill for a better view. There it was near the crest, a ball of black and white fluff curled in the grass. I approached carefully, not knowing at first what it was, then a head popped up, followed by a sharp yap and even louder whining. It was a wee pup tied to a shrub!

A bit of oatmeal and water and a few kind words and the pup was happy. There were no settlements nearby, so I decided to find someone along the way who wanted him. Even with a full belly he weighed only a few pounds and fit nicely in the folds of my plaid. He soon snuggled and fell fast asleep.

* * *

By early evening I had reached the camp at Loch Ainort, a flat area with a stony beach flanked by large hills. The strath leading to the loch was full of cattle resting after the day's march. The most welcoming sight was the warm fire, ringed with drovers and dogs, all under canvas held up with driftwood poles.

I had offered the pup to several drovers on the way, but they laughed and said no one wanted pups this time of the year. And they suggested I put him back on a hill to die. One drover shook his head and said, "*Mí ádh, mí ádh*." My Gaelic being close to non-existent, I asked his friend what he had said.

"That the pup will bring bad luck," the friend translated.

"How so?" I asked.

"The dog was given to the fairies, and 'tis bad luck to steal from the fairies. You'll see," he said with a wry smile, leaving me unsure if he was jesting.

"Then what is the word for "good luck" in Gaelic?"

The drover chuckled and said, "Good luck is *ádh mór*, and you will need it now that you have offended the fairies."

So, I decided to call the pup "*ádh mór*" or Adhie for short because he was one lucky dog to have chance intervene in his favour, and some would say luck defines us in our brief lives. At least he weighed little, and I hardly noticed him on my side when he needed to be carried.

The folk at the camp did not like my dog but I bought their goodwill by sharing my horn of whisky as we dried by the fire while the dogs met each other with a round of sniffing. Soon enough, among the men, singing became disputation, and a few ended up with fists flying and plaids askew on the beach. An enjoyable time was had by all.

By morning, good sense had returned, and I suppose Adhie decided life with me was not all bad, so when we left, he trotted proudly behind, tail in air.

* * *

Sligachan sits in a flat of rocks and heather, guarded by mountains both round and craggy, and this day speckled with cattle. It is a major crossroads on the narrow waist of Skye, with only a few miles separating Loch Sligachan on the east coast from Loch Harport on the west. It is also the crossing of trails heading north-west to Dunvegan, north to Portree and the Trotternish peninsula, and south to Broadford. And it is the meeting ground of the three major clans, the MacDonalds to the north-east and southeast, Clan MacKinnon to the east, and Clan MacLeod to the west.

The Sligachan Inn stands amid this barren landscape as if it were mistakenly built there by lost masons. It was a surprisingly well-maintained L-shaped building of whitewashed stone and thatched roof, set among a few weathered-wood buildings for necessities and animals. The pup and I had made good time despite the tough climbs and his insistence on walking much of the way and stopping to smell everything. Luckily, the weather had improved to mere sprinkles with the sun peeking out sporadically, a splendid day by Scottish standards.

There was a drover camp on the other side of the small river across from the inn, with an ancient stone bridge at the crossing. I headed straight for the inn, hoping that a room was available. I would deliver the letter given me by Captain Wilson to the innkeeper, and perhaps he would trade a boon for a boon and let me sleep indoors. Failing that, it would be me and Adhie romantically cuddling under the stars at the drover camp.

The woman at the desk said there were no rooms available and nodded in the direction of the tavern part of the inn when I asked for the innkeeper. She said with a hint of contempt to look for the "big, ugly brute." The tavern was dark panelled with a few windows and lit by tallow candles set in sconces on black wooden posts that held the roof in place. The several tables were occupied. A bar fronting a door led to the kitchen. All but two in the room had the weathered look of drovers, and those two had the best seats in the house close to the hearth and its inviting peat fire. The man facing me by the fire was massive, the size of a boulder and just as rough-looking, with a jowly pock-marked face and thinning grey hair. He was in grim conversation with the other man, a tall blond, dressed in Lowlander clothes.

"We've no more rooms today," the big man shouted through the crowd when he noticed me, "and get that dog outa here."

I ignored him and kept walking, Adhie trailing happily behind. The innkeeper gave me a sour look and got up from the low chair. I removed the letter from my pouch and offered it. "A letter from Captain Wilson," I said.

He grumbled and took the scrap in his paw, daintily opened it, and read the few words scrawled therein. He looked up, gave me a quick once over and said, "Welcome to the Sligachan Inn, brother."

I had no idea of the contents of the letter, but a warm welcome was better than a punch in the face, so I nodded and asked if he might provide hospitality.

"No rooms...full of paying customers, but Eileen can set you up in the storeroom. Couldn't turn out one of ours, could I?" He clapped me on the back and shouted for Eileen. Meanwhile the other fellow at the table rose, offered a hand, and said his name was Niall Morrison. Said he was on his way to Fort William and could see I was a fellow countryman and would be honoured if I would join him for supper. I didn't quite understand the overly friendly welcome but agreed, then was escorted by Eileen to a room barely big enough to lie down in under the dead animal corpses and hanging herbs and barrels and crates of everything needed to run a tavern.

"I'll bring ye a blanket, an' pot, an' basin, an' bucket 'a water," said Eileen, a slovenly woman of middle age at that time in life when disappointment replaces hope. I opened my pouch to retrieve a coin and thanked her. She favoured me by lifting her frown slightly. I laid out my blanket to dry and bought some kitchen scraps for Adhie, then had a wash in ice-cold water with special attention paid to the back of my scalp that had been itching all day.

* * *

Back at the tavern, Niall was once again in discussion with the innkeeper, who introduced himself as Iain Mackinnon. "You wear our plaid well, for a Lowlander; but your foreign tongue gave you away," Mackinnon said sardonically as I pulled up a stool.

"The plaid was a gift from a witch," I replied, in my laughable version of a Highland accent.

"Gormal of Broadford? More bitch than witch, that one," he chuckled.

That was the truth of it, and I found myself pleasantly settled by a warm fire being served heaping bowls of cock-a-leekie soup and fresh bread with ale. After days in the harsh elements subsisting on oats and onions, it was gastronomic heaven.

"And who are you then, if not a fellow clansman?" Mackinnon was direct and I liked that, so I told him my name and origins and where I was going and what had happened, including the shipwreck, and poisoning by Gormal. Mackinnon gripped an over-sized mug as he listened and rumbled in mirth a few times. Niall was listening quietly; a strikingly handsome man with wavy short blond hair and a masculine face with heavy cheekbones and a mouth that always seemed in half-smile, as though he were laughing at the world. Over six feet tall, with broad shoulders and muscular arms that stretched his waistcoat, he was a bonnie man, as most women would agree.

"I've a few more days walking to Dunvegan," I finished my story and could sense Niall had something to say.

"You will be welcome there, I am sure," Niall said with a smile that brought wrinkles to the corners of his grey eyes. "I am from Dunvegan and know the laird is not the strongest of men and needs the best of medical care, and our resident physician is getting on in years. And Elspeth...well, she isn't truly a physician, is she?"

"Elspeth is professionally trained, but no, women cannot legally practice in Scotland, at least in the cities, without special permission, and she's not received it. But we'll do our best," I started to explain the limits of our abilities, but he raised his hand and smiled again.

"And she will *not* get permission, will she, especially with the charges hanging over her head? We've been recommending for years that our laird move to the city for better care, but he won't listen." Niall leaned back from the table, brought out a pipe and offered tobacco. I dislike smoking, so I politely refused.

There was a pause as the men lit their pipes, coughed, and spat. Then Niall continued, "Of course, you know Elspeth is my cousin. You will find most are related there. We are very, emm...close." He coughed again, then drew in another puff before saying, "That poor girl got herself in a lot of trouble."

"The witch thing?" I asked.

"Aye. None of us who are educated believe in that nonsense, but there are stories and allegations."

"Then she needs to clear the air, so to speak." I pushed my stool back to escape the cloud of noxious smoke, as they vied to produce the biggest puff.

"I hear you've also attracted some bad luck," Niall said.

"The dog?"

They both laughed and coughed. "Nay, the troubles in Edinburgh last spring," Niall explained.

He was referring to Professor Turnbull, Head of the College of Physicians, and his attempts to stop our research into a cure for smallpox. It had resulted in a confrontation and men had been killed, regrettably some by my hand. "'Twas not bad luck at all," I replied. "An inoculation to provide immunity to smallpox is a realistic possibility and we proved it. But there are always those who resist change, aren't there?"

Niall nodded. "Aye, change is a good thing, if there is no other way." I found myself agreeing but wondered if his meaning was other than mine. It was easy to like Niall, with his affable demeanour and quick mind.

Mackinnon called Eileen to remove the dishes, then tapped Niall on the sleeve. "Did you not mention a sickness in Drynoch?"

"Aye, they turned me away as I was riding through," said Niall. "I seldom stop there but for an ale and a piss. But there was a man on the road, said there was a fever and to keep going."

I thought a moment as the two stared at me, waiting perhaps for an instant diagnosis. "A fever seldom frightens people," I said, "at least not enough to turn travelers away. Must be more to it. I should be there by tomorrow night." That seemed to satisfy them because they nodded and continued smoking. But I had not heard reports of any major infectious diseases in the Highlands recently. I determined to get there as soon as I could. "Are there any horses about that I can buy or rent?"

"Just my pack horse, but she's as slow as walking, and Niall needs his to get to Fort William. You are better off walking. 'Tis not far."

"Would lend you my horse," Niall interjected, "but I have important business and I am leaving first light."

"I understand…worth a try asking," I said, and just then a flea jumped off my head and onto the table between the three of us. I hoped the others had not seen it, but no such luck. We all stared at the tiny brown intruder. Then Mackinnon raised his fist and hammered it so hard I thought he would break the table.

"Damned dogs," he muttered.

Niall deftly changed the subject. "Did you say you are from Torrport? MacDuff land, isn't it?"

"Aye, and I'm the laird's physician, and that's where I met Elspeth. She was working there as a healer."

Niall nodded and tapped the remains of the tobacco into a bowl. "Then you likely met our clan chieftain when he was there this spring past…that meeting with…emm."

"The meeting with the Tsar of Russia? No secret now…and I did meet your chieftain, Norman Macleod. Seemed a pleasant fellow. Didn't say much but I could tell his presence disturbed Elspeth." I was watching his reaction and there was none.

"Worse was the lack of results from the meeting," Niall mused while putting his pipe back in the leather pouch on his belt. "The chieftains walked away with nothing…complete waste of time. But I am sure you know more than me."

"I gather the tsar wanted Highland mercenaries to fight the Swedes," I replied. "Maybe try the Highland charge on them to break their lines. The clans wanted weapons, but the tsar didn't think he could get them past the Swedish blockades, and then there are the Royal Navy patrols."

"Could have used better leadership on our side, though," Niall said. "A deal could have been made. 'Tis a damned shame!" Niall left me wondering who he meant to criticize.

Mackinnon had leaned closer, mitts fidgeting with his cooling pipe.

"I know little more than that," I nodded. That was not quite true, but I did not want them to think I was a Lowlander spy. "I am just here to help with medical problems, if I can."

Niall shrugged. "Well, you will find Dunvegan a depressing place. Half of it is falling to pieces. Not enough money to fix it. So, says the laird, anyway. The cattle thefts continue, and many crofters aren't paying rents, yet the famine is long past…so no excuse." Niall's face changed as he said that, pleasantly affable replaced by a look of anger.

"Surely you can help change the situation," Mackinnon exclaimed. "'Tis a shame to see a proud clan brought low like that."

"We tried," Niall said. "I do not want to disparage, but we are at a critical stage. I trust God will help us." I was not sure what he meant but remembered Elspeth's letter and her worries that someone was trying to overthrow the laird. I did not know which side Niall was on, so thought it best to remain silent.

"And that affects our cause as well," Mackinnon said. I looked at him to explain but he said nothing more.

"He is with Laird MacDuff at Torrport," Niall said, nodding at me, "and is one of us, notwithstanding his family name. He must know full well of the arms shipments. And he is not stupid nor blind, so we can speak openly. Besides, 'tis common knowledge hereabouts, anyway."

"Can't be too careful…I'm the one they'll hang if the redcoats find the muskets in the shed," Mackinnon said, chuckling nervously and looking around to see if anyone had overheard his indiscretion.

"Aye, most everyone at Torrport knows of the arms shipments," I confirmed. "The castle is full of lads from the countryside being trained. Word gets around. I just hope there is no cause for war."

"Yet the English are determined to annex Scotland, aren't they? And we will *not* allow ourselves to be their vassals." Niall's cold grey eyes glinted fiercely.

I shook my head. "It won't come to that. It can only be done with the consent of the Scottish Parliament."

"Pfft! That bunch! Traitors and cowards, the lot!" Niall said forcefully. It had grown silent in the tavern now. All eyes were on our table.

Thankfully, Mackinnon intervened to divert attention. He bellowed, *"A round for all on the house!"*

A roar went up and I saw Niall instantly change back to the affable friend. I realized I had been holding my breath.

"So how did our dear Elspeth end up in Torrport?" Niall asked.

"Well, as I understand it, she went to Edinburgh and asked her cousin John Beaton to help find a position. He suggested Torrport, partly because I had just moved there. John is a close friend. We attended medical school together at Leiden." I was glad Niall had changed the subject, and by the look on his face, so was Mackinnon.

"Ah, Cousin John. Pleasant fellow if a bit florid like his father Angus," Niall chuckled.

I added, "Like a ruddy Scots cherub. But a finer friend no one can have."

"His good father has a position at the College Medical School in Glasgow, if I remember correctly. Those Beatons seem to have your profession locked up, don't they? The old doctor at Dunvegan is a relative as well. You will meet him soon enough. Herold Bethune is his name. You'll be even more confused by names when you get there, as every second one is a MacLeod. Our clan has problems but we're good people, mostly," Niall said.

A man of passion, I mused listening to him. But passion can lead in many directions, good and bad, and then there is fortune and fate.

We sat quietly for a moment, I listening to the surrounding conversations which mostly concerned cattle, money, women, and weather. The usual fare. Niall seemed lost in thought and Mackinnon was scowling at Eileen who was ensconced behind the bar pretending to clean mugs. I resisted the urge to scratch the back of my scalp, thinking I must have lice in addition to the more recent gift of fleas from Adhie, when Niall said, "That Elspeth," then stopped. I was expecting another question, but he leaned toward us and said in a conspiratorial voice, "She's a passionate one."

"A passionate one?" I responded, thinking I had heard wrong.

"Indeed, she had quite an infatuation for me several years past...couldn't get rid of her. I had half a mind to deflower her...as punishment." Niall shrugged as if he would have had no choice. "It was embarrassing. She's a homely little thing, not to my standards at all." Niall smirked as though that should be obvious to anyone. But it was cruel to say that about her, especially to me. Surely, he knew Elspeth and I were friends and colleagues. I found myself disliking him for the first time. Men should not speak that way about ladies, especially their kin. But it was getting late, and we'd all drunk too much, so I excused myself before I said something regrettable. I walked unsteadily back to my "royal suite" for a night's rest among the supplies and fleas.

I was undressing when a gentle knock came at the door, followed by the sound of a feminine voice calling my name. "Aye, come in," said I.

The door opened a crack and she peeked in. "I'm Isla," she said, blushing,

"Eileen's daughter." Adhie wiggle-bounced to greet her. She laughed on seeing him.

"What is it you want, Isla?" She was young, mid-teens by the look of her, with wavy dark hair, glistening green eyes, bare feet, and only wearing a long shirt.

"Mackinnon sent me. Compliments of the house, he said." She blushed again and knelt to pet Adhie.

* * *

It had taken only a few hours to cover the stretch from Sligachan to Drynoch and I arrived early, the morning light sufficient to see the villagers mending their nets, hauling peat, and repairing huts, readying for another bitter winter. It had been an uneventful walk over mostly flat land, following the small streams which flowed into lochs east and west. To hurry, I had carried Adhie most of the way and he had slept content after the evening of play with Isla. And no, I had not bedded her. Far too young, and I was infested with lice and fleas, so I gave her some coins and suggested she entertain and feed Adhie while I washed and re-organized my pack.

"Where's the sick family?" I asked the old woman stooped over a bucket of vegetables harvested from her garden.

A sour expression accompanied her advice. "Don't want to go there, sonny."

I started to leave, then she said, "Four down, then left and theirs is the one with the broken cart on the side." I nodded. She said something in Gaelic to the vegetables.

* * *

The smell of rotting human flesh is unmistakeable, and I could not help but notice it as I ducked my head to enter the derelict stone hut. The fragrance, if you can call it that, is not at all like the normal off-smell of sickness, but magnitudes worse, like a combination of feces mixed with rotting meat and seasoned with a few drops of that cloying perfume many ladies often wear but should not. I am not normally squeamish, but this made me gag. I halted to let my eyes and stomach adjust to the dimness and stench. The hut was mostly empty but for the five of them: a woman by the central fire with two small children lying at her feet clutching each other closely, an adult on a pallet by the far wall, and a man hunched on a stool by the only window. I could hear the man on the pallet wheezing and mumbling.

The peat fire hissed as the woman prodded what little was left of it. The cottage was clean but bereft of any welcoming warmth and devoid of anything beautiful. But then illness turns everything ugly, at least in my eyes. "Is the one on the pallet sick?" I asked, kneeling by the woman who looked too old to be the mother of the children. I reminded myself that it is often the poor and malnourished who birth healthy children, whereas many pampered city women have difficulties. Perhaps the meek will inherit the earth after all. While I was musing, she turned slowly to me, her face gaunt, with that listless look of starvation I had seen far too many times.

"He's got the fever," she said eventually, as though it were an everyday event, then glanced back at the pot simmering beside the fire; in it a broth of old bones and skin with some unidentifiable plants. At least it did not add much to the cottage smell.

"What happened? Who got it first?" I asked, scanning the hut for any signs of food or drink beyond the foul soup.

She thought, then nodded in the direction of the man on the pallet. "His brother...buried him two weeks ago. Got back from the continent. Served with Wellington, you see...till the injury." She sat straighter as she said that. A wan smile flickered on her lined face. Maybe she was proud of what he had done and was remembering better times. The War of the Spanish Succession had been going on for several years and men from the Highlands willingly served to supplement meagre family incomes. But sometimes they did not come back, or returned like this, ill and broken.

The children were fussing on the stone floor, scratching their heads, reminding me of my own worsening condition. "I'm a doctor from Edinburgh," I said to the woman, while trying to mentally block the itch. "Mind if I have a look at him?"

"Please yourself," she shrugged, then whispered something to the children and they stopped scratching.

It was only a few steps to the man on the pallet, but the closer I got, the worse the stink. I knelt beside him and observed as best I could in the dim light. He was on a bed of matted heather, clothed in a filthy plaid with a blanket pulled over.

"My name is Malcolm. I'm a doctor and here to help." I could see he had a sheen of feverish sweat but thankfully no signs of smallpox. What could this be? And what was causing the foul smell? He did not react, so I shook his arm and spoke louder. He tried to look at me, eyes searching, but it seemed he could not see nor focus, then he gave up and just muttered the name of someone I did not know. I took this as consent and pulled his blanket down then opened his soaking wet shirt. He was very thin, his chest covered in rash. I investigated further and found a gangrenous sore located near the pelvic bone by his belt. It was sunken rotted flesh, blood-black in colour and about three inches in diameter. I quickly had a look at his legs, feet, and arms, as he continued muttering and moaning incoherently. There were several of these gangrenous sores interspersed in a field of rash that looked like it covered at least seventy percent of what I could see of his body.

I felt his pulse. It was weak and rapid. His forehead was burning. He was in serious trouble. I sat back on my haunches. This had the look of camp fever:the rash, the delirium, and even the gangrenous sores. It all fit. If I was right, it was that ancient killer which went by many names including jail fever or ship fever, but with these common symptoms, the result of poverty and over-crowding, spread human-to-human. His brother likely had brought it, having contracted it on the troopship home. I could do little, and with the disease unchecked, his prognosis was poor.

Who should live and who should not? It is often a heart-wrenching decision. This patient would not survive without considerable support, and the support would put others at risk. I had to protect those still healthy, especially the children, even if it meant sacrificing him. I found a small vial of laudanum in my medical bag and tipped the contents into his mouth, enough for a few hours of respite, then replaced his blanket and silently wished him God-speed.

The woman had her back to us the whole time. I went to the entrance where I had dropped my pack, took out what was left of the food and set it in front of her. "For you and the children," I whispered. She looked at it as though it might not be real or perhaps a trick of the fairies. "It's yours, but you must listen carefully." She reached out and touched the cheese lovingly, then looked up and nodded.

"Is one of these men your husband?" I asked.

"The useless one, there." She lifted a weak finger of blame and pointed at the one hunched by the window.

"Why are you starving?" I had to know how they had found themselves in this situation, starving and diseased with only a stranger willing to help.

She shrugged; her mouth twisted in bitter sadness. "The fish...didn't come like they used to this summer, and they said my husband stole, so they wouldn't share with us. They didn't think of my bairns, did they...my innocent bairns," she explained evenly, emotions long spent.

"And the man on the pallet?"

"Husband's cousin. They hate him too, as do I. 'Twas him who started it." She looked back at him in disgust.

"Have you been tending him?"

"Nay. Husband has, and I keep the wee ones away, always."

That was good news, at least for the children. They did not look too emaciated, so she had been feeding them as much as she could.

I looked in her tired eyes. "This is what you *must* do." She listened and I went through it slowly, simply. I told her she needed to keep herself and her children away from the men. I told her that the man on the palette would soon die and when he did, she should have her husband wrap him in a blanket and take his body to the door to be removed and burned. I assured her that the village chieftain would look after it. She gave me a look of disbelief, but I assured her that if they did their part, the chieftain would too. Then I told her to feed herself and her children and wash themselves including hair with the fresh water the villagers would bring.

I dug into my pack and found the bottle of scented wig powder that included pyrethrum. "When you are clean, put this powder in your hair where it itches. It will help rid the lice. Shave your heads if that doesn't work." Then I leaned close and whispered, "Feed your husband only if you have leftover food, and for God's sake stay away from him."

I finished by loudly announcing that their home was quarantined for forty days and that no one must leave or enter, except a physician. Only the woman was paying any attention. She smiled and mouthed, "Thank you."

* * *

I admit it was a relief to be out in the fresh air where Adhie greeted me in puppy fashion by jumping on my leg. I picked him up. He seemed to enjoy my new smell as we cuddled, and I whispered a very sincere apology fore I had given away the last of our food. I had an intense urge to purify myself and the dog, but I had to finish the job here, so I shouted to whoever could hear, "I am a doctor and I need to see the village chieftain!" That brought a few curious souls and I explained again what I wanted. Eventually a girl brought him.

"What's this about, then, eh?" I assumed the man speaking was the village chieftain, but he was not the picture of a Highland chieftain which would come first to mind. He was short and pudgy, looking disheveled in stained brown trews and yellow linen shirt. He looked like he had been dragged out of bed and was none too happy about it.

I introduced myself and told him that Niall Morrison had asked me to stop by and see to a sick patient. The sickness was serious and could threaten the entire village. He tilted his head toward the hut behind me then coldly said it must be God's punishment.

Nothing irritates me more than those who use religion to justify bad behaviour, so I knew I must keep tight rein on my tongue, or this could unravel quickly. "I understand you are a man of faith," I smiled warmly, "and will consider my request with love and fairness, as would our Saviour." He nodded slowly but I could see he was wary. "I'm sure you agree that The Holy Bible tells us that children are innocent and beloved by God and that it is our solemn duty to protect them, as Christ would." A small crowd had gathered and what could he do but agree? "Sir, I have no quarrel with your authority or justice but there are small children in that hut who could die without your help."

There was a murmur of agreement in the crowd. The chieftain stood listening and considering. Then he said, "But we'll not help the men! Nay, never...not after—" He spat in anger and the crowd seemed to agree with that, too. He faced me defiantly, hands on hips, head tilted back.

"Then we have agreement." I took a step toward him. "Everything will be done to save the children and of course you must include the mother, or you'll be left to care for orphans." He made his stand and we had found the middle path without bloodshed. I was satisfied it was the best we could do. He agreed. The crowd applauded. Then I took charge and told them what must be done, including enforcing a forty-day quarantine, bringing food, water, and blankets, and removing waste and the dead for cremation. It was grim business, but I gave reasonable assurances that the village could be saved.

When my lecture was over, the chieftain pulled me to one side and whispered, "You have our sincere thanks for helping us, but I was nay un-Christian. That family has been despised for generations, and they were caught stealing from our nets, and not for the first time! They were lucky we didn't kill them on the spot."

I knew it is not easy leading even a small village like this. There are many tough choices, and then there are the imponderables. I did not envy him. "Just help the children. Give them a chance," I said sincerely.

"But one thing, good sir...we are all in the same boat, so to speak. There were few fish this year and no help from the MacLeod. We have little enough food for our own children."

I knew he meant it. Most in the crowd had that lethargic, emaciated look. "Can you buy food to get you through the winter?" I asked.

"Aye, but we've no coin and without repairs to boats and nets, no future, neither." He shrugged.

I had little money left, the trip having taken far more than expected. But I'd be in Dunvegan soon and Elspeth would provide, so I handed my small pouch to him and said, "The MacLeod will pay me back...but if I hear you've let those children die, I'll visit in the black of night and slit you from belly to gullet...understand?" I hoped the confidence of authority was enough to ensure compliance, but fully realized I was standing there holding a wee puppy who continued to lick my face. Not very intimidating. I trusted his piety and word but resolved to get them more help as soon could be.

* * *

It was afternoon and I could hardly wait to leave that benighted village. Camp fever is frightening like smallpox, but potentially even worse in these crowded villages over winter. I was left with that creeping feeling of being contaminated, the stench lingering in my nose, my head itching from lice and God knows what other vermin, and I had handled an infected patient. And it was not just my body. I felt spiritually dirty too, after having made the decision to sacrifice men for the children. It is not easy to let someone die. And then there was the risk that they might give it to one of the villagers helping them.

I stopped at the first secluded spot by a shallow stream, stripped, waded in, and imagined the frigid mountain water cleansing body and soul. The cold hitched my breath when I submerged. But it was such a good feeling laying there floating on my back as the water flowed past. I gazed up at the patchwork sky speckled with birds gathering for the flight south. Adhie was yapping on the streambank, no doubt worried, yet afraid to dive in after me. I stayed in for several minutes, till the cold reminded flesh of its frailty. But it was good, in a way that re-unites mind and body.

Back on shore I dried and dressed, with plaid as both towel and clothing. The pup seemed pleased with his brave efforts of rescue, or at least that is what I imagined him thinking. But perhaps it had more to do with thoughts of lost food. And speaking of food, here we were, the two of us with no food nor drink, no money, no shelter, no friends, and seventeen miles yet to walk through the rough hills and glens of western Skye. I touched my ring and pleaded with Fortuna and to God Almighty not to abandon us. At least the weather was not awful that day. My pack was lighter without the food and drink, and Adhie, after a few days filling his wee belly, seemed more inclined to walk as we followed the drove road to Dunvegan.

* * *

Dunvegan, fortress home of Clan MacLeod held fast to the rugged slab of black basalt as though formed and fastened by unnatural force. We finally reached it, and my heart lifted in thanks to God and good fortune. We had done well on our trip, although my turn-shoes and socks were shredded from rocks and grasping heather. And I had been able to trade medicine for oat cakes along the way, so we were not starving. It had been a long walk with a night under the stars, and luckily the weather had held. I was ready for a hot bath and a fill of tasty food and drink. And it was relaxing to be among people again. The wilderness, at least to me, is a stressful, hostile place, to be avoided if possible. But now that was past, and I happily anticipated better times. We crossed the stone bridge over the ravine linking the village and docks to the fortress mount. There was no obvious gate, just a path that wound counterclockwise around the base of the fortress. I looked up to the battlements hoping to see a familiar face, imagining Elspeth and Janet waving, throwing flowers, and promising a grand feast. Sadly, none of that was evident, just suspicious guards following my progress with their eyes. The only entrance turned out to be an old sea gate on the opposite side of the building. I picked up Adhie and descended steps to a rock-strewn beach with a stone pier.

Nearby, men were scraping the hull of a birlinn hauled out for repairs.

Uneven stone steps ascended to the sea gate. Two warriors stood guard within. I introduced myself and told them who I had come to see. The guard with a kindly face and ample belly held in check by a broad leather belt cocked his head on hearing my name, then excused himself and went into the guard hut beside the gate. He emerged a moment later with a welcoming smile, and said, "Let him in, Keith," then turned to me and said, "Been expecting ye. Follow me, sir."

Up a long flight of stairs from sea gate to main level we went, the burly guardsman in the lead. As we crossed the bailey, I could see that the fortress was in poor condition, with rooves missing and interior walls collapsed. And there appeared to be no one at work making repairs. Niall Morrison's description came to mind, but I hoped all was not as desperate as first impressions would suggest. I did perceive some activity, including servants hustling bags and water, and the clang of the blacksmith's hammer. We entered the ground floor of a building and went left along a short corridor. The guardsman stopped, took the ring of keys from his belt, and unlocked the door. He smiled and said warmly, "They wish ye to stay here awhile afore they officially welcome ye, sir."

The room was small, clean, and simply furnished with bed, table, chair, and a sea-chest on the floor. The guardsman lit some candles and said it was good to have another guest. Strangely, there was a round iron grate on the floor, hinged on one side, and from it came a whiff of odour I recognized at once. Adhie yelped and I did not turn fast enough, and the guardsman caught me on the back of my head with the butt of his sword. I fell to my knees, stunned. Then the guardsman must have kicked me hard in the back because I felt intense pain and ended up face-down on the stone floor with an immense weight on my back. He was grabbing my arms and clamping metal on my wrists, all the while swearing at Adhie who was barking frantically.

I struggled and ordered the guardsman to desist and forcefully told him I was the son of a Scottish lord and that he would be made to pay for this outrage. He leaned his face closer. I could sense his hot breath on the back of my neck as he snarled that this was not a mistake, but by direct order of the MacLeod of MacLeod, Chief of Clan MacLeod and the only authority that mattered hereabouts. My family name and connections mattered not, nor the fact I had come to help the very person who had just imprisoned me!

The guardsman laughed amiably as I implored him to find Lady Elspeth, that this surely was in error. But it soon became evident that he would not relent, and I would not gratify him by begging for my life. So, there I lay, Adhie licking my face, and me wondering what would come next. It did not take long to find out because immediately he called for more men and said to them with a note of glee that I was to be imprisoned indefinitely in the dungeon, its entrance being that iron grate in the floor and the dungeon below the source of the evil smell.

Chapter 7: Elspeth

Someone or something was crying softly. I pushed myself up from the rows of herbs in the bailey garden and searched for the source of the sound. The smell of turned earth, crushed rosemary, and peppermint hung about my skirts as I stood. Two gray-and-white cats sprawled atop the sun-warmed stone walls leading to the sea gate below the bailey groomed themselves, licking their splayed nether parts indelicately with the supreme indifference of their species.

The crying sound seemed to float up from the sea gate, the only entrance into Dunvegan Castle. The narrow steps leading down to it were purposely built just wide enough to permit passage for one person. A single warrior at the top of the steps could defend the constricted opening. There is no roof over the passage steps except for a few feet at the bottom. Any enemy beyond that small shelter was also vulnerable to attack from above by defenders armed with spears, arrows, sticks, stones, boiling pitch, flaming brands, and the contents of chamber pots. All well-considered defenses.

The crying sound came again, and the cats paused a moment before resuming their ablutions. I brushed my skirts free of earth and green things and started down the uneven treads to the sea gate. Vile epithets and a single terrified yelp came from above me as a black-and-white puppy tumbled down the steps, followed by a large man, foot upraised for another kick.

"Stop!" I screamed. He stilled abruptly. Unwashed flesh, onions and ale fogged the air in that walled space. His greasy dark hair fell lankly about his shoulders and his beard and plaid bore traces of past meals. The enormous hand of the guard gripped a claymore, better suited for dispatching an armed opponent than a wee dog. He knew me at once. I had cared for his kith and kin often enough during the past weeks. He gawked at me, lowered his weapon, and peered uneasily back up the passage.

"You were going to kill the wee thing? Why? It is but a pup." The dog cowered against the wall, trembling. I stooped. "Ahh, *ceann beag*, little one, come to me." I held out my hand, but the furry scrap shivered and scooted back. I rummaged in my pocket and broke a piece from the bannock bread I had brought for lunch, then held it out. After a moment, hunger overcame fear and the pup slowly crawled on its belly toward my outstretched hand. Its black-and-white coat was full of burrs, mud, and only the gods knew what else. The guard looked nervously behind himself again, then thrust out a scarred nail-bitten hand toward the shivering creature. The pup growled and darted between his hairy legs, fleeing into the old castle-keep. The man shouted something that sounded like, "cursed devil spawned arse-worm," and sprinted in pursuit.

I grabbed my skirts and hurried after them. The puppy was in the entrance room, scrabbling frantically at a metal grate on the floor, whining piteously. It was the iron grate that covered the hole leading to the castle dungeon. The guard lunged clumsily for the puppy. I was quicker and snatched him up first, clutching his filthy body to my breast where he squirmed desperately, seeking escape. We were all breathing hard.

The guard moved to stand defensively over the grate. Another man appeared. Both knew I was the laird's cousin and gossip named me witch, so they regarded me with wary respect. From under the guard's great stinking feet came a familiar voice from below, singing merrily. I tightened my grip on the pup, wondering if I had gone quite mad.

Be merry my hearts, and call for your quarts,
and let no liquor be lacking,
We have gold in store, we purpose to roar,
until we set care a packing.
Then Hostis make haste, and let no time waste,
let every man have his due,

To save shoes and trouble, bring in the pots double

for he that made one, made two—

I had heard those words times beyond remembering. It was Malcom's favorite drinking song! I reached out with one hand and pushed the guard as hard as I could. Surprise took him off the grate. Keeping a tight hold of the puppy, I fell to my knees. The reek rising from the hole made me want to retch.

"*Malcolm...Malcolm*?" I yelled down the hole. The singing stopped.

"Elspeth?" The name echoed faintly off the stone walls. The puppy wriggled and wailed. I peered down, but the darkness was impenetrable. Jumping to my feet, I turned like a tigress on the guard.

My voice was controlled and lethal when I spoke, "What have you done, you great ugly *bawheid*? Why is he down there? Get him out at once! If you have hurt him, I promise that I shall personally reach down your throat and pull your slimy guts out through your nose, then make you use them for garters."

He took a step backward from the rage in my words and blustered, "'Tis by the laird's own wish. I cannot release him with no orders."

"The laird told you to imprison Sir Malcolm?" I asked. "Impossible! I do not believe that for a moment. Sir Malcolm is his friend." The guard's eyes widened when I used Malcolm's title and I felt his uncertainty mount.

"Nay. Word was sent to us to hold him. We but did as told." He shuffled further back, looking at the other man.

"Who? Who told you to imprison him? When the laird discovers what you have done, he will have your head removed from your shoulders and placed on a pike for the crows to pick." My voice was purposely laced with deadly promise.

He took fright at that. Sweat gathered on his brow. "'Twas just a note from him brought to us saying he was a danger and we was to keep him locked up till told different. We but did as told."

I narrowed my eyes at him. "I want to see that note! You will find it and give it to me, but first you will do as I bid! Remove that grate and get him out. *Now!* You." I pointed at the other man, "Help him. Then go for the laird and Lady Janet. Tell her to bring my bag. If you see Lady Mairi, tell her she is needed here." Bringing the laird and Lady Mairi into this muddle cowed the men entirely, and they stumbled over each other in their haste to obey.

No further sounds had risen from the dank hole in the stone floor. I leaned over it and called down, "Malcolm? We are going to get you out. Are you able to move? Do you need help to get up?"

He mumbled something unintelligible. The guard returned and a looped rope was lowered, vanishing into the dark, noisome pit. There were scrabbling sounds and after some moments a shout from below, and the men began to pull the rope up. Two scraped grimy hands, one wearing a gold ring, grasped the edge of the opening, followed by an unkempt mop of dirty brown hair tangled into a matching beard. Deep brown eyes glinted at me through a hairy veil as he pulled himself over the verge onto the floor. The puppy scrambled from my arms and began to bounce and bark in ecstasy, pawing and licking at the grubby face of the prone figure.

The wretch was laughing! The little dog ecstatically attacked him with canine kisses. "Adhie! Good boy." He buried his filthy face in the dog's fur. It was Malcolm but gone the fastidious gentleman. What little I could see of his face was as rough as any peasants from sun and windburn. He was thinner than I remembered, his clothes stiff with an indescribable mix of dried muck. The parts of his body lacking even that dubious protection was scattered with scabbed-over lacerations. His feet were the worst—swollen and crusted with black. I knelt and reached out to touch them, but he jerked them back. His voice was calm. "No, El. Don't touch me. I am filthy and vermin-ridden."

I sat down suddenly and began to sob uncontrollably. That is how Janet and Aunt Mairi found us. The laird arrived a few minutes later, trailed unhappily by the man who had been sent to summon him. He strode in impatiently and loomed over me. "What is this about your releasing a prisoner? What prisoner? We presently have none."

I staggered to my feet and fought to speak. "None? None! Look… just look! How could you do this? You told them to put him in that…

that stinking hole! Are you quite mad? His father will be outraged. I am ashamed to be called MacLeod! How dare you treat a friend of mine so?" I ranted at him, pounding my small fists on his chest. Tears streaking down my cheeks.

The laird took my wrists and gently moved me aside to get to the motionless heap on the floor. Staring down, he regarded the dark eyes in the dirty bearded face for a long moment before stepping back in shock. His face paled to gray. "Sir Malcolm? By all the gods, I will have someone's bollocks for this." He turned his fury on the guard. "Who told you to imprison this man?"

"'Twas ye, my laird. Ye sent a note saying to hold him, did ye not? We found it on the table with the others." The man's voice quavered, but he answered readily enough.

A hot crimson tide erased the pallor from the laird's face. "I sent no such note." He took a deep shuddering breath before turning back to Malcolm. "Sir Malcolm, this is a terrible mistake. I stand shamed before you and humbly ask your forgiveness. By my honor, I swear I knew nothing of your arrival at Dunvegan or that you were subjected to this...this usage. You are a friend and an honored guest and should have been welcomed so. This is a grave and inexcusable error. I promise that those responsible will be severely punished. Not that it will lessen the insult or my fault in this. I pray you can find it in your heart to forgive me." He glared at the guards. "I will settle with you lot after you have made your own apologies. Elspeth, these wretched examples of manhood will do whatever is needed to help you." He gazed at Malcolm, who had not moved nor uttered a sound. "Again, I ask your pardon, although I am undeserving of it. And I will find out who is responsible for this outrage." The laird's strength seemed to ebb, and his shoulders slumped. He breathed in sharply, coughed, then straightened and walked unsteadily away.

Anger fled before the fatigue I sensed in my laird. Every morn he seemed to be wearier and more depressed. His domain was literally crumbling about his head, and he had neither the stamina to control it nor the coin to halt it. He needed both desperately. I had sent for Malcolm because I hoped he could help. But after this debacle, he might well simply return home and not agree to do so. I turned back to the abused one on the floor. I could but tend his hurts, mend his appearance, and pray he would help me find a way to save the laird and Dunvegan. I would even care for his scrawny wee dog.

* * *

After the laird left, Aunt Mairi laid her hand gently on my shoulder and suggested we use the laundry to care for Malcolm. It was close by and would be easier to clean when we were done. And there was no better place in the castle to contain whatever pests Malcolm might be hosting. She tapped her staff across the floor, knelt by him, touched his forehead with tender fingers, then rose. He gazed up at her, his dark eyes lit with an unholy humor dredged from some untouched strength inside himself. She poked him gently with her wooden rod, told us he would do well enough after a bit of scrubbing, commanded him to attend her when he was decent, then left.

I sent for soup, fresh bread, cheese, and ale, and bullied him into eating a little before leading him to the laundry room. His former guards were anxiously feeding the peat fires and heating huge pots of water. A tub they had placed on the floor in the center of the room was almost filled with steaming liquid. I asked Malcolm to strip. He held up a delaying hand and dug into the rags he wore, bringing forth a black sporran which he laid on the clothes press, then pulled the gold Fortuna ring from his finger and handed it to me. He offered us his backside as he undressed and gave his reeking plaid to a guard with a terse command to burn it at once. When he was naked, he wrapped a towel about his narrow hips and turned toward us. His body was whip thin but not cadaverous. He was not as slim as I had first thought, but wiry. Clearly defined muscles ridged his body, lean but fit from whatever he had been through these last weeks.

The nits on his chest were visible tiny white flecks against the dark tangles of hair, as were those of his head and beard. Not so visible were patches of reddened skin which patterned his torso. A flea hopped on my arm as I walked around him. "He will need to be shaved and well scrubbed. There is no help for it," I sighed.

"Not completely!" he blurted.

"No. We can deal with your hair and beard, but it will be easier to shave some parts of your body..." I felt myself flush. Why was I reacting this way? 'Twas only Malcolm. "That would eliminate the need for salves there," I muttered. I had a salve, made with equal parts of powdered *olibanum* and clean lard, to kill lice, but it took several days of continuous coverage to work. I would wash his long wavy hair with rosemary shampoo and use the lice comb. It would take longer but serve his vanity.

Cawdie had stalked into the laundry and stood, arms folded near the door. At my comments, he snorted. "Nay. Ye cannae do that! Ye are a maid. 'Tis nae fit!"

I laughed. "Cawdie, I can well assure you that Malcolm has no more than I have seen many times. He is only a man like any other."

"Aye, an a wee one, too, ah see." He looked at Malcolm, expecting a ribald response, but strangely there was none. Janet was pouring more hot water into the tub and ignoring both men. After glancing at her, Cawdie sighed in resignation. "Ah dinnae like it. Ah will stay here and watch yon blaggard." He leaned against the wall and scowled menacingly.

I laid an old blanket on the floor, placed a stool on it and asked Malcolm to sit. Janet stood before him and began to separate smelly clumps of oily vermin-ridden hair, pulling them away from his head while she cut, piling the filthy hanks to be burned later with the discarded clothing.

"I rather liked your long hair. 'Tis a pity we have to mangle it so," said I. While Janet clipped, I dug into my bag for a razor to shave his body. He eyed the instrument with some misgiving, then closed his eyes and took a deep breath. I drew blood only once.

Shaved, he stood, shook himself and stepped gingerly into the hot bath, then submerged himself till the water covered completely. He uttered a moan of profound relief and lay motionless a few moments before sitting up. We moved toward the tub to wash him. Cawdie let out an audible snort.

"No!" Malcom's voice was sharp. "Let me soak awhile first to soften the scabs. I'll wash myself next, at least what I can reach. The treatments, I'll leave to you."

We waited. And when he finished, we washed his hair thoroughly before making him change to a second tub of clean warm water to wash again. He was much too passive while we tended him. The explosion would likely come later. Janet tried and failed to smother a laugh as she scrubbed his back. I was far more concerned about his feet, which were layered with half-healed scars, cuts, calluses, and half-open sores. I doubted he would be able to walk without pain for a time and would require some sort of soft slipper.

We added pyrethrum-water to the final rinse, dried him and applied soothing salve to his mistreated body. He complained that his teeth felt filthy, so I gave him a small jar of sage and salt tooth powder and a square of cloth to rub it in. When we had done, he was noticeably drowsy. We guided him to a clean bed in a room in the servants' quarters and tucked him in like a wee bairn. Talking could come later. I left the door slightly ajar as we left.

The pup, who had been tied outside, was howling unhappily again. Cawdie surrendered and brought him to the laundry. The two of us removed burrs and gave him a bath in Malcolm's still-warm rinse water. We rubbed him as dry as possible and dusted him with pyrethrum powder. As soon as we permitted him to escape, he darted up the hallway to find Malcolm, nosed open the door, and jumped onto the bed. There he curled damply against his sleeping master, joining him in the arms of Morpheus.

The guards cleared and cleaned the laundry. The one who had chased Adhie approached me cautiously. "My lady, be there more ye want done?" As he spoke, he held out a scrap of paper and a worn sling pack. "'Tis what he was carrying, my lady. And here be the note ye wanted." He shuffled nervously. "'Tis all there. Ye can see we but followed orders."

I took both items and read the proffered paper. As the guard claimed, it named Malcolm, warned that he was dangerous, and ordered him imprisoned when he arrived. I frowned. There was no signature.

"I will keep this." I looked at the man. "You put him in the dungeon without knowing who gave the orders?" He looked genuinely puzzled.

"'Twas from the laird, my lady. We get such from him often." He shifted uncomfortably. "'Tis all in there. The laird's own words." He pointed at the note.

Suddenly I understood. "You cannot read!" He flushed guiltily. "How do you know what it says? Who read it for you?" He shook his head frantically and turned the color of whey.

"'Tis not a problem. There be some who can read amongst us." He hesitated, evidently unwilling to say more. "'Twas some time ago. I dinnae remember, my lady." Fear tied his tongue. He was terrified of whoever it was.

* * *

Malcolm was wearing clean garments and pacing the floor impatiently when I met him next morning. Aunt Mairi had somehow acquired a new plaid and a linen shirt for him, and Cawdie loaned him a belt. Until his feet healed enough to bear shoes, the soft slippers I had been making for the laird would do, despite a few unfinished embroidered blossoms. He was presentable, if not his usual stylish self. It was enough. I returned his backpack. He whirled angrily, almost stumbling over the puppy. "God's bones, woman. Your laird kept me imprisoned and now keeps me waiting. I want to see him and leave this misbegotten island as soon as can be. I've come through much on what seems to be a fool's errand. Please tell me what you want, Elspeth." He took a small box from his sporran and pushed it roughly into my hand. "Take this, too. Take it! One of your so-called healers named Gormal gave it to me for your Aunt Mairi. Said it would heal the laird."

I did not reply, just opened the worn lid of the small, beautifully painted box, and unrolled the linen cloth that held a palm-sized flat rock. "The Brightstone?" I gripped the fragment tightly, sensing and absorbing the heat it had collected from Malcolm's body. Some objects took from the body, and some gave. In my hand, the stone appeared to be a piece of common gray rock until it caught a shaft of sunlight from the window. In the shifting beams it flashed with hundreds of silver glints. "Gormal gave you this? 'Tis a thing used only by the *cailleach chneastas,* the white witches, because it carries the light. I wonder how she came by it?" I folded the cloth back around it, put it into the box, and held it out to him. "Please see Aunt Mairi and the laird, Malcolm. I rather desperately need your help. Please. I beg you. I am too involved and upset to think clearly. There is so much happening. Please, as my dearest friend, Malcolm, help me sort things." I was ashamed to be begging and to hear the entreaty at the edge of tears in my voice.

He groaned. "You know quite well I shall," he grumbled, "but I will not accept hospitality from one responsible for my less-than-gracious reception. It grates at me, notwithstanding his apologies." He began pacing again. "Cawdie told me that in the village there's a small inn and tavern that takes boarders. I will try that, but make no mistake, Elspeth, I'm here to help, but ready to leave at once if this turns out to be one of your imaginary problems. You prattle on such too often."

"It is not one of my starts! Go to the village, then. I care not where you stay. The tavern may well be more appealing in many ways." I was certain he would find the red-headed innkeeper much to his taste. "Only please remain nearby till I can see clearly what is happening and what needs to be done." I said no more. It would serve no purpose. He would do as he pleased no matter what I might say, but at least he would stay awhile.

* * *

I returned to my room. Aunt Rhona was sitting up against a heap of bed-pillows. A long woolen arisaid of white, with fine red and blue stripes, warmed her painfully thin shoulders and hid her swollen legs. Her sweet face was tinged with the peculiar whitish gray that marks the faces of the seriously ill. I sensed her slipping away from us. Aunt Rhona and Aunt

Mairi are sisters of my mother's mother. They also had two brothers, both dead.

She smiled a bit anxiously at me and patted the coverlets next to her. "Come, child. Sit with me a moment. Bring the basket of wool yarns I gave you." I carried the heavy hand-woven container to her. It was filled with balls of dyed spun wool. The worn wooden niddy noddy she used for measuring the strands lay unassembled amid several finished skeins. She tipped the contents of the basket onto the blanket before her, and the balls bounced and rolled in every direction. Except for one saffron yellow sphere that refused to follow its escaping fellows. It plopped solidly onto the coverlet, where it lay inert. She picked it up and began to unwind the strands. A faint smell of heather and the vinegar used to brighten dyes drifted from the wool. As she unwound it, a dark ball emerged. It was a stone sphere carved with triskele symbols! I leaned closer to see it better. The intricate spiral patterns on its surface were not exactly like those on mine, but similar.

No one knew from whence the balls came nor understood their purpose. I had been told that they were powerful talismans and must be protected at all costs. According to the old tales, each of them had belonged to and been guarded for centuries by women of the clan. The women were the entrusted ones. I have vivid memories of the ceremony following my first flowers when I became part of their circle and given a stone ball to guard with my life. It had been Aunt Rhona's. Aunt Mairi had a second triskele ball, my mother a third, and Erika, my sister, a fourth that I believed had been lost when she died. And Una Talisker was said to have another, making five in all. This one on the bed must be Erika's! I stared at it, shaken. Aunt Rhona lifted my hand and closed my quivering fingers about the warm surface of the stone.

My breath caught when it touched my skin. "Where did you get this, Aunt Rhona? Erika has been dead for almost four years!"

She looked at me sadly. "No, child. I have tried to tell you otherwise so many times. You most of all should have known Erika lives. Your refusal to use your gift has cost us all dearly. You, the strongest yet the weakest would have known she was not gone had you not closed your mind and buried your talent. And then your sister suddenly stopped using her gift too. We no longer sense her clearly, but she is not dead. Not yet." She continued, "A message was given to me by an old man from the keep at Talisker. He said his life was forfeit if his master discovered he had done so. In the message, your sister told me she had concealed the ball in a hidden niche known to both of you as children, in this room, at the back of the fireplace. She told me to safeguard it and give it to you. I removed the ball from its hiding place as I felt myself becoming ill. And Ysabell had begun to visit far too often with the excuse of tending the fire. I caught her searching among my things. You were children together, and I feared she knew of your secret place." She shifted painfully. "The communication was from Erika. Touch the stone!"

"No! No, Aunt Rhona. She is dead! It is not possible she could be living. You are wrong...wrong!" I jerked back.

My aunt looked at me sadly. "Elspeth, child...take this." She thrust it toward me, forcing it into my shaking hand.

I reluctantly closed my fingers around the ball. There was no doubt that it had once belonged to my sister. Part of her still lingered within it. Aunt Rhona had helped Janet with our care after mother died giving me birth, for Janet had been much too young to be responsible for a newborn babe and a lively child of two years. As we grew older, Aunt Rhona ceded much of our care to Janet. Erika and I were close when we were young. I remembered once when we made a planned escape from the castle and what we understood as unfair punishment for eating only a few—no more than a dozen, surely—pieces of marchpane made for the laird's name day. Unfound and unrepentant, we remained hidden for an entire day in a small opening on the mountainside, too small to be called a cave but just large enough to hide two wee girls. Hunger and thirst ended our rebellion. No sweetmeats could fill our stomachs for long. Half the castle and village were looking for us and the laird declared we had ruined his name-day with worry. But his dour face was belied by the twinkle in his eye when we were found.

Janet was not so lenient. Erika and I shared the well-deserved switching without shedding a tear. Janet hated to punish us and wept more than we did when she had to do so. But she made certain we had something to eat before being sent to bed.

The carved stone ball felt like a living thing in my hand. I went to my trunk, retrieved my own stone from the concealed compartment inside and laid it on the bed to compare with Erika's. Both were about the size of oranges and differed in the number and size of bumps. And each was ornamented with the winding spirals of the triskele symbol and strange symbols like ancient runes. The patterns reminded me of a massive carved rock I had happened upon while meandering through a meadow one wet misty day. My mind reached out to the memory.

The air around me shimmered in the odd hazy light. Today I am ten and two. This morning Erika pinched one of the two sensitive little corms growing beneath my nipples and laughed. She said it was a sign that I would soon bleed and be a woman. I told her they hurt. She looked at me for a long moment and said, "being a woman often hurts."

I am restless and anxious for no discernible reason and further from the castle than I should be, drawn to a curiously shaped boulder sitting alone at the edge of the field. My fingers look strangely small as they stroke the cold grey slab, tracing the ancient cup-and-ring carvings covering every part of its surface. Mist pleats itself into raindrops that gather in the dimpled depressions on the table-like stone. Each cup is surrounded by carved circular rings or channels. The cups fill and overflow into grooves cut randomly across them, creating runnels connecting other rings before falling over the edge of the rock or sinking into natural fissures.

The downward path of the water becomes convoluted before reaching the ground or the crevices in the rock. I am bespelled by the sparkling silver filling the channels. Touching the wet slippery surface with my fingertips, I wonder whose hands had created the laboriously carved the mysterious designs.

A glint of color caused me to look up. Through the grey gentleness of rain, a man leaned over the stone from the other side, one arm extended above it. He did not look my way. A small dirk glowed in his other hand. He murmured something and sliced the blade across the inner surface of his extended limb.

Crimson blood dripped from the wound and began to fill one of the cups. He held himself motionless above the stone depression, his eyes following the direction of the red stream as it overflowed the cup. Blood blossomed along its course, painting a red pattern in the channels. The stain flooded nearby rings and grooves before falling off the edge and pooling at my feet, sinking into the earth like an offering to the old gods. The man looked across the streaked altar at me, bowed his head and touched a leather bag hanging from his belt.

I sank into the blackness that overtook me and must have lain in the suddenly heavy deluge for some time before regaining my senses. I was shivering and soaked through. There was no man nearby and no blood except that of my first flowers. I had become a woman.

I jerked back into the present and frowned at the triskele. Why was I remembering that? These were spirals, not cup-and-ring designs. It is true that cup-and-ring carvings were sometimes found with spirals and grouped in threes like the triskele, but that meant little. I moved the two stones about in my hands, trying to discover some relationship, but nothing came. Perhaps the one Aunt Mairi had would be helpful. I would show them to Malcolm, too.

"Aunt Rhona, may I keep these?"

She exhaled slowly and nodded to me. "I thank you, child. 'Tis a relief. You will know what to do." She lay back on her lavender-scented mound of pillows and closed her eyes, her breath coming more evenly, and slept.

* * *

Aunt Mairi was not in what we generously called her room. It had once been a closet, an austere cell-like place used for storage. The laird had insisted she take it so she would not need to return to her cottage in the village in harsh weather or late at night. It smelled cleanly of new limewash and held but a small cot, a wee wooden chest, and a stool. I suspect she agreed to use it only because it was near the stillroom where I found her. She tilted a blue-green glass beaker, carefully pouring liquid into a simmering pot, concentrating entirely on the task at hand. When she finished, she used a wooden stirrer to mix the ingredients, then spoke without turning, "Tis in there. Second shelf, cobalt glazing." She inclined her head toward a large cupboard. I opened the door and found a fat pot labeled "Stinging Nettle" gathering dust at the back. I lifted it down, removed the fitted cork stopper, and dug into the dried contents. My fingers found a round stone ball nestled in the desiccated foliage. Dried nettle no longer stings. How she knew what I wanted was beyond my ken.

"Most clever, Aunt Mairi. May I borrow this? We need to talk."

"Aye," she muttered. I could smell the mint she added to the hot liquid, stirring it several times before finally looking up. "You have three now. They are part of the key. Guard them well."

I rubbed the ball free of clinging bits of withered nettles, my fingertips tracing the carved surface. "I have come about Malcolm. Perhaps it was a mistake. He wants to leave, and I have drawn him into danger. Am I being selfish? Perhaps I was wrong to have asked him. There is so much he will never understand and is vulnerable because he does not. Did you sense it? Someone tried to bespell him. He said it was Gormal and Doideag. If he stays, he must always be protected. I would ask Cawdie to guard him, but he is so content with Janet." Startled, I looked down. I had tapped the Fortuna ring on the stone ball and received a slight shock.

"Then give him back the ring, child," she said. "We have less need for such. Fortuna protects unbelievers as well. I will speak with him. It will be as it was foreseen."

"You have seen it?" I was bewildered. "When? How?"

She gave me one of her rare frowns. "Cease being childish, Elspeth. You are what you are. You cannot hide forever. Do as Rhona asked. Open your mind and look for yourself! 'Tis long past time you took your place as one of the active entrusted ones. I am old…and…ill, as is Rhona. You are our hope for the future. Malcolm will stay, and you must be fierce for all of us."

It was a scolding. I put the ball into a pocket beneath my skirt, kissed her velvety cheek, and left.

* * *

Malcolm had company. As I walked down the hallway, a flash of belling fabric vanished behind the closing door. I walked faster and thwacked the scarred door hard. There was a short silence before it opened. Ysabell stood there. She altered her expression from sleepy-eyed seductress to one of arrogant mock-merriment. "Ah, Sir Malcolm, 'tis our little healer."

"Come in, Lady Elspeth. Lady Ysabell brought me a present." He still looked tired and glanced between us as he held up a flagon.

"Lady Ysabell," I mimicked her sweetly in return, "how kind of you." I gave them both a savage smile, brushed past her, took the vessel from him, and examined it. "Ah, 'tis sorry I am." I held the flagon out to Ysabell. "I suppose you did not realize that this vintage has become sour. Such a pity. So much work for nothing. 'Tis not even fit for cooking." I stared coldly at her until she took the flagon. Rage surfaced in her eyes for a moment.

"Oh, do forgive me, Sir Malcolm." She leaned closer to him and let her breast brush against his arm, an old whore's trick that made me flush in anger. I badly wished to slap her. "I will find an unspoiled one for you," she said, then looked at me defiantly and swayed out.

I watched Malcolm's eyes follow the graceful swing of her buttocks and tried to think of a way to warn him. But of what? My suspicion would seem but female venom and jealousy. Nonetheless, I had to try. "Malcolm...you must be wary of...things here. They are not always as they seem." I pulled the Fortuna ring from my finger and offered it to him. It felt hot. "Like this. Please wear it. It will afford you some shield from those who might seek to influence you. I know you do not believe in such powers, but others do. For most, simply seeing the ring on your finger will be sufficient to warn them away. And it will please me greatly if you accept it."

He looked at the gold and carnelian circle and shook his head, but finally took it, albeit reluctantly. "It may work in some instances, Elspeth, and because of that, I'll do as you ask. Old beliefs are powerful forces, and this is a backward, benighted place." He placed the ring on his finger and changed the subject. "I hope we don't have travelers from Drynoch. God help us if that happens. We need to discuss the situation there and send help."

"What is wrong? What about Drynoch?"

"There may be a typhus outbreak. A family…it may have come from a returning soldier. I quarantined them…but they need assistance before it spreads."

"You are in no condition to do anything now. If you promise to rest, I will go and speak with Dr. Bethune."

"It's urgent, Elspeth."

I could see by his grim look—the same one he gave me when the smallpox epidemic began in Edinburgh—that he meant it. "When I leave, I will find him, tell him of your concerns, and ask him to meet with you at once."

* * *

Aunt Rhona was sleeping when I returned to our room. Sitting cross-legged on my bed, I retrieved the three stone balls and placed them in a line before me. I rotated them, running the sensitive pads of my fingers over the surfaces, trying to discover differences and similarities. All were made of sandstone. In addition to the bumps, the carvings varied on each one. But each had at least one spiral or triskele figure as part of its design. And they were slashed with runes that might be understood by someone familiar with them.

I studied them closely and was reminded that triskele spiral designs are sometimes depicted as running legs. The MacLeod armorial had three flexed legs in a triangle joined at the upper part of the thigh, in the form of a triskele. The drawing of the knot garden Uncle Angus gave to me in Glasgow showed spiral herb and floral beds, but his plan had four sections, not three. Four…I frowned. What had four parts? The number four was considered lucky by many. The Loch at the shipyard at Rubh' an Dunain is shaped roughly like a four-leaf clover. Sir John Melton wrote, "If a man walking in the field find any four-leaved grass he shall, in a small while after, find some good thing." I laughed to myself. I was growing silly.

I gave up for now and wrapped the stones in soft cloths. Three were too heavy and too many to put back in Aunt Rhona's basket or in my travel chest with the grimoire. But they needed to be hidden. Erika and I had always used the hollow in the hearth. Ysabell had ceased her care of Aunt Rhona now that I shared her room. So, our hearth hiding spot would be more secure and would have to do for now. Brushing hot coals away from the back of the fireplace, I used my sgian dubh dagger to pry out the sooty stone concealing the cavity, gingerly pushed the balls inside, and replaced the blackened rock. Another turf to the coals angled to the scorched wall obscured all traces of the hollow.

I was about to leave, my hand on the door of my room when I heard voices in the corridor. One was Ysabell, the other a man. His was that masculine treacle voice which slid down a woman's spine igniting a pleasurable burn in the belly. It belonged to a friend from my childhood, Niall Morrison. He used his voice like a weapon. Years had passed since I last heard it, but it was unmistakably the same. Appealing and devilishly handsome, Niall was an irredeemable flirt who had once turned his attention to me. I had fancied myself in love with Ranuff Talisker at the time, so I was almost immune, but not entirely. He pursued both Erika and me, I think more to annoy Ranuff than from any lasting affection for either of us. He and Ranuff had competed fiercely since childhood, and it was mere sport to them, akin to the card games we played.

I closed the door and leaned against the rough wood. Niall's voice brought back old and almost forgotten memories of Niall, Ranuff, Erika and me sitting before the fireplace in the laird's library, playing Bragg. Erika, her pale, delicate features enhanced by the soft gleam of candles and the rich green color of her gown, was easily charming both men. I bloomed late, but she was already in possession of her formidable beauty. She was everything I was not, had everything I thought I wanted—including the man I loved. Envy twisted in my gut. I was shamefully jealous. I tried inexpertly to dally with Niall, hoping to make Ranuff take notice. Niall, surprised and amused, responded gallantly to my awkward advances. He was kind, a superb gamester favored by Dame Fortune and a master of deception, often driving Ranuff to fling down his cards in disgust. He told so many clever half-truths mixed with half-lies that it was impossible to discern which was which. It made him doubly skillful at the subtle management of the game of Bragg, which involves the art of bluffing about the cards you hold.

That evening his artful manner was intended to convince us all that he was going to bluff or out-bounce us with a hand of low and insignificant cards. He feigned a seemingly reluctant Bragg of half a crown, but an almost concealed glint in his eye warned me to throw in my modest hand. Erika and I ceased the Bragg. Ranuff was determined not to be out bounced. It became a war between the two men. The stakes might have gone beyond a hundred crowns had not the laird, passing behind Niall, let out an indiscreet and involuntary grunt of surprise upon seeing Niall's hand. Ranuff was instantly alerted and immediately ceased Bragging to avoid further loss.

Instead of low cards, Niall held two natural Aces and the Knave of Clubs, making his hand the greatest Pair Royal that could be dealt! Ranuff took it badly, tossed his purse on the table and stormed out of the library. That ended the game. Erika jumped up from the table and followed Ranuff to soothe him. I was left with Niall, who decided to return my inept flirting, in lieu of taunting Ranuff. But I was no longer interested. When Ranuff left with Erika, there was no longer a point to the pastime. I glared at Niall and left him standing there with his mouth slightly agape. Minutes later I curled forlornly under the covers of our bed, weeping in resentment and frustration, and wishing Erika to the devil. When she finally came to bed, I pretended to be asleep.

* * *

The next morning Erika and I had woken feverish and vomiting. In three days, the flat, red rash of smallpox appeared on our faces. Dr. Bethune cared for us as best he could but was soon overwhelmed as others succumbed to the terrifying disease. Erika rapidly became worse, and they moved her out of our room into a makeshift infirmary. I was one of the fortunate, soon recovering with but a few scars on my belly and left cheek as reminders. Erika suffered greatly, the disease ravaging her body until no trace of her exquisite loveliness remained. I dragged myself to her bedside when I was permitted to do so and sat for hours staring helplessly at her and laying cool rosemary-infused cloths on her hot, weeping skin. I spoke tenderly to her, repeatedly telling her I was sorry and that I loved her. I asked her forgiveness, but she seemed unaware of my presence.

Ranuff was ever-present. He hovered over Erika, or sat, or paced restlessly about the infirmary, lost in his own agony. But she grew steadily weaker and died one night after I had returned to our room for a few hours of sleep. When I returned the next morning, they told me Ranuff had taken her body away to be buried near his home. I had not been there for her in the end. I wished her gone and my wish had been heard. God had punished me by giving me what I desired. Aunt Mairi said I had the gift of feeling others, but I had caused Erika to die with my spiteful thoughts. I did not want such a "gift." I resolved to keep it buried within myself and never use it again. In death Erika could never absolve me. I would have to live with my remorse the rest of my life. Thereafter, guilt was my constant companion. I desperately needed some way to redeem the culpability I now perceived within myself. Eventually I became enamoured of becoming a healer and decided I would devote my life to helping others—that way I might someday forgive myself my sins.

Over the years, my aunts trained me in their various arts, but I craved some near-impossible goal to further my penitence. I read constantly, seeking to lose myself in the written word. The locked cabinets in the stillroom were filled with handwritten herbals and manuscripts, and I devoured them all, committing much to memory. When that no longer helped, I pored over every tome in the castle library. The old laird watched me, perplexed for some time, then one day handed me the key to the muniment room where he kept Dunvegan's most valuable volumes and family records. I absorbed them all. I planted unusual herbs, searched for others, created new salves, experimented with different concoctions, made copious records, and began my own herbal. But I remained restless and unhappy. I became a thin, quiet shadow that flitted about the castle at all hours.

Despairing of my well-being, Janet went to Aunt Mairi. She in turn went to the laird and persuaded him to send me to Italy, where being a woman would not hamper my study of medicine. He agreed. It was decided.

Two weeks later, Janet, Cawdie and I set sail for the *Schola Medica Salernitana* in Salerno. I spent three glorious years in the *curriculum studiorum,* which included the study of texts of ancient medicine and the new science of surgery. Women were permitted to teach a variety of subjects as well as study, and in my time there I learned much more than medicine. Often, I slipped quietly into the men's lectures on theology and law, just to hear the discussions, but they were never as fascinating to me as my own studies. Those years changed me and my life.

I shook myself out of my reverie. It was time to do something besides relive old memories and dreams. I would do what I rarely did—invoke help. It had been long years since I had asked the spirits for assistance.

I removed the grimoire from its hiding place in the false bottom of my small chest and carried it and a few other things to the stillroom. This grimoire is a heavy volume with raised, tooled-leather covers and elaborate metal decorations. It was given to me in Italy by an old woman whose daughter I had safely delivered of twin babes. When daughter and babes were safely resting, she opened an old chest, removed the book, and pressed it into my hands with the promise that one day it would help me find what I was seeking. This was a perfect time to see if that were so. And mayhap I would find clues to help me decipher the meaning of the stones. I placed the grimoire on the table, closed the stillroom door, dropped the pivoted wooden bar into the slot in the jamb, and pulled the dangling latch string inside so no one could enter.

The grimoire had been written in the sixteenth century. The soft fabric used to protect the skin and metal had taken on the characteristic odor of old books mixed with subtle spices. Had ever there been anything inscribed without or within the cover, it was no longer visible. The manuscript had been written in three different hands and filled with a jumble of Christian prayers, ancient spells and conjurations, advice for making amulets and talismans, and herbal lore. Many pages bore illustrated charts, marked circles, drawings of spirits, and diagrams designed to keep the summoners safe.

The church had divided such knowledge into what they called white—or natural, and black—or demonic, magic. White witchcraft was used solely for the greater good, calling on God, his angels, saints, and the benevolent old gods of natural forces. But such spells may not be evoked to cause harm. Most healers practiced some forms of natural or white magic. Black magic calls on the Devil and his demons, with malevolent intent. These spells are strong, but white invocations defeat black ones if the invoker is pure of heart and intention. But should a white witch summon dark spirits, she loses the power to use white magic and can thereafter call only on the Devil and his cohorts.

There is much written and discussed about witchcraft by learned men. I had read *A discourse of the Damned Art of Witchcraft* by Perkins, a believer, and *A Blow at Modern Sadducism* by Glanville, who maintained that there was no such thing as witches and witchcraft. Neither was entirely correct. The ancient ways have adapted and survived. Where it could not oust them, Christianity absorbed the old gods and feast days into its own ritual. Outside the cities, people openly worship God and the gods in equal measure. Women pray to Saint Mary, wear amulets of a goddess beneath their clothing, and visit the local wise woman or witch to ask for help during birthing. Ancient figural carvings representing the hag and other symbols of the old ways still adorn churches and sacred places, familiar and honored by women. You have but to look closely.

The grimoire contained both black and white magic, as though the authors had not yet determined which path to follow. The worn leather cover of the old book absorbed light from the candles I had lit, hiding the elaborate designs. I opened it carefully. Power seemed to waft from the folios. For a moment I thought I heard faint chanting. Shaking my head free of illusions, I searched the volume for a Finding Spell I knew to be there. Some of the pages were difficult to read, faded from having water poured over the words of the invocations inscribed on them. After flowing across the spells, the water was believed to contain the essence of the words inscribed on the page. The spell-infused water was then poured into a flask. Thus, spells could be carried about in small containers, to be used in lieu of the volume itself.

I found the leaf I sought, a white invocation for finding. Then I gathered from Aunt Mairi's locked cabinets and my own bag everything for the invocation. I retrieved a pure beeswax candle, Holy Water from Rome in an exquisite ancient iridescent glass bottle, rosemary herb, and a bag of common salt.

Silence thickened the air around me. Aunt Mairi had taught me well, and I remembered. I emptied my mind of everything but the now. With the lit candle on the floor, I opened the bag of salt. Focusing on the ritual, I faced the east, turning sun-ways south, north, and west, pouring an unbroken line of white crystals around me as I revolved, drawing a protective circle of salt on the floor. I placed a single rosemary branch at each of the four cardinal directions and scattered precious drops of Holy Water within the ring.

The MacLeods have a banner known as the Fairy Flag. Legend says that the silken banner was given to the MacLeods by Tatiana, the wife of Oberon, King of the Fae, or fairies. That tale had intrigued me as a child, so I chose to call Oberon first. Then came Mycob, Lilla, and Rostilla, spirits from the grimoire to the other three corners.

I knelt facing the east and recited the list of prayers and petitions to invoke and summon. When done, I added my own prayer to Saint Brighid:

Bright One, hear me.
I call your light into my hand,
All shapes of evil thus are banned.
Illuminate darkness, find what I seek.
Open my eyes to see the spark.
Protect the flame from darkness's reek.
Show to me the hidden land,

Unlock my mind so I may see.

As I have asked, so mote it be.

Wind puffed at the north arc of the circle, but it held. I waited patiently, knowing that those who called Oberon often were ignored. The child in me shivered to think I might see the fae.

I knelt in silence for more than an hour. Nothing happened. Then discouraged, I rose and stepped out of the circle, swept up the salt, and brushed away all signs of the protective ring. The herbs I burned, the Holy Water bottle restored to my bag, and the candle and salt secured in the cabinet. I closed and picked up the grimoire and my bag, looked around one last time to be certain no signs of my failed attempt at summoning remained, then lifted the bar on the door and pulled it open.

Mere feet away, my father stood framed by the doorway. He had lost none of his presence. Tall and dark of complexion, his shoulder-length auburn locks streaked with bands of white repeated their colors in his short beard. A new scar, barely a hair's breadth from the outer corner of his left eye, divided his face from temple to chin, marking a faint path through the stubble. His dark blue gaze searched the room, lingering on the faintest trace of salt glittering on my slipper. I stared at him in shock.

"'Tis past time you returned home, lass."

"Father?" My tongue seemed unfamiliar in my mouth. "When...why are you here?" I had not seen him in several years. He had been absent most of my life. One of the tales I had been told was that when I was born, and my mother had died giving birth, he went berserk and destroyed two rooms in the castle before being subdued by several of his kinsmen. According to the story, he ruined himself with drink for a month before the laird sent him away to the colonies in America. During my childhood, Erika and I had seen him seldom. I knew exactly how many times: I kept count in my journal after I learned to write. I recorded but five visits in seventeen years. He was not cruel when he was here. But he never looked at me, even when I was with Erika. I cried in Janet's arms many times over whatever I was lacking to deserve his affection. She made no excuses for him but simply stroked my hair and told me I was loved.

I looked at him, waiting for his answer. One hairy auburn-and-white brow rose at my question. "'Tis my home, is it not? 'Tis ye who have been away of late. I but returned this day from Uig." He looked directly at me for the first time I could remember, his gaze assessing. "I have something for ye from your mother, lass. Before she died, she made me promise to give it to you at the right time, should she leave us. 'Tis time now." He reached into the depths of his plaid and pulled forth a small leather bag. "I have carried this since your mother was taken from me. Now 'tis yours." He held the bag a moment longer, as though he could not bear to part with it, then thrust it roughly into my hands, turned, and was gone before I could respond. I stood frozen, holding the bag, staring at the empty space where he had been.

The bag was warm, small, and heavy, scarred from years of guarding its contents. I fumbled to open it. The old ties broke as I pulled at them, and a circle of leather fell open to reveal a carved ball! My head swam. It was my mother's triskele ball.

The old woman who gave me the grimoire had said it would help me find what I was seeking. Had the Finding Spell from the grimoire worked after all? I slid bonelessly to the floor.

My father! He was here. He had spoken to me as though the intervening years had not been. Some deeply buried place inside me swelled with elation. I pushed it ruthlessly down and rose shakily to my feet. Through the open door I perceived a dark figure detach itself from the corridor wall and become one with the shadows. I placed the stone back inside the bag with trembling hands, clutched the grimoire tightly to my breast, and fled to my room and Aunt Rhona.

Chapter 8: Malcolm

Cawdie snorted as I started re-telling the story of how he had found the courage to ask Janet to marry him. It was my ale-inspired version, of course. Cawdie was my "brother" since he had stopped a bullet intended for me during the smallpox riot in Edinburgh last spring. I owed him my life, and in return I gave him his beloved Janet. Well, not exactly, but let us say I was the goad who made him move. Cawdie was one of those overly-large men the Highlands seem to breed in abundance—several inches taller and half-again bigger than me, and I am not puny, by any means. He sat there with a silly smirk on his battle-scarred mug, a face that none but Janet would think handsome.

"You should have seen the look on his face when I told him I'd take his woman if he didn't find the courage to ask her. Precious!" said I, teasing Cawdie and nudging Captain Wilson who had joined us for a drink at the inn. In truth, Janet was an attractive woman, a blue-eyed redhead with the translucent skin of a northern lass, a warm heart, and a lust for life that drew me as a moth to fire. And I was half-serious. I might well have taken her, and he damned well knew it. Janet remained a constant friction between us, and I had to be careful of his feelings. Cawdie was a volatile brute, and Janet the woman for whom he would kill and die. Good thing Lady Elspeth was here to soothe abraded feelings with abundant verbal salve.

"Nay as comical as the sight of Malcolm being bathed by the lassies," Cawdie countered in his broad and almost unintelligible Highland accent, then released a guffaw that shook the room.

"I think you're right," I replied, not taking the bait. "It was a bit embarrassing, wasn't it? That was Elspeth's punishment for the trouble I've caused."

Cawdie laughed as we both remembered the washing, scraping, and trimming to get me clean. I was a shocking mess. I could see it in their faces. And then they threw the dog in after me, to clean him up. We made quite a pair of vagrants.

Captain Wilson looked at me askance. He, the same captain who wrecked on the coast of Skye a few weeks back, had miraculously appeared a few days ago with a grin as wide as a belly after a feast, presenting my sea chest intact. The MacDonalds had fled after they realized I had escaped, leaving the captain and crew to make speedy repairs and be on their way without further harassment.

"Aye, captain, I seem to cause everyone trouble. Ask around Edinburgh."

"You were no trouble for us, good sir. Saved one of me boys, you did." The captain smiled. He had told us earlier that they had stopped at Portree to buy cheese and woolens for the Glasgow market and found plenty of buyers for his goods. Expected to make a tidy profit. *If he makes it home,* I thought, rubbing my Fortuna ring, and silently wishing him good luck.

We were having a fine evening drinking, the three of us. I was yet itching from the bug infestation, now more a memory. But I felt much better, clean, and back in my tailored Lowlander clothes. I had spent a week or more in that filthy dungeon. It was cunningly designed, a bottle-shaped hole in the floor, about ten feet in diameter at the bottom and a dozen deep, tapering up to an entry hole about four feet wide. Cut by hand out of black rock centuries ago, it bore the residues of countless unfortunates. They kept me good company, those poor souls, or so I imagined. It had been impossible to climb out. I tried. Hopeless without a rope. So, after the first day of rage and claustrophobic anxiety, I decided to make the best of it. I never honestly thought I would rot there forever. Someone would notice, surely. I resolved to bide my time and ready myself for the next opportunity when I might escape and gain revenge. Sometimes it takes only a wee slip on their part.

But the days went by, and I became thankful for the trivial things like the light from the candles kept lit in the room above, and the servant who lowered my food and drink and raised my waste, without abuse or comment. I was especially thankful for the pail of ale she lowered in the evening to help me sleep. In a few days I had become reasonably content with my lot. I could stay warm wrapped in my plaid, and the kitchen scraps they provided were better than oats and onions. I could rest all day, and sleep—blessed sleep—if I wanted. I needed time to recoup, and if it meant on the bottom of a stone hole, well, God be praised!

Then one day I decided to sing. It was a drinking song I had sung with the drovers and yet stuck in my head. I could not get rid of it. It kept going, round and round, endlessly. It desperately wanted to come out, so I let it. My singing was horrid, but the shape of the dungeon made it sound grand, like I was in my own private concert hall. My audience of one was not so impressed and in awhile I heard the guard ordering me to shut up. Of course, I did not. Sang louder, in fact, just to annoy him. What could he do? Come down and gag me? And it turns out it was my not-so-melodious voice that saved me, as my dear friend Lady Elspeth happened by one day. Caterwauling, she called it later, in derision. But whatever, that day my caterwaul drinking song saved me, and I was grateful.

* * *

"Doctor Forrester, Doctor Forrester!" I opened my eyes and found myself hanging over the edge of the bed in my room at the inn, staring at the wood-grain pattern on the floorboards, wondering what they were and what hellish fiend was waking me in the middle of the night. "Go away. Back in morn'," I grumbled and rolled to the other side of the bed, hoping he would go away.

"'Tis late morning already, sir…almost the noontime, and you are needed by Doctor Bethune."

"Oh God," I muttered. "Herold Bethune!" I remembered now. He was organizing the relief for Drynoch, and we agreed to meet this morning. I rolled back and pushed myself to sit on the side of the bed, my head ale stupefied. "All right tell him I'll be there soon. Bring coffee, will you?" Our evening of carousing had ended with Cawdie staggering home and me flopping contented on my bed with the intent of sleeping till noon. I almost made it.

* * *

The sun was wicked in its intensity as I left the inn a half hour later. I shielded my eyes as I made my way slowly along the path to the castle, thanking Elspeth for the padded slippers she had adapted for my battered feet. In the sunshine the castle looked almost cheerful in its black and grey with dark slate roof, the light burnishing angles in the stone. The few trees nearby were a delightful red and gold, contrasting with the grasses green amid richly mossy rocks. As I crossed the bridge, I saw women below in the flats harvesting produce from the garden that adjoined the southern aspect of the castle. It was a fine day, and but for a bout of well-earned crapulence, I was pleased to be alive and free.

Three carts were parked in front of the castle, just past the bridge. Men were lowering sacks of grain down the castle wall, and women were bringing baskets of produce up from the garden. Elspeth was there with Doctor Bethune. She was inspecting the contents of a leather medical bag on the first cart while Bethune was having discussions with the lead cart driver. I snuck up behind her and gave her a playful poke in the ribs.

"Ai!" she yelped. "Your lordship has decided to join us?"

I put on my best haughty look and said, "Thought I'd see how you were doing. I know you can't manage without me."

"'Tis true, Malcolm. Women always need a man to direct them."

I nodded in agreement, and she gave me a swat on the arm.

After I had been released from the dungeon, I told them about the dire situation in Drynoch, and surprisingly old Doctor Bethune jumped at the chance to help. He said it was the least he could do as they were kin. And what else could we do but let him lead and offer our full support. But if I was right and it was camp fever, then we all needed to be afraid and vigilant. "I am not sure what else we can offer for medicine," said Elspeth. "You gave them the best advice when you were there, Malcolm. But will they take it? Perhaps if Herold can stay awhile with them?" She looked around as if trying to decide if there was something she had forgotten to put in the bag.

Thoughts of typhus were sobering me quickly. "We need another pair of eyes there," I said. "I assume Bethune has seen typhus. Maybe I am wrong about the diagnosis. In any case, we need him there to watch the progression. I agree he should go alone, although I know you are worried about that. If it *is* typhus, no point risking anyone else."

Bethune joined us—a sturdy man in his sixties, with a crooked walk, the result of a hip injury from a fall off a horse. His unusual gait was matched by an endearing, lopsided smile that made him look kindly as he dispensed his dreadful-tasting elixirs. He may be past it as far as the latest medicine was concerned, but I knew as soon as I met him why he was a popular doctor.

"We will be ready to leave within the hour," Bethune said, wiping his hands on an embroidered handkerchief. "Just need a few more sacks of wheat and some carrots and cabbages from the garden." He was a man on a mission, and I admired his take-charge attitude.

"If this is camp fever," I said to them, "we must stop it at Drynoch. Can't have it coming here. The castle and village are even more crowded and vulnerable."

"Don't have to tell me that, sir," Bethune retorted. "We've had the smallpox." He gave Elspeth a look which suggested sympathy, but her focus was on packing the medicine sack. "I will do what I can to prevent the spread of whatever it is. You have my word." He straightened his crooked stance briefly and looked me in the eye.

"I know you will, sir. And now with Lady Elspeth's approval," I teased, as we both looked at her in expectation of a droll rejoinder, "your expedition can begin."

It was our staring that must have caught her attention, because her eyes snapped to us and she said, "I know what we are missing—wait!"

* * *

"Walk me to Janet's?" Elspeth said with a weary look that made her seem older than her years. "I need to bring her some of these herbs for supper."

We had stayed to see the carts off to Drynoch. The sun was lowering in the sky, bathing all in a warm glow. But feet felt heavy on the path and toes caught some of those stones placed randomly by the fairies to make one stumble. "Your feet still hurt?" she asked.

"Aye, but we need to talk." I took her fragile hand in mine. We had known each other several months only, but I felt a connection—perhaps it was her intelligence, maybe our common interests. We had experienced a lot in those months, from surviving a smallpox epidemic to being captured by smugglers. And we had grown close—not in a romantic way, mind you. She was not my type and I suspect she felt the same. But we had a deepening friendship that was both satisfying and challenging.

"Thank you for coming to Dunvegan for me."

I stopped and turned to her. "It wasn't just for you, you know. Father wished it, as well."

"Your father? Ahh, he is worried about the Highland clans?"

"Always." My father is a lord in the Scottish Parliament and connected on some level I do not quite understand with Queen Anne and her government. He seems to know everything of note that is happening in Scotland and seems especially concerned with the Jacobites and their plots to overthrow the government.

"Malcolm, he is wise to be worried. I am as well. Not that I care so much for the Crown, but there is too much suffering as is." She flicked a strand of hair out of the way and looked up at me.

"Captain Wilson's birlinn will be ready to leave in a few days, and he offered free passage to Glasgow and enough coin to get me home."

"You wish to leave...already?" A look of surprise crossed her face.

"I can stay, but not if I'm unwanted. I survived, but I can assure you I did not appreciate the welcome your family bestowed."

"Oh Malcolm, the laird apologized, and he *was* sincere. I've known him since we were children, and he is a good man."

I shrugged. "He may be too good. There are rumours that he's weak, not just sick."

"Yes, I know, but he is young, and we need to assist him. I believe he will be a fine laird."

"You miss my meaning. He is what, twenty-one, and with an even younger wife?"

"Aye, about that."

"And he's surrounded by older women who are able to give orders to his men?"

"Mayhap it might seem that way. He certainly does not heed Aunt Mairi."

"He needs to be in charge, Elspeth, and seen to be so. He cannot let women run things. It makes him look weak, and most Highland clans would eat a chieftain like that alive. They respect strength, above all."

"We must support him, but when does support appear to be control? Perhaps that is part of the problem?"

"You are naïve, my friend. Perhaps some in his family intend to make him look weak."

The men who had been loading the carts greeted us as they passed on their way back to the village. Elspeth seemed to know them all, though she had been away for years. "Let's continue to Janet's," I said. "My feet have had enough for one day."

"I have to say, you do look better in your clean waistcoat and breeches. 'Twas appalling seeing you come out of that blasted dungeon. And those padded slippers do look smart," she teased.

"Are they not the latest in style?" I chuckled. "Well, at least they're comfortable."

"I am glad."

"You two made quite a mess of my hair. Good thing I have a tricorn hat to hide it. Perhaps I'm vain." I grinned at her.

"Perhaps?" she said, laughing. "You are, but 'tis comforting knowing you have some faults."

We were coming to the outskirts of Dunvegan village, south of the castle. It is strung out along a dirt trail that follows Loch Dunvegan south to Drynoch. There also is a drove road from the village that heads east to Portree. "The village looks well tended," I noted, in contrast to the castle. I remembered the rumours on my trip of rents not being paid or not reaching the laird and wondered if this was further proof.

"It has improved since I lived here last," she said.

"Your laird doesn't look well. Who is treating him?"

"Now that is difficult to say. Doctor Bethune, officially, but Ysabell has enormous influence and may be giving him something. I am not certain what is going on. That is why I needed your help."

"I see…too many cooks spoil the broth?"

"Mayhap some are fully intent on its spoil. But I am too close to it and not able to be detached…part of the problem, I fear."

"Indeed, it's not easy dealing with kin. Memories are long and often unforgiving," I offered, remembering well my own family troubles.

We entered the main part of the village, the inn and Janet's home nearby. The beginnings of a village green were being constructed, with the native rocks cleared and a few trees and shrubs planted. It was a start to make a fine village, and perhaps we needed to get on with our work as well. Enough introspection. "What do you want from me, Elspeth?"

She smiled and reached over to squeeze my hand. "Please examine the laird and his family. I want your unbiased assessment. Then we can proceed to help them if we can. I trust you, Malcolm…and please see Aunt Mairi, too. She knows the history and people much better than I."

"Be careful who you trust, Elspeth. We are all enfeebled in certain situations." I grinned. "Offer the right kind of woman and I am doomed!"

"I know your weaknesses. They are of the mature redheaded variety. I shall protect you."

We both laughed, then she told me of the birth of the laird's son Norman at the end of July, past. The baby and mother were doing well, but the year-old bairn John was not thriving. "I have been helping Lady Anne and her babies, but the laird has been reluctant to seek my help, and I fear he has other troubles beyond consumption."

"And what of Bethune?"

"He thinks the laird may grow out of his health problems and recommended a change of climate and gave him an expectorant to ease his cough. He uses the older term *scrofula* for this condition. It is the same as consumption or tuberculosis."

"Some say a dry sunny climate is better for those with this complaint, but let's have a fresh look and see if we concur with Bethune. Now tell me about his other troubles, as you call them."

She told me about his symptoms. He had many. Fits of coughing, abdominal pain, neck and back stiffness, anxiety, and increased perception. She told me of the gloves he often wore that had a strange residue inside; and that she had serious concerns about Ysabell.

"Elspeth, we need more facts. Suspicions are not enough."

"That is why I wanted you here. The laird will listen to you. He was educated in Edinburgh, as were you. He will respect you much more than he does the locals."

"I'll do what I can, but we need to be united in our professionalism. I know it's hard when it comes to family."

"I will try, but this place is filled with memories," She smiled rather sadly at me. "It is very difficult for me."

"And me, also, when it comes to my family."

"I remember well," she replied.

We stood there looking in each other's eyes. I was thinking of the hours she sat by my father while he suffered through smallpox, and how she and Janet nursed me back to health after my near-death experience at the hands of Captain Mackmain. I had no choice. I must help her family. "Then it's settled. I will stay and interfere with your family and die an inglorious death at the hands of some Highland witch."

She laughed, then promised I would not die if I wore the ring of Fortuna. I held it up before her face. We both smirked like silly children.

"If all it takes is a little ring to live forever, I'll gladly wear it."

"Please do, if only to send a signal to others."

"What do you mean, exactly?"

"You will see," she said. "Oh, I forgot to mention...Sir Ross Campbell and his man Gregor have been here."

"Oh?" That raised my interest.

She continued as questions filled my mind. "They arrived right after us...in July. He has been coming and going, since."

That explained his mysterious absence from Torrport, I thought. "What in hell is he doing here?" I blurted.

She clasped her hands and swayed back and forth with head tilted, smiling in a way that suggested a girl about to tell a special secret. "I think he is interested in me."

"What!"

The sweet smile left her face. "You think I cannot attract men?"

I sighed. "Of course, you can. But he is much older and...well, I don't trust him."

"I rather like older men, but I don't trust him, either. That is what makes him of interest."

"I see. You are playing each other? A dangerous game, Elspeth."

"But a most pleasant one."

"Be careful of your heart, dear friend."

"I shall be most careful, Malcolm. Besides, I rather prefer his servant Gregor. Charmingly dangerous, is he not?"

"Och, God's teeth! Is there no end to the foolishness of the human heart?"

She frowned at me. "I have been thinking it would be nice to have a husband, one who would let me work in medicine. Sir Ross would indulge me, and we have many interests in common. And I will tell you another secret. I loved holding Julianne's baby last spring."

"Aye, you need a husband and babies, too, if you are so blessed. But Ross, or even worse, Gregor?"

"You are a fine one to be giving advice on this subject, Malcolm...with your mother fixation. Janet knows full well why you lust for her."

She was right, of course, but faults in others seem self-evident, don't they? While our own are obscured in mists of desire and delusion. "But truly, Elspeth, what other reason could Ross have for being here? Hmm... you know I met one of your relatives at Sligachan. Niall Morrison."

"He was there? He comes and goes often. But we were wondering where he went."

"Aye, and he was chummy with the innkeeper, who all but said he had a shed full of guns meant for the Jacobites."

"I have seen no new weapons here. Nor has the laird recruited any lads for training recently. It is quiet in the bailey, as you may have noticed."

"I suspect Ross is a Jacobite agent. So be careful, Elspeth. You are playing with fire."

"And you with Janet. We must be drawn to flames."

"Duly warned," I conceded and chuckled at her reference to my preference for redheads.

As we walked past the village green, we came near Cawdie and Janet's little cottage. Elspeth must have noticed it, too, because next she told me how beautiful Janet was at her wedding and how well the couple danced. She watched my face carefully as she spoke, but I was careful to show no sign of jealousy. That must have reassured her. Cawdie was outside, sitting shirtless on a stool, repairing a broken chair. Our consultation concluded, I said, "Tell the laird I can examine him and his family at his convenience, and I will see your aunt, too."

"I will, Malcolm, and thank you for staying."

"Only if my brother will protect me," I said in a voice loud enough for Cawdie to hear.

He looked up and grinned. "Ye need protecting again? Who's it this time? Some kiddies make ye cry?"

"Not this time, Cawdie, but I see your goodwife has domesticated you already. She'll have you on your knees scrubbing floors next." At that, he threw the knife he was using at me, missing my beautifully embroidered waistcoat by mere inches, the blade embedding itself in the tree stump behind me. On hearing Cawdie's complaining, Janet came out and gave Elspeth a warm hug and a friendly greeting to me as well with those beautiful blue eyes. As we chatted amiably, I worried that I had been invited into a fine Highland muddle.

* * *

Captain Wilson was looking pleased when I joined him for supper. He was eating in the tavern part of the inn and being served by Teresa, the owner, a buxom woman with strawberry hair and glib tongue. The inn and tavern occupied a two-story, dark-stone structure that looked like it was originally two buildings, united by the upper floor, leaving a walkway through the middle of the bottom floor to access the docks from the trail. It was nearing the end of the droving season and I was able to get a nice room on the upper floor with a window, offering a view of the docks, the loch, and hills on the other side. Adhic had joined me and approved of the inn with its kitchen full of delectables. He was a bad boy for constantly begging, but I did not have the heart to correct him. One problem at a time, if you please.

"Cleaned it special for you, sir, since you are a gentleman and staying awhile," Teresa had said proudly as I was inspecting it. In truth, I would have accepted anything that was out of the weather and reasonably warm. This room even had a fireplace and a cupboard for clothing, along with two chairs and a small table. It was large enough that I could even see patients within.

"This meat pie is delicious," Captain Wilson opined, I think to please Teresa, who was standing nearby at the bar. She heard him and smiled. They had been flirting all evening. I was happy to see him that way, a tremendous change from the near-defeated man I had known but a few weeks ago.

"I shan't be going back with you on this trip, but thank you for the kind offer," I explained. "I'll be staying for a while to assist but look for me on your next trip."

The captain stopped shoveling pie and raised an eyebrow. "Might be a mistake. Not much to do here in late fall...a dismal place, this." Then he raised his voice and said, "But for the best tavern on Skye!"

I sighed and smiled. He must really want her. Elspeth said Teresa was a good woman and ran a respectable inn and tavern, so the captain might well end the evening frustrated, poor sod. But that was his problem. Mine was more elemental. I wanted to help them and get out alive, and for that I needed as much assistance as I could get. To that end, I needed the captain.

"This is a letter for my father," I said. "Please deliver it in person. I know it is a bother to travel to Edinburgh, but I assure you it will be worth your while." I slid the sealed letter to him. In it I had asked Father to give the captain a substantial gift, explained the situation here as I knew it, and begged his forgiveness for being away so long. I also told Father when I was due back and provided a list of suspects should I not return. The captain nodded and slipped the letter into his belt.

"Leith is not on the way but close to Edinburgh. If you find yourself there, hoist a pint at the Sand Bar pub and give my regards to Calum Duncan."

"Well, if the trip includes drinking and bonny lasses, I shall do it," he chuckled.

"Can't guarantee the lasses," I said, noticing him glancing at Teresa again, who was joking with a group of men at the bar.

* * *

I had agreed to see the laird and his family, but the days went by, and I heard nothing, so I kept busy exploring the area and helping those in need. Turns out there were few since doctors and healers were in abundance. That left me more a visitor than a practitioner. I did not mind it so much, because Elspeth had lent me some money and the use of a wee pony which I rode often.

There were only a few hundred people in Dunvegan village, but they had most all the necessities and skills needed, with a blacksmith, weavers, builders, and the like. There also were shops set up in cottages that offered myriad products brought by traders like Captain Wilson. Dunvegan looked prosperous. Some of the cottage-shops were even whitewashed and had painted doors and trim. Business must be good, no doubt in part because of the cattle coming through from the Outer Hebrides on their way to the cattle markets at Crieff and further south.

I introduced myself to many of the village folk. Most thought it strange that a Lowlander physician was here, and suspicious that there was more to my story than I let on. "Maybe he's run away from an unhappy marriage," I heard one villager whisper to another. An old woman who made her living emptying chamber pots thought it was an ill omen having me here and loudly protested every time she cleaned mine. But overall, the villagers were polite and helpful, especially when I mentioned that I am a doctor and pleased to treat them, even *pro bono,* or in trade.

It was mid-October, and I was walking by the blacksmith's when I saw Elspeth come out. The brisk wind caught the hood of her cloak so violently I thought it might carry her tiny self away. The weather had been changing—some days nice, but more often a sample of winter to come. This was one of those days.

"You still have a thing for blacksmiths?" I teased.

"Devil!" she laughed. "Not this one. He has a fat gut and a wife seven months pregnant."

"I see. Is she well?"

"Very. We should have a new MacLeod soon."

Elspeth was cheerful despite the wind trying to knock her over. She invited me to tea at Janet's, which was not far. I agreed. We needed some quiet time for discussion. And it was a pleasure to come out of nasty weather into a cozy cottage with a fire burning and smells of food being prepared. "Cawdie is away on an errand for the laird," said Janet, as she started the tea and arranged her few chairs for us. She offered me the one Cawdie had repaired, and I wondered if I would end up on the floor. But it held and the three of us sat by the fire, appreciating its radiant warmth.

"I'm well settled at the inn," I said. "The food is plentiful and the room well-heated."

"And Teresa?" Elspeth asked.

"She's the perfect innkeeper. Keeps my room clean and even allows me to see patients."

"Very considerate. She is a good woman, by all accounts."

"And why are you telling me this again, Elspeth dear?"

"Emm…well you are a titled Lowlander, rather exotic hereabouts and could tempt the best of women."

"You needn't worry. I will not corrupt your women." I smirked and noticed Janet trying to suppress a gurgle of laughter.

Elspeth looked unconvinced and I knew it was time to change the subject. "What's going on at the castle?" I asked. She sighed and said there was much work to do. There were around sixty souls living there, including a garrison of forty men, the laird, and his extended family, and of course the servants. Seems Ysabell had gone somewhere, leaving Elspeth to care for everyone. And Doctor Bethune was still at Drynoch. She had heard from him. He said it was dire, but the people stalwart. They would comply.

"I can treat the villagers and crofters and leave you to the castle," I suggested.

"You will have more to care for than me. I have some I am treating in the village as well…pregnancies—the blacksmith's wife and a few others."

"Aye, you are better at the female complaints than me. I'll send them your way."

"Pregnancy is not a complaint," she chided.

"I know, I know, but it's not a disease either. What shall we call it then? How about "Nature's Revenge" or "God's Blessing" perhaps? Take your pick." I was mocking, and she took the bait.

"I think we should call it 'Women's Supremacy'."

I looked at her, puzzled. I heard Janet choke.

"Do you not think women are better at having babies than men?" Elspeth said with the hint of a devilish grin. She had me there. We spent the next half hour reminiscing about Torrport, with Janet expressing a desire to return someday. I felt the same. I had missed them all, even Cawdie.

* * *

I had been less than honest with Elspeth. Teresa was a distraction, and we both knew it. Perhaps it was just proximity. I was her only long-term guest, and single and rich, by her standards anyway. And as for me, Elspeth was right again, I did prefer older women, and redheads. Was it to do with the loss of my mother as a boy? It is easy to diagnose others, much harder to parse one's own mind. But whatever the reason, Teresa and I found each other inhabiting the same bed one lonely night as gale-force winds kept other customers at home. It was comforting, warm and snuggly, but in the back of my mind I knew Elspeth would disapprove and I was not sure why I cared. And in those weeks, life settled into a routine of seeing patients, exploring the countryside on my pony when the weather allowed, and spending time in the evenings drinking with the men, then snuggling with Teresa. I did not see Elspeth again until that unfortunate day.

* * *

A wee lad tugged on my sleeve as I was sharing a story in the tavern. "Please come, sir. Lady Elspeth needs you," he said.

I looked at him. His eyes were wide. He looked quite terrified as he stood there, bonnet in hand, huffing. "Can it not wait till morning?" I growled. I just had supper and three pints of ale and was in no mood to go out in the rain.

The boy looked around, fidgeting. "Sir...please, sir. She is sick!"

That got my attention. "Lady Elspeth is sick?"

"Nay, someone else...a woman. Lady Elspeth said 'twas someone you know."

"Someone I know?" I struggled to activate my ale-challenged mind.

The boy tugged my sleeve again and cringed, perhaps expecting a slap in return. "All right, all right. I need to piss and get my medical bag. Meet me outside."

The night was as foul as expected, and I was soaking wet and cursing the whole way. At the castle sea gate, the burly guard who had thrown me in the dungeon was on duty, along with another fellow. I was curt, in no mood for anything but the task at hand. The boy led me through the bailey and into a door to the servants' quarters on the ground floor. There was a hallway lit by smoky torches. We turned right and passed the door to the laundry, then went further to a door near the end of the hall. The boy took me into a room that had but a few rough chairs, tables, and shelves. There was a door at the far end. He stopped and knocked.

A voice from within said, "No one enters but Sir Malcolm." It was Elspeth.

I pressed a coin into the lad's palm and tried to send him away, but he refused and instead squatted to wait. The oak door was tight on its jamb, so I had to force it with my shoulder. The small room held two cots and a table between, lit with a single candle in a rusty holder. "Your patient from Drynoch," said she, without looking up. A small female shape wrapped in a familiar cloak knelt on the floor with her back to me, holding the hand of a woman curled on a cot.

"Elspeth?" I asked.

My eyes went to the woman. "Oh God!" was all I could think to say.

Chapter 9: Elspeth

My problems with my father and the sacred stones could wait. The woman lying on the wooden bedstead before me could not. She was so thin she scarce made a dent in the straw-filled mattress covering the ropes. Camp fever had arrived at Dunvegan.

I sent for Malcolm. It seemed the woman had followed him here from Drynoch, bringing her lethal companion. My first concern had been to keep her away from everyone, but I feared it was much too late. She had been helping prepare food in the castle kitchen and sleeping in the servants' quarters, as well as shopping in the village. The disease spread quickly in crowded places.

I heard footsteps and called out a warning as Malcolm pushed open the door. He looked decidedly the worse for wear and smelled of sleep, old ale, and rumpled male. And lemon balm. Teresa loved and grew the herb and used it in everything from soap to salve. She dried it in her kitchen, used it for tea, and filled bowls with it to scent the rooms of the inn. Even her bed linens smelled of it. I pushed that thought aside and turned to him.

"We have to keep her here and find out who she has been with. She has a rash and a hot fever, and she has been vomiting." I pointed toward the contents of the vile smelling bucket. "I washed her and made her as comfortable as possible, but she is terribly ill. Please look at her, Malcolm. If she has what you saw in Drynoch, we can expect others here to show it soon." He groaned, muttered a curse, and put down his bag.

* * *

In four days, it became a crisis. Cook was the first to succumb. She began to cough, her naturally florid complexion growing redder with fever. We put her on the other bed in the room with the woman who had followed Malcolm, and I began to look around for more space to care for the newly afflicted. The Great Hall was large enough, but it was the heart of Dunvegan Castle. People still must meet, eat, and sleep. I went to the laird and asked for the barracks that housed the warriors. The young men would be able to survive in the old, mostly roofless ruins of the castle-keep better than most. The laird readily agreed.

Aunt Mairi worked tirelessly with the clanswomen and servants to turn the barracks into an infirmary. Beds were stripped and linens boiled to rid them of the vermin commonly found in such places. Floors were scrubbed and ropes suspended from beams and walls hung with blankets to provide a modicum of privacy for those most affected.

Common danger united us, as such things do. Everyone contributed what they could, and even Aunt Rhona could not be prevented from rising from her bed and assisting where possible. She was weak but sat serenely in a quiet corner mending and folding laundry or walking with painful slowness around the makeshift infirmary, applying comforting words and cool cloths in equal measure. We coaxed, bullied, cooked, cleaned, and cried over each sufferer. The children were the most painful to lose.

No amount of salve could keep our hands from growing red and rough from the constant scrubbing and washing. Despite my distrust, I could not fault Ysabell's work. She was a fine healer. Her mother, Mistress Una Talisker, who always smelled of peppermint, often labored with me in the laundry and questioned me endlessly about my time in Italy. She was no taller than me and rounded everywhere, her plump face neatly framed by the pristine white of her coif, confined beneath a dark blue bonnet. The ties peeped from beneath two crescent chins, and her smile curved to meet downwardly arched brows. Moon-lidded eyes shrewdly observed everything around her, while large, callused hands did the work of a man. She always wore a delicately knitted shawl of pale blue that lay like fairy work against the rough textures of the rest of her practical clothing.

Mistress Talisker had the healer's thirst for new knowledge. Her wisdom was empiric, derived from a lifetime of experience and experiment, so our conversations benefitted us both. Unlike her daughter Ysabell, she had always been kind to me when I was growing up. She had known my father and mother well and often shared memories of them with me. One of my vivid memories was of wanting to send my missing father a gift to celebrate the New Year. The excuse others gave when I asked about my sire's absence was that he was a soldier, so my ten-year-old self reasoned that a salve to heal wounds might be welcome and remind him of me. Aunt Mairi was away, so Mistress Talisker patiently helped me make a simple balm of garlic, mint, honey, and beeswax. Erika and Ranuff rolled their eyes at the muddy-looking mess we concocted, but Niall helped me wrap it and found a way to have it delivered to my father on the first day of the New Year. My gift was never acknowledged but making it had made me feel better.

I smiled and wondered where my father was at this moment. He had been closeted with the laird for several hours following his unexpected return, and evidently given his old place as the laird's *lucktaeh* as though he had never been away. My father often smoked tobacco widely considered a cure for many illnesses. I rather liked the smell of the smoke and wondered idly if it would help our patients. I saw him offer Sir Ross Campbell and his manservant Gregor a pipe and prayed fervently that none of them would become ill with camp fever. Fully half of those at the castle had fallen to it, especially the servants and guards who lived in close quarters. The MacLeod and his family had been sequestered in their rooms, and Malcolm visited the laird most every afternoon to check on them.

Returning cleaned linens to the laird's rooms one day, I saw Ysabell in the hallway, lingering by the door to the library. She turned a fiery red and fell to her knees, pretending she had dropped something, then escaped down the hall before I could question her. I scratched at the door and entered. The laird and Malcolm were bending over a map on the table, talking and drinking ale. They stopped and invited me to join them, but I refused with a smile, deposited the linens in the oak coffer by the fireplace, and went back to work. I considered telling them about Ysabell, but instead put the incident away to think about later. She was eavesdropping. It was troubling.

* * *

I dreamt of Aunt Rhona that night. In my dream she was minding me in the bailey, and I was a wee lass, trying to plait the green stems of wood sorrel into a wreath for her hair. The crushed foliage had an enticing smell, so of course a sprig found its way into my mouth. My face puckered at the lemon and sharp-apple-peel taste of the heart-shaped leaves. My aunt laughed at my soured face and told me the plant was called *Fairy Bells* and she would teach me how to make delicious soup with it. She promised I would grow to like the flavour. Then she gathered me into her arms and called me her precious lassie and told me never to forget she loved me. The dream faded.

When I awoke, I could not feel her, and I knew she was no longer with us. She lay peacefully in the bed next to mine, her spirit gone, her lips tilted in the same sweet smile she had given me in my dream. I touched her to make certain. Her skin was cool. No warmth pulsed in her throat. Not fever but age had taken her. She had been fragile but well enough, except for the tale-tale swelling in her legs and the weakness that age brings. It was her time. Strangely, I felt nothing. All my emotion hung suspended like an insect arrested in amber. I dressed by rote and went to find Aunt Mairi.

In the corridor I became dimly aware of footsteps echoing mine. Gregor appeared, matching his stride to mine as I searched. He said nothing but his presence was improbably comforting. We found Aunt Mairi in the armory bending over a boy. She looked up as we arrived, her face sliced deeply with gashes of grief. She already knew. The link had been broken. Gregor bowed deeply to her, turned, and vanished back from whence he had come. No words were exchanged.

Aunt Mairi pulled the covers over the sleeping bairn, took up her wooden staff and the covered basket by her feet, and walked with me back to my room and Aunt Rhona. The castle seemed preternaturally silent. She leaned over the bed and studied her sister's tranquil face. The fingers of Aunt Mairi's left hand clenched inflexibly about her staff. Her other hand moved a curl away from Aunt Rhona's cheek and smoothed the white ruffle at her neckline. She stayed with her hand on her sister for several moments, then kissed her tenderly. The furrows in her face settled more deeply and I began to fear for her. I could not lose both!

Looking more wraithlike than ever, Aunt Mairi arranged everything with her customary care.

Six women came to wash and purify the body, then escorted it to Aunt Mairi's cottage in Dunvegan village. After the proper rites were observed she would be placed in the one of the chambers beneath the ancient cairn by Dunvegan's sacred rowan tree. When the castle and village were free of pestilence, her body would be taken to St. Clement's Church on the Isle of Harris, the traditional burial place of the MacLeods.

The loss of Aunt Rhona was one of too many. My numbness faded much too soon, and I wanted to mourn, to scream and cry, but there was no time. We would grieve properly when the gods permitted.

The village had been badly stricken. Malcolm told me that Teresa had converted the inn to a hospital, supported by every able man and woman left in the village. More than a few villagers had fled, and I prayed they did not carry death with them like the woman who had brought it here with her wee bairns, and now lay in stupor amid the chaos she had wrought.

After Aunt Rhona's death I began fearing anew for those caring for the sick. The laird's family were secluded in their rooms, and Aunt Mairi refused to let anyone near them except me and Malcolm who seemed to be everywhere. I knew Teresa made certain he ate properly and had clean clothing. The persistent aroma of lemon balm always hung about him, and I began to dislike it greatly.

* * *

There had been no new cases in the past five days. I had a moment to myself and was on my way to work on whatever was left in the castle bailey herb garden when I saw Aunt Mairi in quiet conversation with the ratcatcher I had first met in the college in Glasgow. His wee servant sat nearby holding the worn wooden box of poisons tightly to his chest. The lad waited patiently with a dirty, odd-looking dog atop the stone wall leading up from the sea gate. All turned as I approached, the ratcatcher bowing obsequiously, his unblinking stare as bold and assessing as it had been in the Great Yard. I nodded to them and continued. I needed a few moments alone and had no desire to interrupt their conversation. The herb garden represented refuge.

After Aunt Mairi left, the ratcatcher came to where I was working and lingered, waiting for me to acknowledge him. When I reluctantly turned to him, he whispered, "I do bring a message fer ye, my lady, from yer uncle in Glasgow." He waited a moment, then added, "'Tis paid for, my lady." He reached inside his vest and placed a much-folded and wax-sealed packet of parchment in my hand, glanced sharply around, bowed, and walked away. I used my fingernail to break the seal.

Undone, the paper held four seeds and a greeting from Uncle Angus. I recognised the seeds. They were the round, flattened hairy seeds of *Nux vomica*. I asked Aunt Mairi later that day what she knew about the ratcatcher, and she rather testily replied that she had known him many years and that he was quite useful and provided certain needed services.

The ratcatcher soon became a familiar sight as he, the lad, and the dog scoured Dunvegan for vermin. He seemed to have no fear of the fever while performing his grim duties, although I did notice that the rats he caught were killed and tossed into the burial pit and not kept for sport or skinned for leather. His tasks seemed to include contact with most everyone at the castle. Late one afternoon I saw him speak to Sir Ross and give him a small packet. Shortly after the exchange, Sir Ross left Dunvegan, returning three days later. I realized belatedly that one of the "services" the much-traveled ratcatcher offered was passing information. It was logical. Who was better positioned to oblige so many? His profession took him from village to village, working from cottage to cottage all over the Isles.

The day the ratcatcher was to leave Dunvegan he came to me again, his pack looking exactly as it had when he arrived—no larger, no smaller. I would have given much to see what was inside. He faced me, the wind wafting his peculiar body odor toward me. He smelled faintly of garlic and of the more exotic things he combined for his work. The musky fragrance of deadly wolfsbane made me feel queasy. He shuffled restlessly and spoke to me as though the words came unwillingly. "Lady, there be much amiss here. I have seen it. Guard thyself and those you love. Evil do sometimes hide behind kindness. Beware of them that worship the dark gods. Remember to always carry thy Rowan." He wheeled to walk away, stopped, and turned stiffly back. "Lady, I serve ye, should ye ask it of me. Ye have only to send."

He felt for some hidden object under his shirt as he finished his words in a rush and motioned to his lad and dog. Hoisting his bag, he picked up his staff and vermin cage, which was empty, and stepped onto the path that led north. He did not look back.

* * *

It was late, and I was tired, but I walked to the inn. I needed to speak with Malcolm. When I arrived at the tavern, I found him sleeping fitfully in a chair before the banked peat fire. Adhie lay beside him. He whined and lifted his eyes to mine, then settled his wee head back on his paws. Malcolm looked so drained and weary that I decided not to wake him. I left, closing the door gently behind me. An almost-moonless night wrapped about me and the feeling of someone watching was strong. Lately it had been nearly constant. My neck prickled. I stood quietly, seeking the source of my unease, but I was unable to sense anything. Something seemed out of place. I looked around the village, silent in the moonlight, then saw it. High on the hill behind the village kirk, an orange flame flashed. It appeared to flare and vanish repeatedly. I turned toward it and as I did so, my skirt caught on something.

Reaching down to tug it free, I touched soft cloth much finer than my coarse skirt. The delicate fabric had been pushed down onto one of the sharp spined rose bushes Teresa had planted. I released whatever it was from the clinging thorns and held it up to the light coming from the inn lantern. It was a man's shirt—no village make, much too fine. My questing fingers found a familiar embroidered laundry mark and I realized it as one of Malcolm's beautifully tailored linens. Lifting it to my nose I smelled sweat, lemon balm, and Malcolm. One sleeve was missing. It had been cut or ripped from the shirt, and several rents pierced the front of the costly fabric. I ran my hands over it for a moment, feeling for some residual emotion, then folded the mutilated garment neatly and tucked it under the belt of my arisaid.

Malcolm would never destroy his shirt, and the damage did not appear to be the result of some tavern brawl. There was no blood or dirt. The cuts were coldly deliberate. What had happened? Glancing briefly back at the inn where Malcolm lay peacefully sleeping, I crossed the road and made my way slowly toward the kirk. The strange flashes seemed to be coming from halfway up the hillside behind it. I loosened my dirk in its sheath and began to climb up the rocks as noiselessly as possible. I could hear the crackle of fire and feel the first edge of its heat. Moving cautiously, I sought the cover of a clump of gorse bushes, crept closer, and knelt behind them to watch.

Three women twirled about a fire, billowing skirts obscuring then revealing the blaze as they danced. One was Ysabell. A circle of pale white crystals enclosed them, glittering on the ground to protect them from what they were summoning. The flickering light illuminated the scene with red gold, bringing into wavering relief the carving on a flat stone slab said by the villagers to have been used by the Druids. A red silk cloth, thickly embroidered with time-darkened silver threads, lay on the slab beneath an opened book. Beside the book was a long piece of white cloth. It was Malcolm's sleeve! They were using it to draw the dark powers they were invoking. Such spells require something belonging to the intended victim. They had planned this with care.

Small bowls and piles of herbs littered the remaining surface. Smoke wisped from several of the vessels. A water-filled scrying bowl used for looking into the future had been placed beside the book, opposite the sleeve. Though the grimoire on the altar looked much like mine, I doubted the contents were the same. I studied the tableaux for a moment, remembering Aunt Mairi's teaching. The spell they were chanting was a common one for invoking harm. But when calling on the old gods, the trained summoner must be very conscious of the *Rule of Three,* and know that whatever actions are invoked, there was always the risk that they will be returned to the sender threefold. But why would they wish to harm Malcolm? As far as I knew he had done nothing to warrant such strong reprisal. That inquiry could wait. Now I had to stop it.

Standing, I stepped into the light. One of the women saw me and stumbled in terror, perhaps believing I was one of the Old Ones they had called. All three ceased dancing and watched me warily. I smiled, gently pulled Malcolm's shirt from my belt, and held it toward them. Clasping the shirt in my left hand, I made a ritual gathering motion over it, then flicked my fingers at the women using the gesture I had been taught to reverse harmful spells. Two of the women fell to their knees, cringing and clutching their chests. Ysabell blanched but remained upright, holding my gaze defiantly before looking disdainfully down at the cowering women. I stepped across their protective circle, picked up the sleeve from the altar, folded it inside the shirt, tucked both pieces back under my belt, then turned and left the hill. The shirt would be mended and returned to Malcolm. More importantly, I now knew I needed to find a way to protect him from such malice in future. And I prayed he had been wearing Fortuna this night.

The path seemed to have grown darker and the feeling of being watched returned. I was courting danger by walking alone and resolved to bring Scathach when next I left the castle at night. She waddles and is huge with unborn pups, but she remains fiercely protective. I made my way toward Aunt Mairi's cottage in the village, instead of going back to the castle.

* * *

I awakened at dawn next morning to find Aunt Mairi pouring tea into a delicate blue bowl. She gave it to me silently. Malcolm's shirt lay neatly mended and washed atop her sewing basket near the fireplace. After I had sipped a little of the sweet-scented brew, she said mildly, "You should not have gone unaccompanied. You remembered the *Ways* and you have dealt with it for now. Ysabell has broken trust. We will need help," she said after a moment. "I shall call a gathering."

She twitched a warm moon-colored shawl into place on her slim shoulders, picked up her staff, and left. The liquid soured in my mouth. *A gathering?*

* * *

The sun was a shell-rose promise at the edge of the loch after I dressed and began the walk back to the castle from Aunt Mairi's. Crisp spangles of music floated from the rocks near the bridge, where a man stood limned against the kindling dawn, slender-fingered hands moving caressingly over the satiny curved body of a lute. I shivered.

He stopped playing as I approached and turned his face to me, removing the ribbon that held the lute on his shoulder. I avoided looking directly at Gregor. His eyes, and the impervious reserve he wrapped about himself disturbed me. This time I remained still and forced myself to examine him dispassionately. He had accepted the tsar's recent decree that bearded Russian men should become fashionably clean-shaven or be taxed. It made him look quite different. Caught by the wind, strands of his dark hair fought with leather strip that severely confined them at the base of his neck. The style exposed elegant patrician ears that lay flat against his skull, and a broad forehead. Deep creases separated his thick upward-slanting black brows, and a long straight nose slashed down between prominent cheekbones to an unsmiling mouth. He had a decidedly cleft chin already shadowy with beard growth. I wondered idly if the cleft was difficult to shave. A small sickle-shaped wheal on his left temple broke his hairline and did nothing to dim my startled discovery that without his long beard he was an impossibly handsome man. As though he heard my thoughts, his mouth relaxed and curled into a mocking smile. I felt hot blood rise in my cheeks as he turned fully toward me, the black material of his robes briefly defining his great muscular body.

"My lady?" he bowed.

"A strange place to find you." I lifted my chin and gathered my wayward thoughts.

"And also, you. Your absence from the castle was noted."

"I was...I had something that needed attending."

"Ahh. May I be of service? You are aware that I am always yours to command, are you not?" There was a brief pause. "Sir Ross has decided that it be so." His voice was dry and devoid of inflexion. He might have been reading a bill of lading.

I hesitated, then decided to give him the truth. "Would that you could, but I fear I need someone learned in the magical arts, one who can help me control unclean sources. Do you even know what a grimoire is? Or of any protective invocations that will safeguard others?" I asked waspishly.

"You mean such as those found in the *Clavicle of Solomon* or the *Emerald Tablet*?" he asked with a wry, questioning smile. "Has someone put ashes in your footprints, my lady, or cast a spell over some article of your clothing? Perhaps they have secreted magical roots and grasses in your home?"

I gaped at him, stunned, then looked around to see if anyone could hear us. I touched his arm and whispered, "Come with me to a place we can talk." I almost dragged him toward the castle.

* * *

It was late. Gregor and I had spent much of the day going over our combined collection of grimoires, seeking what we needed. I came back to my room to rest, and removed my clothes quietly to avoid awakening Janet, then crawled into bed, aching with weariness. I pulled the covers up and stared into the darkness above, thinking about what I had discovered.

Gregor was a *koldun* or Russian witch. I had not realized that Russian witches tended to be men. It was exhilarating to exchange information with a man who understood such things. His knowledge far surpassed mine and his anecdotes of Russian witchcraft were fascinating. As a lad he had been present when Prince Golitsyn and his friend were accused of using astrology and magic on the then seventeen-year-old Tsar Peter!

Gregor and I worked together and decided on two protective invocations to try. His inclinations ran with mine. We would use a spell from my *Book of Oberon* and one from *The Heptameron* which invokes the archangels of the seven days of the week. Visions of the defensive diagrams drawn in the grimoires rolled about in my head. I idly compared their powers and shapes with those of the ancient duns and other round stone structures left by those who came before us. I was so tired; my thoughts began fading into sleep.

I was seeking Erika endlessly through shifting spaces filled with choking miasma so vile I wanted to stop breathing and retch. I could feel her nearness, but she stayed just beyond reach, her voice leading me deeper into nothingness.

"You must come now, El. I am tired, and he will kill her when I am gone. Please! Now El, now!" Her voice grew faint, and I felt myself spiraling away and losing her, becoming frantic with fear.

"Tell me where, please, where?" I mumbled as I awoke, chilled and trembling. "Please, don't go—tell me, Erika...Erika?"

Chapter 10: Malcolm

It had been a long day, but Elspeth wanted me to see her Aunt Mairi as soon as I could, so I was at the south end of Dunvegan looking for the right cottage. It was easy to find—mid October and faded flower boxes framing a front door gaily painted with leafy tendrils and strange symbols. *This must be Aunt Mairi's cottage,* I thought as I raised my hand to knock.

The woman who greeted me was old but moved like a woman much younger, as though her wrinkled skin was slipped over a girl's body. Elspeth believed Mairi was so healthy because she never had a man to rule her and children to ruin her. I reserved judgement. Some of us age well, others do not.

"Whisky?" she asked, pouring herself one from a cut-glass decanter on a side-table set with glasses, cups, carved boxes, and the like. I recognized one of the boxes immediately, the one holding the Brightstone, and the reason for my visit.

"A large one...been one of those days," I said, removing my much-traveled tricorn hat and looking for a suitable place to perch.

She pushed a protesting cat off the rocking chair by the fireplace. "Try this one," said she, pointing to it and handing me a crude pottery cup filled almost to spilling. I thanked her and took a slurp to avoid having it run down my fingers. It was good, rich, and peaty, an easily acquired addiction. She sat close on one of those low stools used by women for spinning. The room was spare but tidy, the floor swept, the fireplace clean, a beautifully crafted bed in the corner. "Tell me of the epidemic," she said, smiling in a way that suggested she already knew the answer and wanted to know if I did too, like the game parents play with children. I did not respond. Elspeth had told me to trust her, but I had learned to be wary of her kin and their machinations. The space was quiet but for the hissing fire and the gamboling children outside. She sat very still, composed, waiting, her lined face glowing, and framed seductively in waves of white hair. *She's attractive even now*, I thought as I studied her and took another sip of whisky.

"We are treating everyone as best as we can," I said, regretting my defensive tone.

"Over forty sick so far and several dead," she shrugged, "and but two weeks since your woman arrived."

"My woman?"

"Forgive me if I have erred, but was it not you who interfered at Drynoch?"

"Interfered?"

"Aye. The chief there— the one you publicly humiliated— had decided to shun them and save his village. But gallant Sir Malcolm rode in to save the damsel, and now look."

"I did not *ride* in, I walked, and it is my *sworn duty* to help those in need." She was aggravating, and I suspected that was her intention. "You would have left them to die? You call yourself a healer?" In a pique of anger, I threw the half cup of whisky in the fire. It exploded, sending a shower of burning peat sparks onto the floor and on my fine breeches. I slapped the sparks out as they ate tiny black holes in the fabric, reminding me that life is largely fashioned by cause and effect, but we do stupid things, regardless.

"Your bad temper wastes good drink," she muttered, then swept the embers back to where they belonged.

"That woman should've stayed in Drynoch, as instructed," I said.

"But she didn't, and perhaps you should have foreseen that."

"How so? I can't predict the future. Can you?"

"You were the only kindness in her unfortunate life. She followed you, like that other stray you found."

I said nothing for a while, letting my anger settle. This woman knew how to provoke me in the most effective way, with logic. "I'm sorry I wasted your whisky, but I am *not* sorry I treated that family. Consequences be damned! It is what I was trained to do. I swore an oath."

Mairi reached over and placed her veined hand on mine. "I know, dear. I can sense you are an honourable gentleman. And I would not have left them to suffer either."

I was shocked to hear that. "Then why do you criticize?"

"I do not. Merely observed. Life can be unpredictable, but less so if one is observant…and shall I say…wise."

I nodded.

"More whisky?" she offered.

"Thank you, but I've misused your hospitality enough."

"Not so, Malcolm. What little I have is yours."

"Then I shall have this fine cottage," I teased.

Her laugh was surprising in its passion. "'Tis not mine, but a friends. And I am certain she would approve."

"You are very kind—"

"Not kind. 'Tis our way. But we have difficulties to discuss…several in fact, don't we?"

"Do we?"

"The first is that the community blames *you* for bringing typhus to Dunvegan. They have heard the story. Few secrets are kept here for long, and these rumours are hard to refute."

"I cannot change what people think."

She slapped her knee. "Of course, you can! We must counter these lies with truths."

"It does look as if I need a better reputation hereabouts, so I will accept your kind offer to repair it," I chuckled.

"Done! That brings us to our next problem…the laird and his family."

"Indeed. I've been waiting weeks to examine them."

"The laird has wanted to give you time to recover and adjust, and he is a cautious man."

"Aunt Mairi, are you still up?" It was Elspeth's voice from outside, at the door.

"Aye, Elspeth. I have a gentleman caller," Mairi said, winking at me.

I love a good prank too, so I gave a few manly grunts and muffled curses.

"Oh? I will come back...in the morning...late morning," Elspeth said.

"Och, no...come in, child. 'Tis your Sir Malcolm with me." The old woman laughed herself into a cough and Elspeth was beside her in time for a helpful pat.

"As usual, just in time, Elspeth. We were about to discuss the laird's health problems."

Elspeth sat cross legged on the floor, looking haggard and ill-kempt. I knew why, of course. Long hours tending the sick and the stench of death make it hard to keep down food and drink. I had Teresa to care for me. Elspeth only Janet, and she was distracted by love. But we had been in a worse state during the smallpox epidemic last spring.

I reached over and grasped her tiny hand. Our fingers interlaced. I could feel her weakness. "You need to eat more. Mairi, please convince your headstrong niece to have some nourishment before she leaves."

Mairi nodded. "Fresh bread and ale will perk her up, and please take some for Janet and Cawdie."

I smiled at Elspeth. She sighed in resignation. Mairi set a plate of bread and a half-eaten onion on Elspeth's lap and poured her an ale and me another whisky before returning to her stool. We both stared at Elspeth until she acquiesced and began nibbling on the bread.

"Now about the laird—" Mairi started.

"The laird and family show no signs of camp fever. We have them isolated in their quarters on the upper floor of the castle," Elspeth said between chews.

"And the castle servants?" I asked.

"Many are sick. We are using the barracks on the ground floor as an infirmary. The warriors have moved to the old castle keep. 'Tis not been easy for them, roofless in the rain. But they have rigged some cloth for shelter and peat fires for warmth. Fortunately, few warriors are sick. It has mostly been the servants and children the Drynoch woman encountered."

Mairi shifted on the stool then asked, "And new cases?"

Elspeth took a large swallow of ale. "Many have left Dunvegan. We tried to keep them, but they went at night to their families. I am sorry, Malcolm, but you are seeing the tragic results in the village. But to answer your question, there are few new cases in the castle now. We are maintaining quarantine of the sick. Beyond that, it is out of our hands."

"Aye, the number of cases in the village is rising," said I. "The infirmary at the inn is overflowing and the cottages dangerously crowded. God knows what is going on in the crofts surrounding Dunvegan," I added.

Mairi had retrieved a comb from the folds of her arisaid and was pulling the tangles from Elspeth's long hair. Meanwhile Elspeth had begun eating and drinking voraciously. I was beginning to understand their relationship. Sometimes the healer needs a healer.

"I know you are both very tired," Mairi commented, "but the time has come for Malcolm to see the laird and family."

Elspeth was slowly slumping to the floor, looking as though she would fall asleep, the bread and ale having their effect. "We will, we will," she muttered as her head descended to Mairi's lap.

"Goodnight, Malcolm," Mairi said. "I will take care of this wee lass. Please return soon, we have much more to discuss."

I had been dismissed and welcomed it, for I was as tired as a drover at day's end.

* * *

Caring for the sick is very time-consuming. Cleaning, disinfecting, treating rash with herbal washes, administering cooling baths and medicines for fever, hand feeding, and cleaning again, always cleaning. It never ends—well it does when the patient either recovers or dies. And we were in the thick of it now, Teresa and me. I did not want more help if it increased the risk of further spreading infection. It was bad enough for Teresa. We had been sharing a bed for weeks, but it was nothing remotely romantic, as we were taking shifts sleeping and caring for patients. And she did most of it at the inn while I prowled the village. At least I had not been required to remove any gangrenous body parts, but we had lost several patients, mostly the old and weak.

Disease is like that—nature's culling, as some call it, ordained by God. But I did not believe it. We just did not know how to cure some diseases, and that is why we had tried inoculation for smallpox last spring. Seemed to work, too, mind you with a small number of us physicians as volunteers. Could the inoculation method work with typhus? Hard to know, and I was too overwhelmed to give it much consideration. If anything happened to those of us skilled enough to help—the ones who would try the inoculation first—this disease could burn through here like a grass fire.

"It breaks my heart seeing you on your hands and knees cleaning." Janet poked her head through the door at the inn as I was sopping urine off the floor from a chamber pot that had tipped.

I glanced back on hearing her familiar voice. "You are welcome to help, you know."

She laughed in that earthy, sensual way she has that instantly reminds me of sex. "Lady Elspeth requires your presence at the castle this afternoon. Can you come?" she teased.

"Will there be cakes and tea?"

"Emm...maybe rash and vomit."

"I have enough of that here."

"Seriously, Malcom, she needs your help with the soldiers and to examine the laird."

"All right, I can be there late afternoon. We are busy, as you can see."

"Aye, same in the castle. Do you want anything before I go?"

I chuckled, "There are many things I want, but few I need. Convey my greetings to your husband and tell him we must go fishing when this is over."

"Your needs have a reputation of their own," she giggled. "Could use some fresh fish, though."

I returned to my smelly task and heard Janet share a joke with Teresa as she left.

* * *

The castle bailey gardens were churned to mud and the forty or more warriors were trying to stay dry in their makeshift shelters within the ruins of the castle-keep, poorly warmed by sputtering peat fires and body heat. I nodded to the sullen boy cooking a pot of stew over a smouldering fire amid the muck in the bailey. The scene was depressing, and the ground floor of the castle was no better. In happier times the castle housed soldiers in the south wing barracks. The north wing were the servants' quarters and work areas such as the kitchen and laundry. I had entered through the door near the kitchen and could hear people working inside, metal on metal, women muttering, feet scuffling. But there were no joyful sounds, no one laughing, no one singing. It felt grim. And down the long hall, were the unmistakable sounds of misery coming from the barracks. I headed in that direction.

This time it was Janet on her knees tending a patient. The room reeked of sickness. Ysabell and an older woman were chatting in whispers as they restocked bedding and towels from the laundry. It was good to see them helping. I wondered if Ysabell was as wicked as I had first assumed. Perhaps Elspeth's fears were unfounded and Ysabell truly was trying to protect the laird.

"I'm here," I said, kneeling at Janet's side, observing the patient, a heavy-set man with an ample belly and round face. It was Keith, the guardsman who'd cold-cocked me and thrown me in that damned hole. I had to restrain my mirth.

Janet glanced over at me. "Our newest guest," she said.

"Then give him the royal treatment," I said loudly.

His fevered eyes opened wide and imagined horror must have exploded in his mind, because he blurted, "You!" and tried to sit up.

Janet pushed him back gently in that well-practiced, firm-but-gentle way she has, and suggested that he would enjoy the cooling bath she had made special for him.

Of course, we would take the best care of him. But let him live in fear for a while. He deserved it. "Has Elspeth seen him?" I asked.

"Aye. He is well cared for. You need not worry."

"That's a relief," I quipped back with a grin. "Now, where is she?"

"Second floor above us. Stairs are right there," she nodded in the direction of a wooden staircase against the end wall. I resisted the urge to hug her before I left. But those days were long over, and I had to be careful of my affections.

The second floor was quite different than the first. Oak paneling replaced cold stone and cracked plaster, and a cheerful fireplace blazed in the shared area by the stairs. Well-dressed women and girls were having tea and doing needlework. They stopped talking when they saw me and one of the young girls blurted excitedly that I must be Sir Malcolm and offered to take me to Elspeth. I had been here before, but the castle is a maze of poorly lit corridors and doors leading to who knows where, so I gratefully accepted her offer. It was nearby, and in this case impossible to get lost because Cawdie was squatting in front of the door, lovingly stroking his claymore with a chunk of black rock. I thanked the overly helpful girl and patted Cawdie on the shoulder.

"Guid day brother," he said in his broad Highland accent, hardened like his sword by years of hardship and service. "The women be in there. Better ye knock afore entering They could be up ta anything."

"Good idea. They could be naked and frolicking, couldn't they?"

Cawdie gave a lusty guffaw. I knocked on the door and waited. A voice called, "Come in!"

The room was small and sparsely furnished. Elspeth and her Aunt Mairi were there but someone was missing. Elspeth must have noticed my questioning look because she said, "Aunt Rhona died…a few days ago now."

"Ah," I said. "Typhus?"

"I am not certain. She had a slight fever, nothing more. She was old, Malcolm, and tired, and—," she had a catch in her voice, "and I shall miss her so very much."

"I'm sorry." It was all I could say. We were becoming numb with grief.

That is how physicians deal with it. We shove those feeling deep and hope they do not resurface at an inopportune time. Aunt Mairi was perched on the edge of the bed searching for something in her bag. Elspeth was seated on the room's only chair, shoulders drooping, a blank look on her face.

"I ordered a mass grave dug at the kirk," I said. "It's best to have the bodies touched as little as possible." They nodded, and I could see tears forming in Elspeth's eyes. She dabbed them away with the end of her sleeve.

"My sister will *not* be thrown in a mass grave," Mairi said with firm defiance.

"Where is her body?" I asked.

"Where she belongs...with her family," Mairi replied.

I glanced over at Elspeth. I did not want to provoke a fight, but this was important. Infected dead bodies can spread pestilence as well as the living.

"We took her from here to our cottage in the village to prepare for burial and visitation," Elspeth said reluctantly.

I sighed and shook my head. "You of all people should know better."

"Malcolm, please let us do it our way. She was a revered elder. When the rites have been observed she will rest in the cairn beneath the Sacred Rowan Tree, until such time as we may take her to St. Clement's."

That is how these things get out of control. Everyone wants an exception. They are special. I took a deep breath to calm my frustration. Elspeth closed her mouth tightly, refusing to sob, but I could see tears track down her cheeks. What could I do? We were all on edge, warring emotions exacerbated by a lack of sleep, and it must be much more difficult for her, watching family members die. I knew the feeling well, that helpless desperation. They needed me to be the dispassionate physician, now more than ever, so I changed the subject: "I am here to examine the laird. Is he ready?"

Elspeth blinked and tried to stop weeping. She blew her nose and rose, steadying herself on the nearby table. "Aye, Malcolm. He should be ready. Aunt Mairi, have you any suggestions before we go?"

Mairi had been staring out the window, seemingly lost in thought.

Elspeth's question brought her back. "I do. Our laird is like many men. He discounts the advice of women. Examine him thoroughly, Malcolm. We will meet afterward to discuss your findings, and I hope you will be open to opinions other than your own." It was a rebuke and perhaps I deserved it, but in any case, Mairi had yet to learn that I am not easily intimidated, especially by women. I nodded in the direction of the door and took Elspeth's arm as we headed to the stairs up to the laird's apartment.

* * *

Norman MacLeod of MacLeod—a strange name for a strange place. But it fit. He was a few years younger and a few inches shorter than me, fine-boned, with broad shoulders and well-developed arms. His face was unlined and round, set with blue eyes and capped with thinning sandy hair. I had met him first at Torrport last spring and again briefly here after my release from captivity. Both times he had said little beyond what was required. I assumed he was just shy or quiet. But this day he was far from reserved, offering an engaging smile and warm handshake.

We were standing, in those awkward moments of introduction when no one knows what to say. Across the room, Elspeth was speaking with Lady Anne who was holding her new bairn, with the year-old babe at her feet wanting attention. Two young servant girls were preparing tea and cakes by the fire. The apartment had fine views of the village to the south and the loch to the west and north. Oak-paneled walls were decorated with tapestries and paintings which harmonised with the elaborately carved dark-wood furniture. The overall effect was one of wealth and good taste, equal to any royal dwelling.

I recognized the piece at once and took a few steps closer to touch it. My fingers caressed the carved wooden side-table that depicted a boar hunt on its front panels. Do fingers have memories? I think they might, because my mind instantly filled with images from long ago, of family and laughter and being held lovingly by the fire.

"Wonderful, isn't it? Brought it back from Edinburgh. Belonged to some noble who'd fallen on tough times," the MacLeod said, then snapped his fingers for the servant to bring us drinks.

I nodded. "That happens. It's beautifully made. Must have cost a fortune."

"Hellish to get it here in one piece, I can tell you. The transport was as much as what I paid for it."

"Do you mind if I ask where you got it?"

"Not at all," he smiled. "Lady Myreton...she owns Corstorphine Castle near Edinburgh. She is a friend of Aunt Mairi and often visits in summer. She thought it would look better here. Rustic, she said, and knew I was looking for quality pieces."

I forced myself to look away. I was certain now that side table was my mother's, before she died, and Father sold out and moved us from our family home in Corstorphine to Edinburgh. I could remember as a child intensively studying that carved man on horseback as he was about to spear the wild boar. But maybe not. Memories play tricks, don't they? I had to remind myself that it is only a piece of wood, after all.

"As much as I love admiring art, I've come a long way to be of service," I said, restoring focus.

"Indeed, you have, and 'tis appreciated. But I assure you I am quite well. Women worry to excess, do they not?"

Elspeth and Anne had stopped chatting, no doubt listening to us. "It's wise to seek wider counsel," I said, "and I can assure you that if it is inconsequential, I will tell you."

"I am certain that whatever it is will pass," he said, trying unsuccessfully to suppress a cough. "'Tis nothing," he muttered, hawking up phlegm into a handkerchief.

I was not sure of his intent at this point. Was he delusional or did he honestly think nothing was amiss? It seemed he was not going to be forthright in front of his women, so I asked if there was a private room where he could be examined.

* * *

Moments later we were in a small room one floor up that he called the "Fairy Tower." The room smelled of leather and gun oil, with a whiff of old whisky and tobacco. It was spare, with stone walls, one window, a desk, a few well-worn chairs, and wooden and glass cases filled with an odd assortment of what he called family treasures. Not jewels and gold, but objects like an old drinking horn, a tarnished tankard big enough to quench the thirst of a giant, and an ornate box he said contained an ancient flag. *One man's trash is another's treasure,* I thought. This looked like the kind of private room where men like to drink and smoke and plot revenge. I liked it.

"You can cut the shite and tell me what's going on," I said, watching as he leaned on the desk facing me, arms folded. He let out a harsh laugh and said something delicate ears should not hear. I laughed, too. It was a good start.

It is always best to begin with taking a patient's history, since it is often informative and relaxes them. Most people love talking about themselves. But the laird was not one of them. It was like getting gold from a miser. He answered every question, but with few words and no elaboration. I had to practice patience on this patient, not one of my strong suits. In the end I discovered he had a long history of illnesses, colds, influenza, even an infection from sword play gone wrong that almost ended in amputation. And he knew what people thought of him—that he was weak and no Iain Breac MacLeod, his legendary father who had lived large and well.

"Tell me when the cough started," I said, directing him back to more recent times.

He shrugged and looked out the window, sighed, then turned back to me, "Must we?"

"Your family loves you. We must try."

"For them, then. It was early summer, right after that meeting in Torrport, sailing home from Glasgow. Maybe I got it from one of the sailors. It was crowded. Some were coughing."

I thought it unlikely symptoms would appear so soon but did not disagree. "Please remove your shirt, so I can listen to your chest."

As he did, I found my notebook in the medical bag which thankfully had survived my trip. I had already noticed a sheen on his skin that suggested a slight fever, and his laboured walk up the stairs to the Fairy Tower. He was more ill than I expected. "A deep breath in, then hold it. I want to listen to your heart."

"Nothing wrong with my heart. I'm as strong as the best."

"Sure," I mumbled, as I moved my ear on his chest from place to place. It sounded fine, but for the elevated heart rate. "Now breathe normally." I looked in his eyes. They appeared sad and fearful. He knew I was about to discover the truth. In his chest, I could hear that crackling sound typical of consumption or lung infection.

He coughed while I was listening, sending a spray of droplets on my head. "Sorry," he said, wiping his mouth on a blood-stained handkerchief.

"Does it hurt when you cough?"

"A wee bit."

I knew by his expression that it was more than a bit. "Eating and sleeping well?"

"I try."

"Please explain. Are you *not* eating well?"

He shrugged. "It is the pain I get in my stomach, and…the bloody shits if I eat more than a little."

Those symptoms were not caused by consumption. I made note. "Any other pains, other than your stomach?"

"I've noticed that the back of my neck is stiff and sore sometimes. But maybe I need more exercise. I should get out riding…" His voice trailed off.

"How about urination?"

"Emm, no problem there."

"Are you sure? What colour is it?"

"Yellow, of course," he chuckled.

"Dark or light yellow?"

"Like the gold of your ring." He pointed at Fortuna, and I was beginning to believe he needed her more than I.

I finished the exam by feeling his forehead. It was slightly feverish, as expected. Next, I palpated his abdomen. It showed signs of tenderness. "You can put your shirt back on." I wrote another note and waited. "Now tell me again when these symptoms started."

"Early summer, after I returned from Torrport."

"All the symptoms…stomach pains and diarrhea included?"

"Aye."

"That's over three months past. You are a tough man to have endured so long without complaint. But you need help. I'm going to confer with Elspeth and Mairi, and we will devise a plan of treatment."

He nodded.

"Norman, do you agree, and will you comply with our plan?"

He laughed. "Provided 'tis not a humiliation."

"Always remember your family loves you and I would *never* do that."

"Some would," he said. With that ominous thought stuck in my mind, we rejoined the ladies for tea and cakes. The laird ate little and excused himself shortly thereafter.

* * *

"I believe he has consumption," I told the women in Elspeth's room. "A cold or flu would not last so long, and he's fevered and coughing up phlegm and sometimes blood, and obviously losing weight. Can't rule out catarrh or a simple inflammation of the lungs, but my coin is on consumption which is more common in Scotland than those other complaints. Either way, he has a serious lung problem."

"Aye, and I have watched him get worse, too, these past months," Elspeth said. "Anne says he sleeps poorly and sweats a lot at night."

It was getting late; the day's light having fled the advancing dark. We were very tired, but this needed resolution. "Then we have another set of symptoms," I added, "seemingly unrelated…the stomach and neck pains and diarrhea." I looked at Mairi, who had said nothing so far. She was staring down and slowly twisting the walking stick between her hands like she was trying to start a fire in the floor.

"The ratcatcher was here," Mairi said, finally.

"Aye, and those darned scented gloves." Elspeth muttered.

I was at a loss.

"In your considered judgement, could those unrelated symptoms be caused by poison?" Mairi asked.

"Could be. But remember, we have symptoms, not proof. Other things cause stomach upsets, as you well know."

Mairi banged her stick on the floor and demanded, "Then what do you recommend, doctor?"

Dealing with consumption was hard enough but throwing in an unknown illness made our plan tenuous. I considered it carefully for a few minutes while retrieving my notebook, quill pen, and ink. "We need to pool our knowledge and experience to serve the laird properly. Here is what I would do...but I am open to your suggestions as well." I proceeded to lay out a step-by-step plan to alleviate the symptoms of his consumption in the traditional way by using an expectorant based on coltsfoot to clear his lungs and a willow bark analgesic to reduce fever. But that would not be enough. Ideally, we needed to find a way to cure, or at least encourage his disease to go into remission, and to that end I recommended a diet of fresh milk and oatmeal, along with more exercise and sunlight.

"Aye, he spends far too much time in the castle, taking rich meats and drink," Elspeth noted.

"A dubious benefit of wealth. So, have we dealt with the consumption part of the puzzle?" I asked.

"Aye, but what of the other symptoms?" Aunt Mairi asked.

"The problem is that we don't have a probable cause. It may be poison, but what kind? And many have access to him and his food and drink. It would be better if we could isolate him for a time to see if he improves. Failing that, we could just treat his symptoms."

"The symptoms are similar to those produced by strychnine and arsenic...in a small dose, obviously," Elspeth said.

We both looked at her. She shrugged and added, "Poisoning is more common in Italy where I went to school. Ratcatchers use it too, and he was here recently."

"Be careful, Elspeth," I warned. "Rat catching is an honourable profession. Having access to poison doesn't mean he is poisoning the laird."

"Nay, but perhaps there are others with motive," Elspeth countered.

While we were discussing ratcatchers and poison, Mairi was digging in her bag. "Here it is," she said, holding up the worn, engraved, and painted box I had brought to her from Gormal. "The Brightstone," she said, opening it carefully. The stone was folded in a plain linen cloth which she spread open. The stone itself —as I knew from having seen it before—was dark grey, probably common basalt with imbedded flakes of another mineral which sparkled in the torch light. It was unusual, but what did it have to do with all this? Mairi smiled at me, her eyes seeming to probe my mind. "I have an idea to help with the laird's consumption and his mysterious ailments, both."

I shrugged. "I believe in objective truth, as best we can perceive it. If a rock can help the laird, then let's use it. Now tell me about this Brightstone."

"'Tis very old," Mairi started, launching into what was to be a long story about Vikings, the Isle of Man, and the early MacLeods. The Scots love to tell their history. But in the end, it turned out that the Brightstone had accompanied the MacLeod healers for centuries and reputedly gave them the power to cure.

So much for legends, I thought. *Try treating camp fever with a stone.* I listened to it all while Elspeth sat quietly, a wee smile on her lips. I hoped she was proud of my patience. And I had heard much of this before from Gormal when she gave me the box.

"I see you are feigning interest in our history," Mairi smiled. "Listen now and I will tell you how we can use the Brightstone."

I admit it was a cunning plan. She told us of Loch Siant, north of Portree, reputed to cure consumption, and how we must take water from its spring and place the Brightstone in it for full effect, then carry the healing water sun-ways around the loch before having him drink it. Sounded like bizarre superstition, bordering on witchcraft, but they assured me the laird was a believer in local traditions, despite his city education. And it was the perfect excuse to get him away from his kin for a time so he could be completely in my control. I agreed wholeheartedly. "Then we have a plan. We are going on a trip to that healing spring. But we need time to prepare. I'll make a list of necessaries." I was taking charge, and they did not seem to mind. That made me worry.

* * *

Before we left that evening, Mairi had invited us over for supper the following evening. "It will be a feast," said she, with a grin. A feast of what was not made clear. Perhaps I was the one to be roasted. In any case, I was famished after working all day and when Elspeth collected me, I was relishing the prospect of an evening of tasty food and stimulating company. Adhie had been invited as well and was happy to search out new smells on the way.

The cottage was gaily decorated with sprigs of pine and heather and even some bright red rose hips Mairi had found in a bramble. The meal was better than imagined, a feast of fresh-caught fish served with boiled potatoes, drowned in herb-butter. This, along with berry pie and endless ale, soon had us sated and sleepy.

It was Mairi who brought us rudely back to reality. "We must discuss your trip to Loch Siant, Malcolm," she said firmly. I knew there must be good reason for this meeting beyond fattening us, so I sat up straight and nodded. "You could have trouble," she said.

"I'll be ready."

"Perhaps not," she replied.

"Then educate me," I said, not sure I would like her form of schooling.

Mairi told us that there might be some who wanted to replace the laird and they might stop at nothing, including attacking us on our trip. I heard this before but decided not to tell her what I was thinking. I would play the ignorant schoolboy for now. "Who are these people you suspect?" I asked.

"Perhaps Ysabell and some...ahh...and some other witches," Elspeth replied, "but we mustn't say. 'Tis sensitive, and we have no proof...nothing but rumours."

Mairi nodded in agreement.

"Witches like Gormal and Doideag?" I asked.

"Perhaps so, and more," Mairi added.

"You know I am not a believer. These are just deluded old women wanting attention," I said.

Mairi gave a condescending smile and cleared her throat. Elspeth touched Mairi's sleeve and shook her head almost imperceptibly. "As you say then, Malcolm. But please do not underestimate them."

"Nor should I fear them. I am more their match, as they have experienced." Perhaps I was tempting the fates by saying that, but I wanted her to know I was not afraid to deal with a coven of silly old women.

"Be careful, Malcolm," Elspeth continued. "They know the land and culture better than you. They will have you disadvantaged because of it. I know some of these women...they have methods to deceive such as you have never seen. Your poisoning at Broadford was but a gentle example," she explained.

"Then tell me how is it that these women had the Brightstone and gave it to me to help the laird? Is this not proof that your ideas are based more on unfounded suspicion than reality?" I confronted Mairi squarely. I had to know if there was substance to their fears before I set off.

Mairi's eyes flashed fire. She opened her mouth to speak, then stopped. "Aunt Mairi," Elspeth interrupted. "Malcolm needs to know. 'Tis not impertinence, but intelligent planning."

I laughed. "Thank you, Elspeth. You are quite correct, especially the intelligent part. It's enough that I'm working in a culture I barely understand."

"Forgive us, Malcolm," Mairi said. "We guard our secrets closely. 'Tis our way. The Brightstone was given to Gormal a few months ago to treat a close member of the laird's family who had taken ill on the way to Fort William. I've been trying to get it back since. When I heard you might be coming to Dunvegan, I asked my friends, healers throughout Skye and beyond to provide aid should they come upon you. I most certainly *did not* ask them to poison you. I also asked Gormal to give you the Brightstone or deliver it herself, that it was urgently needed, and that she would not be forgiven if she failed to do so." Mairi looked to Elspeth for support.

"Malcolm," added Elspeth, "this is complicated by the fact that these women are, or were, our friends, and we are uncertain of their loyalties at this point."

"So, let me summarize. There are so-called witches and others who may or may not wish us ill, and you want me to take the laird to a sacred healing spring with a sparkling rock to heal him of a disease which has no cure?" I knew I was being facetious, but their plan sounded that idiotic.

"Yes!" Elspeth chuckled, and even Mairi laughed politely.

"Now, that is my sort of quest!" We shared another round of nervous mirth while I wondered how many times, I could get away with dipping my toes in that well of peril.

"And that is only the half of it," Mairi said, then reached over and took our hands in hers. "Do you remember what I told you earlier? The story of the Brightstone and Clan MacLeod history?"

"Aye?" I said, feeling my stomach tense as if expecting a blow.

"The part I left out is known only to a few. It has to do with where the Brightstone and your Fortuna ring originated and why they have such power." Mairi paused for our reaction. "Malcolm, you must never reveal to anyone what I am about to tell you."

I did not agree. I do not make promises like that. Elspeth turned to Mairi and said, "You can trust him."

"Very well, child. He is what we have been given to work with—sent by destiny and protected by Fortuna, one who is not tainted by greed, one who descends from Captain Forrester of old and who terrifies witches more than hellfire. I will tell you now the great secret of our clan."

It was a stunning revelation to hear of the Viking treasure brought by the first MacLeod from the Isle of Man hundreds of years ago. The Brightstone and Fortuna ring were but a minor part of that treasure hidden in a place known only by cryptic signs left to the elders and passed generation after generation in their safe keeping. "There are some who have discovered a few of the clues as to the location of the treasure," she said. "We must stop them."

I took a deep breath as Mairi finished. So that was it. We were facing those who not only wished to replace the laird, but also to steal the MacLeod Viking treasure. I knew this was the decisive moment, why I had come. I turned to Elspeth, my good friend and colleague. I was not sure I wanted to know all this and to be drawn further into their web of tribal intrigues.

Elspeth's green eyes reflected black in the firelight as we sat holding hands. I had come at her request to help the laird with his illness and now I knew there was much more to it. Elspeth had hinted as much in her terse letter. I had a choice. My father would wish stability, provided the clan remained out of the hands of the Jacobites. Elspeth and Mairi wanted my help. The laird agreed to be treated. But what did I want? Sometimes there is no clear answer. I had nothing to gain and my life to lose. It was an easy decision.

"I will do it," said I cheerfully. "Thank you for the lessons, Mairi."

Elspeth leaned over, hugged me, and whispered, "Thank you," in my ear.

Mairi scraped leftovers into a bowl for Adhie and minutes later we left, stomachs full, my mind equally full of tasks yet undone.

* * *

Those days before our trip dragged on slowly, as time does when one is waiting. Cawdie was tasked with gathering our supplies, which included two riding horses and a milking cow. We started the laird on his new diet and medicines immediately after our decision had been made, to give him time to adapt. We did not want him sick on the trail. The trip would be hard enough with forty-odd miles of rugged terrain and little shelter. The cow could walk but several miles a day, so it could take us one to two weeks for the round-trip. It could be a dangerous too, and I asked the laird for suggestions to enhance our protection. He had one and we agreed to take it with us, although it would be an extra burden for the horses.

The typhus epidemic was waning, and Doctor Bethune had returned from Drynoch with good news—only six dead, much better than we had feared. He was a stalwart and richly deserved praise from the laird and from his fellow healers. He offered to help at the inn once he had time to recover. All seemed well in hand now with Elspeth, Janet, Mairi, Ysabell, and her mother working at the castle, and Teresa and Bethune at the inn, with Adhie doing his doggy best to cheer everyone with endless kisses. It was time for us to go.

* * *

"Gonnae war, brother?" Cawdie dropped the weapons on the table in the tavern. I was sitting contemplating life or resting, as you please, before our trip to the healing spring which would begin the next day. I had asked Cawdie to sharpen my cutlass and dagger, and oil my pistol, and provide plenty of powder and balls.

"I hope to avoid it," I grinned. Cawdie was the only one I had told of my plan, and he did not approve.

"Got the laird equipped," he said. "Takin' a musket. Bonnie with silver engraving." Nay sure if it shoots straight. An' what of that other thing? Don't troost it. Looks like it coods blaw up in yer mug. Ah still think ah should go with ye." His massive weight was threatening to flip the table he was leaning on, as he scowled down at me menacingly.

"No. Stick with the plan. You must stay with the women and children in the castle. If anyone threatens them, you have my permission to slice them from gizzard to groin."

"Hah. Well, ah hope that bastard who flirts with mah Janet has a try. Be mah pleasure ta cut him in two."

I laughed. Cawdie could be funny, in a murderous sort of way. "I hope you've been spreading the word, too."

"Aye, all folk from the baker to the barber knows by noo. Damned foolish, if ye ask me."

I had asked Cawdie to spread the word about our trip, where we were going and when. I wanted everyone to know. "We've done stupider things," I reminded him.

"Och, that time we faced doon the mob in Auld Reekie, ye almost got me killed."

We were still laughing about it when Elspeth came roaring in, fury in her eyes, "What in the name of? Why are you two miscreants telling everyone when and where you are going? Are you insane?"

Cawdie and I looked at each other then burst out laughing. Elspeth fumed. I took her hand. She pulled it away. I knew she would be even more upset when I told her of our secret. "Elspeth, calm yourself. We have a plan."

"What plan?" She looked confused. Cawdie and I were grinning like schoolboys who had discovered a cask of whisky.

"The plan whereby I lure the laird's enemies out to the moors and kill them."

Chapter 11: Elspeth

Malcolm had gone quite mad. Evidently, he had some wild plan to identify and stop the troublemakers causing our problems. I was not certain he understood how dangerous they were. I had listened and agreed reluctantly. But there was no stopping him, especially after he somehow persuaded the laird to take part.

The camp fever epidemic had abated, leaving its worst victims only in our memories. After Aunt Rhona had succumbed, Janet moved back into the empty spaces of my days. I was too drained and too grateful to object yet, but I would when I regained my strength. Cawdie always seemed to be at hand to help as well. It was selfish of me not to insist the newly wed couple spend all their time together, but I needed them, and persistent dreams of Erika kept me from sleeping well.

The laird ordered the yellow warning flags of contagion removed from the battlements and ships began to call at the castle again. Pedlars and chapmen resumed bringing their wares in packs and baskets to our doors. From the depths of their cleverly designed hampers, pockets, and totes magically appeared pins, needles, fine threads, rainbows of colored ribbons, brass, and silver oddments, chatelains, a small selection of silks, all manner of exotic spices, and objects that were easily conveyed and much desired. But the most important items weighed nothing. Gossip, rumour, reports from courts and campaigns, fashions and fantastical tales from the Americas were as avidly sought as material stuffs and paid for in coin or in kind.

When travel resumed, Sir Ross and Gregor packed numerous chests and took their leave, pledging to return soon. As they left, Sir Ross claimed my hand and bent gracefully over it. Gregor, his handsome, saturnine face still and unemotional, only bowed and placed a packet in my palm. We had agreed on several things that would be effective against black magic and the forbidden dark arts. His knowledge of the occult was formidable, and he had devoted hours of his time, patiently teaching me the proper use of arcane hand patterns and signs from sources written in Sanskrit. Later, I discovered the packet contained a silver disk skillfully engraved with a gryphon embracing a circle that contained a triskele, and cup and ring symbols. The protective amulet was suspended from a heavy silver chain. I put it around my neck and immediately imagined I felt better.

My father was not permitted to go with the laird and so he began regularly mustering the clansmen for training in arching, wrestling, jumping, putting the stone, throwing the bar and all manner of exercise. It was good for them, and the lasses soon began to gather to watch, and the warriors responded to their presence with added effort.

Everyone still worked long hours recovering and adjusting, but the overwhelming sense of helplessness was gradually replaced with the resumption of normal daily tasks. It was near midnight when I completed my rounds and went back to my room. Now that the camp fever had abated, Janet returned to her cottage in the village and Cawdie. As a result, I was alone in my room for the first time in weeks.

Someone had thoughtfully left me a tray with a cup of ale, two slices of buttered bread, and a bit of cheese. I dutifully ate most of it. The ale tasted flat but perhaps it would make me sleepy. It was safe enough here with Scathach. I peeked into the whelping bed where she lay licking her four new pups. She had birthed them the previous night and the wee bonny balls of fur tumbled clumsily about her, snuffling for a teat. I slipped to the floor and picked one of them up. It nuzzled me hopefully, smelling of warm fur and straw. I savored the miracle of the wee pup and returned it to Scathach to suckle. But I was too exhausted to settle. Mayhap a walk would clear my head. Closing the door carefully behind me to keep the puppies inside, I walked to the bailey and down the steps to the sea gate.

The guard allowed me to pass.

Starshine silvered the winding pathway around the castle. I would ask Saint Brighid to clear my heart. Wind whispered messages on the breeze. It seemed to sough vague warnings through the swaying grasses and bushes along the way. Shadows shifted and spun around me. The sacred rowan tree thrust its ancient branches upward to couple the earth and sky. The tips of its heavy boughs murmuring across the top of the cairn wherein Erika and Aunt Rhona rested.

"Enemies here—beware," the wind seemed to sigh. I felt the danger, but dully, as from a distance. My thoughts grew jumbled. Was someone following me? Hesitating, I lifted my head and tried to see and hear better. Everything blurred, and I reached for the blessed rowan tree to steady myself.

Ysabell stepped lightly from behind the thick gray trunk. What was she doing here? She did not worship the lady. I stepped back and was blocked by someone behind me. A large hand reached around my waist, holding me still, while the other covered my nose and mouth with spongy wetness. The noxious odor of henbane overlaid with the sweet charred-blossom scent of opium and herbs was overpowering. It was a combination I knew well and used myself to make patients sleep during surgery. I fought desperately to avoid breathing in the sickening fumes, stomping down viciously on a leather-shod foot, and digging my fingernails into the hand clasped over my mouth. A man grunted and cursed. Was it Ranuff? I could feel the warm wetness of blood where my nails had rent skin, but his hand held steady. I was growing weaker. I needed to breathe! Where was everyone? My mind screamed for Malcolm, Cawdie, Father...anyone. My body surrendered and sucked in the fumes. Ysabell's satisfied smile was the last thing I saw as I fell into unending night.

* * *

It was too dark to see. I reached out as far as I could on both sides. Straw prickled. I was lying on a thin pile. My fingers touched a coarse cloth bundle next to me in the foetid room. Nothing else was nearby. I lay quietly, seeking my wits. Flittering memories of being roughly thrust into a cart surfaced. Aches and incipient bruises told me that part had been real enough. I groaned as I tried to sit up and rid my head of haze. One thing was certain—I had been drugged by someone who knew how to make a soporific sponge. And had there been something added to the ale left for me in my room? I recalled feeling unsteady before Ysabell appeared. And I think Ranuff had been there! I looked around. I thought I recognized the room. It was the dungeon in the laird's keep at Talisker, held by Ranuff for the MacLeods! Why had he brought me here?

My parched mouth tasted like something best forgotten. I had no idea how long I had been lying there, semi-unconscious in the stinking filth left by prior tenants. There was an intake of breath near me, and then I heard "El?" I knew at once, over the span of years—it was my sister's voice, weak and changed, but uniquely hers.

"Erika?" I rolled over and bile roiled, trying to escape my abused belly. I swallowed it back and reached shakily for the swathed shape lying near me, my hands searching the coarse surface of a blanket. It felt hollow, the fragile form beneath patched with wet. This could only be a terrifying dream. If it were not, I would have to accept that I had failed my sister yet again. Once because of jealousy, and a second time by cutting away my apparently useless talent when I thought she had died. If I had not, I would have known she was alive and felt her, as my aunts had insisted. But I had doubted them. It didn't seem possible.

I rolled closer in the darkness and pressed against my sister. A flood of grief surged from deep inside me. It was a cowardice I could no longer afford! Fear and disuse slowed me as I stripped away my defenses, seeking that precious place Erika and I had shared as children. I begged her forgiveness without words. She opened to me at once and we clung to each other as we had always done in childhood, accepting the missing pieces of ourselves, reveling in the old loving completeness. I poured my strength into her ravaged body as we communicated. Finally, we slept peacefully wrapped in each other's arms.

* * *

I awoke feeling stronger and pushed myself carefully away from Erika. She was very weak. I had to find some way to for us to survive. I needed light. A slightly brighter patch in the surrounding blackness drew me and I crawled toward it stopping once to vomit. The faint glow came from a window that had been boarded over. I pulled myself up and tried to peer through one of the narrow cracks between the boards. I could see stone walls nearby and slices of purple mountains and green swaths in the distance.

I sank to my knees and crept back to Erika and was reaching down to check the sheath holding my dirk when a door opened. Light flared blindingly from a lantern. I jerked my hand back. Ranuff walked in. "Ah... Is it not touching? I have reunited the loving sisters," he sneered. "She is more stubborn than you, Elspeth. But now she is less than nothing, despite her precious *gift*. In the end it did not serve her. Is she dead yet?"

"Dear God, Ranuff. What have you done? Are you mad? She is ill, dying. You are killing her." I blinked, trying to see his face in the glare. The lantern's light reflected sunken eyes filled with incipient madness. His sartorial splendor had vanished beneath soil and sweat.

"Not I. She kills herself by choice. I have been more than patient. Kindness did not work. I loved her! Cared for her. I even let her have that bastard child and kept them both in comfort. Yet she refused to help me and was too stupid to understand and meet my needs. Now, I have you, and she no longer has value." He paused, then recalled himself, "There is no further time for pleasantries. I *must* have the MacLeod treasure at once! And she knows where it is. As do you and your aunts. It is rightfully mine. I am the true laird, not that weakling Norman. Everyone knows it...everyone! I will have my treasure, or you both will die."

I stared at him. His face wavered in the flickering illumination. I was yet affected by the potions he had given me and could not think clearly, so I tried bluffing to give myself a little time. I coughed and sniffled, then spoke, "Ranuff, there is *no* treasure. We may have believed it as children, but 'tis only a fable invented and embroidered to entertain. Surely you know that?"

"The fable is that Norman is laird. I am the true laird, the MacLeod of Talisker! With the treasure I will restore Dunvegan to its former place. I must have it and you will give it to me. I will take care of you, even marry you. We will rule together."

I stared at him. He was quite mad.

Ranuff hung the lamp on a hook by the wall, his nostrils twitching at the stench of the place. "We have bread, cold meats, and water, but since you chose to lie and defy me, I shall not reward you." He looked down at Erika who had not moved. "Elspeth, you claim to be a skilled physician. See if you can heal her!" His voice shook with rage. He laughed shrilly and left us, forgetting the lantern in his anger. There was the heavy rasping slide of the bar sealing us in, then silence.

I moved back to Erika. Her face was clearer in the glow from the lantern, dulled skin painted over elegant bones, and once-shining red-gold curls now faded to dry straw. I placed my hand on her flushed cheek. Her anxiety and pain had already begun to affect me, but I forced myself to ignore it. Pulling back her blanket, I began to examine her dispassionately. Her breath came in labored, uneven gasps. My hands read the downy hair and dry, cracked skin that came with starvation. Her wrist was as fragile as the bones of a wee bird, her pulse weak and erratic. I sat back to think. She needed warmth, water, and food. I pulled her into my arms, using my skirts to add a layer of warmth, feeding her my heat, holding, holding, blending. I should not have defied Ranuff. When he returned, I would take whatever was offered and do anything he demanded of me. Later I would kill him for this.

He was right. I could not save her. I lay holding Erika for hours. She was broken beyond repair. Tears spiked my lashes and dripped unheeded onto my cheeks. Why had I thought becoming a physician would serve anyone or anything? Nothing I had learned could save my sister without water and food. Death the final adversary and always the victor.

She stirred in my arms and spoke faintly. "El, I have a bairn, a lass. Find her...take her away from him. Save her. She will be the most important of our kind. He threatened to kill her...and claims he has assassins in place at the castle. To kill Aunt Mairi and...and others...if I tried to contact them... he will kill my babe. She saw him, she saw..." Her voice quivered then began again. "She lives because he needs our secrets. I refused. He would have killed us both after I did so. She is not Ranuff's child. I loved her father deeply, will love him into forever."

I touched her face gently. "Erika, I will tell him. Who is it?" My fingers traced her cheekbones, tight and sharp, pushing to erupt through her skin.

She coughed, the breath crackling in her lungs, then spoke again. "Her name is Solas. She will bring comfort to all she touches. Free her. She is everything to me. El...the stones. He wants them. Oh, my wee lass, my babe..." She was raving, her fading words meaningless. I could feel the pull of the darkness that had come for her.

I was weeping uncontrollably. Surely all this was madness. I wrapped her tightly in my arms and tried to empty my life into her. I prayed for her deliverance and asked the gods to take me in her stead. I no longer desired to live. I would not leave her again. A glow grew around us. Erika sighed and reached out to embrace it, a smile calming her face. I held her tightly, determined to follow wherever she led. But then I felt an angry wrenching jerk that cut the tie between us. I cried out in anguish, but she was gone.

* * *

Next morning, I was fully lucid. Sunlight cut through the narrow spaces between the warped boards of the window, laying thin golden stripes across the floor. I sat up. I could see more clearly now. We were in a cold, bare space with stained stone walls. It smelled of hay, human and animal waste, sickness, and something sweet. I looked down at the husk of my sister. She had left me behind, and lay motionless, mouth slightly open, eyes fixed and glassy. I sank down again and held her, weeping for all the things done and undone that death prompts us to remember.

When dry of feeling, I covered her dear face with the blanket and vowed

Ranuff would die by my own hand for this. The careful walls I had raised about myself had crumbled. They would not be rebuilt. The pain I was feeling was a welcome flog to stir my hatred.

There had to be a way out. I had promises to keep. The heavy wooden door was barred from without, and the withdrawn latch string made it impossible to open from within. The lone window offered another possibility, but I needed something to pry lose the wooden planks covering it. My *sgian-dubh* was still in the sheath on my calf. I removed it and tried to lever one of the boards. It did not move. Then I pounded and pulled with my hands. The only effect being the blood from my ripped fingertips darkening the wood. I sank to the floor, waiting for whatever was to come. Time telescoped; I heard the bar on the door lifting. Ranuff came in, looked at the covered body on the straw and shrugged. The hatred inside me writhed like a living thing. I detested him with all my being.

"It took longer than I thought. She was foolishly obstinate." He noticed my hands. "Poor, wee Elspeth. Does your witchcraft not work here?" His lips stretched over his teeth. "In this place I am the one with power. 'Tis simple. You will give me what Erika would not, or I will kill the child. No one can stop me...no one. I am the true laird."

"What child, Ranuff? You speak in riddles." I lowered my eyes so he could not see what was smouldering in them. "I know of no child nor of any treasure. What fantasy have you woven? Have you been partaking of the poppy?" He kicked at the pitiful bundle beside me. I sensed his insanity. My gift does not enable me to read minds, but I feel and share emotions with those around me if I do not shield myself constantly. My protection was gone, yes, but my gift was stirring. I focused my thoughts and tried to send a slender thread of fear and doubt toward Ranuff. He jerked as if burned.

"Are you sure there is no one with more power than you, Ranuff?" I asked quietly. He looked around wildly as though he were not certain where he was, lurched out of the room, and slammed the door. The iron bar crashed down.

* * *

It had been two days. I had nothing to eat or drink, but I was not hungry nor even thirsty. Ranuff had not returned. Erika's body had the faint, sweet odor of death. My long-buried senses were bare and raw. I had attempted to use them to tell Aunt Mairi that I was in the keep at Talisker but felt no connection. I was on the edge of sleep when I imagined Aunt Mairi standing over me. She reached down and touched my face, then turned and nodded to someone behind her. Only Gregor wore that blankness like a shield. I looked up into those obsidian eyes, felt an unexpectedly soothing and gentle touch, then my eyes closed, and I slept.

Ranuff came that evening, but he was not alone. Ysabell hesitated at the door. She glanced around the bleak room, inhaled the ripeness of the bundle that had been my sister, and backed away, avoiding my eyes. "I cannot do this, Ranuff," she choked out the words, turned, and vanished down the dark stairway.

"Go then," he said to her retreating back. "I can." He turned to me. "Have you decided to tell me where the treasure lies, or do you choose to extend your stay? I will be generous, Elspeth. Perhaps I will even let you have the child, although you may not want her after you see the deformity. What is that saying? Beware of what you wish for lest you get it?"

I flinched. He laughed, walked over to me, and backhanded me across my right cheek. I neither reacted nor spoke. Blood from my lip dripped on the dirty stones of the floor. I licked some from my lips silently, my eyes never leaving his face.

"Speak! I grow tired of this farce."

It was the last thing he said.

Strong fingers encircled his neck from behind, tightened and held him motionless until he ceased to move, then dropped him heedlessly to the floor. The hands belonged to Gregor. He knelt before me and used his thumb to gently wipe blood from my mouth before offering me a flask. I accepted it greedily, retaining enough common sense to sip sparingly of the ale it held, knowing full well I would vomit if I drank too much at once.

"How did you find us? And get inside?" My hands were shaking. He took the flask.

"Your Aunt Mairi showed me, a girl from Talisker came to her, and Sir Ross and I have been in Talisker many times, courtesy of the old laird, who used our services often." He looked around the noisome space. "We do not have much time, my lady. Are you able to walk? We must leave here at once."

"Not without the child...Solas. Do you know about the bairn? And... and Erika. Is Aunt Mairi here? I thought I was seeing things...dreaming or hallucinating. Ysabell. Was she here, too?" I was having trouble remembering, I was so tired.

Ranuff's body twitched, and I could hear faint breathing sounds. He was not dead! I wanted him dead! I struggled to move toward him, hands taloned in fury, but Gregor gripped my arm. "No. Not now. Save your strength. There is much else to do. We must find the child before he fully wakes. I promise you, my lady, I will see to your sister... and to him."

He was right. "Aye, I know you are right. I believe I can walk. My sister's bairn is far more important." He helped me to my feet, supporting me as we left the foul chamber. Gregor paused as we left to drop the heavy bar across the door. Ranuff could keep company with my sister this night. As we made our way down the staircase I wondered where Ysabell had gone. The passage at the bottom opened into another hallway and thence to Ranuff's library. It was a strange mix of luxury and decay. The walls were exquisitely paneled with richly carved but worm-eaten wood. Furniture covered with rich fabrics and soft rugs filled it.

A gnarled gray-haired man staggered into the room, laden with a load of peat. He dropped it in surprised confusion when he saw us and cowered back at the sight of Gregor. I knew him. Willis and his wife and daughter have served the MacLeods for longer than I can remember. His words tumbled out of his toothless mouth as he made haste to speak. "'Twas none of my doing, my lady. I be telling you plain enough. Me daughter be the one that took Lady Mairi a note. Come quick now. The wee one be below. Me wife and I cared for her as good as our own. Even do I be hung, 'tis happy I am you have come for her." He looked anxiously behind me for signs of Ranuff, then placed his hand over a wooden boss carved with twining leaves at the top of one of a set of matching columns decorating the sides of the fireplace. He twisted a concealed door in the elaborate paneling on the left to open. Motioning for us to follow him, he closed the panel and led us down a winding flight of stone steps to the old caverns concealed beneath the keep. He lifted a bar and opened a thick oaken door. It was a cell. The opulence of the furnishings could not conceal that. A small child of about four years sat quietly on a sheepskin rug in front of the stone hearth. Firelight licked along the curving strands of gold and red curls tumbling over her shoulders. I thought I had made no sound, but her head turned sharply toward me.

"Mother?" The purple blue of her eyes fixed on my face. It was a moment before I realized she was blind.

"No, I am your Aunt Elspeth…child." My voice floated lightly in the room, fading as I spoke.

"Oh," she said sadly. "Mother said you would come." Her eyes turned unerringly toward Gregor and the old man. "And Willis has brought you and another one." She turned back to me and held up her arms. "May I take my dolls?"

* * *

Willis did not lead us back through the castle to the entrance but down a hidden tunnel that exited on the stony beach, the entrance obscured by a tumble of rocks obscured with shrubs. Gregor picked up Solas and we began to walk. Willis stayed behind, carefully concealing the opening. Near the main entrance to the keep, two horses waited in a copse. Gregor seated me securely on one and placed the bairn on the saddle before me. She calmly let him wrap her in a plaid tucked trustingly into the shelter of my body. He handed me a flask of ale and some oat cakes and cautioned me to go slowly.

For several hours we followed a trail visible only to Gregor, then took the drove road north for a while before stopping to eat sparingly. I remember little of the trip back to Dunvegan except for trying to stay awake and holding Solas and listening to Gregor cajoling and urging us on, although I have no memory of his words. They were lost with the hours.

* * *

When we reached the steps leading to the sea gate at Dunvegan, welcoming torches were spilling light over a crowd from the village and castle. Many had been part of the frantic search for me, and several hands took the horse's reins and tried to help me dismount. I slid and fell stiffly off the horse into Cawdie's waiting arms. Janet embraced me next, reek and all, then took the child from Gregor, and sent others to prepare food and a bath. Cawdie made a strange guttural sound when I looked up at him, and he picked me up and held me closely. He nodded to Gregor and carried me up the steps to the bailey as though I were naught but a bairn.

Within the castle bailey, Sir Ross was waiting with several others. His mouth became a grim line when he saw my abused face, then softened as Janet brought up the bairn, her red-gold hair shimmering in the light of the torch flames. Malcolm and my father stood on the other side of Sir Ross, wearing masks of calm. Cawdie placed me on my feet in front of the laird and Aunt Mairi. To avoid soiling them with my filth, I bowed. "Thank you, my laird," I managed to say. He looked worn and pale but reached out to touch my bruised face.

Aunt Mairi noted the bundle in Janet's arms. "Welcome, child," she said.

"Her name is Solas," said I.

* * *

After I bathed and dressed in clean linen I slept, waking only to eat and drink. Janet sat close by, making certain I did both. She refused entrance to anyone but Aunt Mairi, Malcolm, and the laird. Janet said they would not leave on their journey till I was better. I asked her about Solas, and she said the lass was safe with Aunt Mairi and was wantonly stealing Cawdie's heart with her charm. The healing slumber I enjoyed those few days, I suspect was induced by one of Aunt Mairi's concoctions, and it did its work. One morning I awoke feeling myself again. Gregor was standing beside my bed looking down. My heart jumped. Evidently, I had recovered enough to be vainly horrified that he found me in a crumpled nightdress, my hair unbound.

He was unsmiling, darkness tangling his words. "I have come to tell you I have failed. I brought your sister back as promised and gave her into Lady Mairi's hands. She has been placed in the cairn with Lady Rhona until other arrangements can be made." He paused, a brief look of embarrassment crossing his otherwise passive face. "Forgive me, Lady Elspeth. Sir Ranuff has vanished. You are yet in danger."

Chapter 12: Malcolm

"Take off *all* my clothes?" Norman MacLeod of MacLeod, the Chieftain of Clan MacLeod and owner of everything that could be seen in all directions wore a puzzled expression on his face. It was our first day on the trip to the sacred spring and we had stopped at a small fresh-water loch to rest and water the livestock.

"Tradition calls for it," I bluffed. "One must not be a haughty pilgrim dressed in finery. It offends the gods."

He laughed, "You would have us in sack cloth and ashes, barefoot and flogging ourselves with willow switches?"

"Almost," I said in jest. "Come on. We must do this. Strip and bathe. Quickly now, before we freeze."

He must have thought I was mad but proved a good sport, and soon we were naked and up to our necks in water so cold that every appendage wanted to flee inward. My purpose was simple. I wanted him clean of any trace of poison—intended or otherwise—which he might have endured these past months. And to that end I wanted to be sure he was rid of his usual clothing. We scrubbed, shivered, and scrubbed again; hair included. I got out first and retrieved two sets of belted plaid from my pack. One I threw on the ground for him.

"Take your Lowlander clothes and put them in the saddle bag. These belted plaids will be used for the rest of the trip."

"Och, you mock with these rags. Methinks, you enjoy humiliating," he protested, but I could see by the look on his face that he was liking our lad's adventure, so far.

"I promise I will not flog you…provided you behave. But to be serious, 'tis safer not to look like a couple of fops out here."

"Indeed, Highland clothes are more practical for travel, too. I used to wear them when hunting with my father."

Elspeth had found us some well-used hunting tartans in muted shades of blue with yellow stripes. We quickly donned linen shirts then rolled into the plaid, adjusted it, cinched the belt, and pinned the upper part by the shoulder. Next came the wool socks and leather turn-shoes, and finally the leather sporran and generous wool bonnet. We turned to each other and grinned. We must have looked a sight in our matching garb.

* * *

Several hours before our bath and change of clothes, we left Dunvegan with as much pomp and ceremony as could be mustered in a small village. The whole community came to see us off, the piper piping, the men bowing as we passed, the women throwing kisses, the children frolicking. I felt like a conquering hero as I waved to everyone and threw some of Janet's sweets to the children, who had to fight off the chickens and dogs for them. The only ones not cheering were my friends, the ones who knew the truth. They stood by Mairi's cottage near the edge of the village, holding hands. I thought I could see a wee tear roll down Elspeth's cheek as we passed, or maybe it was the dust in her eyes. She had survived capture by that damned fool Ranuff, and it was difficult leaving her and the other women. But this had to be done. My eyes glistened as I waved them farewell. Moments later, we crossed a bridge and were alone and I prayed that all would be well till our return.

Cawdie had outfitted us well with two sturdy riding horses, mine with a milk cow tied behind. We had packs full of everything imaginable for a two-week trip, including plenty of black powder and shot, and the laird's special instrument wrapped in oilcloth. It would be a grand time provided we were not killed. The drove road would take us west, then south to Portree. From there we would follow the trail north along the east coast of the Trotternish peninsula to the village of Digg. Loch Siant and the sacred spring were nearby.

* * *

I admit with a twinge of guilt that I was relieved to be out of Dunvegan. Even for someone like me who should be used to it, disease and death lower the spirits immeasurably. So, it was a delight to be out in the fresh air, rocking gently on the back of a good horse and able to take in the sights without stress or fatigue. I suspect the laird was loving it too, because he unexpectedly became chattier, pointing out as we went what had happened where, the places he had fished, where so-and-so had died, that sort of thing. I listened and nodded and asked questions when I must. It was leisurely, partly because the cow could not be rushed and partly because it pleased us to make our way through the countryside at a slow enough pace to be able to savour every mile.

We stopped early that first evening and decided to camp on a dry pebble bed by a stream. Could be chancy should the heavens open and flood, but we decided the weather looked stable and we preferred dry pebbles to wet grass and moss. We had made only about six miles, but it had been a pleasant day free of rain and wind. In good spirits, we unsaddled and made camp. Norman started the fire with flint and steel and some dry kindling we brought, and there was plenty of deadwood about to feed it. Meanwhile, I took our iron pot and squatted beside the cow to relieve her of milk. This was my first time with her, so I was cautious, half-expecting Cawdie had provided an ornery one for my sins. But she was placid and cooperative, munching grass as I pulled on her teats. After I finished, Norman shouted that I must pour the first of the milk on the ground for the fairies. I did as he asked. No point angering fairies. I thought it a waste, but we had plenty, so it was a small sacrifice. And the needs of fairies reminded me of Fortuna. I looked at my hand and smiled because the ring was coated in milk. It seems she got her share too. Fairies and ancient gods placated; my stomach reminded me it was time to sup. Norman crumbled oatmeal cakes in the milk and heated the mixture over the fire as I erected the tent and made beds out of heather. Elspeth had even provided woolen blankets. We were in paradise!

Before bed, I reloaded my pistol with fresh powder and suggested Norman do the same with his musket. It looked quite safe out here but best to be prepared. Livestock watered, we settled in with weapons at our sides, our backs to the stream and horses guarding the approach. The cow we left on a long leash to graze as she wished. The clouds were high and thin and the wind lightly tickling the bushes. It would be a chilly night, but at least it was dry and free of midges, as good as it gets hereabouts.

"Do you remember when we met at Torrport last spring?" Norman asked once we'd settled.

"Aye, you were hard to miss with that entourage, and Elspeth quaking in her wee boots."

"Quaking?"

"Indeed. She had not seen you since she left for school in Italy. You were but a lad."

"I remember…she left suddenly back then. It was my elder brother's doing. He was chief and fond of Elspeth, but it was all too much for him to deal with. He died far too young. We miss him greatly. I had no wish to be chieftain, you know."

"I suspected as much. 'Tis not a light burden."

We lay there in silence for a time, watching the clouds turn from grey to the warm colours of sunset. The animals were quiet. It was that blessed time of day to rest. Norman turned his head and asked in a half-whisper, "Will I die of consumption soon?"

I had thought it strange at the time, those days ago in the castle when I gave him my diagnosis. Usually, the first thing they ask is how long they will live. But not him. He merely thanked me as though I had told him one of his poultry was ailing. Then we parted, leaving Elspeth and me wondering. I would not lie to him. He deserved the truth. "God willing, not soon," I replied.

"Years, or less?" he asked.

"A year or two, maybe more. It can go into remission with treatment."

"Can it be cured?"

"Rarely, but not impossible."

"Then I will plan on a year."

"That's prudent. And rejoice if God grants you more."

"Malcolm, thank you for being honest with me. I am grateful Elspeth returned and brought you."

I nodded silently, although in my heart I wished a different outcome for him.

"Our secret?" he whispered.

"Aye, but Elspeth and Mairi know."

"I trust them."

Now I understood why he waited till now to ask. Many believe illness is the result of weakness, and clansmen abhor weakness above all. Rumours already were circulating. He did not want them confirmed.

"Your family must be protected from those who wish them ill," I told him.

"I have plans. Keep me alive long enough to see them through."

"I'm sure your friends and supporters will help." It was an evasive answer, I know. I would do my best, of course. It was my duty as a physician. But I could not fully support his goals till I knew where he stood on the Jacobite question. I needed more time to sort that, for my father's sake and, in the end, for all Scots.

"I trust you are included among my friends," he said after reflection.

"Let's continue this trip together and see how many enemies we can kill."

I could sense him grinning.

* * *

It took three days to reach Portree, a village of a few hundred souls on the east coast of Skye with a fine harbour fringed by cliffs. The land was much too rough for farming, but the locals were thriving on fishing and trading. Portree was MacDonald country, and I was on edge as we descended into the village. Norman mocked my concerns. "The days of clan wars are long gone," he said. But I had more recent experiences with the MacDonalds and hoped my Highland tartan would prove adequate disguise.

The trip so far had been easy, and I noticed Norman's health and temperament much improved. Fresh air, exercise, and simple foods do wonders, what nature intended before mankind decided to improve on her wisdom. We stopped at MacNab's Inn. It was quiet, with few patrons. The woman who greeted us was shocked when Norman introduced himself. I was duly ignored when introduced, as she focused her fawning on him.

We unloaded the horses and found the stable out back. I watered and fed the animals while Norman carried our packs to our room, which turned out to be wonderfully comfortable, with a large four-poster bed, washstand, and two upholstered chairs by the single window. The wool-stuffed mattress felt like I was floating on a cloud compared with our prickly heather bed on the trail. *Feather better than heather*, I laughed to myself.

We selected a table in the tavern by the window overlooking the harbour which was scattered with wooden fishing boats undulating in the swell. All was good, and the ale and roast chicken with potatoes superlative, well at least for me. Poor Norman stuck with his bowl of oats and milk. I tried not to laugh.

"Where ye gents heading?" It was MacNab himself who made an appearance after hearing the great MacLeod of MacLeod had graced his establishment.

"Loch Siant," I said.

MacNab looked at me like I was speaking out of turn. "For the healing waters?" He was one of those rotund, florid types, who looked overly fond of his own drink.

"Aye. Join us for an ale?" I asked, refusing to be silent.

MacNab glanced at Norman for permission to sit. Norman nodded, then MacNab shouted for the woman to bring three ales. With a flourish he plopped his fat bum on the bench, too close to Norman, who in turn slid away enough to avoid having his privacy offended.

"We haven't had a MacLeod chieftain here in many a good year," MacNab said while running his fingers through his thinning grey hair and glancing across the room at the woman pouring the ale.

"Not since my father came to a wedding, I think," Norman offered. "And that was many years past."

"Before my time," MacNab nodded.

"Any troubles here recently?" I asked.

"Such as?" MacNab responded.

"Such as anything," I replied.

"The usual," MacNab said.

He was not being helpful, so I decided to be more direct. "Any other strangers stay here recently?"

"We don't want no trouble, sir. But a few of them…err, women were here a few days ago with a small man…a dwarf, I think, and a black dog."

"What kind of women?" I persisted.

MacNab looked at Norman, who told him with a stern tone, "Answer him."

MacNab flushed, then said, "They looked like them witches people talk about…older, oddly dressed But I don't know for certain."

I smiled. Gormal and Doideag. I was hoping they would show up.

"Are they still in the village?" I asked.

MacNab replied, "Don't think so, or folks would be gossiping."

"Good." I smiled at Norman, who was eyeing the buxom woman coming with the ale. He had not had an ale in weeks, and I approved of this little reward for steadfast adherence to his diet.

"Slainte!" Norman said loudly, and the three of us raised our mugs.

The ale was particularly good, but I needed more from the innkeeper. "Any reason we should worry about traveling in MacDonald lands?"

MacNab shook his head in mid-slurp, "Not since the clan war a hundred years ago."

"What was that about?" I asked. Of course, we had studied it in school, but I wanted to hear the local version.

"They insulted our chief's sister," Norman said.

"How so?" I asked.

Norman told the story. It started with a feud over land, since the two clans were uneasy neighbours on Skye. To end the feud, Rory Mor MacLeod, who was chieftain, offered his sister Margaret in marriage to Donald Gorm Mor MacDonald, Chieftain of Clan MacDonald. Problem was that as the years passed, Margaret had no children and had lost sight in one eye. Her husband Donald was not pleased and sent her back to Dunvegan riding backward on a one-eyed horse, accompanied by a one-eyed dog and a one-eyed servant. It was intended to be a humiliating insult and begged retribution. Rory Mor MacLeod was forced to declare war on Clan MacDonald. Who could blame him?

"War seldom ends well," said I. "And how *did* it end?"

"With our victories at Carinish and Coire na Creiche," MacNab interjected. "Many here still celebrate those times."

"Hardly!" Norman blurted with surprising passion. "You won at Carinish only because your devious Clan Ranald men led our brave warriors into ambush on the holy ground of a kirk, of all places."

MacNab cringed and I could see a droplet of sweat form on his temple. I was wondering if I should intervene when Norman added, "And the last battle lost because our leaders were away when the MacDonalds attacked. They knew it to be so. 'Twas shameful!"

Norman was almost shouting, so I put my hand on his arm. "Steady now," I whispered.

He leaned closer to me and said, "The MacDonalds are known for their treachery."

"Shush! Not here, Norman," I cautioned. Fortunately, there were few others in the tavern, and they were engrossed in their own heated debates.

Norman raised his voice in defiance. "As we learned in school, there was no victor in that war. The Privy Council intervened and, thankfully, there has been peace since."

Norman glared at us and was about to say more when MacNab announced, "To peace!" and raised his mug in toast. I smiled and joined him. Norman, still livid, did so as well.

I thanked our host for the excellent food and drink, paid him, then suggested to Norman that we had enough fun for one evening. We all laughed while realizing that beneath the oil of peace that calmed these Highland waters was a deep well of grievance and distrust, and all it would take was one unfortunate stirring to bring it to the surface.

MacNab rubbed his grizzled chin. "Ye would be wise to stay with us a while."

I did not understand his meaning. "Your hospitality is appreciated but we'll be on our way in the morning, provided the weather is suitable."

MacNab just shook his head and looked at us both. "'Tis All Hallows Eve tomorrow. Best to stay with us and enjoy the festivities."

Norman had a look of surprise on his face and was about to say something, but I cut in, "We're not afraid of ghosts or fairies if that is your meaning. And we don't wish to have this rare period of pleasant weather wasted on merriment."

Norman mumbled something in Gaelic, then nodded in agreement. MacNab shrugged and made a face as though to imply we were about to make a grave mistake. But we had found out enough to know we must remain on guard till we returned to MacLeod lands. My not-so-subtle invitation had been broadcast at Dunvegan, and we would soon discover who had come to our party at the sacred spring. And we could not depend on the locals for defence. We were on our own, as expected.

* * *

MacNab told us to follow the trail north to Digg, about ten miles up the coast. We wanted to push hard to get there before by dusk, and because of that we left the cow at Portree, tended by a wee boy recommended by MacNab—one of his relatives, no doubt. Leaving her made it a one-day trip instead of two. The trade-off was no milk for Norman. He did not seem to mind after having his fill of ale the previous evening.

It was easy travel like that of the previous days, mostly across a scattering of meadows and crofts and fast-running streams flowing to the sea. Along the way, Norman recounted some of the local lore about All Hallows Eve. It was amusing to hear his stories of mischievous fairies and long-dead souls coming out of graves to walk among the living. He clearly was a believer and told me that his old nursemaid would be horrified knowing he was disrespecting the spirits on such a day. I responded by saying that we were not disrespecting anything or anyone and that I hoped we could have a friendly meeting at the sacred spring with some witches—to resolve our differences. Failing that there could be a more forceful solution. I said that last bit while patting the package tied behind me. And by the resolute look on of his face, he was relishing the prospect of what was to come as much as I.

* * *

The views near the village of Digg were splendid, the sea on one side and grasslands rising to rugged mountains on the other. An ancient crofter we encountered grunted and pointed further north when asked directions to Loch Siant. It turned out to be only a half mile from Digg, seaward off the trail.

We dismounted and descended the trail to the small loch. It was unremarkable, just another fresh-water loch among hundreds on Skye. On the west side was a steep slope covered in a thicket of hazel. The seaward side was meadowland which undulated down to a stony beach. But it was the water of the loch itself that was unusual. In the light of early evening, it seemed to glow an eerie colour that reminded me of luminescent blue moonstone. Perhaps that was its attraction. But it was too late to explore, so we decided to camp beside the trail on the southern end of the loch.

* * *

They came after dark. A gibbous moon lit the still night. We had carefully placed our camp in plain view, horses tied a few yards away on the side with the overgrown slope and left saddled to allow easy escape should our guests arrive in force. Our campfire had burned to embers, a lingering drift of smoke rising straight into crisp air. There was enough moonlight to see into our two-man ridge tent to descry the lumps we had made to look like sleeping bodies. Meanwhile we crouched on the other side of the horses, hidden in the shrubs, fully armed and wrapped toe to nose in wool plaid. We watched and waited. I had set some simple trip-ropes on both approaches to the campsite, more to alert than harm. It was one of those that rattled first, and then we heard a muttered curse which sounded like a male voice.

"Ready?" I whispered, nudging Norman. He nodded imperceptibly. I gripped my pistol, breath held, body coiled to pounce. But nothing further happened till minutes later when I felt a light touch on my shoulder. I turned my head and saw beside me the almost formless grandmotherly face of a woman, hooded, with strands of blond hair escaping. It was Gormal, the healer from Broadford who had poisoned me those weeks ago. I flinched on seeing her.

"Are you expecting trouble?" she whispered.

I glanced to the other side, to Norman. He was staring ahead into the dark. I thought I could see a dark shape rising behind him. I leapt up and vaulted out of the bushes, grabbing Norman by the arm on the way, making him tumble face-first into the grass. I turned and knelt in firing position, both hands steadying my pistol, checking the bushes from whence we had come. Norman had dropped his musket and was scrambling to right himself and draw his sword. "Come out of there!" I shouted into the shrubs. There was silence. I glanced at the nearby horses. They were alert and watching, showing no telltales of fear.

"Come out or I will fire," I repeated, the continuing silence making me distrust what I had seen. I held my breath and listened. I heard Norman stifle a cough. I heard one of the horses shift a hoof. I heard a crackle from the remains of the campfire.

"You would not shoot an old woman, would you?" her whisper loud as a shout. My head swivelled so fast my neck spasmed, and there she was again, so close I could smell her.

"Damn you, Gormal. Cease these silly tricks!" I reached behind and grabbed her cloak, pulling her closer and shoving the dangerous end of my pistol under her chin.

"Malcolm?" It was Norman, his voice oddly pleading.

Holding Gormal firmly, I looked back to see a dark-hooded shape holding a musket to Norman's head. "Checkmate," said she, flipping her hood back to reveal the face of Doideag, her wild hair glowing hot bronze by the moonlight.

"Hang on to your damned weapon next time," I said to Norman in frustration. That was unfair, I know. It was I who had planned this, I who had not expected an attack from behind. I was more to blame than he.

"Put down your weapon, Doideag. You're no match for me and you know it," I bluffed.

"I know Captain Forrester," Doideag said. "We request a friendly meeting, and that you will not harm us. We are merely village healers who have come to serve the laird."

I watched her cautiously for a few moments. I could see the muzzle of the heavy musket sinking gradually as it often does when held by a small woman. I had a choice. Stall, and wait for a chance to overcome her when the musket muzzle had sunk low enough to be off-target or agree to her request. I looked at Norman. He seemed neither afraid nor readying himself to attack. It was up to me. "A truce it is, then," I said. "We will parley, and I will not harm either of you...this time, provided you agree to the same."

I heard Gormal exhale and felt a slight shiver course through her body. "Agreed," they both said in uncanny unison. I smiled reassuringly, but in the back of my mind, I knew we had forgotten someone—that male voice we heard and the report from MacNab of a male dwarf. Must be the same one Doideag had with her on the drove road near Kylerhea. I knew he must be out there, perhaps armed, and with the dog. He was their protection, as the laird's package was for us. I had assembled and loaded it in the dark and placed it between the lumps that were our fake bodies in the tent. I did not know where the dwarf was hiding. But talking is better than fighting, so I decided to give them a chance and invited them to join us for polite conversation around the fire.

I made sure to sit first, my back concealing the tent opening. I pulled Norman down beside me and whispered that he must not let them touch him, nor should he eat or drink anything they offered. The women sat opposite. Norman added wood to the fire and placed a pot of water on, ever the good host. In the light of the reinvigorated fire, we four must have looked a sociable lot, but for the silence that held.

It was Norman who spoke first. "You have my assurance that our village healers will be protected from harm or prosecution, within the law, of course."

I was readying myself for a lecture when Doideag spoke up. "That is precisely the problem…the law," said she.

"The law?" Norman asked.

"The law that allows innocent women and even some men to be persecuted for helping others."

"May I remind you that many have committed evil deeds and confessed to them?" Norman objected.

"Indeed, that is irrefutable. Some of those poor souls undoubtedly have been deluded and others have confessed under torture," Doideag said.

"Torture is an accepted method. It is accepted—" Norman argued.

"Well, I suggest you let me torture you and we will see if it is only truth you tell," Doideag said. Gormal snickered.

"Nonetheless, these people have evoked magical and demonic powers forbidden in our lands," Norman said with a tone of assurance.

I was listening to this exchange carefully, glad to see him standing up to these hags, notwithstanding their wiles. My mind was on our surroundings, too. There was a dwarf out there, perhaps with evil intent, and I did not want the distraction of conversation to give him advantage.

"I can assure you, Laird MacLeod, that no one who has been put to death on charges of witchcraft possessed any magical or demonic powers whatsoever." With that provocative statement, Doideag sat back smiling.

The two women functioned as twins of benevolence; but I knew otherwise. I waited for Doideag's cunning logic to complete.

"That is impossible. It has been proven!" Norman blustered.

"With respect, 'tis not impossible. Consider this: If you possessed such powers and found yourself one day facing prosecution or death, would you not use those powers to force your persecutors to desist, or failing that, use your powers to escape? I submit to you that preservation of self is the prime use of true power...otherwise the rest is for naught."

I laughed aloud. "You are far too clever for us, Doideag. But take this *logic* to its conclusion. You stated that all who have been charged, convicted, and executed for witchcraft have been innocent." I looked at them and they nodded cautiously. "I'm glad we agree on this point." I turned to Norman and could see he was about to object, so I held up my hand. "Wait, there is the promised logical conclusion." I paused a few seconds. "And what of those who have been charged with witchcraft and *not* convicted or executed? Do you agree that those must the *true* witches, able to use their powers to evade justice?" It was my turn to be smug.

Doideag and Gormal chuckled. Norman looked confused. I whispered to him, "Elspeth is *not* a black witch. This is but wordplay." Then I said to them, "Now that we have proven that if you say you are a witch, you are not, tell us why you wanted to meet tonight?" It was time to get down to business.

Gormal largely had been silent through this, so I was surprised when she took over from Doideag, addressing Norman with her disarmingly feminine voice—a voice that I had learned from experience to distrust. "We are here representing the poor. As you know, there are several healers on Skye and the islands. We see the people—your people—suffering."

"We help those in need," Norman interjected.

"Aye, when you can, but needs far outstrip your generosity."

"In fact," Norman continued, "we sent assistance to Drynoch but weeks ago." He was beginning to sound defensive, and that was not a good tactic with these clever women.

I touched his arm and whispered, "Steady."

"We thank you for your charity, but 'tis not what the people need," Doideag added.

"Go ahead and tell us what you imagine the people need, then." I was being a bit sarcastic, but these two were getting on my nerves.

"They *don't* need handouts from the rich. They need justice," Gormal shot back.

"The crofters are doing much better," Norman said, beginning to put his case forward. "The famine is over and the cattle stocks back to normal. We collect rents, but those rents are put to beneficial use, including to support those in need...like widows, orphans, the sick and infirm. This is not charity, but their due, as is the requirement to pay fair rents to support our way of life." Norman had stated his case well and succinctly.

I was impressed, but the women snickered, and I could hear Gormal whisper to Doideag that it was the laird's way of life that was supported, not the poor. Norman heard her too, and angrily responded, "I invite you to Dunvegan, where you can witness our lavish life first-hand."

The women nodded and smiled as though they may well visit.

"To the point, you two," said I. "My patience is waning, and I'm certain you have not come here to discuss clan economics."

"But good sir, it is why we have come...to enlist the support of this young laird who could do so much good...for the clan and for himself," Gormal said.

"Get on with it, then. What do you want?" I asked.

Norman raised his hand, index finger pointed to the heavens. "Malcolm, please, we agreed to hear them out. I am always open to suggestions if they are of benefit to our clan. What is it you offer?"

I bit my tongue.

"Only wise counsel, dear laird. Nothing more." Doideag smiled warmly.

Soon we will be singing around the fire, I thought, sarcastically.

But Norman said, "I accept your wise counsel gratefully."

I was not sure if he were a complete fool or much cleverer than I had assumed. I waited for the probabilities to sort.

Gormal started first and told us that it was well known that there was a vast treasure hoard owned by the clan, and that should the treasure be shared equitably, there would be no poverty, and everyone would live in health and ease.

I smiled. Of course. This was all about that damned treasure.

Doideag took over and explained that they could help locate the treasure, before "others" with less altruistic motives got to it first, thus vouchsafing it for posterity. They made it sound like the right and honourable thing to do. After all, most of us who knew of a way to alleviate suffering would do so. They were convincing, but not quite.

I glanced at Norman, and uncharacteristically, he seemed about to explode in laughter. Instead, he coughed and spit phlegm into the fire before speaking. "Logic is only as valid as the basic assumptions on which it relies," Norman said while chuckling. "I learned that at college."

The women stared at him in silence.

"And if the basic assumptions are false?" I asked, thinking I knew where he was going with his argument, since I, too, had attended those philosophy classes long ago in Edinburgh.

"Indeed, Malcom. You assume there is a treasure to distribute," he said to the women. "What if there is not?"

"But...we...we know!" Doideag said.

"Do you think the clan is populated by saints? Think on it. Would my ancestors have let Dunvegan Castle sink to ruin had they access to vast treasure? Surely not! Your basic assumption that a spendable treasure exists, surely is false, is it not?"

"Perhaps just lost—" Gormal offered weakly, but I could see her posture sag on hearing the laird's logical refutation.

"Not lost," he replied. "Do you not think we know of these things? How arrogant to assume you can help find what is *not* lost."

I was becoming evermore impressed with this young laird. He was no fool. "You've received your clear answer," I said. "If you've nothing further—"

"We know of your sickness, young sir," Doideag interrupted.

Norman shrugged, "Many know, and I am receiving the best of care."

Gormal smiled. "But not a cure."

"Perhaps not. One can only hope and trust God," Norman replied.

"*We* can cure you," Doideag said decisively, "and not with a ridiculous Brightstone."

"Nonsense!" I cried.

"Is it? Have you proof we cannot?" Doideag replied.

"The burden of proof is on those making unsupported claims," I responded, wishing to end this discussion.

"We only offer to serve the good laird and clan. If our efforts come to naught, what is the harm in trying?" Gormal said.

"I can think of much harm. If you do have a cure for consumption, then let us see it. Find a sick wretch and show us. But I will not let you work your spells on the laird and his family," I said.

The women laughed, then Gormal leaned closer and said venomously, "But we heard you enjoyed experimenting on people, Malcolm." It was a well-deserved dig.

"I assure you that I, myself, was among the first to endure those smallpox treatments. Perhaps Doideag can use you, Gormal, in demonstration of her cure?" I sliced back.

"We often use each other so, for the benefit of others. You play the hero because you have done it once. You are but a neophyte in these matters," Gormal countered.

"This be profitless debate," Norman interrupted. "My health is improving, and I have made it clear as tonight's moon that there is no treasure of use to be had. It is time to end this parley before we are provoked to withdraw our offer of truce."

"The gods forbid that the Macleod of MacLeod and the great Captain Forrester suffer provocation from old women," Doideag mocked.

"You continue to taunt, Doideag. Your tongue will be your undoing. And as for you, dear Gormal, how did you manage to sneak up on us tonight?" I asked.

She looked at her compatriot and grinned, then explained, "'Twas nothing. We arrived before you. The villagers at Portree told you we had passed through, did they not? You were foolish not to expect we would be here. We waited and watched as you set those childish traps, and when darkness fell, we tripped one to distract, while our little friend crept close."

"We see what we expect and ignore the rest," I mused. "Clever of you. And the face I saw was not yours, but the dwarf's, hooded and wigged."

"His face is round, like mine, and in the dark—" Gormal added.

"Your dwarf is out there yet?" Norman asked.

"I am sorry to say he is, and he has a wee pistol pointed at Captain Forrester's dark heart as we speak," Doideag responded.

"Of course, he is your protector," I said to Doideag.

"As Fortuna is for you, our lucky dwarf is for us," replied Doideag with a nod.

"'Tis not Fortuna who protects me, but I her." I had had enough of these manipulating women and leaned away from Norman to reveal what was behind me: the cruel steel maw of a blunderbuss pointed directly at them. "Only a fool would bring a wee pistol up against a blunderbuss." I waited for the shock and protestations of innocence to subside, then ordered the dwarf to come out of the shrubs. He did indeed have a wee pistol, one of those that women carry. Still, it could have done me damage at this range. I was angry and pointed my finger at Gormal while the dwarf and dog settled cautiously beside them. "Gormal, I want you to remember this well. Tonight, I have spared your life a second time. There won't be a third."

Gormal said nothing, but her pale face twitched. But Doideag was defiant. "We have done nothing but assure our own protection. Can you blame us, considering? Behold that hideous weapon. Would you use it on innocent women who only wish the good health and prosperity of the laird and his family?"

"You are far from innocent, the pair of you. Now be off before Captain Forrester reappears," I threatened. It was done, and I wanted them gone before their deceitful words infected the laird's vulnerable ears.

* * *

Dawn broke frost rimed. It had been a frigid night and we had let the fire go out to lessen the light. We had little sleep, shivering and alternating watches. Norman retrieved a pot of water as I restarted the fire. We sat waiting for the water to boil. "'Tis All Saints' Day," Norman muttered, rubbing his tired eyes.

"A good day for healing, I would say."

"An interesting All Hallows Eve. At least we had some hags and a dwarf appear," Norman mused.

"Don't forget the black dog. God knows who he really was."

"I think a dog…and black."

"I suspect you're right, and the hags were more lawyer hags than the magical version," I quipped.

"Aye, but we need to be careful of them. They are on the scent of gold and will not be deterred easily. I am not as ignorant a fool as some may think. Mairi has kept me apprised, but my hands are tied until they break the law, and as you witnessed last evening, they cloak their desires in the garb of helpfulness."

"Still…you and your family are exposed. I noticed your unusual symptoms have abated since we left Dunvegan. You know what that could mean."

"I have noticed it as well," he nodded. "But many things have changed. My diet, clothing, exercise, our good Highland air—"

"Or you could've been poisoned."

"I know, Malcolm, but who of my kin and friends would do such a thing?"

"Gold and power corrupt the best of us. And surely you know who in your family are tempted."

"There is little gold and less real power. 'Tis more a burden than a blessing. And as for my family, there are a foolish few who aspire. I am not deaf to rumours."

"Then there is the treasure."

Norman looked at me and smiled, his blue eyes sincere. "I told them the truth last night. There be nay treasure…as they assume. At least that is what I know of it."

"Mairi and Elspeth seem to think there is."

"Parse my words carefully, Malcolm."

I thought back to what he had said. He had told the hags that there was no treasure to distribute and none to spend, and just now he had not denied the existence of a treasure, just one as they assume. But what if there was another kind of treasure? One of value, but one that could not be spent. I thought a minute then asked, "Do you know where this treasure that cannot be spent is located?"

"Nay."

"Is there a way to find this treasure, should you so desire?"

"My brother said as much. Mairi, the chief healer, is the keeper of the signs, but I have never asked."

"There may be others looking for it, perhaps those close to you in the castle. And we know not whether they are collaborating with Gormal and Doideag. Do you know what this so-called treasure is?"

"Not exactly."

I could sense he was reluctant to discuss it further, so I ended by saying, "If there is a treasure, it could be under threat of discovery. There are several who know of it, and they will not be put off by your assertions that it is not spendable. Most everything has a value. We need to get back to Dunvegan as soon as possible and speak with Mairi."

Norman sighed, "Just when I was beginning to enjoy this." We both laughed aloud. "At least we managed to avoid bloodshed," he added.

"I rarely bite, Norman. Early on I discovered that bite leads to bite back, and sometimes the other dog has bigger teeth."

"When you showed the gun to them, I had visions of being known as the chieftain who slaughtered old women with a blunderbuss."

"That would be a unique epithet," I replied, and we laughed again. But then a harsh voice entered my mind, that of Captain Forrester, telling me I was weak and may have missed my chance with those devious witches, reminding me of my goal. *But we had a truce, and they are women!* I argued in defence, then cursed him and sent his voice away.

The water was simmering, and I crumbled in some oat cakes and gave a stir with my dagger. Norman found our spoons and clean bowls, and we quickly had our fill. We had one task yet to accomplish before departing, that of locating the sacred spring and availing ourselves of its fabled healing waters.

* * *

"'Tis here!" Norman shouted.

I brought our freshly cleaned cooking pot and the Brightstone. Norman had walked clockwise around the loch, and I the opposite way, looking for the spring. It was small and trickled from rocks on the steep part of the hazel copse. The spring flowed into a pool that in turn emptied into the loch.

Our instructions from Mairi were concise: Norman was to place the Brightstone in a pot of sacred spring water, say some words beseeching the gods to heal him, then drink his fill. Then he was to circumambulate the loch three times sun wise, and finally tie some strips of cloth on a nearby hazel bush. To honour Mairi, I think, more than the old gods, we did this faithfully, laughing through it all as it seemed so silly. The most difficult part was the circumambulation. It was a scramble through muck and over slippery moss-laden rocks, and by the end we were a muddy mess. Mairi also had warned we must not cut any trees or take any fish from the loch. Also, we decided that washing our filthy clothes there might bring offense, so we quickly de-camped and made off, looking like a couple of disreputable beggars.

We made our way back to Portree, stopping but once to clean ourselves and water the horses. There had been no sign of our haggish friends, strange considering we had horses and they did not, but perhaps they had taken another route to avoid being overtaken. We arrived back at Portree by nightfall, eager for proper food and a soft bed. The innkeeper was attentive as the MacLeod delighted us with a tale of bravery in the face of insurmountable odds. He did not exaggerate too much and had us splitting our sides in mirth as he described the look on the hags' faces when they found themselves staring down the barrel of that ugly blunderbuss.

"'Twas a foolish thing," MacNab opined. "Ye were lucky 'twas sacred ground or the fairies would've made mischief and the hags had their way with ye."

"But they didn't, and we paid proper respect to the old ways, didn't we, Norman?"

"We did, including drinking of the spring and saying prayers. I feel much better already," Norman said with a wink.

"It may have more to do with a belly full of oats and milk," I teased, for while he supped on that meagre fare, I gorged myself on feather fowlie soup, mutton pie, and crofter's plum pudding.

We intended to leave early and make haste to Dunvegan, and to that end we decided to give away our cow to the boy tending her. It would save a day or two in travel time. Norman would have to make-do with oats and water. He was reassuringly forbearing and as keen to be home as me.

* * *

We had just crossed a shallow river called Snizort, several miles from Portree, when first we spotted them—several riders a mile or so behind us, gradually closing. We stopped. Norman retrieved his spyglass.

"Looks like...hmm...nine of them, Highlanders...dark red plaids, likely MacDonalds."

Damn, I thought.

"The one in the lead is side-saddle," he added. "Must be a woman."

"Could be my friends from Sleat," said I, remembering the wreckers who had tried to kill us.

"Did you not say you killed one of them?"

"I did. Rory, his name was, the creature dressed in seal skins."

"If it is that lot, they may want revenge."

"Their blood has cooled, surely."

"Not them. The MacDonalds never let it go."

"My luck, then, but they started it." I stared down the road. We had a choice: ride hard for Dunvegan or stand and fight.

"I know what you're thinking, Malcolm, but I'll not run from a MacDonald."

"'Tis many more than one."

"Nevertheless, if we flee, I am no longer worthy. And besides, I know these horses—dependable and sure-footed, but too slow for rapid escape."

"If we stand and fight, we could die."

"Rather that than dying in bed of consumption."

I knew by the grim look on his face that the matter was settled, and with or without me, he would stay and fight to preserve his honour. I hoped it would not come to that, but we were exposed, the rocky land open and dressed simply in late fall colours. There was nowhere to hide here at Loch Snizort Beag, edged with willows and sea grass on one side, and rising low hills on the other. "We don't know yet who they are nor their intent, if any. Let's find a defensible position off the drove road and hope they pass without incident."

We kicked our horses to a gallop. Half a mile further we found a steep-sided glen with a shallow rocky stream and a tumble of boulders along both sides. For a place to fight, it was favourable. We wanted them forced to bunch together on attack, so we could cut them to shreds with the blunderbuss. That was the plan, anyway. But plans often fail, and by the look of this glen, they could send men up and around and attack us from behind and from both sides. It was a gamble, but we needed a quick victory, not a siege.

We tied our horses, so they would be protected behind us, then selected the best cover behind some boulders with our backs to the glen wall. Next, we unloaded the weapons and ample powder and shot. I assembled the blunderbuss and leaned it behind the boulders. It would be our answer, should words fail.

"Where did you find this thing?" I asked, while loading the blunderbuss with a handful of lead shot.

"A gift from the tsar last spring in Torrport. He did not come empty-handed. Remember Aiden the blacksmith? He was making a new gun for the tsar. But I rather like this one...makes a lot of noise, if nothing else."

"Cawdie and I tried it," I said. "It makes more than noise. Devastating at close range, and it can use pebbles as shot when lead is not available."

"But if they charge, we get but one shot before they are on us."

"Then let's pray it's enough."

* * *

The wait was long, and we were hopeful they had passed us by. It was before noon, and we could yet make many miles on our trip home. I was about to suggest that I make a foray to the glen mouth for a look, when there he was, crouching and scrambling from rock to rock, trying to stay hidden, a MacDonald in muted red tartan carrying a musket. He must have seen us when we saw him because he gave a loud "Whoop!" I nudged Norman. He had seen the man, too, and was cocking his musket.

"Let me do the talking this time, Malcolm," he whispered.

"Agreed, but if we spot them trying to get behind us—"

"Then we go down fighting."

"Not exactly what I was thinking. We retreat up the glen. Leave the horses. Maybe that'll be enough."

"Or we go down fighting," Norman said again. He certainly was stubborn, but then I had not been offered the death sentence that was consumption.

"Or we go down fighting," I agreed. We grinned at each other. Was it amusing or perhaps just the prospect of death? I have thought of that moment many times since, and I suspect, like Norman, I too wanted an honourable death with a sword in my hand. It was the wish most men share, along with the love of a good woman.

'Twas not long before the rest of the MacDonalds arrived. Some had muskets, a few pistols, and all wearing sword-steel. "We wish you no ill, Laird Macleod." It was a woman's voice.

"Then be on your way!" Norman shouted back.

I readied the blunderbuss to lift into position.

"'Tis that damned Lowlander we want," she replied. "We offer ye safe passage."

"This damned Lowlander is under my protection. You'll not take him without me," Norman responded. I could hear them muttering as though debating the issue. Norman spoke again, a hint of frustration seeping into his voice: "My mother is a MacDonald. We are kin, for God's sake. Leave this to me and I promise to pay the blood-wite."

"We seek not gold. 'Tis blood for blood we want. Rory was my youngest and dearest. I shall have the young Forrester in recompense," she cried.

I whispered to Norman, "Take the offer. Save yourself. I'll fight it out with them, end it where it began."

"Never!" Norman growled at me. "The MacLeod *never* surrenders."

While we were speaking, I noticed two MacDonald men pull back from the group and thought I glimpsed one starting up the glen side. I curse found my breath. "While we chat politely, they plot. If we are to fight, it must be now."

Norman gave me a steely-eyed nod. "Come get us, Lady MacDonald, if you are brave enough!" he shouted.

"A debt will be paid this day," she shouted back.

Then there was that ominous quiet before battle. The clouds had lowered and darkened, threatening rain. It would be grim business, but better done now than let them get behind us.

The first shot was from them, not even close. Perhaps a distraction. "They'll soon be ready," I muttered.

"Aye, 'tis time," Norman answered. Then inexplicably, he rose, dropped his musket to the side and said calmly, "Cover me, if you will, good sir." He unsheathed his ceremonial claymore and with a mighty war cry vaulted over the boulder and ran headlong at the MacDonalds.

Oh, for God's sake! I thought. *That fool is going to get himself killed.* What else could I do but follow? I got off a shot with his musket. That made the MacDonalds duck while he splashed his way across the stream. From the other side of the water the MacDonalds fired a volley and missed. Nerves at the start of battle make even the best men shoot wild. That is one reason battles are unpredictable—we have our plans and then there is fate and fortune.

The MacLeod bellowed and pressed his advantage. While he distracted them, I took the flank, hoisting the ten-pound blunderbuss and sprinting crabwise along the side of the glen. Another volley came, some balls in my direction this time. They had seen me. Norman drove at them, flinching back just before he was on them. I wished him well, but I had my own work to do. I ran into the stream and knelt, raising the fearsome weapon to my shoulder. Norman was swinging his claymore in powerful sweeps, grunting, and growling with each. The MacDonalds were panicking, trying to reload or draw steel before he hacked them down. Shouts and cries filled my ears. Norman was fending off several, with the woman behind them screaming obscenities.

I aimed, careful not to hit Norman. There was a group on my side, furthest from him. One turned when he saw the muzzle locked on him. But it was too late. I caught him face-on and two of his countrymen on their sides. The recoil was powerful, felt like it tore my shoulder. I steadied and rose, my vision blurred and ears ringing. Amid the smoke I saw Norman pressing forward again, in a bloody rage. Men writhed at his feet, cut open and dying. I dropped the blunderbuss on the streambank, drew my cutlass and dagger, then yelled and charged their flank. I hit them hard, slashing and gouging in steel flurry. Bloody-minded wrath filled my soul. I killed repeatedly. There was shouting. Men fled.

We finished off the MacDonalds in minutes, all but the woman. I found her behind a boulder fumbling to load a pistol, swearing in Gaelic. She raised the pistol, her aged face filled with feral fury. I swore and punched her hard on the temple with my cutlass guard. Norman was nearby, standing stock-still, his claymore imbedded in a flinching corpse. He coughed and spat blood.

It was over, for now, but the Devil's poison that makes us kill coursed in my veins, and I knelt beside the unconscious woman, my body shaking, and I wept, not tears of grief, but of exultation. I had killed and loved it. *God forgive me, I am evil!*

I heard a faint moan, then saw a slight movement on the ground. He was close. I crawled over blood-slick rocks. He was one I had shot, and yet alive. My training thankfully over-rode the Devil's malicious drug. I rolled him over. The side of his head was gone, his brains a mass of pulp. I rolled his head back to hide the sight of it. His seeing eye opened. He blinked and must have seen me because he moaned again. I knew what must be done. I found his sword and placed it in his hand. He gripped it tightly. I turned his head to the side, to expose his jugular. "To Valhalla, arsehole," I whispered as my dagger sliced clean.

I slumped beside him, watching his life-blood flow to ground. I felt empty. The Malcolm I knew and respected was gone, replaced by a Devil's intern. I felt sick in my gut, soul poisoned. "Are you all right, brother?" It was Norman hovering close, a hellish ghoul made real.

I turned my head to see him better as he collapsed.

* * *

Norman had been shot in the upper chest and had many small wounds on arms and hands. As for me, Fortuna had been kind and I had little but bruises and a damaged conscience for my sins. The young laird was much worse off. I had opened his shirt and stopped the bleeding, cutting up my shirt to use as packing and bandages. It was the bullet wound that worried me. It had not penetrated the lung—there was no pink frothing to indicate. But the bleeding had been copious, and it took a while for it to clot while I pressed my shirt on it with both hands.

"Trying to kill yourself, were you?" I asked, trying to make him laugh.

"Almost worked," he chuckled, then winced.

"Next time let's try retreating when faced with overwhelming odds."

"I am sorry, Malcolm. Did you not enjoy the entertainment?"

That stopped me. It was man's shared guilt. He knew it. I knew it. Man, like few other predators, loves to kill for sport. It is thrilling, and I think innate. "Perhaps some wine and women instead, shall we?" I responded to change the topic.

"Och, I cannot. My darling Anne would not approve, and she hates me drinking, too."

"Must be something she favours?"

"Children and reading the Bible."

"A good woman."

"She is." He hawked up some blood.

He seemed in better spirits now, despite the pain. The wound was staunched, but I needed to find my medical kit to get that bullet out before we left.

"Stay here. I'll get the horses," I stood up.

"I won't move."

He looked a mess lying there, his white linen shirt stained red, his tartan mottled with mud and blood. Yet he was alive. A chill gust caught me off-guard, reminding me I was shirtless. I looked up the glen. No horses. *Perhaps they've been spooked,* I thought. I walked back to where we had tied them. There were hoof marks, but no horses or gear, just the spare powder and shot we had hidden behind the boulders. My heart sank. It must have been the two men, those I saw climbing the side of the glen. I tracked the horses further. They had followed a trail out of the glen. I followed it and reached the top, then spun around looking, hoping. They were gone.

I ran back to Norman, fearing the worst. Thankfully, he was still there, unharmed. But what of the old woman? I searched. She was gone too. *When will you learn to kill them when you have the chance?* Captain Forrester urged me. I shushed him and continued my search for horses. Minutes later I slumped beside Norman and gave him the dreadful news that our horses and supplies were gone. And there were two men or more and that damned woman out there wanting us dead. "Of course, they would not leave any horses. That and cattle is their gold," Norman explained.

"Of course. My fault. Should've known." I felt defeated. We had nothing—no shelter, no food, no fire, nothing. Well, we had our weapons, but that was it. Norman was seriously wounded, and we were miles from friendly territory. I knew if we stayed, he could die of the cold. If we left, we risked ambush by the MacDonalds, or Norman could bleed to death before I got him to safety. For surgery, all I had was my dagger and it was too risky to try to get the bullet out with no medical supplies. We had no acceptable choices. Then it started raining hard, and even worse it was cold and mixed with ice that pelted and soaked us. Thank you, Fortuna.

* * *

At least Norman's legs worked, and he was game for it. We decided to keep going and seek shelter on MacLeod land. Norman thought it could be several miles further. I remembered the trip over on horseback. There were no real settlements, just a few stone shielings scattered in the wilderness. This time of year, the drove road was empty, crofters and drovers having returned to the comfort and safety of their villages for winter.

I packed our weapons and filled my powder horn and sporran with shot and wadding. With the blunderbuss on my back, and Norman's musket, it was all I wanted to carry, since the laird was my priority. We left the rest, but for an extra plaid I took off a corpse for Norman.

Mile after mile we trudged through rain, ice pellets, and buffeting gusts. My hands and arms were numb from cold. And then the drove road left the warm embrace of the sea and turned west. It was afternoon, and the temperature started dropping. We walked on, leaning into the wind, me in front. We would stop every mile or so to rest. I could hear Norman's breathing worsen as we went. But he never complained.

For hours we walked, seeming to make no progress, the gorse, heather, grass, rocks, and low hills the same in every direction. It was desolate and discouraging, our energy expended to little end. The further we went, the slower our pace until we were at a crawl. I put my arm around his shoulder and felt his bandage. It was soaked. The wound must have opened from the walking, and he was losing blood. He said he was fine, so we kept going, me hoping for respite, he quiet in his thoughts. Then he stumbled and went to his knees.

"Put your arm over my shoulder," I suggested while helping him up.

"I am all right, just stubbed a rock," he stubbornly refused. Then a half mile later it happened again. He relented only when I told him he could carry me next trip.

From there on it was agony. He was having trouble lifting his feet and I had to drag him, stopping every fifty feet or so to catch a breath. And then Norman let go. I turned quickly. "Leave me, Malcolm. Save yourself," he mumbled while on all fours.

I crouched beside him and took some deep breaths and in that weak moment the Devil spoke to me again: *He is right, save yourself. He will die soon, anyway. Why risk your life for a doomed man?* The Devil often tells the truth when it is convenient. In my mind I cursed, then said aloud, "Since when does the MacLeod of MacLeod quit?"

"To save his loved ones," Norman replied with logic of such power I was stunned, and at once ashamed of allowing the Devil in me.

"We are almost there…a few more miles. We can do this."

"You are such a liar, Malcolm."

"Aye, but a good one. Now get up. Can't do this without you. Your lovely wife and children await."

I took his arm, hauled him up and we tried again. It was nearing darkness. He felt weighted as a corpse on me. We were breathing heavily, fighting for every step. Then the ice pellets turned to ice crystals. They assaulted my skin like thousands of tiny needles. My body screamed for it to stop. I was exhausted, soaking wet, frozen, and tormented. *Will God show no mercy?* I cried in my mind.

And then I saw a flicker of golden light. It was the ring on my hand that was holding him. I saw the image of Fortuna and I started to pray to her and Jesus and anyone else who might care about two lost men on the precipice of death. No one answered. I could go no further and fell to the ground, taking Norman with me. I lay there, awaiting death. Not just awaiting but welcoming it. I thought of my family and friends I would never again see. I closed my eyes and was back at beautiful Torrport, in the coffee house, with the rich smoky smells and delicious baking. The smoke, the smoke. I shook my head. Was it real? Aye, perhaps there was smoke! I crawled slowly to my knees and looked around. Then I saw it. A wispy trail of smoke rising from behind a rock face. I yipped and shook my fist at the stinging ice.

"Norman, Norman...we made it! Get up, we've been saved!" It was what I hoped, at least. I struggled to my feet then helped him off the ground and draped his chilled body on my back, then forced myself to walk. It took forever to get close to the cottage, but it gave me time to think. I did not know what we faced—friend or foe—but we were in dire need. We had to take that cottage, by force if necessary.

There was firelight in the window and two horses tied in a shed. I let Norman to the ground and whispered, "I need to ready the blunderbuss. There might be action. Just hang on to me, right?"

"Don't kill my people," he said, his voice stronger.

"I don't often kill them," I laughed too loudly.

I pulled Norman up. He wrapped his arms around my neck, his chin on my shoulder. That freed both my arms. The blunderbuss was cocked and pointed at the door, but my hands were so cold I was not certain I could pull the trigger. I knocked.

"Who's it?" came the reply, in melodic baritone.

"'Tis your laird. Let us in," I demanded.

The door opened a crack. I kicked it hard, sending it flying back on its leather hinges. And there we were, his ruggedly handsome face and tousled blond hair to the muzzle of my hideous blunderbuss. We glared at each other a second, my frozen trigger finger tightening, his face registering shock, then Norman said, "Niall?"

"Who is it, darling?" the woman on the floor behind Niall said. She was sprawled by the fire like a cat, and like Niall, wearing little more than a linen shirt.

"Ysabell?" Norman said as though not believing his eyes.

I had enough of awkward introductions and dragged the laird past Niall, who stood dumfounded.

"Get Elspeth. Now!" I ordered.

Chapter 13: Elspeth

"Cawdie has fallen in love with someone else." Janet looked across the chamber to her husband whose great shaggy cranium almost touched the melted-gilt curls of his angelic companion, Solas.

"Aye, Janet." I hid my smile. "'Tis plain you have been replaced for the nonce, but I think you will soon be gifting him with something she cannot. A bairn of his own."

Janet's face flamed. "I am not yet completely certain. Please, El, say nothing, I beg you." She placed her hand tenderly over her flat belly. "I have felt no movement. And until I do, I dare not tempt the gods with hubris."

"Of course not, but promise you will tell me if anything is wrong? Have you been feeling well? Do you need a tisane for your mornings? I prepare one for Lady Anne each morning. I could add another easily."

She flushed. "Nay, ginger and mint work well enough."

We were in the laird's library. I felt physically well enough again after my mistreatment and enforced stay in Talisker. My scars were not the visible sort. Everyone had been markedly kind to me. Even Una had come bearing one of her famous puddings. But she looked unwell; the roundness of her face thinned in her bonnet. Her tending of the village had been unstinting. I was grateful for the care, but I was being treated like a fragile piece of crystal and it had begun to irk.

Janet gazed thoughtfully at the two figures angled over the wooden chess board before the fireplace. Adhie, Malcolm's puppy, had succumbed to Solas as well, and he drowsed contentedly against the child's foot. Cawdie was speaking earnestly to Solas as he moved her hand and the chess pieces around the board between them. He had incised thin grooves between the squares to outline them and gently guided Solas' tiny fingers along them as he explained the rules of the game. It was a loving gift of time.

Solas's sightless purple-blue eyes seemed to look directly into Cawdie's own even though I knew the wee lass could not see. Sir Ross leaned back in one of the large wing chairs observing her intently. He spoke to the lass. "The horse is the only piece that can jump over another piece. Remember that. 'Tis an important advantage to be able to bypass an obstacle."

Solas turned her head to him and nodded in understanding. Everyone loved Erika's daughter.

Cawdie glanced over at us frequently. He had not forgiven himself for being absent when Ranuff had taken me. While I was sleeping away the effects of my stay at Ranuff's keep he had paced the corridor outside my room refusing to return home, telling Janet he could not fail me again. She knew her man well and wisely let him be, knowing some time must pass while he dealt with his demons.

Janet insisted that she must share the guilt and watch with him. One of them was always close now. It was wrong of me to want them nearby, yet it did help me heal. My emotions were still too fresh to control completely. When the memories faded all would be well. Meanwhile, having Cawdie and Janet here felt right, especially with Malcolm and the laird away. There had been no word from them since they left. "They have been away too long. The weather is so uncertain." It came out as a whine. Hard winter approached in alternate chunks of freezing and cold fall days. And the waiting lay leaden inside me. I glanced down at the garment I had been stitching. It had somehow become crushed in my hands. I hastily shook it out and noticed Gregor regarding me with intent from the corner of the library where he sat reading. His thin ascetic face was without expression.

* * *

Niall Morrison returned from one of his trips, opening his cottage and resuming his usual place in the clan. The general camaraderie built around preparations for the Martinmas celebration on November eleventh had started and Niall was a braw laddie. Females young and old, giggled, blushed, and flirted with him as they devised dances, games, and parades. The older women contented themselves with memories and preparations for the customary festive dinner of roast goose and veggies from freshly stocked larders. The men used equal time to compare the recently brewed Saint Martin's ale with that of former years. 'Twas a dedicated task requiring multiple tastings, often ending in the insensibility of the tasters.

Many days had passed, and pretence was useless. We all knew something was wrong. Malcolm and the laird had been gone too long. Unease curdled my belly. I surrendered, folded the crumpled tunic I was making for Solas and returned it to my sewing basket. Scathach lifted her head expectantly from nursing. Her pups had been named for the four fae spirits I had attempted to evoke with my finding spell. But the pups could scarce be less fairylike, all tumbling balls of vigour and mischief, but the names fit. After all, their mother was an immortal female warrior, in name. The pups answered to Oberon, Mycob, Lilla and Rostilla, the four already claimed by my father, Aunt Mairi, Cawdie and surprisingly, Gregor.

I reached down to ruffle the warm fur on Scathach's great head and turned to Janet, attempting to distract myself with chatter. "'Tis passing strange. I have examined Solas countless times and can find nothing to account for her blindness. She has not always been so, for she speaks to me of things and colors and something she calls "the before time." She describes Erika, Willis and his wife and their daughter perfectly." I frowned. "Loss of sight can be the result of a head injury. I asked if anyone had hurt her, but she denied it. And she bears no signs or scars of such. Except for the blindness, she is perfect."

Janet turned to me. "Have you spoken with Aunt Mairi about it? Or Malcolm?"

"Nay. But in the ancient texts, there was a talk of such a condition amongst Roman warriors after battle." I exhaled a breath I did not realize I was holding.

Standing, I went to the window. Patterned frost obscured the stormy landscape below. I rubbed away the rime on a pane of glass and peered out. Sleet blew about but the clouds had set the moon free for the moment. Distant mountains glowed silver white in the light, fractured across the unsettled landscape below. A thick coating of ice coated everything, the storm adding more and the temperature dropping as the cloud cover thinned. I shivered. It was cold. So cold. Where were the laird and Malcolm?

This weather was unusually harsh for early November. It boded ill for the annual Martinmas celebration. My head ached. Cooling my palms against the iced pane, I pressed them to my throbbing temples and turned to leave the window. I felt faint and stumbled. Janet saw me. "What? What is it?" said she. Before I could answer, the door to the hallway exploded open. A great male body thrust into the room. It was Niall, his handsome face ashen above clothing haphazardly donned. He slewed to a halt in front of us seeking enough air to speak. Melting sleet puddled around him. Weeping red scrapes painted his knees where his breeks had been torn from numerous falls.

"'Tis the laird! He has been shot. Mayhap dying…so much blood. Malcolm sent me." His eyes met mine. "You are to come at once!" he gasped. "Bring your bag, and whatever else you need for surgery. And dry warm clothes and blankets. I can help. Show me what you need to carry back." He drew in more air. "We must carry everything or perchance I can pull one of the carts or a sledge. Horses are nay good on the ice. I tried. They cannot stand on it. Mine may have to be put down." He looked helplessly down at his shins then back at me.

Janet and I were moving before he finished speaking. My vertigo vanquished in the moment. Cawdie plucked Solas from her cushion by the fire and placed her solidly in Sir Ross's lap. "Take the wee one. Ye can tell her tales about the other pieces and how they move. Mayhap teach a move or two, like yer leapin' knights." Sir Ross blinked, eyes widening in consternation at the unexpected intimacy with the child.

I grabbed Cawdie's sleeve. "Find a hand cart or sledge with a basket. The ones we use in the orchard will do. Niall, Cawdie will show you what to gather."

From behind me, Gregor spoke, "My lady let me locate carriers and take them to the sea gate. I will bring as many sets of ice crampons as I can find as well."

"That would help greatly. I thank you, Gregor. And will you stay at Dunvegan? You are needed to protect Lady Anne and the children."

"Yes, my lady. I am yours to command." He bowed his head to me and swiftly quit the room.

My heart gave an odd twist as he left. "Meet at the sea gate. Janet and I will collect my bag, medicines and bandages." I called to Niall as he left the room. "Where is our laird?"

"The bothy, the one outside the village on the drove road to Portree. The way is treacherous." He coloured hotly, adjusted his soggy clothes, and scurried after Cawdie.

* * *

We scrambled along the frozen path, the crampons we had tied to our boots providing some measure of safety. Cawdie and Niall pulled the sledge behind us, and Janet was at my side carrying a light pack. Pellets of sleet pummeled us, and safety lay in moving. By the time we arrived at our destination we had all acquired an icy shell. I never felt so chilled in my life. My arms were frozen and occupied so I kicked at the door, the sudden movement causing ice to crack and splinter off my skirts. To my surprise, the door flew open.

A steamy mixture of heated smells wrapped around us as we fell into the blessed warmth. Slabs of peat smouldered hotly in the fireplace. Medical bags deposited on the floor; I began to shed melting outer garb. The laird lay before the hearth on a pile of straw and sheepskin, covered in a shabby blanket and plaid. His bared feet jerked spasmodically in the warmth of the flames; eyes closed. And astonished, I saw his head was resting on Ysabel's lap! Of course. That explained Niall's presence. They were trysting. She sat brazenly cradling his head, looking up at me, eyes flickering defiantly for an instant before transforming into contrived innocence. Did she believe I had not seen her with Ranuff, or running down the stairs outside the dungeon at Talisker? I pushed the memory aside. Questions could come later. Cawdie helped Janet remove her cloak and they quickly began unpacking. Niall averted his eyes from the scene and left to retrieve the contents of the sledge.

Malcolm sat before the peat fire wrapped in a woolen horse blanket. He spoke first. "Our supplies were stolen. I could do nothing but try to stop the bleeding and get him here." His voice rasped wearily into the heavy silence. "He has a bullet lodged in his upper chest and lost much blood and is half frozen. Get to work. Help him, Elspeth."

"You brought him home. Thank you, Malcolm. Now 'tis our responsibility. Rest, please." He shuddered as I laid a comforting hand lightly on his arm, then carried my bags past him to kneel by the laird. "Ysabell, move! Put his head on something and get out of my way. Did he speak? Say anything about pain. Tell me what has been done."

"We could do little but warm him and offer food and drink" said Ysabell defiantly while placing a worn pillow beneath his head to replace her thighs. The firelight revealed the laird's face patched with the pinkening white of frostbite. It was expected. Parts of the exposed skin were starting to regain color. Matching mottled hands lay atop the makeshift coverings, fingers twitching with the excruciating pain of returning sensation. But frostbite was not my main concern. The gunshot wound was.

My hands pulled some of the none too clean makeshift bandages away from his upper body. Blood-soaked remnants of a man's shirt had been tied over the bullet wound on the side of his chest and clung to his body. He seemed insensible, which might be a good thing for now.

"Janet, we need to soak these before we can remove them." She had already hung a kettle of water on the crane over the fire and was laying out clean cloths. "Help me examine him." We raised the laird slightly and I skimmed my hand over his back feeling for other wounds, finding nothing that could not wait. The lesser damage on his arms and hands had long ceased bleeding and had crusted over.

Ysabell spoke, "As you see, I removed his wet clothing but not the bandages…tried to warm him with hot soup and a bit of ale. He took little and has been silent for the most part, except for a few curses and groans." She glanced at Malcolm. "Him, too."

The door creaked open again. Cawdie and Niall, burdened with more bundles, entered on a blast of frigid air. "Separate out what we might need, Cawdie. Put it within reach next to us. Another blanket for Malcolm, too, please."

Janet moved to the laird's other side as we soaked the blood-stiffened cloth with warmed water, then peeled it off. The last piece we lifted revealed a narrow furrow which began at the middle of the laird's rib cage and deepened into a gash that entered his shoulder below the clavicle. The angle probably saved his life while cracking a few ribs along the way. The running laceration had bled profusely, and scarlet seeped from the edges of the bullet hole. The laird had been keeping his eyes closed but grunted when my fingers explored the open wound. He was not unconscious, then. "Careful lass," he mumbled.

I smiled. "Janet, let's clean him up a wee bit more before I do anything that will truly earn his ire." The kettle now steamed, and a pile of cloths stacked nigh a chipped basin. I rinsed the wound with a mixture of wine, boiled water and honey and bandaged it lightly for now. We bathed his abused body, being especially careful of cuts and painful thawing flesh. When he was washed and enfolded in fresh blankets, I went back to his chest wound. The bullet hole was inflamed where ball entered flesh and came to rest. I sponged away the slow drain coming from the opening and leaned down to smell it. There was no stench of decay yet but the bullet and whatever it had dragged into the wound would need to be removed. To do that, I had to find it. The laird made no further sounds except for a few bitten off blasphemies, but what I had to do next was going to be painful. Cawdie and Niall might be able to hold the laird, but if they failed to restrain him, I could cause more harm.

My bag contained a soporific mixture to induce unconsciousness, a concoction I resort to with reluctance. *It was kin to what Ranuff had used on me,* I thought grimly. Ysabell watched me prepare it, her face closed and blank.

Rather than use a sponge over his face, I gave him the liquid dose for a man of his size and waited for him to drift into deep sleep. Next, I flushed the bullet hole using a syringe, then inserted a long silver probe with a rounded tip to locate the ball. The probe vanished inside the laird's body for several inches before I felt metal shiver against metal. Depth and angle placed the ball just beneath the clavicle. I noted the length, retracted the probe, and Janet handed me the bullet extractor.

Slanting the tip of the extractor into the wound, I closed my eyes, focusing on touch as I angled the instrument slowly inside and up. I felt the decisive tick of metal on metal when it reached the ball. Widening the forceps jaws slightly, I eased them around the slippery lead, grasped it firmly and withdrew it cautiously. It emerged with a sucking sound, followed by an outpouring of thick clotted matter. Fragments of linen from the laird's shirt had been pulled in with the ball so I let the blood stream freely for a moment to cleanse the wound, then applied pressure to control it. When flow ebbed to ooze, I packed the wound with a salve of honey, garlic, cinnamon, and beeswax.

"Janet, I need to close this and embroider part of the furrow." She pushed a tray with threaded needles, scissors, swabs, and salves toward me. Minutes later I leaned back, finished, then watched as Janet applied fresh bandages. We examined him carefully for other injuries. There were none that mattered, and only a few cuts were treated. And thankfully, the frostbite was superficial. 'Twas not yet full winter. There should be little lasting damage to feet and hands. Time would tell. We left the laird to sleep. Consciousness would only bring pain.

My next patient was Malcolm. He had refused to be helped before the laird, but Ysabell had evidently ignored his surly words, covered him with a blanket, removed his frozen shoes, and insisted he turn his bare feet and hands to the fire. His skin bore the same dappled white and pink color as had the lairds. And I could sense misery too, his plaid so covered with dirt and dried blood that it was impossible to tell if or where he was injured. I filled the basin with fresh warm water, picked up a soft cloth and went to him. He pushed me away. "Let me be. I'm fine. I'm up. I'll be well. Concern yourself with him not me." his voice came out a froggy croak.

I smiled at him overly sweetly and turned to Cawdie who had been feeding the fire. "I think you might have something Malcolm would prefer to my tender ministrations?"

Cawdie snorted something uncivil and rummaged in one of the bags he had crammed, retrieving a squatty bottle of whisky. Cawdie pulled the cork and lifted it to Malcolm's lips. "Have some brother. Dae ye guid," said he. Malcolm tilted his head back, sucked an ungodly amount from the contents, leaned back against an old wooden chest and closed his eyes.

He gave only token resistance when Janet and I began to remove what was left of his filthy clothing. To my relief, most of the blood was not his. He had used his shirt for bandages, but the plaid had protected him reasonably well. I smiled down at my friend and entertained a moment of guilt for involving him in my family problems. HeHis injuries were those often seen after clan battles, deep bruises, abrasions, and haphazard slashes. I stitched up two that needed closing, then applied salve. We bathed his damaged feet and hands despite his grumbling, dressed him in a clean shirt, covered him with another blanket, and in a few moments, he was slumbering as deeply as the laird. The gods only knew when they had last slept.

Pushing myself to my feet, I brushed uselessly at my soiled skirts and walked to Ysabel. It was time to deal with her. "What are you doing here? Where is Ranuff hiding?" I could hear the bitterness coating my words.

She glanced quickly at Niall who had kept to a corner of the cottage, well out of the way, only helping Cawdie bring water and peat. She feigned surprise. "Ranuff? What say you? I've not seen him, nor have I stirred from the village in weeks, except to be here with Niall." She stared at me with determined candor. "Where do you imagine you saw me?"

I met her look coldly. "You know exactly where I saw you! You were there, in the dungeon where Ranuff held us captive and killed Erika. You helped him!"

Something shifted in her eyes. Was it guilt, perhaps terror? She held my gaze and saturated her voice with spurious sympathy, hiding beneath her beauty as she had always done. "Elspeth," she said kindly, "you are distraught. You have not been well. I am so sorry for what my brother did. He is a beast. But I had no part in it. You must believe me." She lifted a hand to me and affected distress when I stepped back. "Are you certain you were not having one of your dreams? Why would you imagine I was with Ranuff? Ask my mother. Ask Niall." She turned to him for confirmation.

Niall looked from her to me and nodded slowly. "She speaks truth. I have been with...seen her here. Are you well, Elspeth?" he asked solicitously. "You have been through much recently. Mayhap the strain has affected your memory and you are confusing things imagined with things real?" His voice strengthened. "Ysabell has been here with me."

I sensed he believed what he was saying, and his concern genuine. Both puzzled me. I recalled the scene at Ranuff's keep. Ysabel's look of horror as she turned away from the door, the sound of her running down the stairs. Had I been ill enough to conjure her there? But she had helped Ranuff at the sacred rowan tree, as well. I realized now that the food I found in my room had been drugged, so that my memory of that could be suspect. I sighed. It was possible. The mind does strange things. Could I have been drugged, weakened from starvation and lack of water, emotional, and hallucinating? I would think about it later. Mayhap she was right, and I had imagined it all.

For now, of most importance was getting the laird and Malcolm to the castle and caring for them properly. I would talk to Malcolm. But not tonight. All of us needed rest. Cawdie pulled Janet nearer to the fireplace and wrapped them both in a dry blanket. Niall lay next to Ysabell. I sat alone, staring into the fire, watching the laird and Malcolm until exhaustion forced me to join them in sleep.

* * *

Morning glittered under a cloudless sky. The sledge would transport the two injured men home. Cawdie cut through the back side of the creel and flattened the cut section to form makeshift seating. We padded both seat and cart with everything we could find. Filthy or clean was not as important as soft, as the journey back would not be pleasant for our patients.

Niall and Cawdie laid the laird on the cushioned sledge and covered him snugly. Malcolm resisted being drawn but frostbite left his hands and feet sensitive to pain., and he finally succumbed to common sense. We left Isabell at the bothy. Others would return for her and the things we left.

* * *

We were gathered in the library trying to restore some semblance of a normal day. The laird's bullet wound was healing without infection. There had been a few frostbite areas that had blistered on both men, but they were beginning to slough off revealing pink skin beneath.

Adhie lay across Solas's foot. He had assumed the role of her guard and was practicing growling at her slipper. Solas patted the dog's neck to quiet him. They stood as one and began to walk across the room. Adhie was trying to be her eyes and often put himself between Solas and low obstacles. The child hesitated before a carved wooden panel on the right of the fireplace. One wee hand lifted and brushed down the dark surface. She frowned, turning back to Cawdie. "Cawdie open door, please?"

He smiled at her. "Nay, lass. Nay door. 'Tis wood covering stone."

"Door!" Solas insisted. She was nearing her fourth year and becoming quite determined. Adhie whined, sniffing, and scratching at the paneling. Janet and I went to the child. Solas's hands moved resolutely over the geometric designs on the panel. I knocked. It emitted a hollow sound. Janet and I looked at each other and began tracing the contours. There was a sharp creak, and a gap large enough to accommodate a man opened. "Bad man there!" said Solas, burying her face in my skirt. Carrying a candle, Cawdie pushed his way through the opening. He told us it led to a narrow passage that stretched in both directions. He turned left but returned a few moments later.

"There be nothing. Save this." He held out a shred of cobwebbed black fabric. "Did ye ken the passage here?" I shook my head. The ancient building was riddled with secrets. This was but one more we had not discovered when we were bairns, or simply forgotten. I knelt and pulled my trembling niece into a fierce embrace.

"Solas, my heart... All is well. You are safe. You never need be frightened. We are with you. Who was it you saw?" I held her close, her delicate body quivering against mine.

"Bad man hurt mother. He is there." Her finger pointed unerringly at the opening in the panel, tears pooled in her eyes. I glimpsed something else shockingly hot and ancient in their depths. Cawdie swiftly took her from me, cradling her to his chest and covering her fragile body with his plaid. I reached into the dark corridor with my senses and my blood iced. Ranuff was in the castle! Discovered, he fled. Solas had known. I had not, till now.

I asked the laird if there were records or lists showing the number and position of such passages in the castle. He reluctantly admitted there were, and even more reluctantly told me where to find them. After retrieving a cumbersome packet of mostly unintelligible notes and hand drawn maps spanning centuries, I tried to make sense of those nearest the laird's chambers. The drawings showed a hopeless warren, a stone maze that was as likely to take you to a blank wall as a door. But I did learn that most began and ended inside the buildings. Those leading outside were few.

After that night I kept Cawdie and Solas close by. Adhie slipped like a shadow among us, always with Solas and barely visible against the bulky darkness of Scathach. Cawdie drew the bairn into the circle of care he shared with Janet and me. In return she gave him the unqualified love that children give their fathers.

Janet had not yet told Cawdie or anyone else about her babe, but one day I saw Solas lay a chubby hand on Janet's belly, murmur something, then smile up at Janet. When I asked Janet what Solas had said, she looked at me with awed amazement and replied, "He is awake."

* * *

The castle and village were now well into preparations for Martinmas, or St. Martin's Day. A patron saint of beggars, drunkards, and the poor, he understandably retains a loyal following despite Protestant urges to curtail veneration of Catholic Saints. Martinmas also was a Scottish term day when rents and contracts fall due, and it was a time for feasting and preparations for winter. But through this activity, there had been no further signs of Ranuff. Cawdie stayed close and Gregor closer. I was hemmed about by overly caring men and one wee bairn who clung tenaciously to Cawdie. Janet went about with a soft glow overlaying her usual competence. And I fretted as a growing need to discover the secrets of the stone balls pulled at me.

It was my turn to watch Solas, I brought her to my room where she promptly curled into a nap among the downy pillows on my bed. I removed the stones from their hiding place and sat near her, laying the balls on the coverlet before me and staring at them. Each of the round spheres had the triskele symbol carved somewhere into its surface as well as many other marks and bumps. The three coils of the triskele are a mark so ancient that the original meaning has long been lost. Some say the whorls are the three faces of the goddess, maiden, mother, and crone. And the rule of three is a powerful belief for it shapes the past present and future and insures both good and evil are returned to their source threefold.

I was musing all this when Solas awakened and crawled over to me, laying her chin against my thigh, gazing at the balls which I had been arranging in different patterns. I smiled, smoothing the curls away from her face. She leaned over, touched each of the stones, stopped at the one my father had given me from my mother and tugged at it. It was heavy and a bit large for her to move. I picked it up for her and felt it warm, almost hot.

"This," she looked down and pointed. "Aunt Elspeth, here." I placed the ball where she pointed. The conformation with the other balls seemed vaguely familiar. I searched for things that might connect them. All four had circle motifs on their surfaces in the form of bumps which varied in number on each ball. As well, mine had a triskele surrounded by what appeared to be symbols like runes. The other balls had triskeles, circles, and lines, along with the symbols. Each ball was unique but made of these elements. I rotated one ball a little and there it was. The strange herb garden design Uncle Angus had given me weeks ago, with the design resembling the combined pattern on the stones. He had told me garden design was a copy of an older plan for a knot garden at Dunvegan. How did the child know where the stone went? I turned to ask but she had crept back into her nest of pillows and was sleeping. I pulled my wooden chest nearer, rummaged through the contents and removed the knot garden design. Most certainly it closely matched the design made by the balls when they were properly oriented. The plan was beautifully drawn and notated, a written list of bedding plants beside each section. There were four lists of plants. One for each quadrant of the garden. Yet they made no sense. Many could never be used for outdoor gardening in this harsh climate. Fully half would not flourish. Why plan a garden that could not thrive? And what did it have the do with the stone balls? Mayhap a cipher? Many hid their secrets in ciphers. 'Twas an old ploy.

I inspected the garden plan with new interest. Was it an acrostic? The first letter of each flower? Every other letter? Sentences with nulls? I began to write down possible combinations. Flowers had special meanings as well. I went down the list for the third plot and tried to recall what they represented. Heather, aloe vera, and dill were common and used medically. All four granted the wearer protection from evil. Acacia meant hidden treasure. *Lisianthus* promised an everlasting bond or promise. Roses signaled hope, and gowan daisies had many meanings, according to context.

Rue declared repentance. Rosemary pledged remembrance. In combination they could mean "I am sorry. I will not forget." The last two were hellebore, which was one of the four deadly poisons, then poppy which stood for eternal sleep. So, repentance and a promise of retribution? 'Twas a killing combination.

With so many meanings how could anyone be certain which was intended if anything? The message may lie in the list, the spelling, the position of the words, or only in certain letters. I needed someone more knowledgeable to help me. I made a copy of the plants for each section and put it in my pouch. Aunt Mairi and Una Talisker were both wise in such things, and Gregor too.

After covering Solas with a shawl smelling faintly of Aunt Rhona, and concealing the balls, I placed Adhie on the bed against Solas and told him to stay. Gathering my wooden basket and shears, I asked Janet to sit with Solas while I went in search of advice.

In the bailey, Una Talisker stood glaring down at the dead and dying herbs. She startled when I greeted her, then smiled wanly at me. "Ah, lass. How fare ye? Glad to see your father? Looks well he does. Still a braw lad, he is." She sighed, shook her head, and laughed, her thinned cheeks reddening. "Tis a bitter thing that we women don't wear so well as the menfolk. Did you known we two walked out a bit when we were young? But after your mother came, his eye saw no other." She faltered then went on, her words melancholy with yesterdays. "Your Aunt Mairi was caught in a storm and not able to get there for your birthing." Her words wisped in the air. "I have oft wondered if the midwife pulled the after burden too soon." She caught herself, stopped speaking and noted the wayward strands of auburn curls escaping my braids.

She upped the corners of her mouth and looked down at the sad remains of the garden. "We must make more salves soon, child. The rosemary still be good, and the garlic. If you give the oregano and thyme some cover, them, too." She stopped speaking and stiffened as the door from the kitchen corridor swung open and Aunt Mairi stepped out, followed by Lady Myreton.

Aunt Mairi greeted Una. "'Tis glad I am to see you. Are you prepared for the Martinmas gathering?" Lady Myreton nodded respectfully to Una and flicked an assessing glance over me. Three of the most learned women of the clan stood before me. It was my chance. I hastily pulled the herb garden design and list of flowers from my pocket. Told them I was curious of garden lore. An hour later I had many answers, more questions and new hope. Una and Lady Myreton confirmed much. Aunt Mairi contributed that to "have the gowan under one's feet conferred safety," but aside from that she was unusually silent, letting the other women talk. At least I knew that whatever the cipher meant; it clearly was draped in meaning. I attempted to discuss it further, but Aunt Mairi hesitated and gave me a warning glance. I took myself off.

* * *

Martinmas had arrived. The harsh weather had cleared into what is known as St. Martin's Summer halcyon days. It might last three days or three weeks. The village was alive with fluttering fabrics and strange faces. Rented stalls united foreign fishmongers, woolen and linen drapers, glovers and white tawyers who made pale creamy leathers cured with alum and salt instead of tannin. Butchers and ale sellers verbally vied with vendors of timber and faggots, while in the middle of the road camped those offering coarse bread, earthenware, and coals. The ever-present reek of human and animal waste mixed with the fragrances of the Martinmas Fair and melded into something between intolerable and intoxicating. Rushes, sweet hay, brooms, thorns, and bushes lay next to offerings of meal and seeds. And cheese, eggs, milk, butter, peas, and beans embroidered scrubbed wooden surfaces.

Despite myself I was drawn to the bags and packets of seeds essential for making medicines and meals. My father found me haggling happily and waited patiently to walk me back to the castle. He took my bundles and twists, saying bluntly, "We need to talk, lass. Now is a suitable time. I will be returning to the Carolinas soon, and I want you and Solas to come with me."

I ceased walking and turned to him, stunned. "Return? Father to what? And why would I go with you? There is nothing for me there. I have a life here." A hot blade of pain ripped my belly and shrilled my response.

Color washed him red before he found his voice. "Things change, lass. I am now long in years. In Carolina I have land, servants of my own, and two houses. One is in Charles Towne." He stood taller. "You would share it with us, lass. 'Tis new land, rich, unfilled, and needy. You would be welcomed as a physician as you will never be here." He paused, took a deep breath, and expelled the final phrases. "My wife Amanda would welcome you, as would your wee brother Iain who needs you."

Breath escaped me but no sound. I had a wee brother? My father had left us and began a new life abroad. He had remarried and produced a priceless son to replace his two useless daughters. His first family had not been enough to tether him, but now he wanted us to follow him.

"Think about my offer, lass. I could use you."

Use? I stared at this stranger who was my sire, bleeding self pity and childhood illusions. The loving father I had imagined was just that. Imaginary. I felt sick. I was going to faint like some dainty demoiselle. Then a firm hand grasped my arm. It was Gregor. Support from him flowed into the empty place where my dreams had lain. My legs stiffened and resumed holding me upright. Gregor and my father measured each other before my father nodded, handed my purchases to Gregor, and walked away.

"I will take you back to the castle," said Gregor.

"Yes, please," I said, dutifully taking his arm. He restored the blankness he carried about him. I no longer sensed him, but Gregor had briefly revealed himself. I did not care to pursue that revelation yet. We passed a stall proffering hanging geese, and to my surprise he recited:

If ducks do slide at Martinmas

At Christmas they will swim.

If ducks do swim at Martinmas

At Christmas they will slide.

He nodded toward the small pond near the kirk where several ducks circled. Coldly indifferent Gregor was attempting to make me smile. He succeeded.

* * *

In my room I fell across my bed, slept dreamlessly, and awoke at a knock on the door. Lady Anne clutching her child was looking frightened. "He is not eating. May I speak with you?"

I pushed at my unruly hair and bade her come in. "Of course. Ah 'tis wee John." The sweet smell of child and sour milk warred. He had been born last year in late of spring. The bairn fixed round eyes on mine. I took him and felt a cough shiver through his wee body. He was solid and warm in my arms. Anne's face was drawn in premature pleats across the fine bones of her face.

"Can you help him, Elspeth? He is coughing much and sleeping little. I cannot soothe him, and I fear for him. 'Tis like his father."

I examined him. His symptoms appeared to mimic those of his sire, which made her concern understandable, but he was no sicker than any other infant with a cold. The laird was another matter. I handed the babe back to her. "Lady Anne, he should be fine, but we will watch him faithfully. Give him as much breast as he will take. You might try giving him sops as well. He is growing and hungry."

I gave her a soothing syrup of honey and lemon for the bairn's cough and a packet of herbs to make a posset warmed in wine for her own worries. When she left. I found my grimoire and began to write.

Chapter 14: Malcolm

"Will you not tell me what is wrong with you?"

I glanced up. Elspeth stood over me, arms folded, and wearing a concerned frown. Cawdie was trying not to laugh. "Nothing wrong," I replied.

I knew she was exasperated. I did not blame her. Women do not understand and there is no point trying to explain.

"Then why in the name of all that is holy have you been sitting here for two days staring at the fire?"

It was a good question. I did not fully understand myself, but I knew that no medicine could cure what ailed me. And despite her good intentions, she was making it worse. "I'm fine, Elspeth. Cawdie, please take her home."

Elspeth groaned loudly, her exasperation made plain, then told Cawdie to be sure I ate something and that she was perfectly capable of finding her own way home. She was gone in a mutter-filled swish, leaving Cawdie perched on his low stool by the door and me on another by the fire, neither of us saying a word.

They had moved me to Aunt Mairi's cottage after we returned from our near disaster of a trip to the sacred spring. I was glad of the move since I did not want to burden Teresa. There was nothing much physically wrong with me, a bit of frostbite on my hands and some bruises was all. It was my soul that was sick, I think, if there was any of it left after that ordeal.

Cawdie grunted and went to the table where Elspeth had left some bread, butter, cold beef, and ale. "Better do as she says. Don't want her rage at me, coz the goodwife will too, then poor Cawdie gets none." He grimaced at the thought as he made up a plate for each of us.

I laugh quietly. Poor Cawdie, indeed! That is what it comes down to for men: sex or lack thereof. "Alright Cawdie. God forbid, don't want you doing without."

"Kind of ye, good sir," He grinned and slid a plate and ale mug to my side of the table.

We ate in silence. Cawdie's a good friend, knows when to help and when to keep his damned mouth shut. The last thing I needed right now was unwanted advice.

"Good food. Thank whoever made it."

"Me Janet."

"All the more. You are a lucky man."

He smiled.

After I had picked through the food and eaten enough to live, I lay down on Mairi's tiny bed. It was far too short, but soft and warm with its hair mattress topped with linen sheets and wool blankets. The cottage had been touched by the hand of woman. All was tidy and decorated. The sole window had clean white curtains, there was a gaily patterned rug by the fire, and the sideboard had small paintings and silverware artfully arranged. It was comfortable and tasteful, but these easy surroundings did not cheer. I curled on the bed and wished I were home in father's study listening to the clock and his fitful snores and sipping brandy after a day of tending the sick. It was my place, where I was respected and felt good about myself.

Cawdie cleaned the plates and packed the basket then resumed his watch by the door. He had been with me two days and nights. Tedious duty and I felt sorry for him. "Thank you for being with me, Cawdie. Now go be with your wife. 'Tis late."

He slowly shook his shaggy head, "Nay, the laird told me tae look after ye till ye are weel."

"I am well, Cawdie. Please go home."

"Nay."

I knew better than to argue, so I rolled over, pulled the blanket up and fell asleep.

* * *

I awoke in a panic, sweat soaking my shirt, fury unsettling my mind. It was another awful dream of slaughter, anger, and joy. I lurched up. It was dark. Cawdie was watching. "Need to take a piss," I told him.

It was cold and blustery, and I immediately regretted not using the chamber pot inside. The cold woke me fully. Back inside, Cawdie was up putting fresh peat on the fire and starting the kettle. "Gonnae back tae sleep?" he asked.

"Nay, I'm up now. May as well do something useful."

"That's a start," he replied.

He was right of course. I had been brooding too long. Time to right the ship and sail on. It was still dark as we shared tea and leftover bread and butter. "How do you manage it?" I asked.

"What?"

"The killing."

He shrugged and pulled on his beard a moment. "Is the horror ay killing bothering ye?"

"Partly."

"What else?"

"That I came to love it. I think. I'm not sure."

Cawdie tore off another chunk of bread. He ate silently then wiped the crumbs off his hands and said, "Ye sure it be the killing ye love?"

"What do you mean?"

"Could be the joy ay surviving. That is natural and right, isn't it? The auld preacher said God wants us ta be happy and alive."

"Maybe, but still..."

"Still?"

"Do you ever go looking for it?"

"Tae kill?"

"Aye."

"Once, but it was needing doing."

I nodded. That was my excuse too.

"What happened tae ye, brother?"

"I went out to kill and did."

"For nay reason?"

"I had good reason, but why did I choose that way?"

"We are men."

Many would say that Cawdie was correct, and I had the perfect right to defend myself and the laird, and any joy I felt was because I had succeeded and survived. But I knew in my heart it was not that simple. Life is characterized largely by our choices, and I had chosen the path of violence, consciously or not, and it sickened me to know what I had become. Reality had confronted delusion and won. But there was no way forward but forward, and Father Hammett, my priest at Torrport, undoubtedly would counsel forgiveness and atonement. I smiled thinking of him with his wheezy chest and gentle ways. *I'll try to do better,* I said to myself, and prayed I meant it this time.

"I think I should see some patients today."

Cawdie banged the table with his fist. "About time! Noo ah can go home tae me Janet."

I laughed aloud for the first time in days.

* * *

It was November, that regrettable month. The blustery wind brought cold showers and I was well-chilled when I reached the castle. This time the reception was somewhat warmer, the guards providing a polite welcome. The bailey was all mud and smoke with a few young warriors standing close to the building entrances trying to stay warm. I pitied them.

"You are up," Elspeth said with a look of uncertainty as though she did not know what to expect from me next.

"You needn't worry, I'm not here to kill anyone."

Elspeth reached out and touched my arm. "Och, Malcolm. I am so sorry."

I could see she was about to tear-up or say something sentimental, so I smiled reassuringly, "All is well. I need to get back to work. Give me some patients before I go mad from boredom."

Her concern brightened to a smile. "The laird will be so pleased to see you. Start with him and I'll find some menial tasks for you later," she teased.

I pulled her to me and gave her a hug and whispered, "I'm all right, truly. Just needed a few days to recover."

She hugged me back and said, "I know, and I'm sorry if I was a nuisance. We were worried."

I looked at her a moment, her face uncertain but hopeful. We parted with well wishes.

* * *

I found Laird MacLeod in his private study in the Fairy Tower. He was seated at the desk, writing. "You are still alive?" I smiled. He struggled to rise and greet. His right arm was in a sling over a linen shirt which covered the bandage on his upper chest. He looked a lot better than a few days ago when I dragged him into that trysting hut.

"Aye, and I heard you've been sitting hang-dog by the fire," he mocked.

"From dragging you around. Wore me hollow."

We both laughed.

"'Twas a near-run thing. I thank you for bringing me home." He looked out the window to the leaden clouds that pressed the grey waters of the loch.

"You shouldn't thank me for foolishly risking your life. Getting you home alive was more Elspeth's doing. I'm sincerely sorry for your wound."

"Foolish fun till the MacDonalds arrived. You couldn't have known of that, surely?"

I shook my head and remembered the agony of those hours on the trail and not knowing if we would make it. "Nay, I was worried about witches then past deeds caught up."

"Happens to those of us who dare the fates."

He was right. Avoiding risks makes for a smooth life. But we took the hard road and paid the heavier toll. I thought of Fortuna or God who may have saved us that night and uttered a silent thanks, especially for protecting the laird. I removed my cloak and opened the small medical bag Elspeth had provided. "I should have a look at your wound, if it's convenient."

"Aye, just catching up on some letters. One of interest to you, I expect."

I helped him remove the sling and open his shirt then unwrapped the bandage, all the while listening to him tell me what he was writing to the Chief of Clan MacDonald.

"His name is Donald MacDonald, lives in Glasgow. Rarely comes to Skye. That's part of the problem. Clans need a firm hand and—"

"And distance doesn't allow it."

Norman shrugged. "I'm writing to complain of our rough treatment by his clansmen, that we were forced to kill some, and that the woman and some of her men are still at-large. We may have to pay compensation if Sir Donald demands it."

"Don't forget compensation for the wife of the sailor who was killed. She lives in Glasgow."

"Ahh, thank you for reminding me."

The wound was clean, not infected, a few tidy stitches had closed it. I wiped away the seepage then applied more honey. "Does it hurt?"

"Only when I laugh."

"Of course," I chuckled at the old saying. "Can you lift your arm without pain?"

He tried it and flinched. I knew the answer before he opened his mouth. "Keep the sling on for a few more days. Elspeth said the bullet entered from below and glanced off a rib."

"Aye, he was crouched behind a rock. I was coming down on him with the claymore. Didn't see he had a pistol till too late."

"Could've been worse…much worse. Next time leave the Highland charge to your warriors."

Norman looked out the window again and shrugged. I think a part of him wanted to go out as a warrior should, not on a sickbed. "Highland chiefs should lead from the front," he said quietly, I think more to himself than me.

I put on a fresh bandage and declared his wound healing well. He was buttoning his shirt and asked, "Remember our discussions about the future?"

"Uhm. Your prospects?"

"Aye, and more."

I nodded and waited for him to continue. He pointed to a finished letter on top of the pile. "This letter is to my wife's family near Inverness. She and the wee ones may favour a change of scenery come spring."

I smiled. It was a wise course. "Inverness is quite lovely then. I'm sure she would like to see the flowers…and her family—"

"And have them away from here while I do what needs doing."

"Your health has improved. The unusual symptoms gone, and your consumption has abated…for now."

"I have you and Elspeth to thank for that."

"I assumed it was the Brightstone and the sacred spring." I tried unsuccessfully not to smirk.

"Quite so. By the way, whatever happened to that stone?"

"Last seen in my medical bag. That and almost everything else, stolen by the MacDonalds."

"I must include it in my letter to Donald MacDonald. 'Please return our charmed stone'…or some such.'" It was good to see him in buoyant spirits so soon after.

"But seriously Malcolm, despite the ugly hole in me, I am feeling much better, although I still find it absurd that someone would poison. If anything, I am too kind-hearted and generous."

"Perhaps that is the problem. To some 'tis a sign of weakness."

"Then no more," said he, with a set to his jaw.

"Then no more," I agreed.

"I intend to use my remaining time to put things right and ensure the safety of my family. Sir Malcolm…" He rose slowly from his chair, a wince of pain creasing his fair countenance, then took a step toward me, tilted his head in my direction and said, "I may need your help again."

I leaned closer and in a mock conspiratorial whisper replied, "I know, but this time I too have stipulations."

He grinned, then stepped back and bellowed, "Girl, more peat for the fire and two mugs of our best whisky!"

* * *

Over the next hour of drinking and laughing, we made our *secret* agreement. I would stay for a few months and do all I could to help his clan, to set things right as he wished. In return, he agreed to keep Clan MacLeod out of any conflicts with Her Majesty's Government and to provide no support to the Jacobites. He could not guarantee all his clansmen would comply, but I was certain this was enough assurance to satisfy my father. There would be no MacLeod Chieftain with his several hundred warriors to contend with should there be war. But the other side of the agreement was on me, and if I failed, this promise was worthless.

"You know I will do all I can to protect our clan," Norman repeated for the fourth time. We both had consumed too much whisky, slipping into that maudlin phase which precedes the obligatory nap, when an urgent knock came at the door.

"If this is about our lack of malt again, go away!" Norman said with a testiness born of our drunken state.

"'Tis Murdoch MacLeod, sir," the man at the door said in a self-assured voice.

"Do enter, Murdoch." Norman's face lit up and he rose unsteadily from his chair. I got up as well and turned in time to face a rugged man with tanned face and trimmed auburn hair shot with grey. He looked military but kitted out in an eclectic assortment of British red serge and beaded buckskin. Could this be Elspeth's father?

"Have you two met?" Norman looked at us and seeing no affirmation said, "Malcolm Forrester, meet Murdoch MacLeod. You know our dear Elspeth…rather well, I expect." Norman laughed at his attempted jest. But at once, Murdoch gave me a threatening glare.

"Not that well. We are friends and colleagues in medicine," I clarified.

Norman grinned, "So far."

"You may be skilled in many things, Norman. Matchmaking is not one of them," I ribbed him back. Meanwhile Murdoch was taking my measure and evidently not liking what he saw, for he growled, "My Elspeth is far too good for the likes of a damned Lowlander."

"I quite agree," I said while moving around him to make my exit.

"Too many cocks in the barnyard, I see. Malcolm, please stay awhile, we three have business to discuss."

I returned to my seat and watched Murdoch listen deferentially as Norman explained the situation and his recent decisions.

"As you know, Cawdie has been assigned to protect the women. And according to Sir Malcolm, I am not able to travel."

Murdoch nodded and retrieved his pipe tomahawk and tobacco. I could not remain silent. "If you please, sir, the laird has enough problems with his lungs."

Murdoch looked to his laird, who smiled warmly and said, "I am afraid our visiting physician is right. My lungs are not the best. You may smoke in the bailey with the men." Murdoch put his pipe tomahawk away and glared hatefully at me again, then Norman said, "I hear that pipe has a fascinating history." Murdoch nodded. We waited. He said nothing further. Norman laughed quietly and said, "I will not command you Murdoch, but ask as a friend. Can you help us while here at Dunvegan?"

A wee smile formed on Murdoch's lined face, "'Tis better coming as a command not a request my laird, if you don't mind me saying."

"Malcolm, this fine gentleman was my father's best friend those many years past."

"May God rest his great soul," Murdoch muttered.

"Indeed. They say my father was the perfect Highland chieftain. I may never measure-up—"

Norman was about to say something deprecating in his semi-inebriated state, so I interrupted, "Different times, and your life has yet to unfold."

Murdoch grinned, "Iain Breac was not without his faults. Ask me sometime when my gut is marinated."

Norman laughed, "Yet he was much loved. Mayhap there is hope for me."

"Always, my laird, always," Murdoch said solemnly.

Norman gave me a sly grin, "I know Elspeth loves to talk about her personal business—"

"She does not!" I protested. Murdoch choked, a gleam in his striking blue eyes.

Norman held up his hand, winced, then continued, "I will let Murdoch fill-in the details, but after the sudden death of his wife, my father bought him a commission in the colonial regiment stationed at Charles Town in the Carolina Colony. There he was promoted to Major, prospered, and took a new wife who bore him a fine son," Norman stopped and looked to Murdoch for affirmation.

"My wife is Amanda and me boy, Iain."

"Father would be pleased," Norman continued, "and now I assume you have returned to secure your military pension."

"One must petition the government. 'Tis paid based on rank and years served. I have received a land grant in the colonies, but without the pension for expenses 'tis lacking value," Murdoch explained.

"And what of Elspeth?" I asked.

"She remains my daughter."

"I can assure you, she will not agree to be owned or commanded, if that is your meaning," I advised.

"Nor mine. My first wife and I spawned strong-willed women. All I meant was those bonds remain in my heart and if she so chooses, we can be a family again," said Murdoch clearly.

"And yet you left her and her sister when they needed you most," I chided, because I wanted the truth if I was to collaborate with this man.

He thought a moment, then said to me. "I was heart-sick, and they wee girls, and I could nay take them to America, could I?" I knew he would not weep, but I could see by the flush forming on his face that his emotions were held in check by strict military control.

Then Norman interjected, "My father would have made the right decision, for you Murdoch and your children."

"I pray 'twere so," Murdoch offered.

"The past is past, and we have new challenges that await. Sir Malcolm has agreed to assist us awhile longer and I need your help as well, Murdoch." We both nodded then waited while Norman searched through his pile of letters. "Here they are," he announced then read the names on each. "One for you, Murdoch, and here is yours Malcolm." He handed us the letters then sat back as we opened them. Mine was a letter of introduction and request that the bearer be given the respect and assistance due an official agent of the Chieftain of Clan MacLeod. I looked up in time to catch him smile.

"You both know my situation and the personal agreements we have made. I may not live to see my clan through this, and my family protected. I trust, in my stead you both will assume the cause should my health fail."

I had agreed to stay and help but this seemed to go well-beyond. When does helping become being held responsible? "Are there not others? I am not of your clan," I asked.

"'Tis a sad state when my two most capable and trusted men are from away. But 'tis so. Many here are blinded by greed and self-importance."

He was right, of course, and this often was the case with families fighting over position and treasure. Reluctantly I said, "I will do what I can, but my future lies elsewhere."

"Mine as well, in the Americas. But I will protect you and our clan while I am here. You have my word."

Norman cleared his throat loud enough to make his acceptance obvious, then said, "It is settled! I can smell supper cooking. Let us join our friends in the dining room."

* * *

The dining hall was on the second floor directly above the kitchen and pantry with a staircase on the end-wall connecting the two. It was wood paneled with high ceilings, wood beams decorated with religious paintings, a few large, glassed windows, a door to the castle bailey and another to the adjacent library. When I arrived the room was filled, the thirty or more souls evidently happy to be together and sharing a meal.

I did not have time to dress properly for dinner, my doctoring clothes stained with body fluids would have to suffice, along with a hearty appetite. Lady Anne, who was dressed in black silk trimmed with yellow, was buzzing around like a bee in a field of heather, greeting, chatting, and directing guests to assigned seating. It was her sport. She said she loved entertaining and told me she enjoyed mixing and matching people to see what kind of explosions would happen. Her words and intent, not mine. This time I was seated next to Sir Ross Campbell on the side nearest the head table, with Ysabell Talisker on my other side. I laughed, thinking Lady Anne may well have her explosion. I knew them both, of course, and not overly fond of either.

The laird arrived moments later, looking resplendent in MacLeod plaid with all the accessories. He smiled warmly and made his way through the room, looking hale and hearty as he personally greeted everyone with a handshake or bow. This from the man preparing to die but hours past. I was impressed, and when came my turn I stood and bowed as though to my laird. The salutations over, the laird and lady settled themselves at the head table, with their bairns between Anne and the wet-nurse.

The tables for the rest of us were arranged like three tines of a fork extending from the head table, with me on the tine nearest the library. On every table were tallow candles which gave the silverware a rich glow. And the serving girls had already set out flagons of ale and pitchers of French wine along with platters of sliced bread with butter and cheese. Everyone was helping themselves as they chatted amiably.

Across from me, on the furthest row of tables, were Elspeth with her father, and Niall Morrison on her other side. Flirtatious Niall had pulled his chair close to Elspeth so that their elbows touched. Across the table from Elspeth and Murdoch were Una Talisker and another woman I had not met. I sent a friendly smile to Elspeth who seemed flustered trapped between her estranged father and an old heartthrob whose hand was creeping close to hers.

At our table and across from Ysabell was Mairi MacLeod and facing me, surprisingly, was Lady Myreton of Corstorphine. I gave her a questioning nod of recognition. In return she silently mouthed, "We must talk…later," and pointed her finger toward the library. I bowed my head in agreement but had no notion of why she was here and wanting to meet.

The rest of the extended family and guests filled the tables, with women and infants near the ends of the rows furthest from the head. Janet was there with wee Solas who was half-asleep on her lap. Both were seated by the door to the bailey near Cawdie who was standing guard with his intimidating claymore. And beside Cawdie was Sir Ross Campbell's manservant Gregor looking as unyielding as a rock. They were a pair. One in a Highland MacLeod belted-plaid, the other priest-like in black coat and trousers with a collar of white linen at his throat. I turned to Sir Ross and noted, "Your man has shaved his beard."

"'Tis the required fashion in Russia now. The Tsar has ordered it," Ross replied.

"He looks less villainous shaven."

Ross chuckled, "And the ladies seem to prefer it."

With that, the burble of conversation was cut-short by the entry of the first course of soup, brought in engraved silver tureens with matching ladles. A woman nearby, over-stuffed in her many layered frocks, said it was that awful soup again, as her face twisted in exaggerated disgust. Her husband made a point of looking the other way. I almost offered to take her on a romantic outing to the sacred spring but instead suppressed those cruel thoughts and said loud enough so she could hear that I was looking forward to having a large bowl of it. I know I was being daft, but I had too much to drink already.

Once the girls had placed the tureens and re-filled everyone's glasses, the laird rose and pounded the table. "Friends and family," he shouted, waiting for the last of the children to quiet. "'Tis is an immense pleasure to feast with you...and as you can see, I have recovered from my wee foray into MacDonald country." He raised his arms and did a graceful pirouette in the style of a Highland dancer. There followed laughter, rude comments about the MacDonalds, and a round of enthusiastic applause for the laird. "But enough of me. I am not the only one who has suffered trials these past months. The pestilence we have endured has ended. But it has taken many of our dear friends and family. To honour them, we will have a memorial service at the kirk this Sunday. Also, I have ordered our birlinn readied to take our Great Aunt Rhona and our Cousin Erika to their resting places in the family tomb at St Clements's Church at Rodel. As many of you already know, our Captain James MacAskill fell victim to typhus. We will greatly miss his firm hand on the tiller." The laird stopped for the scattered condolences, then continued. "Today I am proud to announce that his son William will take over his late father's position. William, please come forward." There followed applause as the laird pinned a silver broach with the MacLeod crest on William's plaid.

"I have kept you from your supper long enough," the laird tried to continue but was poked by Lady Anne who whispered something to him. "Ahh...my goodwife has reminded me that we have planned a grand ceilidh for the week after we return from Rodel. And...and we have commissioned the MacCrimmon, our illustrious piper, to write a new song in honour of those fallen to the dread typhus, and—"

Just then a chill gust of wind came from nowhere and the candles at the head table blew out. Many gasped, some muttered it was an evil omen, others made the sign of the cross. Meanwhile, servants scrambled, and the candles were promptly re-lit. The laird remained composed throughout then said, "And this reminds me of my last point. Our good friend and clan factor Niall Morrison reports that this fall's cattle auctions exceeded expectations, and we will have enough money to begin much needed repairs. As a result, I have ordered supplies so the masons and carpenters can seal our windows and doors, so at least the candles will remain lit."

Fear born of superstition was replaced by cheering and laughter. It was a wonderful performance, filled with confidence and wit. All faces but a few were joyful as we started on our soup. One who did not seem happy was Ysabell, who sat quietly not eating, her hands fidgeting with a cloth on her lap. And I, having had too much to drink and crapulence brewing in my head, could not resist a jibe aimed at her. "The laird's improved health has spoiled your appetite?"

Ysabell's head snapped out of private thought, and she looked at me as though I had made an unpleasant smell. "Nay, we all wish our laird good health and fortune," she said then lifted the cloth to her nose to stifle a sneeze or hide a sneer.

"Obviously, and that must be why you had me imprisoned."

"My mother is very protective of our laird and when she heard Elspeth had invited a Lowlander...well you know the rest," the anger flashed in her kohl dark eyes.

"Someone was poisoning him. If your fondest wish were to protect him, you could've done better," I said, criticizing her openly this time.

"'Tis only evident in hindsight, and even now unproven. His symptoms have cleared, that is true. If you and your little Elspeth have proof of wrongdoing, then present it."

"We intend to...in due course."

Her expression of disdain changed to uncertain fear. Head tilted back imperiously, she gave her lustrous raven hair a flick with her hand before answering, "Perhaps 'twas Mairi with her vile spells, or others of her ilk—"

"Or the powder you put in the laird's gloves each day."

She flushed. "At *his* request, sir!"

"I doubt he requested poison with the powder."

"You...you are insulting in your insinuations. Did Elspeth not tell you that the poisons are kept locked by Lady Mairi in her stillroom?"

"And available from the ratcatcher as well. He was very accommodating when faced with the noose." I was bluffing, of course. We had no proof of who might have poisoned the laird and no information from the ratcatcher. But sometimes it is fun to poke the hornet's nest.

Ysabell's mouth turned to an unflattering scowl and her body tensed making the veins in her neck bulge. Would she flee or fight? I welcomed both.

"If you will excuse me, I am needed elsewhere," She stood abruptly, flipping her dress so it hit my face, then pushed her chair back so forcefully it toppled over. I could not help but grin.

Across the table, Ladies Mairi and Myreton had been involved in private conversation and were startled by Ysabell's dramatic departure. There were questioning looks. "She must be having her courses." I smirked. Mairi rolled her eyes and muttered something. Lady Myreton giggled.

Sir Ross touched my arm and whispered, "You have upset the lady?"

"No more than she deserves."

"She and Niall have many friends."

"Those who pretend to support the laird?" I asked, wondering which side he was playing.

"Many are worried of what will come," he said giving away naught.

Across the way, Ysabell reached her lover Niall who had given up on Elspeth. He instead was flirting with a pretty woman with coiffed blond hair, too much cleavage, and not enough experience to know his intentions. Ysabell tugged Niall's shoulder to break his gaze from the woman's chest, then said something which made him glance at me questioningly.

I returned my regard to Ross. "And you? I am surprised to see you here."

"And I you. Perhaps our Elspeth had something to do with both our appearances?"

"I am here solely to help the laird...and you?"

Ross slurped more of his soup then wiped his hands fastidiously on a napkin before answering slowly, "I am here...because I care...and to further my business."

"You are usually not so obtuse. Are you saying you have romantic interests in Elspeth?"

I smiled remembering last summer. Elspeth and I had treated his anal fistula, so we three were on rather familiar terms, to say the least. I was surprised by his coy response, "Interested indeed," he said carefully, "but I would not describe it as romantic. She seems to prefer my manservant

Gregor in that regard."

"I've noticed that as well. Strange."

"Not especially. Gregor has certain...emm...skills that attract. But she may find him disappointing."

"How so?"

Ross smiled, "I cannot say, but I've known him a very long time."

"I see," said I, but did not. Ross was beginning to annoy me with his lack of clarity. "So, you've come all this way—"

"I've come mostly on business, not to steal your Elspeth, I assure you," said Ross, then raised his hand and ordered more wine.

I decided not to react to his dig about Elspeth, but I did need to know why he was here, because it was Ross who'd worked on behalf of the Jacobites to introduce the Tsar of Russia to the Highland Chieftains. It was to be Russian guns in exchange for Highland warriors, but fortunately nothing had come of it for logistical reasons.

"You have business dealings here?" I asked.

"Many and long-standing ones."

"If you mean Jacobite trade, you are too late."

"Malcolm, ask your father. I am not disloyal, nor do I work for the Jacobites if that is your meaning."

"You were not being loyal to Queen Anne when you invited the Tsar to interfere in our affairs," I stated testily.

Ross sighed and shook his head, "You know but the half of it."

I barked a laugh, and those around us stopped to listen. But that did not deter me, and I asked, "Which half do I know? The truth or the lies?"

"Malcolm, please...another time...I will be happy to explain."

He was right. This was to be a celebration and I had abused both my dinner partners. Lady Anne had been watching and when she caught my eye, winked, and laughed.

Meanwhile, Ysabell and Niall had left, leaving Elspeth chatting amicably with her father who seemed pleased by her attentions. I noticed Lady Anne glancing at them too and wondered of her intent. But then the second course of roast meats arrived. The over-stuffed lady who had complained of the soup had been right after-all. It was an unidentifiable mixture of vegetables that tasted well-past their prime. I had a few spoonsful and decided to leave the rest for the pigs, a decision shared by most others in attendance who had politely pushed their full bowls to the side. I would have a quiet word with the cook later.

If the soup was a disappointment, the roast meats were superb. There was beef, lamb, and poultry in abundance, all heaped on silver platters. Even the serving girls were impressed as they joked about the weight of the platters and the wonderful smoky aromas. Niall and Ysabell returned in time for the meats, with Niall making a place at the end of the row amid the fidgeting children and mothers trying to control them. *Niall and Ysabell were where they belonged,* I thought, uncharitably. Conversation among the adults became minimal as everyone used their mouths as nature intended. It was a suitable time to observe.

Janet brought Solas to sit in Niall's empty place beside Elspeth who was busy serving her father. The four of them made an odd family. I silently wished them well. They would need a good helping of luck to thrive. Warm thoughts of family must have reached Janet because she smiled then made a bountiful plate of meat and bread for Cawdie who remained steadfast with Gregor by the door. The two men shared the plate of food in male bonding which seemed to please both.

Beside me, Sir Ross was picking fussily through the meat, selecting only the leanest cuts, and leaving the rest to Lady Myreton who had a surprisingly hearty appetite. The two contrasted with Mairi who consumed little but bread and whisky. As for me, I can never turn down good meat and drink, a habit that no doubt someday will kill me.

Our appetites were almost sated when the dessert of baked apple tarts arrived. I was too full by then, but others evidently were not, because the tarts quickly disappeared. Soon thereafter, the laird thanked everyone and invited those who wished to stay for coffee and brandy to join him in the library. The usual disorder of goodbyes and well-wishes ensued, as many, especially the families with little children, made their way home. This was my opportunity to have a look at that foul-tasting soup before it was served to the warriors who would be eating next.

* * *

"The soup?" Elspeth said from behind as we entered the kitchen.

"Aye, the soup," I repeated, staying clear of the well-practised ballet of serving girls returning the good china and silverware from the dining hall for washing.

The kitchen itself was a room which appeared too small for the immense industry it hosted. It had walls of white-washed plaster, smooth grey stone floors, and three wooden doors: one to the hallway, another to the pantry, and a third to the stillroom. Along one wall was the huge open-hearth fireplace with iron turnspits for roasting meats, and levered hooks for holding pots. And to one side, a stone oven with cast-iron door. In the center of the room were two oak preparation tables and above them rows of iron hooks for hanging pots, pans, and the like.

"She is head cook. Her name is Deborah," Elspeth whispered, pointing to the florid woman encased in a white apron and matching bonnet. When we entered, she had been scolding one of her helpers who had over-baked a tray of tarts. Deborah promptly greeted us with a cocked eyebrow and half-smile.

"Do you want to deal with this?" I whispered to Elspeth before the cook had come close enough to hear over the din.

"Nay, best from you," Elspeth replied with a sly grin.

"Deborah, I need a word," I said in a tone that meant it was not for her to question.

"Sir?" she responded.

"Send your girls away. This is private."

The cook flushed then clapped her hands and said in a commanding screech, "Git tae the dish washing, the sir wants a word!"

She turned to us as the girls fled. "Ah pray the supper was to yer likin'."

I smiled and laid a hand on her arm, "Deborah, 'twas a meal fit for a king...but for the soup."

"The soup?"

"Aye. Please show us the pot from whence it came."

"There be two. One on the floor, yonder." She meant the large black pot by the door to the hallway, set there for cleaning, "That was fer the dinner served to the laird and his guests. Other pot is on the fire ready fer the boys." Her mouth shut like that was all there was to be said about it.

Elspeth was already on her way to the pot by the door when I asked the cook, "I can see from here there is much leftover."

"Aye, dunno why, 'twas hearty soup," Deborah said in a defensive tone.

"Tainted, something bitter too," Elspeth said after leaning down to smell it and having stuck a spoon in it to take a cautious sip.

"What about this one?" I asked, looking at the pot on the fire.

Deborah got a bowl and spoon. The three of us stared apprehensively into the simmering pot. "You first," I said to Elspeth.

"Of course. I am most expendable," she jested and scooped several spoonsful into a bowl. "Doesn't smell the same, does it? The other pot smelled of mint with a bit of sage. Malcolm smell this."

I stuck my nose closer. There was no off-smell, just savoury herbs, beef broth, and vegetables. "Seems fine," I said. "Let's try the other one again."

Elspeth was right, the soup on the floor tasted foul. An expression of horror gripped the cook's face and she started to babble an incoherent string of apologies and denials. But I knew it could not be her. She would be the one whose neck would be on the block if anyone were harmed. But who did this? Was it an accident or intentional? Ever-practical Elspeth started with a suggestion to take samples of both for study, then told the cook to dispose of the tainted soup in a cess pit far from humans and animals. The cook nodded in fearful agreement, then yelled for help after wiping her eyes and composing herself. I put my arm around the cook's shoulder and whispered, "I know it wasn't you, but we must find who did this and why."

While the cook was instructing the girls in the proper method of disposal, I spoke with Elspeth. "We don't know if the soup is poisoned or just foul tasting, nor do we know how it came to be so."

"And we mustn't make assumptions without proof," Elspeth added, then went to the stillroom door and tried to open it. "Locked," she muttered, then turned back to me, "As far as I know, the healers are the only ones with keys."

"And they are?"

"Mairi, Una, Ysabell, and me."

"We shouldn't assume it was poison from the stillroom. Could have been rancid meat or rotten vegetables," I said.

"Not a clever way to poison. Too obvious. But thankfully few ate enough to do any harm beyond spoil the appetite. That soup was disgusting," Elspeth said, inserting stoppers in the two jars of samples.

"Perhaps 'twas not meant to poison but send a message?" I mused.

"That they could poison us if they wished?"

"Aye, something like that."

I waved the cook over and asked her who had been in the kitchen at any time while the soup was being prepared. "Me and me two girls, a course," she said, "and...and" A deeper flush came over her already ruddy face and she spluttered, "and...Una and Ysabell!"

Oh, for God's sake! I thought then glanced at Elspeth who appeared ready to explode.

In as calm a voice as I could muster, I said, "Deborah, did you see either of them near the soup or doing anything to the soup?"

"Lady Ysabell...she is always so nice and was showing her lovely, beaded bag—"

I reached over and shook her by the shoulder, "Deborah, please answer my question."

Fear filled her eyes, and she began to cry. Then between sobs she said, "Ah dunno, ah was looking at her bag."

There was no point in brow-beating her. We now knew that two people with access to the poisons in the stillroom also were near the soup when it was being prepared. Not much in the way of proof, but it was something.

* * *

No one in the castle library showed any sign of illness. After our kitchen meeting, Elspeth and I split up, she, making the rounds of families living in the castle who had attended the dinner, and I to the library. The room was welcoming with its hazy peat glow from the large fireplace reflecting light from oak walls and silk tapestries. Several notables had stayed, including Sir Ross Campbell, Lady Myreton, Murdoch MacLeod, and the old doctor, Herold Bethune. The laird was ensconced in the place of honour, warming his back before the fire, and entertaining everyone with the story of our encounter with the witches at the sacred spring. I poured myself a well-needed brandy and sat in a brocade chair near Lady Myreton, who had offered a quick smile on seeing me enter. She was beside Murdoch too and listening to the laird who had come to the part where I revealed the blunderbuss to the astonishment of the witches.

"And Malcolm was very calm about it too. Good thing because it only would have taken an errant twitch of the finger to end badly," the laird chuckled at the notion.

"Or well. Time will tell," said I, bringing a snigger from Sir Ross.

"No need for unnecessary bloodshed," said Murdoch, while scowling at me.

"Especially if it is our own," Lady Myreton quipped.

We listened as the laird finished the tale, with him giving away a perfectly good cow to make haste home. "You should have kept the cow to trade with the MacDonalds," Herold Bethune said, grinning.

"Had we known," the laird replied, then got off on his favourite rant about the old clan wars. Meanwhile, Lady Myreton nudged me and mouthed, "Come, please." I dutifully followed her to the far corner of the room where she sat herself on a chaise, pulled her silk skirts in around her legs, and patted the space she had made. I admit it was a pleasure being close to her. She was a refined and exceptionally beautiful woman, stylishly dressed, her face made luminous with powder and rouge, her hair like spun gold flowing past a delicate neck controlled with a silk bow.

"I have something for you," she said with a knowing smile as she noticed my eyes drawn to the rise and fall of her bosom. A rather long moment passed then she broke gaze, dug into her handbag, and whispered, "I would have preferred to have given you this in private." She handed me a rolled packet tied with string, then told me to open it. Inside the paper cover were bank notes and a letter from my father. "I trust the bank notes can be used here," she said. "I brought coin for you as well…in my room…please come see me later."

She said more, but my concentration was on the letter from my father. It was short, with no expressions of love or longing. He said to trust Lady Myreton, that she and her deceased husband were old friends; and to be wary of the Talisker family, there were rumours about them. That was all. Lady Myreton reached over, touched my hand, and whispered, "I am available if you need me."

Then with a violent thud and creak, the dining hall door flew open and banged against its stop. Aunt Mairi strode in, fury in her eyes, the cook and her two helpers sucked behind in her wake. Mairi pounded the floor three times with her staff. All conversation ended. She reverently placed the wooden box she was carrying on a small table near the laird, took a step back and pointed to it in a way which both honoured and accused. I knew that box at once. It was the painted one, ancient, with scenes of the saints. It held the Brightstone and was the box I had last seen in my pack that day we lost it and almost everything else to the MacDonalds.

We looked at the box, then to Mairi. She glowered but said nothing. Then one of the cook's girls bleated, "'Twas 'em witches. Saw 'em with me own peeps."

Mairi turned on her angrily and growled, "Shush girl."

I went to the box, opened it, and saw the familiar cloth covering and shape of the stone. I looked at Mairi and asked, "How?"

"More to the point, why?" Mairi answered. "'Twas found in the stillroom…a *locked* room. Only a few of us have keys, and all have denied doing it."

"And how did it get from that MacDonald woman into the castle?" I asked while handing the box to the laird who had indicated he wanted to see it.

"'em witches—" the kitchen girl insisted. Mairi stopped her with a glare.

People were beginning to squirm. Sir Ross twisted his handkerchief but remained quiet. Murdoch arched his brow, his hand gripping his belt near the pistol as though readying himself for combat. Herold Bethune's pleasant smile was replaced by a look of puzzled consternation. Lady Myreton left swiftly. The door to the living quarters swung shut behind her.

The laird went to his feet, facing the others in the room, and lifted the box high. "'Tis a blessing from God that the Brightstone has been returned. In the hands of our healers, it has cured the sick for untold centuries and will do so for many more." All stood and clapped as the laird held the box aloft. Then he handed it with a curt bow to Lady Mairi and drew his dagger, holding it out before him. The room silenced; our attention held. Then in a chill-calm voice, the MacLeod of MacLeod swore, "By God, if any evil ones have entered our home and done mischief, I will find them and bring them to justice...and that most certainly includes those foul witches."

Cries of support and outrage followed until Mairi pounded her staff on the floor once again and announced, "There is more. Poisons have been taken from the stillroom."

Chapter 15: Elspeth

On further study, we discovered the foul soup was laced with mushrooms that could harm those who consumed overly much of it. That and the deliberate addition of wormwood provided the sickening bitter taste which forestalled severe injury. I studied the spotted gelid remains of the fly agaric mushroom. Some guests might have been plagued with strange visions they attributed to the over-consumption of ale, and any stomach sickness might be passed over as food poisoning. So why bother? Did they simply want to show that they had both access and power? The return of the Brightstone certainly proved both and I felt a frisson of cold fear. Poison is such an easy path to murder. I dumped the disgusting mess into a pail to be taken to the midden. "It was never meant to kill. The wormwood was added to prevent that"

Malcolm grunted. "Not this time. But definitely a warning." He stood in the window embrasure, arms folded, studying the wet cover of wooden trunks waving up the side of the hills. "To frighten us?"

"Aye, they may be toying with us. Trying to slow us down or stop us from moving forward with the search for the treasure. Someone thinks we are getting too close."

Aunt Mairi tapped the stone floor with her staff. "We must move swiftly. This attempt to poison means others know we are near to discovering it." She turned to me. "Have you told them?"

"No. I waited till we would all be together." The creased paper crackled as I pulled it from the pocket inside my woolen skirt. "The list of plants for the knot garden were the key that yielded its meaning." I saw Malcolm's expression and rushed into speech again. "Each of the four knot gardens seems to have a message. The plants make no sense for growing in a real garden, but each has meaning. Look at the mixture in the first section. Mistletoe and white heather next to a thistle? Mistletoe signifies a meeting place where no violence can take place. White heather protection and fulfillment. Thistle is protection and happiness. They are companioned with primroses and hyssop...eternal purity. All are enclosed in an edging of snowdrops and daffodils. Both of those mean beginnings or rebirth. And snowdrops are the flower of St. Bridgit. That combination could point to heaven or a church."

Malcolm glared at me, so I rushed on. "The plan calls for the next plot to be planted with wheat and buttercups, an unlikely combination for a garden but both symbolize riches. An unlikely edging of cloves and rosemary encloses them. Cloves are the symbol of eternal love and are an imported spice not grown here. Rosemary is for remembrance. Snowdrops and daffodils border this bed too, in fact, all four sections of the plan. Malcolm, I believe we are being guided to St. Clements, the MacLeod church at Rodel! St Bridgit is guiding us. Her three-legged sign marks most of the clues. The triquetra symbolizing the triple face of the Mother Goddess as maiden, mother and wise old woman is everywhere, even on the MacLeod armorial," I hurried on to forestall Malcolm's cynical comments about our local beliefs. "The direction is fortuitous for we must go there to honor Erika and Aunt Rhona, even if I am wrong. A time of loss that gives us excuse to search. The birlinn will limit the number of people we can take. We need Aunt Mairi, the priest, Malcolm, and the captain and a strong crew. And Aunt Mairi insisted that Solas accompany us. I argued against it. Thought it was too dangerous. But I was overruled."

* * *

I watched Malcom's eyes measure the depth of Lady Myreton's cleavage as she leaned forward to pick up her glass of wine. Her milky skin perched precariously atop the fine lace trim of her French silk bodice. I fought my inclination to say something unkind and determinedly looked elsewhere in time to see Ysabell quietly slip from the library. I wondered idly where she was going, then surrendered to another surreptitious glance at Malcolm and Lady Myreton. My forehead furrowed and I rubbed at lines which threatened to become permanent.

I had no right or reason to be jealous of Lady Myreton, but I was. She was an elegantly beautiful woman, some years older than Malcolm, but well preserved and presented. I took a cleansing breath and sought distraction. Mayhap something to read. The laird had left a new book called *A Tale of a Tub*, on a table across the room. I retrieved it and stood trying to become involved in the first few pages.

My irrational annoyance with Malcolm had fed something nearby and a touch of sly malevolence sent a shiver through me. I spun around but it was gone. Nothing remained but a lingering pale uneasiness. Scathach lifted her huge head and studied the room, a low menacing growl rumbled from her throat.

Aunt Mairi was watching Solas play with my father, her faint frown mirroring mine. Solas bubbled with laughter as he repeatedly tried tossing her into the air. She clung to him with one hand. The other clutched another of the shell necklaces he had brought from the Americas. It was wound several times around her dainty neck and clicked softly with her flights. Then Aunt Mairi stretched out the small sock she was knitting, eyed Solas plump foot measuringly, and addressed my father. "'Tis your wee lad you are missing? Is he not of an age with Solas? And who cares for your kin in the colonies when you are away?"

Twin slices of red bloomed guiltily on the blades of his cheeks, and he glanced at me before replying. "My wife Amanda." Unwittingly he squeezed Solas too tight, and she squirmed. "I will be returning soon and taking my kin with me."

I choked. "We have spoken of this, and my answer is still no! You cannot suddenly return after all that has happened and uproot and replant our lives to match yours. You left us. Walked away and stayed away for our entire childhood! We had no value to you because we are but women.

Erika and I did not deserve abandonment. We survived. Now you have the son you craved. Leave us be." My voice was ragged. Solas turned her unseeing eyes in my direction then extended a soothing hand. But not to me, to my father. Was she was comforting him? My belly attempted to rid itself of its contents. I stood to leave but Aunt Mairi's voice stopped me.

"Wait!" Her voice came out tired and harsher than she usually spoke to me. "'Tis not true, child. Neither is it your fault nor your sister's. Did I not warn you, Murdoch? I told you to tell her ere this happened."

I swallowed bile trying to escape. "Tell me what?" I rounded on my father who somehow seemed to have shrunken.

Aunt Mairi hummed, put the unfinished sock in her basket and answered for him. "That 'tis he who has been providing for you all these years. Think, lass. When coin was needed for your clothes, books, studies, and travel, who do you think provided it? Not the laird, he had none to spare. 'Twas always your father! Why he would not let the laird tell you, I do not know, but he did not leave you without. You girls were well cared for always. Rhona and I watched and gave you what you needed at the time. And we kept him informed. He was proud of you."

I sat suddenly and stared at my father. His image melted again in my mind. "But why did you not write or send word if you cared enough to support us? Never a note came in response to our letters or the gifts we sent. Did ever get them? Did you not want to hear from us?" Everything had once more shifted.

Candlelight creamed the sudden pallor of his skin. "Lass, will you not let me speak further with ye at another time? 'Tis not proper for us to fight here and now. When we have returned from the church, we can talk…'tis a promise."

I noticed his speech tended to the vernacular when he was stressed. I could but nod and hurry out to find a quiet place to retch. I had never discussed Erika or Solas with my father. It was past time I did so. We were leaving for Rodel in the morning. When we returned, we would talk.

* * *

One of the inexplicable changes in weather common in the Isles came upon us, making the birlinn shudder. The raging sea fought our wood, iron, and sail, seeking its weakness. And troughed heavy waves at the bowed boards of the boat, tried to sink us. Water drenched us all. I and others were sea-sick, the dizziness and nausea emptying our bellies, blurring our vision. Malcolm and one of the sailors pushed away the oars they had been manning and stood. Both glanced at the square sail and frantically grabbed the ropes securing it.

Aunt Mairi turned and thrust Solas into my keeping. Murmuring a curse, she strode sure-footedly on the rolling ship, then grasped the railing. Striking the base of her staff three times on the deck, she raised it skyward. I followed her gaze starboard. Slithering shapes in the stormy water, skin nacreous in the half-light, I saw. As we passed, they appeared man-shaped and a blue like the sea. The creatures went quiet and turned as one to the fragile figure on the birlinn that had interrupted their play. The beings swam upright, after their fashion, bodies emerging from the water at their waists. A strange silence supervened before the largest of them flung one arm up in acknowledgement to the slender challenging figure above him.

Silvery hair flew about Aunt Mairi's head in beckoning wind wound curls as her voice webbed across the water. "Hail, Shony why dost thou greet a friend so?"

A blue head jerked at the sound. His mane sprang wetly, dancing from beneath a cerulean cap. Laughter exploded from sensual fleshy lips at the taunt. "Ahh. Grand sport, indeed. Mairi me precious darlin'. 'Tis your lovely self that steals me sleep and so must with me in rhyme or lose cargo, crew, and ship? Dost, thou agree?" His blue face seamed a smile as his dare blew across the surface of the roiled sea.

I could feel Aunt Mairi relax. She grinned like a young lass and nodded in agreement, her attention shifting entirely to the leader of the creatures she greeted as Shony. He lifted his voice and called the contest. "Your passes o'er my realm, awakening us in your speed. What bear ye of such value that ye would dare to anger me?"

Mairi answered, "I companion tears and sorrow, none of which thou hast a need. Our abandoned husks of loved ones, whom the gods have but made free."

Shony asked again, "What care our kind for human woes when we sleep safe inside each watery cave? You shall be dragged down to serve us when we command our lethal storms to blow."

"Should you dare to battle us, who shall provide the casks of ale you crave? We may gather dulse from ashore, but your favored drink cannot be brewed below," replied Mairi.

Shony's thunderous shout of mirth spumed the space between the blue men and the birlinn. "Ah, clever lass! 'Tis right ye are. I grant ye safe passage then." His voice softened. "Ye no have changed to these old eyes, lass. Still, me beautiful Mairi. Come, be with me again. There be none like ye. I have missed ye sorely."

I saw Malcolm blink away the spray and shake his head. Solas wriggled in my arms, then removed the shell necklace she wore and flung it unerringly to settle over Shony's head. He looked up, finding her face at once, fingered the shells and bowed his huge head to her wee one, and smiling said, "I bid thee welcome, wee lady." Solas beamed at him. Then he bowed to Aunt Mairi, who then leaned over the side of the ship and whispered to him a breathy message. The blue man looked up at Solas in surprise, then vanished into the deeps.

The storm seas calmed. Malcolm and the men securing the sails slumped on their oars exhausted, seemingly unaware of what we'd witnessed. They uttered thanks for the respite and shared a flask of whisky. Mairi joined us and whispered, "'Twas the Blue Men of the Hebridean Sea. Our way be unimpeded now." I nodded. Solas did as well.

* * *

Dead and living arrived safely at Rodel. A carroty sun hung low over the mountains which sheltered what wildlife that dared the November storms. The men carefully lifted the two wooden coffins holding Erika and Aunt Rhona from the birlinn and carried them ceremonially up the path to the ancient church. The rest of us followed the slow progression led by our old priest. He would perform the service before we moved on to the graveyard.

St. Clements Church had been the resting place of the MacLeods for centuries. The stones of the church embraced the hills in a slightly irregular cruciform shape. Enigmatic ancient carved stone statues embedded in the string course circling the west tower projected their messages of power and protection. Three quarters of the way up the south wall, a stone carving of an unclothed female figure nursing a newly born child squatted, casually displaying her secrets to all. One of the old ones, she was worshipped yet, and touched in supplication, albeit with much difficulty by those seeking solace for the usual female birthing fears.

On the north face of the tower, a fully dressed stone man clutching his penis was embedded and awaiting supplicants. Other more decorous images ornamented the church walls. A bishop, a boat, and the MacLeod bull offered visual meanings of their own. And the tombs inside had their own messages which we intended to uncover.

It was a solemn progression with little sound except the swish of footsteps on the path. We entered the chilled clamminess of the church. The bearers placed their beloved burdens before the damaged altar. Through translucent panes and curves of the rose window, shafts of light painted the nave before us. It seemed familiar and I hesitated.

The barest flicker of a similar window seen in the past surfaced and then faded into the present. Malcolm put out his hand. “Elspeth? What is it?”

“Nothing.” I smiled at him wanly. “Only an old memory of me and Erika visiting an old abbey when we were children.” He patted my arm.

Someone had cleaned and dusted the altar. The priest opened his black sack and dressed the altar with creamy linen and lustrous silver candle sticks. Before lighting the beeswax tapers, he looked at Aunt Mairi, who then bowed her head in assent. We became one, as he began to recite the deeply familiar words. Peace reigned when he had done. At an invisible sign both coffins were picked up and carried outside, then sunwise around the church to two open graves within the burial grounds. Erika was interred first. The priest intoned the blessing for the dead then stood back and quietly watched. With ritual, candle and herbs, Aunt Mairi invoked the blessed St. Bridget and gave Erika into her care.

Solas tugged to be free of my hand and I released her. She stepped to her mother's casket, reached into her wrap, and brought out a small rolled-cloth doll that was always with her. It had been molded and fashioned into human form with exquisite stump work. The figure was in a circular nest fashioned of sweet-smelling plaited herbs. Kneeling, Solas placed both on Erika's coffin, crushing the plants so that we were surrounded by the aroma of rosemary and mint. The wee lass stared sightlessly down at the simple wooden box holding her mother. Then she picked up the doll, leaving the herbs, replaced it protectively in her clothing, and returned to me. The men lowered Erika and the garland into the ground.

I knew what was coming next as did the priest. He stood silently, his face completely without expression. Aunt Rhona had given instructions that she be buried with her face pointed down, in the old way of her kind. It prevented the theft of her wisdom through her mouth. What she had not shared during her lifetime, her beliefs, and powers, would now be forever safe in the silence of death.

Aunt Mairi performed the unfamiliar rites in a whisper that could not be understood, casting her prayers to the four corners of the earth. When the rites had been observed, Aunt Mairi spoke to those who had attended. "May the gods grant us their love and protection. May they fill our hearts and hands with healing. May our lives reflect the beauty we can find inside ourselves and others. May we leave this world for the next, content we have done our best. May our faith grow as does the acorn and be as strong as the sacred oak." She lifted her head. "We thank you for your grief. Rhona has asked that I gift each of you with one of these." She pulled one small smokey crystal from a pale leather pouch attached to her belt, for each of us. "They have healing powers from the ancient ones."

I noticed that the priest took one.

Two of the men began replacing the soil over the graves. Some of us stood weeping and others offered condolences to Aunt Mairi. I took Solas to her. She absently picked up the lass. Solas mixed her golden curls with the moon silver of Aunt Mairi's unbound hair and instantly fell asleep.

* * *

Malcolm signaled and we slipped quietly back to the church to search for clues, as planned. Like many churches, St. Clements was shaped like a cross. Inside, shadows hid the differences in the flanking arms that formed the transepts. The arch leading to the north transept was round and constructed of schist, while the south transept was made of freestone. I found myself drawn to the tomb of Alasdair Crotach, 8th Chief of the MacLeods. A canopied stone niche arched over the dark stone effigy sleeping beneath it. Somehow, he did not appear at peace. Wedge-shaped *voussoirs* used to build arches framed elaborate sculpted panels depicting a gamut of activities from sacred to sailing. I searched for anything that seemed familiar or seemed out of place. Stone swirls embossed the black gneiss of an armored knight's helmet. The colors and marks reminded me of designs carved on the stone balls.

"Malcolm, Look! These are like those on two of the balls. I remember because they are runic. Why would they be on his helmet?" I leaned over and traced the pattern with my finger. Malcolm grunted nearby. I carefully considered each carved pane above the recumbent figure of the knight. Nothing came to mind. I stepped back and tried to rethink what I was seeing. There were other recumbent effigies. Two of them also rested on stone slabs, grasping sword hilts in their left hands. A third knight lay beneath the window in the right transept, his sword hilt forever clasped in his right hand. Did that have some meaning or was he simply left-handed?

Turning slowly, I compared the two stone arches on either side of the transept. The one on my right was round and relatively plain. The one on my left, elaborate and pointed. The left tomb was intricately carved with religious figures and scenes. The point of the arch's key stone led my eyes upward. A triskele capped the arch sheltering Alasdair MacLeod! I sat heavily on the cold floor staring up at the three curls of the stone emblem.

It was the only one cut with the ancient symbol. "Malcolm" I could barely get the words out, my throat whispering dry with excitement. "Look! This may be important. Come and help me, please. There is a triskele there." I pointed up. "None of the others have one. What do you think?"

"Damn! Your blasted symbol." He inspected the tops of the other arches, before kneeling to begin searching the arched recess for hiding places. We felt for loose stones and hidden openings in the walls and surfaces till only one place remained: inside the sepulcher. And this meant moving Alexander Crotach MacLeod's effigy, a weighty figural slab atop it.

Malcolm felt along the edges of the sculpted lid. "I can see marks and feel roughness. Someone has already tried to open it. See? Not sure we can shift it. But be prepared for it to be empty. At least the damage looks old, so the witches haven't been here recently."

Malcolm, with maddening male forethought, had come prepared with an iron bar, the kind used by workmen for prying. He inserted the narrow end of the tool between the slab top and the base and heaved. Nothing happened. He moved the bar to the back wall and strained to push the slab forward. A scrape escaped with the slight shift. He forced the tool into the opening to widen and hold it apart. With a prayer for its occupant and a devout request for forgiveness, the two of us managed to get it open enough to see part of a skeletal upper body and helmed head. Gloved hands lay upon the armored chest, one covering the other protectively. We lit a candle and set it on the edge of the tomb. Then Malcolm reached down and gingerly touched the top glove, causing the rotted fabric to fall away, revealing slender desiccated finger bones. A ring encircled the index finger. Carvings covered the ring's head. Were they runes, or a name? I peered at it, unable to see clearly, but with the sick conviction it was important. There must be some message. I wanted to study the inscribed ring. If it proved to be nothing, I would return it.

Malcolm looked at me. "Well? What? We don't have time to tarry. Obviously, there is no treasure in here. Make up your mind." I nodded and removed the band carefully from its owner, pushing it reluctantly into my pouch. I could not make myself speak. Malcolm removed the candle and said, "One more look before we go." Using the candle, he began searching the tomb. "Here, look here," he said, wiping away grime on the inside the tomb by the skeleton's head. "Something is written. Seems to be Latin. Please trace it Elspeth."

While Malcolm held the candle, I did. It was indeed Latin, but we had not the time to translate it. It would take too long, and we had to leave at once. The top slab was levered back into position, and a mixture of saliva and dust blended the marks we had made. We rejoined the others without another word between us. I clutched the Latin notes I had made and felt the metal burning through the leather of my pouch, making me wonder what we had unleashed.

* * *

Lashing winds and torrents of rain began as we sailed home. Huge rolling waves pounded fiercely against the boat causing her to wallow and sink lower into the water. Men cried that we were taking on water! I felt the wetness first, making me glance down, seeing water flowing at my feet. I got on my knees and felt along the seams. Some of the curving wooden planks were leaking badly. I discovered that clumps of fiber had escaped the boat's seams and the rising water was colored with some sort of sooty mud. I imagined I heard the cries of gulls and sounds of female laughter blowing through the winds.

I panicked. "Solas, go to Aunt Mairi quickly. Go now, tis only a few steps." I pushed her toward Aunt Mairi who reached for her and clasped her safely. Then I yelled. "To me! We are sinking! The ship is taking on water through the seams! Captain! Malcolm, hurry." I tossed up my skirts and began ripping my petticoats into strips, stuffing them into the widening gaps, pounding the fabric into the leaks with my dagger. The men took one look and understood immediately. Malcolm fought his way across the pitching deck. "What in the name of hell's hounds happened? Give me the cloth! I can pound it faster. What idiot caused this?"

Others who could be spared from controlling the oars and sail joined our attempt to stem the rising water, tearing off any parts of their clothing which might help seal the cracks. Able women were tied to the mast for safety then worked frantically bailing water. The storm increased to demonic force; the cold downpour so heavy it was often difficult to keep eyes open. The birlinn tossed and heaved, the planks twisting and groaning in agony. Malcolm was beside me and we shortly found that large sections of caulking seemed to be dissolving! How could that be? The shipbuilders combined the experience of hundreds of years. No wooden boat was ever truly watertight, but even I knew that caulking made of wool and pine tar would not disintegrate like that. Had someone deliberately done this?

Despite our combined efforts, it seemed hopeless. The deck slanted. The birlinn began to founder. But we stubbornly worked. This time no blue men came to save us. Then unexpectedly the swells lessened and for no apparent reason the battered birlinn righted herself. The captain grimly held course; his face whiter than the spume on the white-capped waves. We rounded the headland into Loch Dunvegan. There was a short silence as the wind shifted, and an oddly muted crack of slapping sail encircled us.

We continued to make repairs as best we could and struggled home, thanking the gods we had completed our tasks. Cawdie hovered solicitously over Aunt Mairi. Solas scooted down and left them, coming to stand by me, leaning against what remained of my skirts as we made port. We limped the rest of the way to the quay, finding family and village gathered. Sir Ross counted our bedraggled numbers, his eyes lingering on Solas before turning to me. Adhie romped to Solas, and Scathach bumped me welcome. We were home.

Chapter 16: Malcolm

We staggered off the birlinn, soaked with seawater, most of us thanking the unseen ones responsible for getting us home alive. The fierce winds and waves had abated as we neared Skye, and our wee birlinn righted herself once we resealed her tight and sufficiently bailed. But by the time we entered Loch Dunvegan we were spent, arms quivering in fatigue, heads lolling in exhaustion, and mouths uttering sincere prayers. The young captain had done well and survived his first voyage. But if he had any common sense, he soon would be speaking to the village blacksmith to apprentice a more sensible trade. As for me, it was simply one of the worst three hours I had ever spent. And as I slumped to the stone dock in a sea-sodden boneless pile, I vowed never again to leave dry land.

Thankfully, we had a warm welcome that day from the laird, his pretty young wife, children, and many of the castle servants. With them were Sir Ross and his glum manservant, Gregor. And wee Adhie, who came bouncing crabwise to me, giving a cursory lick before skittering back to his new beloved, Solas. Elspeth descended beside me, more a collapse than a lady-like sit, and teased, "Looks as though you lost your dog."

"I'm happy for him. Not my type, actually."

"Aye, I know your type," she replied with a faint smile, the first I had seen in many an hour.

"They make a fine-looking couple. I wish them well," I quipped, trying to get back on my unsteady feet.

"They need each other, so it will work. As Plato said, 'Necessity is the mother of invention,'" Elspeth quoted like the sage she can be.

"And curiosity, the father?" I added, trying to outdo her while offering a hand up.

"Only applies to cats," she responded, grunting as I hoisted her to her feet.

"Then in this case, sired by love." We watched them bonding.

"A child and her dog, can't get better—"

Elspeth was about to tell me the story of her childhood dog again but was stopped when the laird held up his hand and said in a jolly voice that plans were underway for a grand ceilidh to celebrate Martinmas, a few days hence. I was all but certain we intrepid voyagers would have preferred rest and something to settle our abused stomachs. But we were alive and home, and the good ladies had been put to rest at Rodel. Otherwise, we had little to show for our efforts beyond a cryptic ring we could not read and some equally confusing phrases in Latin.

The laird clapped me on the back and made the rounds shaking everyone's hand, even down to the young rowers who had that glazed look of warriors after battle. My thoughts were elsewhere. Beyond sickness of the sea, I also was sick unto death of being attacked, robbed, poisoned, and sabotaged at every turn since I set foot on this benighted isle. Those dark thoughts must have been evident on my face because Elspeth touched my hand and whispered, "It will be better now."

I shot her angry eyes, "It will be better when I find whoever sabotaged our boat."

"We don't know who nor why. No killing, please, Malcolm."

"No promises, and I cannot control Cawdie. He the one who vowed to cleave the man in two who did this to us."

Elspeth leaned closer, "I know, Even I cannot stop him when he gets that way. But it may not have been a man who did this."

"Witches?"

She shrugged. "Mayhap."

I nudged her and grinned, "Well I intend to find out...then tell Cawdie."

"Och, you two!" Elspeth said in exasperation.

* * *

"They appear to be random marks," I said. The four of us had taken turns looking through Elspeth's glass which made the ring appear much larger. We were meeting in the laird's private room in the Fairy Tower.

Mairi disagreed. "To a knowing eye, these be more than random."

"Runes…the runes of our ancestors," Norman offered, with Elspeth nodding in agreement. "Tell me again where you found this," he said.

And so, the women did while the laird asked questions and took notes. I still thought the marks were more likely from ill-use. The ring was old, of corroded metal, likely bronze, and found on the finger of that ancient skeleton at Rodel. Was the ring important? The others thought so. In the interests of collegiality, I went along to play the rational skeptic and protect us from folly, if nothing else. Clan traditions and Elspeth's silly knot garden lead us to Rodel. The ring may lead us further. But where? And then there were the inscriptions in the tomb itself. We made a quick translation from Latin. The one on the left was, "*Protector verbi*," which means, "Protector of the Word," Elspeth explained. And on the right, "*Fidem serva in Deum desuper*."

"Keep your faith in God above," the laird exclaimed.

"You have retained your Latin better than me," I smiled at him. "But what does it mean?"

"One fact is clear," Mairi said, "The founder of our clan was a chieftain called Leod."

"And Leod means ugly in old Norse," Norman chuckled. "You see I did remember something of my clan studies."

"So, the man in the tomb was a successor of Leod?" I asked.

"Aye. He was Alisdair Crotach, our eighth chieftain and the first to be buried at St. Clements after it was constructed," Mairi explained.

"And it is the most elaborate of the tombs and the one below the triskele symbol," Elspeth added.

"And what about 'Keep your faith in God above'?" I asked. "Many religious leaders say that, or something like it, don't they, as well as

'Protector of the Word'?"

I noticed Elspeth's mouth opening, then close again. "What is it dear?" Mairi said.

"Hmm, just an idea. What if the meanings are more specific or literal?" she asked.

I looked at her, "Such as?"

"I don't know," she replied, shrugging her shoulders.

"They may be, but without context, the meanings will have to remain unknown. And then we have the marks on the ring and your enigmatic triskele balls. We still have no idea what all this means and how it might have anything to do with a clan treasure, if it indeed exists," said I.

Our trip to Rodel had done nothing but add to the mystery, and I was considering possibilities when the laird stabbed his notebook decisively and announced, "I know what we must do next." He then announced that we should go to Rubh' an Dùnain on the south-west coast of Skye and speak to an old man called Roderick MacAskill, because he was one of the few remaining who could read the old runes. "You can leave after the ceilidh and use my birlinn and crew," Norman said with a cruel grin. I wanted to say something cutting. But I think he could sense my pique because he added, "No worries, Malcolm, you won't be out of sight of land this time." It did not help.

"Then it is settled. We will follow the signs to wherever they lead and secure the clan treasure." Mairi had decided for us. None objected but my tortured mind. I honestly believed this would end in disappointment. Legends often are exaggerated on re-telling. If there ever was a treasure, it likely was long-gone. And even if it yet existed, was of no worth, decayed with time, or of sentimental value only. But I would not say aloud what I believed. My father wanted me to ensure stability, and if these leaders believed the discovery of this so-called treasure by others would harm the clan, then I would help, up to a point beyond which insanity prevailed.

* * *

Elspeth caught my sleeve on the way out, "A word in private, Malcolm." She pulled me into a small room which looked like servants' quarters, with three cots, night tables with candles, and a shared wardrobe. She sat on one of the cots, I beside her. She blushed.

I thought I knew what she was feeling, so I whispered, "I feel like a schoolboy on my first tryst."

Elspeth's blush spread on her face. "We need privacy. 'Tis not easy in this castle."

"As long a I get a kiss," I teased, noticing her discomfort.

"Nay, but you will have my thanks."

"'Tis enough. Now what is your concern?"

"I sense your misgivings. 'Twas written like runes on your less than enthusiastic face."

"I am not appreciating the trend." She gave me a puzzled look, so I elaborated, "It seems every time I am asked to do something, it requires risking life and limb. It's becoming tedious."

"I am sorry, but that fact shows how dangerous our opponents are and how much we need your help."

"Logical, as always, Elspeth."

"Not always, especially when it comes to family."

"I understand you clearly on that one," I grinned. "If you are worried about my lack of commitment, be assured I am with you fully but as your skeptical partner."

"Then you may keep us safe from family folly."

"Granted, but it is not so much that as the fact we have treacherous players yet on the chess board. Ranuff is at-large, and then there are Gormal and Doideag and whoever may be helping them. I too prefer to avoid violence but if we do nothing there may be some done to us."

"I agree and I am sure the laird does as well."

"And I don't feel comfortable leaving Dunvegan with Ranuff and witches about."

"Then what do you suggest?"

"We have some time before the birlinn is repaired and we can leave for

Rubh' an Dùnain. I intend to use it to advantage."

* * *

I had no plan beyond disrupting our enemies as much as I could. To that end, I decided to pay the shipwright a visit, since everyone agreed he was the one who had inspected our birlinn prior to departure. He lived in Dunvegan village. His name MacAskill, of course, the shipbuilding family of Clan MacLeod. Cawdie knew him, said his first name was Wud, not because he worked with wood but because when he was young, he *would* do anything for coin. Cawdie added that his given name was John. I decided to stick with Wud. When I had asked about him, Cawdie insisted Wud was a fine man and not the one who sabotaged our ship. I was equally insistent we speak with him to verify.

Wud's business was at the south end of the Dunvegan docks, in a weathered shop with double doors facing the loch. Beside it was a slipway where boats could be hauled out for repairs, and beside the slipway, a small sawmill. Wud was standing on a log above the sawpit, one pudgy hand gripping the whipsaw, appearing not as I had expected. Instead of another Cawdie-sized man, he was chunky and short, with a bald pate and a fringe of lanky grey hair with matching scruffy beard. In fact, he looked rather like a Viking dwarf, hard browed and fierce. His nickname fit all-the-more.

"Guid morn tae ye," Cawdie said and offered a hand to help Wud down.

Wud was steaming, the heat from his exertions misting the crisp morning air, his anger made tangible. "Damned log! 'Tis green…ordered dry. Damned Norwegians! Hope the whole lot isn't this bad." Wud refused Cawdie's hand and bounded down as quick as an acrobat then waved his hand at the log pile on his dock. "Paid well too. Should've known when they accepted my first offer."

"My name is Malcom Forester—"

"Ah know who you are and why you be here." He turned his head and shouted, "Billy, get outa the pit, the sawing will have to wait till spring."

Wud was in a bad mood. I glanced at Cawdie who wore a bemused expression. I took that to mean that Wud would not try to kill me anytime soon. "Come inside, I will make coffee," Wud told us then immediately turned and left. On the edge of my vision, I noticed movement then a blond head rose out of the sawpit.

"Wud's boy, James," Cawdie said.

"His son?" I asked.

"Aye."

The reason I asked was that the boy who emerged was tall and thin, almost frail with blond hair and fair skin, the inverse of Wud in appearance.

"Comes frae his mammy," Cawdie explained.

"She must be gorgeous."

"Nay anymore. Dead from pox."

"Ah." I felt a twinge of sympathy, suppressed by necessity. We were here to find out what happened to our birlinn. "Let's have some of Wud's finest coffee."

Cawdie grunted. We entered the shop. Along one wall was stacks of wood arranged by species. There was pine, oak, cherry, and many I could not identify. In the middle was his work area with a large workbench and some partly finished windows and doors. Wud squatted by the fire, whistling, and stirring a dented pot filled with black brew. I took the low stool beside him. Cawdie stood at the ready beside the door.

"Know what yer thinking. Must be ol' Wud done it."

"Just tell us what you know," I said in my matter-of-fact doctor voice.

"Used spun lamb's wool and pine tar to caulk her. Just ask me boy. He did her. Good with his hand's, that one."

"But she leaked...badly."

"Someone must've dug holes in the wool," Wud gave me a small mug of pungent coffee, black.

I nodded and took a sip. It was hot, at least. "That's what the captain thought too, someone covered the holes with clay and soot. It gradually dissolved as we sailed and the rough weather on the way home finished the job."

"Clever."

"Not when we catch him...and we will, you can be sure of that, Wud."

He rumbled, looked away and spat.

"Seems to me that whoever did this would have some knowledge of birlinn repairs and access for an extended time. This was not done in a minute, was it?"

Wud shrugged.

"And that someone must not have aroused suspicion. There were guards on duty at the castle dock, and I am going to ask them—"

"Ah saw Jimmy that night," Cawdie blurted.

"What night?" I asked.

"Afore we left. Thought nothing of it. He's there a lot."

Wud dropped his mug, the black coffee vanishing in the dirt-black floor. He held his head and moaned, "Don't hurt me boy, I beg thee. He's all ah have, and he has a young wife too."

* * *

There are few places to hide in Dunvegan, especially when everyone knows you. Cawdie found him soon enough, cowering behind the hanging meat in the butcher's shed. A wee girl saw him sneak in there, and Cawdie bribed her with one of Janet's sweets. Cawdie had him pinned on the wall when I arrived. The boy clearly was frightened.

"Elspeth doesn't want him killed." I put my hand on Cawdie's shoulder and smiled at the boy. Cawdie was snarling, or whatever giant warriors do before they dismember you.

"Och aye, but she dinnae say ah could nay torture him." Cawdie lifted Jimmy off the ground by his shirt and snarled at him again.

I almost laughed. Poor Jimmy. I could smell his urine. He would be a blithering wreck soon. "Let's give him a chance to redeem himself, shall we? I mean before the torturing. What say you, Jimmy?"

Scared-eyed Jimmy shook his head up and down repeatedly till I told Cawdie to let him down. He slithered boneless to the floor. I knelt beside him, close and fatherly, my hand on his, all concern and love. "Now tell us what happened to our birlinn."

And Jimmy did, in his halting way. He was seventeen and married, his father desperate for grandchildren. They had tried for months, he and his young bride, but nothing came of it. Then an old woman visited one night, said she was a healer and could help them with a fertility spell. They listened. The healer asked for nothing, just a wee favour, one to scare away a damned Lowlander who had brought camp fever to Dunvegan.

"Didn't seem right. Don't want to hurt anyone. Father would be upset. Ah refused the old woman. She became angry. Said she would put a curse on us. Wife would never have children if ah didn't do as she asked. Couldn't bear the thought. Agreed to do as she wished. But ah only made a few small holes in the caulking." Jimmy looked down and sobbed.

"But you didn't think of what would happen in rough weather, did you?" I let go of his hand and stood.

"Nay...sorry." Jimmy was crying now. I looked at Cawdie. A tear rolled into his beard. We both knew what grief life can bring.

"Jimmy, I need your close attention," I said, then gave him a nudge on the thigh with my boot.

He looked up, and in a voice filled with tears said, "Aye."

"Describe that old woman for me." I wanted to hear it from his lips, to have my suspicions confirmed. And they were. When Jimmy finished, I turned to Cawdie and said, "It was Gormal...let's go."

"Wait, there was another," Jimmy spluttered.

I turned quickly, "Another?"

"Another old woman. Ah think 'twas Una Talisker."

"Think?"

"Aye, she was hooded and stood back in the shadows, but I saw her face when the fire flared."

I thought a moment. He could be mistaken, seeing a face for such a brief time. "You have done well, Jimmy. But your debt is not repaid."

He was wiping his nose on his sleeve when he heard that last part. "Huh?" he said naïvely.

"You almost killed us, and it was only the kind hand of Lady Elspeth that saved you from Cawdie's claymore."

He sighed and sunk in on himself, no doubt waiting for the unwelcome news to come. "I want you to immediately tell me if you see that old woman again. Understand?" He agreed, appearing so pathetic that I relented. "Be a good son and husband, Jimmy."

Moments later outside, I whispered to Cawdie, "You did a superb job frightening him but I'm not certain he's completely free of the witches. I want him on the birlinn with us next time we sail." Cawdie chuckled.

* * *

Your beloved needs you in the armoury. Regards, Elspeth.

I folded the hastily written letter and tucked it in my notebook. I had no idea who she meant but hoped it was Adhie. I had seen some patients early and not bothered with breakfast, so I made for the castle in anticipation of a proper meal and some doggy kisses.

The woman was making beds in the armoury, readying it for the return of the warriors who were carrying their personal belongings back from the castle keep. She was the only female. I knew her, but in a regretful way. She, the woman from Drynoch. "Well?" I asked.

She was on her knees and had been tucking a blanket under the wool-filled mattress. "You may punish me if you wish. I came here for me wee bairns."

Everyone has an excuse to justify their acts of cruelty or selfishness, don't they? I am no better. Perhaps that is why it is easier to overlook sin when yours are not well-hidden. "We cannot change the past. The laird should throw you out for what you've done. But he's a kind man and deserves your absolute loyalty."

"I know...but—" she said with little conviction.

"Then why did you ask to see me, if not to be scolded?"

She got off her knees and sat on the edge of the bed, looking not as old and haggard as last time I had seen her, but still too thin for her age. Life had not been kind. "I met my husband in Glasgow," said she in a hushed voice. "He was much older than me…a soldier, and he was so fine looking in his uniform." I was fifteen and my father a dock worker. We had nothing much, often we were hungry, and I would be forced to steal food for me and me brothers. Didn't even have my own bed, did I? Then he told me of Skye, of its beauty and how he could make us a living when he got out of the army. It sounded glorious. So, we married with father's blessing and relief. It was wonderful at first…the army life, and all. Then he left the army, and we went to Drynoch. I soon realized his family was hated, but by then I was pregnant. I should've left him right then. But I had no where to go…not back to father…not with a baby—"

"Interesting story, but I must go…patients to see."

"Please sir. I am sorry, everyone says I talk too much." The flicker of a smile graced her face, and she tucked an errant strand behind her ear. "I don't understand what is going on here, but I have been hearing and seeing strange things."

"Tell me," I demanded. And she did, of seeing old women coming and going. One she knew was Una Talisker, and there were two others. "And a boy or a dwarf?"

"Nay, just the women."

"Describe them." When she did, I knew Gormal and Doideag were among us. It was bad enough having them in the village, now this. And it must have been Una who helped them get in. But how?

"So, you brought me here to tell me you saw old women in the castle?" I gave her an exasperated look. I wanted more.

"They were not servants or high ladies. And they were searching for something. The other servant girls said they were going from room to room looking. They came in here and did the same. I asked one if she had lost something. She said that it was nothing of importance, a trifle. But I knew she was lying. No one looks that hard for a trifle, do they?"

I shrugged. "And so, you saw some suspicious old women. Anything else?"

"One thing. I heard them whispering…about you!"

"And?"

"They are afraid of you…said the name Captain Forrester. Wasn't sure 'twas you till they said your first name. When I heard it, I knew I must tell you."

"If you see them again, come to me or Lady Elspeth at once. Understand?"

She nodded.

"What's your name?"

"Regina Lewis, sir, but I was a Murray from Glasgow." She looked up, perhaps not expecting my interest.

This seemed a day for redemption. It had been on my mind since our encounter with Jimmy MacAskill. Perhaps that is why I responded as I did. "Regina, we are all sinners. The Good Book tells us that, doesn't it?"

She bowed her head and listened without speaking.

"Most would tell you to seek redemption in Christ. I agree…partly. I believe that without acts of redemption, words mean nothing. It is not enough to mouth the words; you must live the life as Christ did himself." I took a step closer. She looked up as my hand reached out to touch her face. "Your act of selfishness has destroyed lives…innocent lives, so in return I want you to redeem your selfish act with those of selfless love and devotion, and perhaps the stain on your life will be removed." Her face was blank. Were my words penetrating her kindness-starved mind? It was hard to tell. But I had more, "To repay your debt, your laird may need you to do something in future, something hard, extremely hard. You owe him your life. Will you do his bidding without question?"

It was obvious by the expression on her face, that my request made her uncomfortable. She looked away and licked her dry lips. It is one thing asking someone to be good and serve others in a general way. It is quite another to make a request like that. I waited.

"What is it? she asked.

"Do you agree, or not?"

She sighed and said, "I will, but please have mercy, I have me wee bairns."

* * *

My unfortunate but necessary coercion of poor Regina Lewis seemed successful. I wanted to turn her from a liability to an asset. But based on her past decisions I was not expecting much beyond another set of eyes and hands to help us with our foes. The idea of redemption was stuck in my head for good reason, so I headed to the village inn to do some belated redeeming of my own.

It was the smell that first beckoned my senses. Fresh baking and meat from the spit, my favourite, and I had not eaten all day. I was drooling like a dog when I saw her, red hair tied and flowing over her back like a river of fire. Or perhaps it was my smoldering feelings re-ignited by her quick smile as she waved me over to meet the men she was serving.

"Malcolm, please meet the MacCrimmon, our wonderful piper…and his two sons," she said grasping my hand and pulling me close.

"Your fame precedes you, sir," I said, motioning for him to remain seated.

Instead, he stood to full height, not much more than five and a half feet. And he was mature with heavy jowls and brows, a wry smile and crinkled eyes that made me think he was considering a prank. "Och, the famous Malcolm Forrester. Our dear Teresa adores you, and I can see why."

He stuck out his hand. I took it for a vigorous shake and jibed that she adored his music as well. Teresa's face coloured and I wondered if there had been more than a love of piping between them. Teresa tried to explain, "The MacCrimmon has come all the way from Boreraig for the ceilidh on Saturday."

There was an awkward silence then Teresa offered a round of ale on the house because we were all such good friends. I smiled, the MacCrimmon shrugged, and his sons nodded. So, I joined them for an ale then more delicious meat pie than I should have consumed. It turned out that the MacCrimmon was an entertainer in more ways than piping, and I had little to do but prompt him with the occasional question to keep the stories rolling. He was pleasant company, and his sons were adoring thralls at court, and I genuinely thanked him when it was time to get back to doctoring.

All was good but I had not accomplished my task of seeking redemption for the callous way in which I had treated Teresa during the camp fever outbreak. I left my coin and sought her out. She was in the kitchen sitting on a stool beside a cat eating greedily from a bowl of scraps. I heard her say, "Oh my handsome fellow." It was what she used to say to me.

"I have been replaced so easily?" I said, smiling at her.

Her head swivelled quickly, "Och, you startled me!"

"He is a lucky boy to have you," I teased.

"Nay, he only cares about meat pies, same as most men."

"I have come to…emm…to say I am—"

"If this is about before, you can stop right there, apologies don't suit you." She gave the cat another pat and stood to face me.

"But I thought—"

"You thought you hurt me? Posh! I'd have shown you the door soon enough, my dear."

I admit I was taken aback. She seemed so fragile when we were together. "Then we will leave it at that." I turned to go. She stopped me with a touch.

"It was delightful. Thank you, Malcolm."

"For me as well…and if you—"

"Shush, no promises."

She came into my arms for a warm hug then whispered, "We need to speak, but not of us…of them, but not here. Can I come to Mairi's cottage tonight after closing?"

I was not sure of her meaning, but knew the inn was oversupplied with ears and eyes, so I whispered back, "I'll wait there."

It was a good parting, as equals, as it should be. I left the inn and almost bumped into Niall Morrison. "Just the man I am seeking," said he, grasping my upper arm tight.

"And?"

"Something nasty going on at a croft north of here."

I pulled my arm away. "Explain."

"Such as shite everywhere. Never seen so much. They smelled of it. Disgusting!" Niall wrinkled his nose as though he could smell it still. "I was there to collect rent. Couldn't get a worn penny out of them."

"I see. Where exactly is this croft?"

"On the trail, about four miles north of the castle. Can't miss it. The only croft on the side by the sea...the one that smells like shite," Niall finished with a guffaw. But it was not funny. Diarrhea can kill.

"I have a few patients to see first, but I'll go right after."

"You can use my horse. Lost yours last time, didn't you? Mine's the chestnut gelding there." Niall indicated the horse tied in front of the inn. "Try not to lose it. Paid well for him."

He was referring to the fact that we had lost our horses on the way back from Portree. I'm not sure why, perhaps it was what I'd suffered or maybe I was jealous, but that remark was petty, and I reacted, "I will protect your horse with my life, Niall. I had best be on my way, then. Oh, before I go." I took a step back and pretended to inspect where he had touched my sleeve. "You didn't happen to touch anyone at that croft, did you?"

He thought a moment. "Why do you ask? I...I may have." I could almost see the panic forming on his handsome face.

I shook my head and said in mock sorrow, "Condolences, Niall. I am so sorry. But please do us all a favour and not touch anyone for several days, especially the ladies. Could be nothing...but..." I took another step away from him, bowed then left before I was more imprudent. When she heard, Elspeth would be horrified and berate me for being unprofessional. I did not care. This was Niall; more worried about his damned horse than me, among his other crimes of conceit.

* * *

It had taken more than an hour to deal with my patients in the village, but with luck there was time to get to the croft and home before nightfall. And Niall's horse was a good one, strong, confident, tractable, and possessing a smooth gait. I had been unfair to Niall. He had offered me his horse to care for his kinsmen, and I had been unkind because of a few unwise words on his part. My education continues, as Father would say. As I rode, thoughts turned to Gracie my rental mare at Torrport. Quite a different creature to be sure. Gracie would never win a beauty prize but all I had to do was say, "Gracie to the castle," and I could sit back and review my notes or have a wee nap in the gig, in full confidence of arriving. She had memorized all my frequent stops. Most days there was nothing better than having a self-driving horse.

I worried this was another case of typhus brought by one of the servants who had fled Dunvegan. But Niall had described massive diarrhea and that was not a typical symptom. It could be dysentery, common in crowded cities, but not out here. So, I was unsure and prepared for both. I purchased left-over bread and meat pies from Teresa and filled a goatskin with fresh water from the village well. Along with my medicines, it was all I could do till I was facing the problem.

The croft cottage was set on a stony cove and hunkered down as if expecting a blow. It was just above the high tide line a few feet from a rickety pier which tethered a small boat sitting on the rocks like a dog on a leash. Fishing nets were strung out on a crooked fence that enclosed a tidy garden. Beside the garden was a hand-dug well with a tripod, rope, and bucket. The rest of the yard was filled with fish drying racks, all empty.

No one was about, so I called out. No answer. I patted the horse's neck and promised to bring him safely home then dismounted and tied him to gorse beside the garden. A woman opened the door. She was young and could have been attractive, washed and in a clean arisaid. But the smell alone emanating from the cottage was enough to ensure abstinence. Niall had not exaggerated. "My name is Malcolm. I'm the laird's physician and here to help."

She stood listless, sunken eyed, and seemed not to have the vigour to respond. I entered when she stepped aside. The room was well-lit by a cheerful peat fire and there were windows on two sides with clean linen curtains. But the smell was choking. *It's only excrement,* I told myself as I cast my eyes about the room and realized it was filled with women and children. And it was quiet, but for the low sighs and moans, a common sign of deathly sickness. "Where is your laird?" I said loudly.

The woman who had let me in said, "He went to Glasgow, trading."

I turned to her, "He? Are there no other men?"

The young woman shrugged and looked away, then muttered, "Brian provides."

There were four adult women in that cottage with many more children. Three were suckling, others sleeping on a soiled bed in a pile like puppies.

"What happened here?" I asked loud enough so all could hear.

One of the older women who had a babe at her breast piped up with, "We got the shits. Can ye not smell it?"

She was on a rocking chair. I went over and knelt beside her. "When did it start?"

She pulled the wee bairn from her teat and lay it on a blanket on the floor. "Three...four days, no more," said she, with an incongruous smile.

"I am a doctor. May I examine you?"

"Aye," she replied, flipping her hair back in a coquettish manner.

It did a quick appraisal. It was not typhus, and there was no fever typical of dysentery. I made my way from one to the other. All were the same, even the little ones had this diarrhea, and thirst, unending thirst, some said, nausea and vomiting too. One woman seemed close to death, curled around a babe in similar condition. She barely responded when I examined her. The others were not much better, without the will or ability to clean themselves properly.

Dysentery was often called the bloody flux because the watery feces are streaked with blood. It was diagnostic, but when I asked, none said there was blood, and oddly some said their excrement was like milk. They said they had plenty of food too. Dried fish and vegetables stored in a dig on the side of the hill out back. "Brian provides," said the women, one after another. But they all looked so weak and exhibiting that grey skin typical of severe dehydration.

I made my way back to the older woman. "I see you have a dug well by the garden. Is that where you get your drinking water?"

She nodded.

"I want to see it...and your latrine."

The older woman looked up at the young woman who was yet standing by the door. “Take him,” she ordered.

Outside, I filled my lungs with fresh air, noting once more the lay of the rocky cove and wondering why anyone would choose to live here. “Bring up some water,” I said to the young woman. The well water was only a few feet below the surface but not foul smelling. I did not dare taste it though. “Now show me your latrine.”

I was expecting a hike beyond the trail but instead she turned and pointed to the board on the ground above a shallow pit. It was less than ten feet from the well and uphill away from the cove. I was stunned. “Who did this?” I turned on her angrily.

She cringed and whispered, “Brian provides.”

I said something rude about Brian and shouted in her face that only a complete idiot puts his latrine upslope and close to his well. The poor girl sobbed. I put my arm around her shoulder and said she must make a new latrine somewhere else.

“But there are rocks everywhere but here,” she protested.

“Better to shit on the rocks or the sea than in your well,” I countered. She got the message but that did not explain their strange symptoms. “Let’s have a closer took at your latrine. Remove the board so I can see.”

I held my breath and looked in. It was nothing like I had every seen. There was a white slime coating the shallow pit. It looked like someone had dumped spoilt milk. I had enough. This was not dysentery, but the latrine had made a dire situation worse.

“Listen…ah…”

“Lorna, me name is Lorna.”

‘Right, listen Lorna. You seem to be the only capable one here, so I am putting you in charge.” She looked at me questioningly. “I don’t want anyone drinking from that well. Come inside, I want everyone to hear what I have to say.”

* * *

On the way in, a woman staggered past holding her abdomen. I knew where she was headed and shouted to Lorna that she had better replace the latrine board before someone fell in. The sense of misery inside was dense. It was not just the smell. I was almost used to that now. It was more, much more, as any doctor who treats the poor will attest. But these people were not truly poor. They had abundant food and decent shelter. They were miserable because of neglect and incompetence.

I pounded the small space on the dining table not covered in dirty dishes and cutlery. The clatter added to the din, waking many. A bairn bawled; others shifted seeking comfort. "Everyone listen," I said with authority, then waited for eyes to meet mine. Lorna returned with the other woman and helped her settle back to her spot by the fire. "Listen carefully! Until further notice, no one must drink water from the well." There was a murmur and I held up my hand to calm. "I have brought water and medicine. Lorna will oversee distributing them. Other healers will come tomorrow with more."

The older woman spoke up, "Good sir, we have no coin to pay. The factor took all we had."

"Niall? Niall Morrison?"

"Aye, 'twas him. Brian provided but enough coin for rent."

I instantly disliked Niall again. He had lied about the rent and taken coin from the sick. But at least he had told me about them. I had to check my temper. "You needn't worry about paying, Laird MacLeod will look after you." That caught their favour. I sent Lorna to fetch the supplies on the horse. Meanwhile, I knelt beside the talkative older woman and whispered, "I sense you are the most respected here."

"Nay, the oldest. Brian is our laird in all things."

"Are you his wife?

She chuckled, "One of many, but not by the church if that is your meaning."

"Soon, there will be more coming from Dunvegan. Tell me how this came about, and it will be easier for us all."

"Nothing much to tell. We four are sisters. Father and mother died of the pox. Brian was father's best friend and said he would provide for us.

He is all we have...men are scarce since the war. And no one wants to live here when they can be in Dunvegan."

"And all the children are Brian's?"

"Who else?" she laughed. I was beginning to like this woman. It is rare to see a sense of humour among the sick.

"I need to know more about your illness. You said it started about three or four days ago. Did you have visitors then...and what was Brian doing?"

She cast her mind back and picked up a long-stemmed pipe on the floor. Then searching her arisaid, she retrieved a worn deerskin pouch of tobacco. "Brian had returned from Glasgow with our rent money and a keg of whisky. He wanted Fiona, the one over there curled up with the babe. He was drunk and took her. Then that daft Ranuff Talisker arrived. They argued with Brian. Then all three rode off to Dunvegan. That's the last we saw of them."

I maintained my professional calm but knowing Ranuff had been here made me shudder. What he had done to Elspeth and her sister was beyond despicable. "Was there anyone with Ranuff?"

"Nay, he's enough, isn't he, always complaining of the laird and lack of respect. Me thinks he came to see what he could steal, but Brian was here."

"Was Fiona the first to be sick?"

The older woman nodded.

Lorna had returned with the skin of water and my attention turned to her. I explained how she should scrub the cups clean with sand and seawater. Each woman should have her own cup, and not shared but with her children. The medicine was a formula from the Pharmacopoeia Edinburgensis and made from gum guaiacum, gum Arabic, cinnamon, and rose water. Its purpose was to sooth the bowels and stop the diarrhea. I had no idea what was causing their illness, but I would not tell them that. When in doubt brazen it out and fall back on the tried and true. In this case, I decided to treat their dehydration and diarrhea and make sure they fixed their latrine and water problem. I could offer little more.

I showed Lorna how much medicine to give, morning and evening. "Pour it in their cup, and mix with clean water," I told her. "And make sure you take yours first, understand? Everyone is depending on you." She didn't look as confident as I'd hoped, so I whispered, "You'll have help from Dunvegan tomorrow. Keep going as long as you can." I was not sure when assistance would arrive, but hope is the best elixir when you have no better medicines.

* * *

I had stayed much later than expected and Niall's horse must have been hungry because he galloped back to his stable at Dunvegan with little prompting on my part. It was well after dark when I got back to Mairi's cottage, my mind fixated on cleaning the stench that lingered on my body.

"You are early," said Teresa, who had set a heaping basket of food and drink on my table.

"You are too," I grinned. She came to me with a mug of brew. "Stay back, I smell like—"

"Like you rolled in manure. I can smell it from here. Go wash and I'll warm the pies and bread and we can talk."

I quickly stripped and stuffed my stinking clothes in the laundry sack, then started at the top and worked my way down, soapy water gradually removing the stench if not the memory. "Do you know Brian, a fisherman who lives north of Dunvegan?"

"Brian Tormund? Of course, I do. Why?"

"Seen him lately?"

"He has a good business selling salt fish. Buys fresh fish from others in the area and salts them. He dropped in a few days ago, had a pint and left... for Glasgow, he said."

"A good business if you have plenty of free hands to cut, salt and dry."

I turned to look at Teresa. She had stopped laying the table and was looking at me thoughtfully. "Is that where you got your new smell?"

"It was, and they seem to live like slaves up there."

"Oh dear. He usually has plenty of coin and buys for his friends. Popular man. I like him, but he likes to touch women. Almost got himself slapped doing that a month ago."

"Well, he may be more than slapped when he returns."

I found my second set of clothes and was bending over pulling on my breaches when she said, "You can leave those off, now that you are clean. The pies won't be ready for a few minutes."

I thought we had said our goodbyes, but evidently, she had changed her mind. I was grateful she had. Afterward, we lay together entwined, holding hands, her glorious hair splayed. Then she told me of her family that had given their loyalty to the MacLeod chieftain long ago. And Teresa's father who owned the inn before her and of his grief on the loss of his second wife. He had no sons, so the inn went to Teresa. It was the gift that she would treasure always. Then she told me about the Talisker family. It was a confusing story with many people named MacLeod and others who were their allies, but Teresa was clear: the Taliskers felt they had been cheated several generations ago out of leading Clan MacLeod. It was a longstanding festering problem, and the current leader of the foment was Una Talisker, born a MacLeod.

"To what end does she act?" I asked.

"I think it is personal, like with us." She turned her head to me and smiled.

"Not much like us," I chuckled.

"They've been at it for years, her, Mairi, and Rhona, fighting over men, power…you name it."

I nodded. Isolated villages are like that, even more than in cities. Grudges are remembered for centuries, unhealed by constant irritation. "What does this have to do with witches?"

"Witches? God help us! All healers dabble. Some take it very seriously. Your Elspeth, among them."

"She is not mine beyond friendship, and if she is a witch, she would say it is for the good."

"You are quick to disown. She would make a good match for you, where I cannot. My place is here, yours is elsewhere and I hope you take her when you leave."

"Elspeth has her own mind."

Teresa rolled on top of me and whispered, "But you can change it as you did mine."

I did not respond to her matchmaking, my mind and body on more immediate problems.

* * *

I was out of bed well before dawn, guilt driving me to the castle. When I left, Teresa was enjoying the warmth of my bed, Mairi's bed, and I wondered if she would have approved of me using it thus. But we had had a sweet time, Teresa, and I, eating, chatting, and cuddling till the wee hours.

I was at Elspeth's door before anyone was awake. I knocked softly and whispered, "Elspeth, get dressed."

I heard someone stir, so waited for her familiar face to emerge. "Why are you here? 'Tis not yet dawn." She was running a brush through her long hair with one hand and wiping sleep from her eyes with the other, her manner the same as wee Solas. It made me smile.

"There is sickness in a croft. Come to the kitchen. We can make tea and porridge."

There was no one up but us. Elspeth stirred the fire and added peat while I filled a pot with water and fetched oats from the pantry. She had an apprehensive look as we sat at the table used by the kitchen servants, "May as well tell me, Malcolm."

"The symptoms are unusual. I was prepared for dysentery, but not this."

"Not typhus?"

"No thank God, but this could be as bad. It came on quickly and they all have it…some close to death." I explained what I had found: the situation with the well and latrine, milky diarrhea, and lack of fever. And then there was the slave-like overcrowding.

The water started to boil. Elspeth poured some in the tea and the rest in the oatmeal and gave both a quick stir. "I have never heard of symptoms like that."

I shook my head. "Treated them for dehydration and diarrhea and promised to return with more."

"You?"

"Aye, me. I've already exposed myself. So, it's down to me. I just need a horse, skins of water and more medicine."

"Och, Malcolm, we've had everything but locusts. When will it end?"

"When we die?" I looked over at her and winked.

"'Tis getting so bad I am having fantasies of being back in my cell at medical school reading those boring books."

"I know what you mean. I dream of going fishing at our croft north of Torrport. All alone, just me and a dog and the salmon jumping."

Elspeth chuckled, "I thought your fantasies always involved motherly redheads?"

"Not always," I chortled. "Oh, there was one other thing I learned at that unfortunate croft."

"Aye?"

"Ranuff had been there but a few days past. And he bought the man who runs the croft back to Dunvegan." I watched her reaction. There was none. She stopped everything, even breathing for a moment. I reached across the table and took her hand. "All will be well," I said with little conviction.

"No, it won't," she replied once her breathing had restarted.

"Elspeth, listen. This is our opportunity to gain the upper hand. We've heard rumours the witches are hereabouts, and now Ranuff. And there will be a that ceilidh tomorrow. A perfect time for them to do what they intend, while we are distracted."

"They want the triskele balls and what we found at Rodel."

"Where are they?"

"In the fireplace in my room."

"Perfect! We just need a plan to trap some witches and maybe Ranuff too."

Elspeth served the tea, and I the oatmeal in matching pewter bowls. I added a large spoonful of honey to mine. Elspeth raised her eyebrow in rebuke. We sat in silence, eating, and thinking, then she said, "I know how to trap a witch." It involved spells and magic symbols and other such nonsense. I opened my mouth in protest but before I could get a word out, she said, "You needn't complain. I know it is not scientific. But these people are believers, and the trap is for their minds."

"Hmm. So, you are saying the trap only works on believers in witchcraft?"

She nodded, "As medicine does for many."

"We can debate this another time, but what if they are not true believers. I have met them. Seems to me they are more interested in money than old beliefs."

"They want money and intend to use their beliefs to get it."

"Then set your trap Elspeth, and I will mine. And be assured my trap involves big men and cold steel."

Elspeth smiled and said, "I would have expected nothing less."

"You know me too well dear friend. Now I must prepare to return to that croft. Can you make the medicine while I fetch a horse and water?"

"Be delighted."

* * *

I was ready at dawn, two skins of water and a jug of medicine strapped to an old mare.

"I'll join you, if you please." It was Herold Bethune calling to me as he rode.

"Good morning, sir. Up early for a morning ride?" I smiled on seeing him.

"Nay, my joints detest riding, but less than my feet detest walking." He laughed heartily then stopped beside me. "I heard from Elspeth."

"Ahh. Just happened along?"

"Nay, she doesn't want you to go. Woke me and I agreed after she explained."

I mounted my horse and spoke soothing words to her. "No idea what this is Herold. But I've been exposed, and you haven't."

"I am up and here. Let us go together. You look like you could use some friendly company."

"Then pray for pleasant weather." He was good company indeed. A pleasant old chap with a vast library of stories, true and invented. He had me laughing before we had lost sight of Dunvegan. The miles went by quickly despite our slow pace. Camaraderie has wings, doesn't it? But soon the croft came into view, and I cautioned, "Stay here with the horses and I'll go in."

He grabbed my bridle and begged to differ, "Nay, 'tis me who will care for my clansmen. You have risked enough, Malcolm."

"But—"

"I am the ranking physician and insist. My wife is dead, my daughter married and gone, and young Elspeth trained and ready to take my place. She needs you…the clan needs you back at Dunvegan. So, go and leave this to me."

He had done the same with Drynoch. Did he want to die? Perhaps not but I sensed he preferred to go while wielding the Rod of Asclepius. I demurred. He was my superior. He had insisted and he was right. I unloaded the water and medicine and called to Lorna.

She greeted us with sad news, "Fiona is dead."

"Be back tomorrow," I said, and left him consoling Lorna.

* * *

"In nomine patris filii et spiriti santi…" Holding her stone-tipped staff, Mairi began the words that sought the help of the Holy Trinity and all the Saints. Then she uttered a litany that also invoked Saturn, Jupiter, Mars, Sol, and the other old gods. Solas stirred beside Elspeth, holding her hand but remaining silent. Mairi ended with asking that they all bind the evil one strongly.

It was the day of the Martinmas ceilidh, and everyone was busy with preparations, including us conspirators. We were in Elspeth's room that she shared with Solas and Mairi. Elspeth had checked and assured us the triskele balls and Viking ring remained securely hidden in the fireplace. Herbs had been arranged around the room to block the window and wall cracks from entrance by witches. The only remaining way in was the door. Cawdie would sprinkle herbs across the door sill once the witch entered the room, so she could not leave. We also were given protective pillows of herbs. Mairi said the witch could try to harm us but could not if we sat on these pillows. And if we did this properly, the witch will be trapped in the room till one of us gave permission to leave.

"That is going to trap a witch?" I was incredulous. "And how will we know if your trap has been sprung?"

"We will know by sensing it, like the vibrations a spider feels on her web when a fly alights. When we come, you must use your herbs. Don't forget." Elspeth explained.

"Sure," I said instead of laughing. Cawdie was supressing a smirk. "We opted for the spider and fly method too, but ours being more tangible than yours. Notice the thread tacked to the top of your door. If you follow it down the hallway it ends in the maidservants' quarters and attached to a feather. Cawdie and two of his warriors will lie in wait. When the feather jerks up, they pounce." I puffed out my chest, winked at Cawdie, and boasted, "Now that is a proper trap."

"Provided you can hold a witch, once caught," Aunt Mairi said with more than a hint of contempt in her voice.

"We have four well-armed men. I have met these witches. They are mortal like us, nothing more."

"Then soon we shall see which is best for trapping a witch," Elspeth quipped.

"Och, but ah still say we round folk up once ta castle is locked and search the lot of them."

"Quite right Cawdie but rounding everyone up and making them strip would spoil the ceilidh and displease the laird. Let us hope one of our traps works, or we will be exposed as arrogant fools who were easily tricked by some old women."

* * *

It was late afternoon and the castle bailey filling rapidly. Everyone had been invited. Tables laden with food and drink had been arranged by the outer wall, and in the middle, a wooden platform for dancing. I was taking advantage by making my way through the throng seeking out patients. Some complained but most were joyful, enduring the day's cold mist with good cheer. The bounteous table and free ale no doubt helped. I stopped to watch some young girls bouncing and twirling in unison. The piper screeched a cacophony while thumping the boards with his boot. But the poorly played music seemed to matter naught to these wee girls as they smiled and happily accepted accolades from friends and family. Lady Myreton came so close I could feel her heat. "I didn't know you were an enthusiast," said she.

"Only to the extent that it makes people happy. I am all for that."

"By the smiles on these girl's faces, I am certain it does. Now, can I lure you away from these wee lassies to more adult company?" she said with a wink.

"Only if it includes you, my dear," I flirted back.

"It might, but I am afraid Elspeth and Mairi want you more. The entertainment has begun inside, and we must begin our vigil."

"You are involved?" I asked.

"Indeed. That is partly why I have come...to balance the scale."

I nodded but did not quite understand and was not sure I wanted to know more, so I said, "Then let us see if the castle's piper is more skilled than this one." I took her arm and lead her through the crowd. She was a silk and lace butterfly flitting among wool moths. More than a cut above but open and friendly, often pulling me to stop to chat briefly with those she knew.

The pipes could be heard before we entered. It was MacCrimmon and sublime. All were watching and listening to a lament played before the laird and his wife seated in the place of honour before the grand fireplace in the library. The room was steaming from the heat of too many bodies clothed in damp wool, and the many candles painted a glow of beauty on all, even the oldest crone. But it was the music which brought the smiles. We were in the presence of perfection, and everyone knew it.

Lady Myreton took my hand and lead me around the edge of the crowded room to Elspeth who was with Gregor. He was bending his neck to hear something she was saying. His gesture looked proprietary. I did not like that. Not from him. Not with my friend.

"I will leave you here to guard the virgin," Lady Myreton smirked. She must have seen Gregor's pose too. "I must protect the laird and Anne. Mairi is on the ground floor with the servants."

I dragged my mind off Gregor and replied, "I'll stay here. Cawdie and his men are in place."

Lady Myreton stood on her tiptoes and whispered in my ear, "Dance with Elspeth. I don't trust him either."

There was little room, but many did dance, especially when the MacCrimmon boys started up with fiddle and drum. I caught Elspeth's eye and mouthed above the din, "Dance?"

Thankfully, she agreed with a quick "Aye!" and excused herself from Gregor.

As we made our way to the dance area, Lady Myreton was slyly dropping herbs on the floor around the laird and his family. Them Mairi returned from the kitchen and ensconced herself by the door exiting to the castle bailey. We were in place and ready.

I took Elspeth's delicate hand to dance. She had let her long hair down. It came to her waist in auburn waves held in back with a green ribbon. I noticed she had powder on her face. Not that she needed it. The rest of her was modestly dressed in a clan arisaid, with a shawl of muted gold and black tartan over a dark skirt. She looked adorable but I could tell by the set of her mouth she was not here to frolic. We tried to dance and chat. It was more like jostling and yelling in that mob, but the food and drink were superb. We changed partners many a time and the evening fled, leaving us sleepy and apprehensive that things had not turned out as expected. Our trap lay bare of prey.

"How was Herold today?" Elspeth asked during a break.

"The wee bairn died. He said one other woman is at risk, the rest are improving."

"And Herold?"

I smiled, "said he was going fishing soon. Lorna is coping well. He will isolate himself for a few days, just in case."

"You know where he is fishing?"

I nodded.

"Oh, please check-in with Cawdie again, and I'll do the same with Aunt Mairi and Lady Myreton. I am feeling something strange. Mayhap 'tis only something I ate."

It was past midnight by the mantle clock and the crowd was thinning, although the music continued unabated and would do so till Laird MacLeod called an end. The door to the residence wing was ajar. I slipped through and went quickly down the hall to the servants' quarters. Inside, Cawdie's men were playing cards while one kept constant watch on the feather. Cawdie looked up and grunted. One boy playing cards whispered, "This had better be over soon before I am skint."

Cawdie smiled. I knew he would give the lads back their money, minus a tax on learning. Nothing to be discovered, I headed back to the library. Elspeth had returned as well and was standing in the middle of the room. She was slowly turning, looking up and down. Odd behaviour, even for her. Aunt Mairi and Lady Myreton converged on her and the three stood in a circle, clutching hands. All dancing and chatter in the room stopped. Then Mairi said in a fierce voice, "They are here!"

I turned and almost bowled over Elspeth's father, who had left his perch beside an attractive widow to see what was affecting his daughter. "Follow me Murdoch," I shouted as I passed him, drawing my pistol.

Cawdie was on his knees pouring a line of herb across the doorsill. "Ah think we caught us a witch," he whispered.

The women arrived within seconds. The door was flanked by Cawdie's men, swords drawn. "I'll take this old friend," I said to Cawdie. "You did the last one." I was fully aware that when you fling open a door you could be facing anyone, armed or not, friendly or wanting to kill. I waited for Cawdie to move the women out of the way of gunfire.

I took a breath, stepped back, and kicked the door in, then charged in pistol first, glancing left and right. Inside was a plump old woman with close-cropped blond hair dressed in warrior kit. She was standing in the middle of the room, mouth open, eyes wide, about to scream or cry-out. I lowered my pistol, then said, “I’m so sorry for the uncivil welcome. I am glad you accepted our invitation, though. Care for a mug of henbane ale, dear Gormal?”

Chapter 17: Elspeth

Three heavy measured knocks on my door awakened me. I scrambled out of bed, immediately alert, and mentally began preparing for whatever emergency called. It is a helpful trait for a physician. Solas was with Janet and Cawdie, and I was alone except for Scathach who growled, her hackles springing upright along her spine. I pushed her aside and ran to answer the rude summons. There was no one there. I looked both ways, but the hall was empty and silent. *Strange,* I thought. Scathach quivered and snarled as I dressed. Her behavior was unusual. She feared nothing of which I was aware. Trying to light my candle, I found my hands shaking too. It was that darkest hour before dawn.

Later, and fully clad, including a dirk on a belt, I sought the one place I knew would be actively embracing the new day. The kitchen was fragrant, warm, and welcoming, humming with gossip about the capture of the witch and the search for Ranuff. Gormal had been imprisoned in a windowless storeroom near the scullery. A guard stood at the door ignoring the furtive peeps of the women. I listened and snatched a hot scone from the peel just pulled from the oven, then tossed it cool before covering it with cherry marmalade. Rumor had it that Ranuff was in the castle, lurking inside the hidden passages, causing delicious shivers in the maids and much talk of manly protection paired with sly glances at the apparently impassive guard. But by morn, all seemed well in hand, so I made my way to the infirmary to make certain things had been replaced properly. Aunt Mairi was there cleaning up a head wound on a warrior who remembered nothing about how it happened. She looked pale and tired but insisted the man stay in the infirmary a while. "Aunt Mairi, please go home and rest. Scathach and I will stay. Supplies need to be replaced and I will finish with him," I said, nodding in the direction of the boy soldier. I rested a light hand on Aunt Mairi's shoulder, feeling bones as delicate as those of a dove.

"Sadly, Elspeth, daughter of my heart, there is much more to come ere we be done." Her voice faded and she left much too meekly.

* * *

'Twas early evening and the laird and his family had retired to their quarters, leaving us to enjoy a few hours without work or cares. Light from the mirrored sconces on both sides of the library desk lit the ivory chess pieces tabled between Sir Ross and Murdoch and glittered off the crystal wine goblets, their ruby contents gifted from Sir Ross. The two men were engrossed in an after-dinner game.

Cawdie sat quietly with Solas. She had settled on his lap listening to him tell tales of his sojourn in Italy with Janet and me, which she found fascinating. To a child who had been incarcerated with her mother since birth, our lives must have seemed endlessly fascinating, although Erika had used the hours well, teaching Solas as much as she could. The hem on the linen apron I was making for the wee bairn was almost done. I enjoyed such simple tasks since there was something soothing about setting stitches. It was a calming time, the end of the day, a time for reflection, with Scathach at my feet attached like burr on wool.

Thoughts turned to Malcolm who had been called that afternoon to assist Doctor Bethune in treating the family with the white diarrhea. Malcolm laughingly suggested that a pretty girl called Lorna might have become a distraction for Herold. She fed him a diet rich of respect and admiration, and he was of that humiliating age when lonely old men crave the touch of young women. I smiled, wishing them both well.

I was becoming drowsy when a slight, very dirty lad put his head cautiously around the door. Scathach lifted her lip in a growl. The boy's eyes, nearly hidden beneath a mop of unclean hair and over-large cap, searched the room, and settled when he spied Cawdie. In a low quavering voice, he informed us he carried a note for "ta big man" from his lady. Something about him was off and I leaned forward to better see him more clearly by candlelight. He trotted across the room and gave a folded piece of parchment to Cawdie. Bobbing his head, he left hurriedly without pausing for comment or coin. A cold shiver washed over me, and I looked questioningly at Cawdie. He stood and carried Solas to Murdoch. She clung to Cawdie a moment then turned to face my father. "Grandfather," she said, patting his beard lightly. He smiled, pulled her closer, and resumed his chess game with Sir Ross.

Cawdie opened the note and read. "Daft lassie wants me ta catch up with her on the mountainside behind the kirk. Said she has something ta show me." His brow wrinkled. "Ah thought she was visiting Teresa." He looked at us for confirmation but none of us knew more. 'Tis coming on night. Best find her." He sighed deeply and walked swiftly to the door, shaking his great head as he left. The room quieted once more.

The fire and low chatter of the chess players had lulled me back to the edge of sleep when Janet walked in and greeted us. I regarded her with disbelief. "Janet. You missed him?"

"Missed who?" Janet said, shaking water drops off her soggy arisaid.

"He received your note and went to meet you at the kirk as you asked. Change your mind?"

She tilted her head in confusion, staring at me. "Note? I sent him no note. What are you talking about? Who brought it? "

Now I was the one perplexed. "A boy from the village, I think. Although I did not recognise him under the hair and grime. Probably belongs to one of the travelers wintering over. But if you did not send him, then who did?"

Murdoch stood, placing Solas carefully on the floor and guiding her gently toward Sir Ross.

"We must find Cawdie," said I to Janet, who was running to the door.

"I will alert the guards. This could be a deception," Murdoch said.

"To the kirk!" shouted Janet. I grabbed our cloaks from their pegs by the door and followed her out.

"Tell them to unlock the sea gate!" I screamed to the guards standing by the steps leading down to the gate. "Tell them to open it at once." By the time we reached the small platform, they had complied and two of them fell into step behind us, weapons at the ready. We flew down the rocky path bordering the castle wall and rushed across the bridge into the village, all of us panting when we arrived at the kirk. There was no sign of Cawdie nor anyone else. And then it began to rain again. The forest which grew behind the kirk was alive with the patter of raindrops on the remaining leaves. The woodland began to stir and whisper.

I turned to Janet. "Listen. You have a choice. Stay here where you will be safe or come with me. But, if you come, promise you will think of your babe and go to ground when I tell you.

The bairn comes first. No argument. Just do it. You know what Cawdie would want. Promise!" She did not respond, her eyes searching our surroundings. The guard gazed alertly into the trees as did Scathach. We had no idea what else the note to Cawdie had said, only what he had told us, that she was behind the kirk. I tried putting myself in his place. He came here and found no Janet, and naturally had become suspicious. What else was nearby? Only the hills, and—

Chilly wind stirred about us. I looked up and saw light flicker through the trees. Grabbing Janet by the arm I began to clamber upward toward the bonfire in the clearing. Red-orange light picked out the ruins of the ancient stone. It was the same place the witches had met before, where I had confronted them over Malcolm's shirt. I motioned to the guard and pulled Janet into the sheltering copse. Flames leapt and sputtered where the fire burned, but no witches cavorted about the blaze. Instead, firelight illuminated the area and reflected from glistening leaves. Boughs shivered, weaving a latticed pattern in the unnatural storm breaking over us. Trunks swayed a ferocious dance lending cover to the movements of anyone concealed among them.

My eyes found Cawdie crouched on the sloping incline above us. He was scarcely visible beneath a stout furze bush whose large thorns wind-whipped blood from his cheek. His attention was focused intently on a shadow slipping between the dark boles of the shifting forest before him. The something moved behind him. Janet saw it and screamed. Cawdie swiveled toward us, at the sound. "Go!" he shouted angrily. "There be naught ye can do here. Go! Do as I bid ye, woman!"

I tugged a resisting Janet behind a gnarled tree and shoved her down. "Do not move. You hear me!" She curled into a foetal position, clutching her belly, while staring at me with terror bright eyes. The guard had slipped away wordless when Cawdie shouted. I knew I could not count on him. Pointing to Janet, I told Scathach to guard. She looked at me anxiously but obeyed, plopping her massive bulk down next to the huddled woman. Rain wept icy tears against the uncaring ground. Thunder punctuated the sky with fearful noise and fitful illumination. Cawdie had turned his attention to the woods. I yelled a warning over the storm. "Cawdie! Ware two! Another on your left." Behind me I could hear shouts and the sound of running feet slapping against the mountain ground. Then a darkly dressed man stepped out of the woods on the right, his milk pale face glowing as he aimed his arrow at Cawdie. It was Ranuff. I stood up, running to place myself between the two men. "Ranuff...No!"

He snarled and switched his aim to me. "Interfering bitch! This time I make certain you die!" He howled like a banshee.

At the same moment, another moving shape transformed as by fairy magic into Robert Myreton of Corstorphine. He stepped boldly from his hiding place, fully armed and targeting Cawdie. *Why is Robert here?* my mind screamed. But I ignored him and darted toward Janet's beloved mate. Time slowed. Cawdie looked at Robert and Ranuff, then lunged toward me, pulling me into his arms and turning his great back to both. The world stopped. The tearing impact of shafts hitting his body vibrated in my own. But he did not fall. Thrice more I felt the shock of arrows finding their mark. A fifth pierced his neck. He staggered. I heard him grunt as air rasped in his lungs, my head trapped tightly against his hammering heart. "Sorry...my lady," he whispered, then dropped to his knees dragging me down with him.

Shouts echoed through the clearing, and I twisted my head and saw an old woman emerge from behind the druid altar, her face obscured by a shawl. *Una?* I thought. Then Murdoch appeared, and on seeing Ranuff, sprinted toward him, tomahawk raised while uttering a blood chilling cry. Turning, Ranuff sneered and lifted his bow. The old woman shrieked. "No. No, Ranuff! Don't kill him!" He glanced at her in puzzled shock, lowered the bow, turned, and rushed away, Murdoch in his wake.

I wriggled from beneath Cawdie, and he let himself sink to the ground on his belly. There were arrows embedded in the left side of his back, two protruding from his right shoulder and one in his neck. Yet he was alive! "Cawdie. My dear one…don't move." My voice was muffled and thick. My mind went cold. I could not afford to panic. He was part of me. I focused on his wounds, his life. Aunt Mairi's hand touched my shoulder.

Cawdie moved then, reaching for my hand, rolling cautiously to his side to keep from disturbing the arrows. I could feel the agony the movement caused him. His voice was heavy with liquid. "Tis all right, lass, as 'twas meant to be." He looked up at us. "Ye cannae deny tha fate." Ah fear fer ye, lass." He groaned, then choked; flecks of blood tinted his spittle. I knew well enough what that meant and fought to stay calm. I also knew there were too many wounds, too much internal damage. Naught could prevent his death. I could feel his warm life running between my fingers. We might slow it, ease his pain, but that was all. Aunt Mairi knelt and touched him. He sighed, face relaxing, then opened his eyes and smiled at her.

"I thank ye, my lady, and know ye will care for me family. 'Tis nay ended but changed." Aunt Mairi bent down and pressed her lips to his forehead in answer.

I crawled to Janet. She had not moved but could see he was mortally injured. I grasped her hands and helped her gently to her feet. We held each other as we walked to Cawdie. Warm moistness mixed with chilly rain as I looked into Cawdie's weeping eyes. They blazed with returning pain and fury tilting into a hot current of love when they met Janet's. He opened his arms as Janet lay down beside him. She sealed her body to his as though to stop the inexorable flow of his life. He closed his eyes and buried his mouth in her braided hair, and fingers locked convulsively on the tartan she had made for him. He pulled her closer. "Forgive me for leaving ye." He shook with emotion, uttering more words of love.

Aunt Mairi was at Cawdie's head. She smoothed the unruly wet curls from his face and stroked it again. His shuddering slowed. We said prayers together to ease him. Janet clung to him desperately. He opened eyes momentarily cleared of agony and regarded us all. The women who loved him poised on the brink of loss. A humorous smile touched his lips. "It will be grand show ye will be makin' 'oer me poor self at the kirk. Ah shall be there watchin'."

"Cawdie, You great oaf…" I could hardly see through the tears. His arms loosened and breathing calming as he continued to murmur comforting words to Janet. Aunt Mairi and I exchanged glances. Everything went silent except for Janet's sobs.

Cawdie sighed. Then a gentle touch of his mind to mine and he was gone. The stiff grass cut into my hands as I crept close to Janet. She lay inert, staring into Cawdie's stilled face as though searching. I pulled her gently back, and two women who had come from the village hesitantly reached out. One of them unfolded a dry plaid, then helped me get Janet to her feet and wrapped it warmly around her unresponsive body. "Come now, Janet," one of the women said. "You need to care for our unborn. 'Tis not good for him here. We will go home now. The men will see to him now and bring him home."

Murdoch returned, grim faced and winded, then knelt beside Cawdie and placed a finger on Cawdie's neck, felt a moment then sighed. His hand went to Cawdie's. He grasped it and whispered, "They have escaped. Please forgive. I vow revenge on your behalf, old friend." Murdoch rose and motioned to some village men who had just arrived. They clustered about Cawdie in quiet sorrow, then began discussing the best way to transport him to the cottage. I spoke to them. "I thank you all. Please take Cawdie home. When Sir Malcolm returns tell him that I need him. And be careful of the arrows. I need them left in place."

They nodded and began their grim chore. Once Cawdie was home, women would take the body and prepare it for burial, but before that I wanted Malcolm to look at the arrows. I wanted confirmation of my suspicions. Nothing must be left to chance or detract from my hatred. My personal pain was contained for now, till this was finished. Then naught would keep me from killing Ranuff. Naught. My bitterness was all encompassing, my passions directed solely to his death. I would live for that. Only that.

* * *

Janet's cottage had that peculiar muffled quiet that attends death. Malcolm had just left the cottage. He had come, held Janet in his arms briefly and grimly inspected the arrows, comparing them with the one Cawdie had retrieved near Corstorphine. And while doing so, he told us that Doctor Bethune had not requested his help and he believed it had been a ruse to have him away while they murdered Cawdie. He took one look at my face and said, "Go and get some rest before you fall down. You look terrible," calm fury in his tone. After delivering this compliment he removed the arrows from Cawdie's body, sparing me the gruesome chore. Then he placed them on a cloth, matching the two sets, and told me he was done, and would see me in the morning.

Lady Myreton came to pay her respects. She arrived as Malcolm left, bringing a posset for Janet, who was sitting in the kitchen near the fire, staring at Cawdie's bloody plaid which was being cleaned in a tub. The folded cloth with the arrows Malcolm had removed lay on a table near the corpse. Malcolm had arranged them by length and fletch design. There were two kinds. Lady Myreton saw them as she entered and stumbled to a stop, an inarticulate sound escaping her lips. She lost all color. As I watched she touched one tentatively and drew back as if burned. I looked a question at her. Had she known her stepson was one of the assassins? Was she friend or foe? She stared at her fingertips and stepped away before I could decide what to do. "I must speak to Mairi at once," her voice shook.

She almost ran from the cottage.

* * *

The village wright brought the coffin shaped wooden board and the body laid on it. Village women, cleaned, washed, and dressed Cawdie's body and hair with pure water and wrapped him in fine linen winding sheets. Three linen straps were placed beneath him. All of this was done in silence broken only by soft weeping or murmurs when instructions were needed.

It took six of us women to lift him into the wooden coffin using the straps placed under him. Men were not wanted nor permitted to help. This was women's work. When we had done, gold gleamed from Cawdie's red hair and from the polished coins that lay on his eyes. Teresa reached into the basket she brought. "I will place this." She walked three times around the coffin and set the wooden bowl containing three handfuls of salt on his chest to ward off evil spirits. Then we began readying the room for visitors. "You are a good friend. I thank you," I said to each of the women, and hugged them.

I walked to the window, opened it for the exit of Cawdie's soul, and pressed my forehead to the cold diamonds of glass he had been so proud of installing. I was calm enough now to tell the bees and opened the door to walk back to the garden to do so. A small hand slipped into mine, and Solas silently asked to go with me. But the bees would have to wait. Lady Myreton had returned with Aunt Mairi.

The lapis ring painted a fire speckled circle on Lady Myreton's finger. Like me, she talked with her hands. "Some of the arrows had the Myreton fletch design, and they were bespelled. I felt it when I touched them. Mairi sensed it too. One of us helped them. One who knew Cawdie. We believe we know who and we are taking precautions."

"I believe I saw your step-son Robert there as well," said I.

A grimaced wrought her face. "I know not how or why, but I will tell you what I can."

"Later," said I, "when hearts have cooled and Cawdie laid to rest."

Lady Myreton bowed her head and addressed Janet. "There can be no forgiveness for your loss, but I vow that your husband will be revenged though I die for it. Your babe will be cared for. He will be brought up as a gentleman and have property that befits him. Neither of you will want for anything I can provide. I will make quite certain of it." She looked fiercely determined, new lines on her face ageing her. Her pain and sadness seemed excessive for one who had not known Cawdie that well, but she seemed to speak from her heart.

I am not certain how much Janet heard or understood. She was drifting along the surface of her emotions, her hand frequently pressing on her belly. She had withdrawn into a place we could not follow. I was concerned she might lose the child. She nodded vaguely at Lady Myreton and returned to stirring the tub with Cawdie's bloody clothes. She bent down to wring the fabric, pausing to note the water had tinted red. She asked for the tub to be emptied and clean water brought. As they took it away, she told them to pour it on the flower beds, to keep him here.

* * *

Cawdie would have enjoyed the wake. 'Tis said that an Englishman would rather attend a Scottish wake than an English wedding. There was much maudlin memory sharing, eating, and joking. After one particularly rowdy recitation from Murdoch, a robust fart erupted from the coffin, startling everyone into temporary silence before a guffaw started another bout of laughter.

Janet slept little. She was present during the sittings during the day and the wake after sunset. I heard her speaking to Cawdie in the wee hours when it was quiet. Solas was often with her. She seemed to be comforted by the child. The wee lass seemed different too, moving about without guidance, but touching Janet often. I wondered if she was regaining her sight, but since she said nothing about it, I presumed it was because her surroundings were becoming more familiar.

Cawdie would be buried near the kirk where he and Janet had been married. A stone had been ordered. Janet asked Sir Ross to design it for her. He had agreed to do so and commissioned it to the local stone mason.

* * *

It poured the day Cawdie was buried. The rain meant he was happy, according to old beliefs. I was not so certain. The coffin was set on two chairs before the door. The men picked it up using wooden rods and began carrying it to the graveyard, walking carefully on the muddy road. I knew they would stop and change bearers along the way several times. And likely some would collapse from overindulgence. Once at the kirk, the coffin would be carried sun wise around the kirkyard before it was put into the ground. There would be no service at the gravesite, although a brief memorial would be held later. Any hint of popish ceremony was not permitted at the kirk, but the old hidden rituals would be observed.

The women did not attend the burial, staying at home to clean away any lingering traces of the wake and prepare yet more food for those who would return to the cottage. We soon finished and Aunt Mairi and Lady Myreton retired quietly to the kitchen fireplace inglenook. I searched for Janet and found her standing in the garden behind her cottage. She was removing Cawdie's plaid from the line. It was clean and mended. I wrapped it about her, covering the swell of her growing babe. She pulled it tighter and lifted one corner to her trembling mouth and wet cheek. In the gathering darkness, we stood, holding each other. With morning, the problem of the witches and Cawdie's assassins must be addressed.

Chapter 18: Malcolm

Laird MacLeod was in a foul mood. We buried Cawdie and it had been a heart-rending experience. I alternated between grief and rage since I knew it was as much my fault as anyone's. I had agreed to trap a witch and not foreseen the consequences of doing so or of holding her. Of course, there would be retribution. Obviously, they would try to get Gormal back and stop at nothing to do so. As a result, we have two answered deaths and the culprits at-large and threatening to topple the clan leadership. Could it get any worse?

We were meeting in the laird's room in the Fairy Tower. The damp grey November skies and smoky fireplace adding to our despair. Elspeth was with us, her eyes reddened from crying. A grim Mairi was standing to the side looking like she was about to smite someone with her stone-topped staff, and then there was me, perched on the edge of the laird's writing table feeling completely useless.

"They say I am weak and perhaps they are right," the laird admitted, slouching in his chair by the window overlooking the loch.

"Nay, nay, you are not weak!" Elspeth cried out from that bottomless well of kindness in her heart. Mairi and I said nothing, in tacit agreement with the laird. We had all been weak, and naive as well.

"Families are always the most trouble, aren't they?" the laird continued. "I grew up in their midst and assumed a love that did not exist."

"There must have been love, Norman. But greed and lust for power often over sways," said I, hoping to make him less morose.

Elspeth crossed the room and knelt beside the laird. She took his hand,

"We all love you Norman, but I agree with Malcolm...this treasure has poisoned our clan. I wish it had remained forgotten."

Norman clasped Elspeth's hand tightly in both of his, "At least I have you and my dear Anne."

The light flashed off the walls when Mairi raised her staff and drove it into the floor, making an ear shocking bang. "Enough of this!" she said in a gruff voice. "There will always be greed. There will forever be those who wish to seize power. Norman, your father was challenged by many and prevailed. You must do the same. Now let us stop this pathetic whining and start planning retribution."

Norman was startled and let go of Elspeth's hand. He stood, looked to Mairi, then said, "Thank you for reminding me of my duty. Henceforth, 'tis I who will lead, and I pledge to hold fast and bring these evil doers to justice and protect our clan."

Smiles broke out as sunlight on a cloudy day. It was time for action, to take the fight to our foes, but I for one wondered if we would all live to see it to the end.

* * *

"Am I well enough to do this?" Norman asked, once we were alone. I had just given him a quick physical.

"You have always been well-enough to lead. You ancestors did so until their hearts stopped beating. Use them as inspiration. But to answer your question...you have plenty of time. You are stable for now. My advice is to do what you must, while you can."

"I sometimes feel weak and spit blood, but the rest has improved."

"Well, you are not being poisoned anymore and your bullet wound has sealed. As long as you have a physician or healer nearby and refrain from unwise acts of bravery—"

"Shall I be so coddled? You will recommend a Groom of the Stool next."

I chuckled. "Nay, I suggest you wipe your own arse, at least till the castle keep roof is repaired."

I was helping the laird with his coat when Murdoch MacLeod entered. "Greetings my laird. I passed Elspeth and Mairi and could see they were happier."

"I would hardly believe so after what happened, but talk of vengeance does cheer, doesn't it?" the laird said offering Murdoch his chair. "Come Murdoch, let us have a wee dram and plot together."

"At last!" Murdoch cried then pulled the tomahawk out of his belt and gave a whoop. That made us laugh.

"You can intimidate the stoutest with that look…the wild Scot gone native," Norman grinned as he poured too much whisky in each mug. "We've all heard the stories of the fierce Indians of America. But seriously Murdoch, I asked you to join us because I want you to take over leading our warriors, on a temporary basis, of course. Cawdie was training two lads to serve as leaders. Perhaps you can finish the job."

"Would be my pleasure," Murdoch said.

"We are going after them. I will not wait passively. They will be brought to justice. You have my word on that," the laird said decisively. "There also remains the matter of the clan treasure. I fully intended to lead that expedition to the shipyard at Rubh' an Dùnain but cannot with those in our midst who wish us harm. I will start by offering a generous reward for the capture of Una and Ranuff Talisker, and that damned witch Doideag. That might flush them."

"And don't forget Doideag's dwarf…and most certainly there was someone else involved. Elspeth was there. She saw Cawdie killed. Some of the arrows that hit him had a unique fletch pattern, the same one used when Elspeth was attacked on the Glasgow Road near Corstorphine. Cawdie took that fletch as evidence. Janet has it still. At the time, he told me that only rich bastards used custom made arrows like that," I explained.

"Elspeth said it was Robert, Lady Myreton's step-son from Corstorphine, who she recognized behind the kirk," Murdoch added. He had been filling his pipe which was the part of his tomahawk on the opposite side of the axe, the wooden handle serving as the stem for drawing in smoke. He noticed me looking at it. "Got it from a Kiawah chief in exchange for…

well you don't want to know."

"Never seen one like that," I said giving him a cautionary glare because I did not want him smoking near the laird. But he did not ken my meaning and continued tamping tobacco in the bowl.

Without stopping his preparations, Murdoch said, "I saw the arrows that killed Cawdie. They were from a longbow, not cross-bow bolts, nor were they short arrows used with a light bow."

"A Scottish longbow is six feet in length and has a draw weight of eighty to one hundred pounds," the laird noted.

Murdoch grunted, "Few women could manage a longbow, and certainly not a dwarf."

"That leaves Ranuff and the owner of that unusual fletch…perhaps Robert as Elspeth maintains. And Elspeth thought she saw Una Talisker too but couldn't be certain because of the dark," I said.

Murdoch nodded. "Aye, a woman's voice was heard before I chased Ranuff. As to the other fellow…"

The laird rose and stretched, impatience suffusing his mien. "I want them all detained."

"Including Ysabell and Niall?" Murdoch asked, one eye arched.

"Nay, not them, not yet. I will give that greedy pair more string to tangle."

"Ysabell may have been poisoning the laird's fencing gloves," I clarified for Murdoch. "Or it was Ysabell's mother, Una, who tampered with the sweet powder."

"We shall find out when they are facing the noose," the laird said, pacing like a caged lion.

"And then there is the matter of how Gormal entered the castle unseen. She was dressed as a warrior, but she would not have been convincing to guards on the sea gate." I had been wondering about that since we captured her. She had not been helpful so far, but then we had been kind hosts and Gormal had not experienced the dungeon.

"There must be another way into the castle," Murdoch said.

Norman stopped pacing. A flush came over his face, "There is."

"What!" I blurted.

"But few know of it, and I never imagined those who did would turn on me."

"Una Talisker knew, didn't she?" Murdoch said in forced control.

"Aye, she did, Mairi too. It is a cut in the wall behind a stillroom cabinet. It leads to the drain that ends in a grate which empties to the sea. It was made for cleaning the stillroom should there be a spill. Provided one has the key to the lock on the grate, one could manage it on hands and knees."

"And Una has a key," said I.

"It is in a jar in the stillroom," the laird explained.

There was no point in recriminations. The laird had been too trusting, as we all are at times. One cannot live in perpetual suspicion. "Now we know and perhaps we can use it on Gormal. But let's focus on necessary tasks," I suggested.

"Agreed. Our first task is to run that damned Ranuff to ground. I offer to kill him gratis for what he did to Cawdie and my daughters," Murdoch said as he bent close to the peat fire to light tinder for his pipe.

"I would take you up on that, but I need you here for greater purpose. And Murdoch no smoking in here. It bothers the good doctor who is overly obsessed with my health."

Murdoch grumpily flipped the lit stick back into the fire. "I understand, my laird. I will stay my revenge and train the boys."

The laird smiled slightly, observing Murdoch suffering his addiction, "I want our men ready to march in a week. We take back Ranuff's keep... there...damn him, he has me saying it too. It is not his keep, it is ours, and I intend to take it back...and Murdoch, I may turn him over to you once he has been emptied."

I knew the feeling of wanting steel justice, but I had to say it, a message from my father the lord and judge, "It might be better to convict them in a court of law."

"Not as satisfying as gutting them while looking in their eyes," Murdoch said. I believed him.

Our meeting of the minds ended that way, with resolve, a half-baked plan, and anger in our hearts. We had been violated and hated it.

* * *

Murdoch was waiting for me at the bottom of the stairs to the Fairy Tower. "A word, if you please, sir."

I could tell by his subdued behaviour in our meeting with the laird that something was bothering him, something beyond clan problems. "I'm on my way to visit Gormal. There is a room nearby used by the women for socializing. It should be free this time of day." Murdoch bowed and followed me along the hallways to the small room on the second floor above the armoury. There was a lit fireplace, a well-placed window overlooking the village, and several upholstered chairs. We settled in close to the fire. A serving girl soon arrived with an offer of whisky.

Murdoch looked in turmoil. "I know many would say I have been a terrible father, leaving my girls like that—"

"You needn't explain nor apologize. It's between you and Elspeth. I just hope you two can heal your wounds."

"It is not that, exactly. I did not intend to come back here. I could have stayed with Angus MacLeod in Glasgow to deal with my pension, but felt drawn back to Skye, and now I am amid it once more, what I sought to leave and forget. Forgive me, this brings back memories." Murdoch looked out the window, as though longing to escape back to America and his new life.

We sat in silence as the girl brought our whisky, then I said, "The past is past, we must concentrate our minds on the present."

"Easy to say."

I smiled, "Aye. But you know it is true."

He tilted his chin in defiance.

"Now tell me what you wanted to say, before we drink ourselves into self-pity."

With that rebuke, Murdoch took one gulp of whisky, put the mug down and sat straight-backed. "'Tis my Elspeth. I just do not know how to help her. Cawdie is gone and now she and Janet have no protector. I cannot be that nor can I leave them. I visited her yesterday. My tongue was as stilled as a shot deer on a carrying pole."

"I may not do any better. I tried too. They were crying. Elspeth shooed me away and said they wanted to grieve alone."

"I understand...but after...who will care for them? They have a child and another on the way."

"The clan, surely."

"Only if they stay here and I am not certain that is her will."

We looked at each other, two men worried about women who may not even want us around. "Malcolm, I know Elspeth admires you, and you would not have come all this way if you had no feelings for her."

I knew that I did this for my father as well, not just Elspeth. But I would not tell Murdoch that right now. I needed allies and he could be a powerful one. "What do you want of me, Murdoch?" I said, finally.

He cleared his throat and gazed out the window again then turned to me with set jaw and cold eyes, "I may be required to do hard things and I need to know someone will look after my women."

"I would do that without your asking, sir," I said without hesitation.

* * *

Gormal was meditating when I entered her room, a converted storeroom off the servants' quarters. It was unheated, windowless, with a cot and a battered crate for a bedside table. There also was a chamber pot tucked under the bed that desperately needed emptying. Her room was locked and guarded. It was a cold, bleak place but far better than the dungeon which had hosted me when I arrived. So far, she had been decently served.

"How is the food?" I asked, then sat on the bed beside her. "Do you have enough clean towels and ale?" I teased. She was staring at the far wall, not acknowledging my presence.

"You know I care about you, Gormal. This could have been much worse for you, had I not intervened."

No response.

"We know how you got in the castle and have set traps for anyone trying a rescue."

Still no response.

"And the only way you can save yourself from being tortured, hung and burned as a witch is to tell me who else is involved and where they are."

She blinked when I said burned. Her head turned. "They say Captain Forrester can never be trusted." She did not look at me directly. Instead, she drew a symbol with her finger in the air.

These witches are exasperating, I thought. "Gormal, I may well be a descendent of Captain Forrester, but I am not evil! Do you not remember when you poisoned me at Broadford? By rights I could have killed you, but I didn't. Then at the sacred spring, I could have blown you to pieces, but I didn't. If I am the captain you fear, would I not have destroyed you before now? But I stayed my hand, and you came to no harm."

I reached over and carefully put my arm over her pillow-like shoulder. She trembled. "Your so-called friends have abandoned you, but I won't." Her upper lip quivered. I gently pulled her into a warm embrace and whispered, "I will care for you my dear and you will help me."

She started to sob.

* * *

"I don't want to push her too hard. I have seen women rebound like a tigress, just when you think you have won. This must be done slowly, or it could go badly," I was explaining the situation to Elspeth. I had come to see her at Murdoch's request, but again she had brushed off concerns and preferred to discuss Gormal, of all people.

"I know our laird is angry and preparing for war. I cannot blame him considering what happened, but I think a less heavy-handed approach would work better," Elspeth opined.

Janet had served us tea and sweet cakes while Solas sat at the chess board alone, with Adhie sleeping at her feet. Solas seemed to be speaking to someone and moving the chess pieces. We all looked when she clapped in excitement and cried, "I won!"

I looked back at Elspeth with concern. She returned my look and whispered, "she says Cawdie is teaching her. We don't have the heart..."

"I understand. Children have creative imaginations. I remember—"

"Nay Malcolm, 'tis not imagination. He is here with us. We need him still and he knows it. He would never leave us unprotected," Elspeth interjected angrily.

"I see," I said, knowing grief can make people believe strange things that have no basis in fact, like angels and fairies. I was even more worried about them now. The last thing we needed was an unhinged Elspeth while combating foes.

I suspect the unease on my face was evident because she added, "Malcolm, you worry without cause. We are practical women. Janet and I have survived alone before Cawdie, and we will again. We just need time."

Janet had been listening quietly on a cushion by the fire, her tear-washed face pale beneath her shawl. My heart pulled to her in sympathy. I understood grief. I have had my share. I wanted to comfort her but could not. Cawdie was a good friend. We all would miss him, especially Janet. They were so happy together. I shook those mournful, conflicted thoughts away and turned back to Elspeth, "The laird must be seen to be strong. He intends to march the warriors to Talisker and take back the keep, by force if necessary. If Ranuff is there, we will try to capture him. In any case, people will see that the laird is willing to act, and further challenges will be met with force. It is the traditional way of a Scottish leader. I support him and I trust you will as well."

Elspeth nodded imperceptibly. "We do but let us pray that goading him into action was not their intent from the start."

"We will deal with whatever comes," I said with more confidence than I had.

Elspeth knew me well and bowed her head in mock reverence, "Of course Malcolm but please remember the last time you and Norman went on a lad's adventure."

I was about to offer a cutting retort when Solas jumped off her stool and announced, "Cawdie wants Malcolm to play chess with me."

* * *

"Open wide," I said to the youth seated in front of me. The armoury smelled of the vinegar that Elspeth had insisted be used to wash everything after the typhus outbreak. Murdoch asked me to have a look at his warriors. He did not want any who were sick or injured being forced to march to Talisker and back. I understood, but it was tedious work. I had almost finished. There were only three not fit to serve. They would stay behind to help the older guards.

The lad's mouth and teeth looked fine, so I asked, "Eating, drinking, and evacuating well?"

He looked at me as though I were speaking French, so I translated, "Eatin' skitin' peein' an' poopin'?"

The boy grinned and replied, "Weel enaw."

"Good lad, "I grinned back.

I was about to have him remove his boots when Murdoch joined us. "That one's fine. Saw him chasing a lassie afore."

I nodded to the boy to leave. Murdoch replaced him on the chair and arranged his beaded buckskins for comfort. "We need a *tête-à-tête*," he said and started filling his pipe tomahawk for a smoke.

"They don't understand French here," I said.

"Precisely, and don't bother giving me any of your sour looks. This be my *domaine de controle*, and I can smoke if I want."

"Picked up some French in America, did you?"

"Had to, the French and Indians attacked Massachusetts and we were sent north to help. Can't blame them though after what we did to them in Acadia last year. And I did learn some French...from a prisoner...nice fellow...said he was from Grand-Pré...a farmer. We had an enjoyable time playing cards, drinking, and telling lies."

"What happened to him?"

Murdoch looked down and shrugged. "Not here to relive those troubled times. Now tell me. What about my lads?"

I had kept notes and was about to go through them when he interjected,

"Don't need more than a yay or nay. Are they fit to march next week?"

"The answer to marching is yes, but not sure what good they will do in a fight, if it comes to that."

"Leave that part to me. I'll make sure they can shoot and fight. Cawdie was training them, and they do have discipline. He scared it into them."

"Then how can I help after I finish this?"

Murdoch had lit his pipe and was politely blowing smoke away from me. He considered a moment before answering. "I hate to ask, but there is no one else. Don't want women on a battlefield and Herold is too old. Mind you he would not say no, if asked. But you are the only one."

"I will tend your sick and wounded. I assumed as much."

"I am sorry. I am sure you didn't intend being stuck in this."

"It's the same with you. We cope," I replied.

Murdoch grunted and lowered his pipe. In a turn of the wrist, that pipe could become an axe. I smiled thinking how interesting drinking and smoking with friends might be in America.

"But that leaves most of the male leadership gone…the laird, you, me. There is Niall, but who knows what side he is on…and the same goes for Ross Campbell," Murdoch stared at me as though expecting a clever solution. I had none.

"Agreed. How well do you know Ross?" I asked.

"Just by reputation. I hear he is avaricious, would sell his mother's only arisaid for the right price."

I smiled remembering his role in bringing Russians to Torrport last summer. "Indeed. He often does seem to be playing both ends against the middle…for profit."

"His manservant Gregor may be a different kettle of fish. I noticed Elspeth's eyes following him everywhere at the ceilidh. Anything going on there I should know?"

"I should hope not. I dislike him. He's not just a manservant. Ross uses him in other ways."

"As his guard?"

"Maybe more."

"Then what in God's Good Name does Elspeth see in him?"

"I asked…she said he shows great sympathy for others."

Murdoch burst out laughing, "Women are not attracted to men because of that!"

"Who knows what women want. In any case, I think he's trouble—"

"But perhaps the best we have to protect the women. I'd rather have a hired killer than a stable boy."

"Provided Elspeth trusts him."

"Agreed. Can you ask her? I am having trouble enough communicating with them."

"I'll try. They aren't speaking much to me either."

Murdoch took another long draw on his pipe. A young warrior entered for his physical, then left, seeing us.

Thoughts went to Cawdie. I felt him sometimes urging me to act. "I wish I'd been here when Cawdie—"

"We all wish things had been different. You know the laird apologized to me for what happened to my girls. God bless him…he's a kind lad."

"But he didn't know about Erika. Everyone thought she'd died of smallpox."

"Not everyone."

I must have raised an eyebrow because he answered before I could ask. "Mairi always said she could feel that Erika was yet alive. Rhona said as much too."

"But no one believed them."

"Evidently not."

It was a tragic affair. I had been with the laird on our trek when Elspeth was captured. Fortunately, she was rescued, along with little Solas. And the man behind all this was that damned Ranuff Talisker.

Murdoch must have been thinking the same because he said, "We did a thorough search of the castle and grounds. No sign of him."

"I doubt he would've stayed after what they did."

Murdoch nodded, then set his pipe to the side. "Most think he went to his keep at Talisker, but if he's smart, he would leave Skye altogether."

“Perhaps. Or he may think the laird is weak and won’t act.”

“He will find out otherwise soon enough.” Murdoch tapped the ashes out of his pipe and stood to go. “We must speak again.”

“We will,” I replied, then called in the next boy to examine.

* * *

The next days were a blur of preparations. Murdoch was drilling the lads in the bailey and having them march through the village and back for hours. The locals were impressed. This was becoming serious. And word had spread about the reward for the capture of Ranuff and the witches. That caused quite a coin-grasping furor and there were line-ups at the sea gate of those seeking to report suspicious activity. One of the servants took their names and information. Turns out most just wanted to settle old scores by having neighbours investigated. And laughably, sometimes it was neighbours reporting each other. But there was one useful account from a drover returning home from Crieff. He said he met a curious pair of women with a dwarf and a black dog walking on the trail near Struan, where the trail east to Sligachan meets the one south to Drynoch. He said he remembered them well because one of the women cursed him for asking if they were healing hags and could they spare any herbs to settle his stomach. He even offered to pay but all that bought was further verbal abuse. Then the dwarf revealed a pistol to confirm their lack of helpfulness.

Later that day, we met with the drover. He seemed completely unaware of what had taken place in Dunvegan but had told the story of his unsettling encounter to his old wife, who promptly escorted him to the castle for a fat reward. After the interview, the laird gave him a nice gold coin and promised more should the women and dwarf be captured. The drover said that he knew those three were bad ones by the disrespectful way he had been treated. As he was saying this, the drover’s wife happily grabbed the coin out of her husband’s grubby hand. The laird glared at the wife and said she would be giving that coin back should the facts prove incorrect.

No matter, she tucked it away in her skirt and gave the laird a glance suggesting otherwise.

We had Gormal locked up. So, Una, Doideag and the dwarf likely were south of Dunvegan and headed either west to Talisker, east to Portree, or south to Eynort and the wild mountains nearby. My money was on Talisker Bay, Una and Ranuff's family home, where they had comfort and support. Even animals run home when they are frightened.

* * *

I was in the castle stables wrestling with an uncooperative pony when Wud called my name. "Over here," I said, "but keep clear of this gelding. He has bad manners."

"Like me and the boy?" Wud replied with a sneer, then snapped his finger and gave the pony a hiss that settled him. "He doesn't like that bucket." Wud pointed. "Ah know this one. Sold him to the laird last summer."

"Is he going to be trouble?"

"Nay, once he gets outside, he will calm. Nay used to be in stable."

I was able to get the bridle on while Wud kept him distracted.

"Next time lead him out to saddle, and he be fine," Wud suggested.

"Noted, but they give me whatever is fed, watered and in need of exercise. Anything I should know before I leave?" I led the pony out to cinch and mount him. Wud followed then cleared his throat suggesting he had something to say. But he did not. Instead, he shuffled his feet and stared to the sky as though begging help from the gods to loosen his tongue. I threw my medical bag over the back of the saddle along with a skin of fresh water. "Well?" I said, raising my left foot to the stirrup.

"Errm, ah want to thank ye for going easy on me son."

I hoisted myself into the saddle. "You can thank Elspeth MacLeod for that. Jimmy is young and deserves a second chance."

Wud nodded then said, "Shoulda come to ye earlier."

"How's that?"

"Jimmy saw someone with Una Talisker...a stranger...a young fellow."

"Oh? When was this?"

"Afore Cawdie was killed. Jimmy shoulda said something but auld Una frights him."

"What did the young man look like?"

"Jimmy said he was lanky with dark curly locks and dear clothes…like a Lowlander."

"And a fancy bow?"

"Dinnae say, but he would've noticed…loves making weapons that one… better than boats 'n furniture."

The shaggy pony was becoming restless, no doubt seeing the familiar trail ahead. "When and where did he see them?"

"Afore Cawdie got murdered. Saw him behind the kirk. Jimmy likes going there to cut saplings."

"Alright Wud, thanks for telling me, but you might have saved Cawdie's life by mentioning it sooner."

Wud said nothing. I was not certain he felt remorse, and his bleak face more likely due to worry about his son. But he did prove they could not be trusted completely. I decided to tuck that realization under my bonnet.

* * *

It was a shockingly fine day, especially for November. The air was dry and crisp and the sea air invigorating. My pony was capable too and managed the trail with little guidance on my part, stopping but a few times to munch his favourite plant which turned out to be a specific kind of grass. Horses can be as fussy as humans about their food preferences, so I indulged him since he was such a pleasant mount.

There was smoke coming from the chimney and a woman outside was bent over searching a sack, an encouraging sign of activity. I hailed. She returned it with, "Welcome, doctor," and a quick smile. She was the older woman I had spoken to before, and today she was preparing a pot of salt fish and potatoes.

"Elspeth MacLeod added some greens from the Dunvegan garden. I'll leave them here with the water and medicine, "I shouted.

"I send her thanks, doctor and to you as well."

"Is Lorna here?"

"Nay, she is up there with Doctor Herold."

"At the fishing bothy?"

"The same," said she with sly a wink.

Elspeth had changed the formula for the medicine, so I needed to advise them. "I must travel further, then."

"'Tis a fine day for it. And don't be worrying about us. We will survive."

I waved as I trotted off, the pony eager. Herold's fishing camp was close-by and this time looking less a derelict hut, the weeds and vines having been cleared, the friendly smell of smoke seeping through the roof, and there was even a blanket covering the door which had lost its wood. *This must be the result of industrious Lorna,* I said to myself. I could not help but smile as I called out to them. I had to be careful here too. Could not afford any kind of sickness with what was ahead. So, I remained in the saddle. It was Herold who poked his head around the door blanket. He did not come out, nor did Lorna.

"Och, 'tis only Sir Malcolm."

"Aye only me with some victuals from the Dunvegan kitchen."

"Ah would—"

"Don't bother getting dressed. Wanted to see how you are faring, and to bring this, and inform Lorna that the new medicine should be given but once a day."

Herold's head popped back in, and I could hear them muttering. Then out came Lorna's head, her hair tousled and a fine blush forming on her face. At least she looked healthy this time.

"My sisters and the children are almost well, so I thought—"

"No need to explain. You have done exemplary work and saved their lives."

Her blush turned deeper when she realized she had opened the blanket a bit too far. I grinned and turned the pony away, then shouted behind me, "We'll send someone up every few days to look in on you."

The last I heard was their laughing.

* * *

What greeted me on return was not only the stable boy, but Elspeth interrogating him. She was stamping her feet, a bad sign. Something was up. She saw me and cried, "There you are!"

"Your world is collapsing without me?" I said, approaching her cautiously.

"Oh, stop it! Can you not be serious for once?" Her little fists were held tight, and her face told the tale of someone immensely frustrated.

"I can be serious, but only once," I said, making it worse.

"You need to help! They might kill each other!" she cried.

"Who?"

"Norman and Niall, of course. Who else?"

She had forgotten I was not part of her family and had no notion of why they might be at odds. "Where are they?" I said, the day's levity having evaporated.

"In the castle. I heard them. Norman threatened to kill Niall!"

"Alright, lets find them. Explain it on the way." I looked about to let the stable boy know I was no longer needing the pony, but he had vanished, so I took Elspeth's hand and we trotted along the trail around the castle to the sea gate. Along the way, between huffs and puffs, she related the details. It was about money. Norman accused Niall of stealing rents. Of course, Niall objected, and a tragedy averted only when Lady Anne intervened to quell tempers.

The laird was in the Fairy Tower study with a boy warrior on guard at the door trying to look fierce.

"Jacob?" I tried to remember his name.

"'Tis Josh, sir."

"Aye, Josh. I wish to see the laird."

He was blocking the door, one hand on his sword, the other fidgeting with his belt, sweat beading on his forehead. "The laird dinnae wish visitors at this time," he said stiffly.

I smiled. "You are a good lad and an excellent guard. But he does not mean me nor Lady Elspeth. Ask him and you will see."

Thankfully, before there was any conflict, Norman shouted through the door to let us in. "Good lad," I whispered to him on the way by, Elspeth behind prodding me forward. The laird was cleaning a pair of dueling swords. "Surely not!" I cried instead of a friendly greeting.

"Surely. He has pushed me too far," Norman said in a measured voice. Men speak like that before they act. Control is needed before the explosion. I pulled up a chair and sat beside him, close enough to touch if needed. I wanted him first to feel my calm presence, but Elspeth could not wait.

"We have known each other since children. It cannot end this way," she pleaded.

Norman glanced at her. I did too and added a sign to shush her. She must not have liked that and turned away to hide her feelings. I fetched some whisky and two glasses, poured us a half-measure. He had stopped cleaning the swords and was looking out the window. I knew that calmed him, so I waited for him to speak. It was several minutes before he said, "He is trying to steal Anne."

I never expected that. I heard Elspeth blurt, "No!"

"How can we help?" I asked.

Then Norman told us. Of how Niall had been stealing rents for years. Getting his rightful portion, as he imagined it. And now Murdoch needed muskets and powder for the men. No money for that according to Niall, and none were available to buy either. And then the final straw. He had been trying to bed Anne when Norman was away. But Anne had said nothing, trying to avoid a confrontation and hoping he would go away. But he was becoming more persistent and grabbed her after the ceilidh. That sealed it.

I listened quietly and let him get it out. He repeated the most hurtful parts. I knew this would not heal on its own. Niall had stolen rents, lied about the muskets, and tried to seduce the laird's wife. How much worse could it get? Well, much worse since we thought to leave Dunvegan and the women in Niall's hands. That clearly was no longer a prudent option.

The laird stopped speaking, then Elspeth turned on us, and in a voice filled with anger said, "Niall must go!"

* * *

Niall did indeed go, but of his own accord, with his prized horse but not with Ysabell. "The tower guard saw him leave as you were meeting with the laird. Thought it strange, so reported it," Murdoch noted.

"Didn't want to risk the dungeon, or worse."

"With the state of the laird's mind...wish he'd left it to me."

"Not when it comes to Anne and the bairns. They are the world to him. That's what set him off."

"Foolish move on Niall's part."

"Niall thinks all women will swoon before him."

"Most will."

"Not Anne," I said, "she is devoted to Norman and her children.

"It changes the game, doesn't it?" Murdoch mused. We were in the bailey by the seawall. Murdock had been working the men when I arrived.

"Did the guard see which way Niall was headed?"

"South, through the village."

"He could double back but I doubt he'd risk it." A sudden gust made me turn my head. It gave me a moment to think. "Norman said something about muskets."

"Aye, most of those we have are ruined. Stored in the old keep and water got in the crates. Damn shame the neglect here. Cawdie showed me... poor sod."

I thought of Cawdie, missing his calming strength the more. "How many are serviceable?"

"Eighteen, or so, and two serviceable cannons."

"So, you are short at least twenty muskets for the men you've trained?"

"Aye, and we intend to take one cannon to Talisker. That leaves one to defend Dunvegan. Not enough. 'Tis a risk."

I considered it a moment. There might yet be muskets at Sligachan. Should I trust the clan with this knowledge? Arming them further might have dire consequences should a new laird support the Jacobites. But what else could I do? We needed to keep our agreement with Norman and hope he would too. "I think I know where to get some muskets…powder and ball too."

Murdoch arched his brow. "You do?"

"Aye…leave it to me, but does the laird have funds to buy them?"

"Niall controlled the money."

"We need to act quickly. The weapons are at Sligachan, one long day's ride with a good horse. If Niall gets to those weapons first, we are sunk."

"What do you need from me?" Murdoch asked. We had already started back into the castle.

"Two pack horses, a few mounted warriors and a decent horse for me."

"They will be ready within the hour. Meet me at the stables."

"Oh…and advise the laird and ask if he has any money for this. I have some but perhaps not enough." We parted with no further words, he to the armoury, me to see Lady Myreton.

* * *

I banged on her door and announced myself. "I am not proper," was her response.

"Then put on a blanket. This is urgent."

I heard some shuffling and her voice. She did not sound pleased. The door opened a crack. One eye blinked sleep. "Come in then. Do you not know it is rude to roust a lady before she has completed her toilet?"

"I am so sorry, I truly am, but I must leave soon and cannot wait for your toilet." I knew what she meant, of course. She was much older looking without her face powder, rouge, wig, and all the other tricks women use.

"Then what is it that requires this humiliation?" She flopped into a soft chair.

"If you have coin for me. I need it."

"Oh that. I was hoping for a better time—"

"I need it now."

"All right. I was hoping to get to know you better, first."

I sighed. "Now...please."

It was in her travel bag. A small cloth pouch tied with string and filled with assorted coins.

I grabbed it from her, offering in return little but a mutter of thanks, my mind racing ahead to the next destination. I heard her say, "Men are rude," as she slammed the door behind me. I would apologize later.

My next stop was Aunt Mairi's cottage. Elspeth had sent a girl to sort my laundry problem. This after complaining of my smell at the ceilidh. In my trunk I found a freshly laundered belted plaid, the one Mairi had provided after my release from the dungeon. I donned it and gathered my weapons, money, the laird's letter of introduction, some oats in a small sack, and a skin with fresh water. That would suffice for a two-day ride.

* * *

A gaggle of friends were at the stable when I returned, and as promised the horses were being saddled and loaded. Elspeth was huddled with Janet, little Solas between them. I noticed the butt end of a pistol protruding from Janet's belt and Elspeth touching the hilt of the dagger she had tucked up her sleeve. *'Tis a sad day when the women feel the need to go about armed*, I thought.

"Does it have to be you? Surely these young men are more than capable of fetching muskets?" Elspeth asked directly.

"No doubt they are fine men. The issue is getting MacKinnon to hand over the weapons. He knows me. I was introduced by Niall as one who could be trusted. And we need to get there fast before Niall spoils the deal."

"This could help." Norman handed me a sealed letter. "'Tis for Iain MacKinnon. In it I promise to make good any shortages of funds." Then he turned to Elspeth and touched her arm, "I am sorry, Iain MacKinnon trusts few, and rightly so. He was to hand over the muskets to Niall, on payment. I cannot risk going myself...not now, but he will trust Malcolm... and with this letter—"

Murdoch interrupted, "The horses are ready."

"Then we must depart," I said tucking the laird's letter away with the other one.

Murdoch leaned toward me. "We *need* those muskets. Much depends on it. If they have fallen into enemy hands, we must know before we march on Talisker." I acknowledged agreement with a curt nod.

"Malcolm, I wish I could give you some coin but what little I have is for the men and our people," Norman said, his boyish face in anguish, "I wish I could go with you...but you have my introduction letter and permission to threaten MacKinnon or take the muskets by force, if necessary."

We shook hands and I wondered if I was the right man for this, being trained as a doctor not a soldier like my brother George. I entertained a fleeting wish he were here to set things right, but instantly banished that foolish thought as I mounted. This was on me. There was no one else.

* * *

It was about twenty-five miles of well-packed drove road from Dunvegan to Sligachan, the same route through Drynoch I took on foot. We were making good time; the weather was holding and our unloaded pack horses content to trot along. It was afternoon and we were about an hour from Sligachan. I had hoped to catch up with Niall. That is why we pushed our horses. But there had been no sign of him, even though his horse was loaded. Perhaps he went south to MacDonald country or west to Talisker instead.

I had little expectation of trouble on the way. Coming back was a different matter. We could be burdened with hundreds of pounds of muskets, ball, and powder. Easy prey for a MacKinnon wanting our coin and weapons, both. On a long ride, thoughts wander and at times find their way into that place in hell called doubt. At least the lads were confident. It was their first real expedition, and they were enjoying it immensely. I would not spoil their fun with my worries.

On the edge of Sligachan, I singled out Josh, the lad who had been guarding the laird. "Follow my lead," I told him, "No response to provocation unless I command it. Understand?"

"Aye, sir!" Josh agreed and passed the order to the other men. He was willing to learn and be led. This would be a good test.

* * *

"Welcome back, good sir." It was pretty Eileen, and she was not looking at me but on the floor.

"Didn't bring the dog. He has a new owner."

"Aww, he's a bonny dog. Ah miss him."

"The girl who has him thinks he's bonny too," I said.

It was late afternoon and I had left the warriors outside to tend the horses. But also, I wanted to see MacKinnon alone. "Is Iain available? We have business."

"Having a nap. But he should get up now and I am sure he will be glad to see you. Please have a seat."

The tavern was full of men needing a drink and a chance to complain with friends at the end of the day. MacKinnon looked like a surly bear as he crossed the room to greet me, minutes later. I smiled warmly and stood to shake hands. Instead, he gave me a hug that almost collapsed my lungs, then whispered, "I hope you have come for those damned muskets?"

"I have," I gasped.

"Then meet me out back. We can't talk here."

I agreed. MacKinnon turned to some men at the next table and roared out a hearty welcome. I set a coin on the table for Eileen, then left.

"Be alert," I said to Josh outside. "I'm meeting with MacKinnon now."

"Should we unsaddle, sir?" Josh asked.

"How are the horses?"

"They seem fine. They've had their oats and water."

"Can we get back to Drynoch tonight?"

"It will be dark, but the weather is good. I think so, sir."

"Be ready to load and go, then."

"Aye, sir."

MacKinnon was pacing when I found him. He had pulled his plaid up over his head and added warm boots. "I hope you have coin?" was the first thing he said.

I decided to save my coin as a last resort. "I have a promissory note from Laird MacLeod and another note to negotiate on his behalf."

"Shite! Is that all? No coin, just notes?"

I handed them to him to peruse. "If you refuse it will be worse for you, believe me. The laird is livid. Niall Morrison absconded with some money. Should he come this way, know the laird will pay for his capture."

MacKinnon snorted. "These muskets have been nothing but trouble. I am risking my life having them. No more. Take the damned things! You can tell him he owes this man." He punched his chest then ambled off, a trail of curses filling the frosty air in his wake.

I ran back to our men and commanded, "Bring the horses round back. We need to be packed and out of here before he changes his mind and comes back with a tavern full of drunk clansmen."

There were more crates and barrels than I expected, but we had brought enough rope and the men had been taught how to pack a horse properly. Thankfully, we were able to get away before the rabble poured out of the tavern. It was satisfying hearing them arguing and cursing the MacLeods as we made our escape. It was even more satisfying that we had accomplished it without bloodshed. Soon enough we reached the safety of Drynoch. We were tired. It had been a long day for man and beast. I told Josh to camp on the edge of the village, then asked a villager to get the chieftain.

"Now what?" said the chieftain, looking as slovenly as last time we met.

"I need some men to guard the road to Sligachan. We have important cargo for your laird."

"This time 'o night?"

"Just do it and the laird will be told of your cooperation."

He stood there like a deaf mute.

I sighed, "How much?"

We haggled and reached an agreement. But honestly, I wanted to throttle him. Next morning early, we decamped and slogged home, the weather having changed its mind back to miserable.

* * *

"I wanted you here because this is of vital importance to the future of our clan," the laird began. It was early morning, the day after we returned from Sligachan. He was standing at the far end of the Fairy Flag room in front of his favourite window overlooking the loch and dressed in formal clan plaid with all the trappings. He also was fully armed as a chieftain going to war and standing behind a table covered with a large vellum map rolled out and tacked in place. The mood was decidedly serious. This was a war council, and we all knew what would be decided today could change clan history. The young laird had our full attention.

Servants had brought enough chairs for us and arranged them in rows before the table. It reminded me of one of the lecture rooms at medical school at Leiden when the only students left were us few in our senior year. It was an honour to be taught by those wizened old men who seldom broke from their research to converse with us mortals. In those days, they were our gods and I wondered if in future would young Norman be remembered in such golden light. Will he be a clan Alexander or Pericles? I had witnessed his potential. With a gift of time, might it be so?

As I was sipping coffee and thinking, I cast my gaze about the room. We were waiting for him to continue. Elspeth was beside me with Solas on her lap. Janet was quietly preparing more coffee and biscuits. Mairi was seated behind us with Lady Myreton, Lady Anne between them, bairn-less for the first time since I arrived. Sir Ross was there too, with expressionless Gregor guarding the door.

"Murdoch will be here soon but let us begin. We have been successful in retrieving enough weapons to arm our men," the laird said, pacing in front of the table. "My dear friends and family, here is the situation. We have one witch in custody. She has not been helpful. Niall Morrison has stolen our clan rents and was last seen headed south. Una Talisker is suspected of being a black witch. She has been working with several others to try to overthrow me and seize the clan treasure, if such exists." There was a pause as Norman seemed to consider his words carefully. "Lady Ysabell remains with us. She claims to know nothing. That is unlikely, but so far, she has done nothing illegal…which can be proven. She will be left to her own devices for now."

I glanced at Elspeth. Solas was squirming on her lap wanting to be set free. I could sense Elspeth's tension and perhaps Solas could too. Even Adhie was restless circling their feet, unable to find a suitable spot to lay. Behind us Lady Myreton whispered something to Mairi. Lady Anne agreed with a whispered, "Aye." I was not comfortable having Ysabell free in the castle in these times and I suspected others felt the same. But the laird would follow the law and I approved, if only rationally. My intuition disagreed. Ysabell was trouble.

A knock came at the door and Gregor let Murdoch in. Eyes turned, smiles came, including mine. He took a seat at the back. The laird cleared his throat, gathering our attention. "Welcome Murdoch. I am outlining the state of our conflict. I will continue. 'Tis Ranuff who grieves me most. Most of you know our history, but for those of you who don't…Ranuff and I grew up together, here at Dunvegan. He is two years older than me, and I looked up to him as I did to my older brother Roderick. Ranuff and I were inseparable, and I am sure we terrorized many, including Elspeth and Janet, in our boyish quests for glory." He grinned at the memory.

Elspeth elaborated, "'Twas more than terror. Remember the time you stuck pine pitch in my hair while I slept?"

"Emm, well you looked better with short hair," he laughed.

"I did not! I looked like a boy, and it took a year to grow back," Elspeth protested, smiling.

"Those were good times, weren't they? My father, Iain Breac, was laird then. Everyone loved him, or so we thought. I know better now. Dark forces were emerging as whispers, then actions un-opposed. Even among us boys. I now regret saying nothing. My inaction has harmed us, and I apologize. Elspeth, do you remember there was a marsh beside the castle? It is the garden now, the stream dredged and land drained."

Elspeth nodded, then finally gave in, and set Solas free.

"We loved to play in that marsh. It was full of fish and frogs and strange bugs. We would collect them in jars. Aunt Mairi had a glass we could use to see them up-close. The colours and patterns were amazing...but it was Ranuff..." Norman turned his head and stifled a cough. "It was Ranuff who started using the glass to burn them with the sun...while they yet lived. That was the beginning, when I was a lad of seven and he, nine. It got worse from there and seemed to become the only reason he wanted to go to the marsh. I said nothing but it sickened me to see him cutting and burning live animals. He told me he wanted to see what would happen and how it felt. And that was the first time he called me weak...because I would not cut open a wiggling frog."

The room had gone completely quiet, and feelings of sympathy poured from my heart to the boy he was.

"And then, a few months later...'twas summer and we were on the road to the village walking home. I was telling him something about trees. He seemed to be listening intently, but suddenly he turned and punched me square in the face. I staggered back, stunned. He punched me again. We grappled. We fell to the ground. He was bigger and stronger than me then and soon he had me pinned. He laughed and slapped me a few times. He only stopped when I ceased resisting. Later, I asked him why he had done that. He said it was to see what would happen and what it felt like. After that I avoided him, but it was hard to do in a castle. He tormented and teased me for years and I said nothing. I knew my brother would kill Ranuff had he known. But I didn't want to be weak and tell on him. That is why I was so glad to be sent to school in Edinburgh."

Elspeth rose, tears rolling down her cheeks. Norman stopped her with a gesture and said, "No. I am no longer that boy. But I want you to know. These things have deep roots. Now I intend to prune them."

There were sighs and sniffles as we accepted the import and share of guilt. Then Aunt Mairi said, "Una encouraged Ranuff too and we did nothing to stop her. We assumed the problem would just go away, in time. We failed you as well, Norman."

Then Anne spoke up, "My husband is not weak. He may be overly kind-hearted. But I know he is strong when it matters."

I agreed then added, "He is most certainly not a coward. I have personal experience." The men chuckled at that, as did I.

The laird raised his arms and cried, "We have exposed the truth and now it is time for justice!"

We clapped and cheered, then with a gesture from the laird, Murdoch came forward and flipped the table on its side so we could see the large map pinned to the surface. He stared at us a moment, put his hand on his belt then started, "Our contingent, lead by Josh," Murdoch looked at me and grinned, "was successful in procuring eighty-seven French trade muskets and six pistols of various manufacture along with enough ball and powder to have serious fun. As everyone in Dunvegan should know, we have about forty young warriors. I have been marching them up and down the road to the village enough times for everyone to see. But till now, those same observers would have easily noted that half our men were armed with wooden pikes and the other half with old English muskets. Not very impressive, were they? This is a rough map of Skye, and we are here." Murdoch touched the map with the pointed end of his tomahawk. "Talisker is down here, and these lines are the drove roads and trails."

We all craned forward for a better look. Aunt Mairi pointed out that the shipyard at Rubh' an Dùnain is another twenty miles or so down the same coast on the west of Skye.

Murdoch continued, "Ranuff may be at Talisker with his men—"

"How many would that be?" I asked.

"Eight to ten which he pays, and a few women servants. And as I said, he may not be there. But it matters not, our laird wants our keep back."

"We have no right to claim what we cannot hold," the laird stated.

Mairi grunted then asked, "Alright Murdoch, how are we going to do this?"

"I will tell you. After today's march, everyone in Dunvegan will know we have forty men equipped with new muskets. This afternoon, I will announce our plan of attack to our men. I intend to leave several here to protect the castle and our families. These, along with the guards, should be enough, provided we seal the castle. In a few days, the rest of our men will march to Talisker, south along the drove road to Drynoch then west following the river to Talisker. It is open country and the glen more a strath, but there are several places for ambush, especially here...and here." He pointed to a few spots marked with an X. "Once the situation at Talisker is resolved, we will leave ten men there to garrison—."

"And that leaves only twenty or so marching back. Splitting our forces is a dangerous strategy, and Ranuff will know you risk losing Talisker or your men on the return." I said trying to be helpful.

Murdoch stood upright and roared in laughter. No one understood, including me. Then he drove the sharp side of the tomahawk into the map and said forcefully, "Well done Malcolm! Now think on it. What would your illustrious brother George do in our situation?"

"Hmm. He prefers the use of overwhelming force. Find the enemy's weak spot and attack," I responded.

"Precisely! Elspeth told me about your experience with that mob in Edinburgh. He could have sent a few men and hoped for the best. But he didn't, did he? Instead, he lined up the whole damned regiment and pretended to shoot at the protesters. Solved the problem in minutes."

"Well, not exactly, but—" I stopped myself short. Those were troubling memories, and I did not want them surfacing now.

Solas was wandering around exploring everything with her fingers, Janet's eyes following her. Elspeth spoke up, "But surely the point is we won't have overwhelming force, if we use your plan."

"Indeed. So, what would you do in our situation?" Murdoch listened. No ideas came from us, then Gregor, who had said nothing so far, spoke a few words in Russian then looked at Sir Ross for help.

Ross smiled and said, "He said to use subterfuge."

Murdoch pointed at Gregor, "He's got it!"

Solas had ambled to the front, Adhie behind her sniffing her tracks. She reached Murdoch, gripped a fold of his plaid, tugged, and burbled something. Murdoch bent over, caressed her head, and whispered, "Not now Solas." Then he stood and announced, "Everyone knows of our troop strength, schedule and route. What I am about to tell you next must remain a secret." He paused. Murdoch's face changed. Dispassion was replaced with fierce resolve. "What most don't know is that Cawdie and I have been contacting our old friends, veterans who have fought in the army. They are ready to help if required and we can use them to stiffen our corps of inexperienced lads."

I had known Cawdie was up to something beyond carousing and telling tall tales with his friends, but this came as a welcome surprise.

Murdoch laughed, then roared, "We will crush these traitors, and I swear the crimes against our laird, Cawdie, and my dear girls will be avenged!"

Solas, still attached to Murdoch's plaid, looked up and screamed, "Nay!"

Chapter 19: Elspeth

I stood quickly to take Solas from my father. Gregor reached her first. She went to him willingly. I studied her weeping in his arms. I was convinced she had regained some sight. I was not certain exactly when, but suspected it was the day Cawdie was killed. In the school of medicine at Salerno, we learned that loss of vision could be caused by an injury to the mind. Rather than see horrors, sight shuts down. It made me wonder if her blindness could have been induced by what she saw Ranuff do to her mother. She was present and Ranuff would not have cared about a wee girl. The thought of what Solas had seen brought bitterness to my throat. The child's reaction to the proposed attack and my father's plan frightened me. Did she know something we had missed? Or foreseen another tragedy?

I glanced at Solas and wondered how it might feel to lay my aching head against Gregor's comforting shoulder as she did. The answer felt startlingly like hunger. He looked to me as though I had spoken, his face cool and aloof, then back to Solas. I realized I was jealous.

* * *

My father insisted I accompany him and the thirty young warriors he and Cawdie had trained. I would be their physician. I could manage that walk, being little more than twenty miles from Dunvegan to Talisker. As instructed, I pretended to the villagers that the young men were the entire force. Meanwhile, Murdoch's veterans provisioned the laird's birlinn in secret. They were to sail down the coast and attack at night, or so I was told.

The men prepared for war, packing their supplies as would be expected. The mostly untried warriors were separated into smaller squads for camping. Every squad oversaw its own site, and each issued its own kettle, axe, flint and supplies to prepare common meals. Janet and I assembled bags of oats, salt, onions, butter, and cheese for those shipping on the birlinn. We kept the packaged provisions hidden in the stillroom in an old fish barrel that would cause no comment when it was sent to the docks. The cannon and powder would be harder to conceal but if passed off as ballast they could slip by. I smiled at one of the goatskin knapsacks we were making for the young lads who would march with Murdoch. "It stinks," I said to Janet.

She laughed, a welcome sound that was beginning to come more often. "As would you if you had been soaked in pee and buried in bark." She lifted her half-finished sack to her nose. "The smell will pass, and the lads will not care. 'Tis an adventure for them. I am putting a rosemary and mint sachet and my prayers inside each one." Her voice saddened, perhaps in remembrance of our dear Cawdie.

Several of the newer lads in Murdoch's corps lacked provisions. And when we gave them their filled knapsacks, they blushed and tied their tongues in twists, but accepted them with the reverence due a sacred relic. I prayed with Janet that the gods would protect them while they learned the harsher lessons of battle. Our preparations now were complete. We waited our orders.

* * *

The dying fire in my room colored the soot-stained hearth dull orange. Should I move the stones to another hiding place before we left? Supposedly the hags had left, but Ysabell was still lurked nearby. And where would I find a safer place than here? Scathach sighed beside me. I chose to protect the hearth with a strong invocation to alert me if anyone tried breeching it. Using the craft worried me but *needs must as the devil drives,* or so said the monk, John Lydgate. I feared the devil was driving.

I added yet more medical supplies to my list, activity keeping grief and anxiety at bay. The men tended to gather in the library, drinking, speaking in hushed voices of various plans and possibilities. We would leave once the weather permitted, they told us fretting women.

Thankfully, Herold had returned to help while we went to Talisker. The castle and village needed a healer on hand, and we could not count on Ysabell. Her loyalties were doubtful.

* * *

Morning found me on a wee pony loaded with supplies plodding through the lashing rain. Teresa had sent word the previous evening that Brian Tormund was there, purchasing pints all around. She said he was paying with good coin and losing much at dicing. I made a hasty decision and sent word back asking her if she could manage to detain him till morning. I could hear her snort in my head. She knew what was to come.

Brian had long befriended Ranuff, believing his claim to be the rightful laird. A disgusting sort of recently ageing male, Brian fancied himself eternally interesting and forever attractive. The laird had let him a derelict fishing croft. It lay across the side of the mountain beyond Dunvegan village. But it was said that he soon tired of the realities of salting fish and caring for women and had turned to less honest sowing.

I tied the pony and stepped into the inn yard, then went inside to the pleasant smell of lemon, stew and baking bread that greeted customers. Brian was folded limply under a chair in a shadowy corner of the inn, sleeping. Double draughts of Teresa's fortified wine had insured he would not be leaving till I arrived. I bent over and shook him. "Brian...Wake up. Time to go home." Teresa joined me and prevailed on two morning customers to lift him up off the floor. His breath was rank and the gas noisily escaping his bowels ranker. I wondered if he had been infected before he left the croft. "Teresa. Thank you. Has he settled with you?"

She held up a purse, pushing it into my hands. "I took what was owed. Give this to the women that must put up with him. He's still drunk as a wheelbarrow and will likely cast up his accounts on the way home."

We threw him on his horse after giving the poor beast some oats and water. I grabbed his reins and resumed my journey to support his women, the offender in tow. Eventually he awoke, soaking wet, and bewildered at his state. When I explained, cursed me and all who'd ever crossed my path. He slid off his horse, wretched, then refused to go any further. "I care not," said I. "You can come and be of use or stay and make yourself a fugitive... because the laird knows of your misdeeds."

His sleeve became the repository of more vomit, then he glanced at me and cried, "The wheel has turned. Ye and that timid laird will be the fugitives, not me." He blew snot out of his nostrils. "Now give up me horse or have a beating when I catch ye."

I was but several yards away and most certainly would not fight him over a horse. A threat and a cajole was the more prudent course. "You may have your horse." I dropped the reins. "But consider carefully. When you go, an implacable enemy will me made. You will have placed your bet. Follow Ranuff now and risk all or play both sides and benefit regardless of outcome."

Brian grabbed his reins and successfully mounted after a few missed attempts. He sat glaring at me. I touched the dagger at my boot. He could see I was not defenceless. But he returned my implication with a hard look, and I wondered what he meant. Was his polluted mind thinking to save himself, or capture me and have his way? I held his gaze while keeping the pistol I had borrowed out of view. But he neither threatened nor rode off, so I tried once more. "Accompany me and help your women, hold what you have, do what is right and fair, or forever be seen as a villainous scoundrel."

* * *

The stench announced we had arrived. The smell of human excrement still hung about the cottage. The door flew open at the sight of Brian. The old woman strode up to him and began a long and descriptive rebuke which began with: "Worthless rogue! Left us sick and dying!" She began to pummel him with small bony fists.

I grabbed her hands and soothed her. "Hush now, we are here. We will unpack our beast and you can feed the wee ones. I also have some chores for him to make your life easier. Come and help me get this undone." The noise had brought others, hastily adjusting their clothing.

Following Malcolm and Herold's recommendations, I showed Brian and the women what needed to be done. We unpacked a shovel, rope, leather bucket and a piece of patched heavy sailcloth to use for dragging dirt away. Brian picked up the shovel and began digging while nursing a piece of bread and cheese in his head, as the saying goes. The excavated earth was dragged to the poisoned well, dumped in, and covered with collected greens. The work seemed to sober Brian and in time and he was doing a passable job. I chatted with him as he worked, more to monitor his mood and prevent further abuse.

As Brian and the women worked on the wells, I surveyed the cottage exterior, then entered. The wee ones were inside. There was barely enough space to set a foot without stepping on someone or something. It was a depressing sight, the crowding, the poverty, but at least the bairns looked healthy. But winter was coming. Repairs obviously needed, and peat cut and stacked. I returned to Brian; my heart tainted with disgust. "There are too many here. This cannot continue. Brian you should handfast with one of the women and avoid putting babes in the bellies of the rest."

He snorted in derision. "And who will salt the fish?" in a mocking tone, he asked.

"Seriously?" I answered, my bile rising. "We Scots are not slaves and if the laird discovers this!" I persisted, and in a more controlled voice, told him there were too many to support, and suggested he take his preferred and let the laird find homes for the rest. That idea seemed to please.

He muttered, "Wonder how much ah can get for 'em? Bet Bethune would pay handsomely fur young Lorna." I held my tongue. A young girl carrying dirt nearby clearly heard our exchange. But she kept her eyes down and thoughts to herself. If that were Lorna, I would not single her out and risk reprisals after my departure. Malcolm had said she was a clever lass and had made herself an asset to Herold, wishing to be free of Brian. Didn't blame her after seeing this. I took pity on them and vowed to help.

By noon, Brian and the women had managed to clear a hole about four feet deep and filled in the old well. "'Tis time for a break," said I. "Bread, cheese, and ale are set. But first everyone must wash their hands." There was an audible groan.

Returning to their chore much refreshed, their water well was soon finished. Next was the privy. The old one had been filled and a site secured away from the new well. Some grumbled that it was too far to walk in winter, while others said that at least it was downwind. Brian ended the discussion and told the women they would make a new privy next day and build a wooden cover for winter. With that decided, I prepared to leave. Brian followed. With uncharacteristic courtesy, he helped me into the saddle, then whispered, "Put in a good word, my lady."

I looked down on him and in my best imperious voice said, "Do your duty and be rewarded. Do otherwise and expect punishment. And you must not leave here till Doctor Bethune has decided this illness has passed." Brian Tormund stood pensive, his eyes watery, mournful, his lips downturned, moving slightly as though wanting to speak. "Aye? Have you something to say before I go?" said I.

"Emm…Ranuff lies in wait. He knows your strength, time, and route. Tell the laird!"

I nodded, then turned the pony toward the trail, my cloak hood hiding a smile.

Chapter 20: Malcolm

The laird wanted a daring surprise attack from the sea in the wee hours of the morning. But according to my brother George, an experienced senior officer in the British Army, that is one of the most difficult attack plans to achieve since there are many variables which cannot be controlled. Minor things like the weather, the sea, getting lost in the dark, men being seasick, and so forth. But here we were bobbing in our little birlinn, crammed like fish in a creel, all of us wishing we had walked to Talisker instead.

We had left late at night. The weather was far from gentle, but at least the sea breeze had carried us south along the rugged coast of Skye with little effort on our part. "I think that might be Talisker Bay beyond the headland," the captain said, sounding not too sure of himself. He was new on the job and had never sailed here in the dark of night.

The laird and I peered through the mist at the dark shape ahead. "Aye, that's it sure enough," Wud said. "Born here, I was. Know that hill like the back of me hand."

"It's time, spread the word. William, bring her round the headland and onto the beach," the laird ordered. I smiled. The young laird was in his element, leading men on a grand adventure.

"Should have done this sooner," he said to me. "Now they may have advantage."

"You were in no condition after our trip to the sacred spring. And we needed those muskets, too, and time to train the lads," I countered. Norman swore. I understood his frustration in having to wait for the pieces to come to play but now we were ready, as well as could be.

The sail dropped and the men took to their oars. No one spoke, knowing the following wind could carry every sound to the enemy. We had sixteen old warriors, friends of Murdoch and Cawdie, plus a cannon from the castle which had been disassembled and lay below as ballast. It would be used if we found ourselves in serious trouble or if there was a siege. But no one wanted that. Sieges are miserable, tedious affairs. Best to have a swift assault with seasoned troops, followed by quick surrender. That was our hope, at least.

Ranuff had fled after the murder of Cawdie. We assumed he had come home to the protection of his keep and to regroup. The laird's scouts had reported more men at Talisker than expected, confirming our expectations. And Elspeth told us Ranuff had taken the bait and was lying in wait. But beyond that, we had little knowledge of what lay ahead. That was why the laird was cursing. We had needed time to prepare, then were delayed by inclement weather, giving Ranuff the ability to strengthen his defences.

Meanwhile, Murdoch was leading his corps of lads, with their new muskets, overland using the drove roads. Elspeth was with them as battle surgeon. They had left a day before us. The plan was to converge on Talisker this morning, take back the village and crush Ranuff and his traitorous band. The greatest risk was that Ranuff would know of our movements and attack Dunvegan Castle while we were away. For that reason, I was missing Cawdie greatly. He would have been the one guarding the women and children. But that was left to Sir Ross Campbell and his servant Gregor, with their uncertain loyalties. And Ross had only a small squad of guards and boys to work with. Could they withstand an attack, or would they surrender? And then there were those left in the castle, like Ysabell and her supporters who might do evil if given half a chance. At least we had blocked the sewage tunnel leading out of the castle before we left. One less thing to worry about.

The gravel beach crunched under the keel as the birlinn came to a shuddering stop. So far, so good. The weather had cooperated, and we had not been flung about like flotsam. Wud was off first, taking a line to secure to a large rock. Next was Norman, then me, glad to be on land. I hoisted my medical bag on my back and instinctively touched my pistol and cutlass to make sure they were there, an old habit acquired through bitter experience. We crouched to consult as the men disembarked. The beach was an arc half a mile wide fronting a wide glen with a stream emptying into the sea. On either side of the glen were rocky hills, too high to climb easily in the dark. There would be but two ways for us to go. Forward up the glen along the stream or back to the sea.

"It's over there," Wud indicated with a nod. "No lights. Bad sign. They always leave torches burning." Wud vanished back into the gloom.

"Assemble the men. We will attack as soon as the cannon is ready," the laird ordered the senior warrior. Men scrambled, belted plaids adjusted, swords slid into belts, and muskets loaded. Whispered orders were passed as the men fell into two ranks, the laird's little army of old men. It would have to do.

Meanwhile Wud, Jimmy and two others had attached a pulley to a tripod rigged near the prow. First came the cannon cradle wheels, then the cradle. They were assembled on the beach and readied. Then much grunting as the small cannon was hoisted and deposited on the cradle.

"Load it with grapeshot," the laird told them. The men knew what they were about, but it was good to hear his voice, confident and in charge. He pointed at two men, "You two will be our advance scouts. See if there is any life in the keep." He turned to the other men. "Don't want us caught on open ground. Single file up the stream bank for cover till we hear from the scouts."

I mumbled to the laird, "No Highland charge please. Let your men do the work."

"If you are frightened then stay in the rear with your medical bag," he answered loudly. I sighed. Some of the men laughed. I really do hate unnecessary bravado. Gets people killed often as not. But I did as he suggested and took the rear, pistol in hand and burdened like a mule with supplies.

The laird took the lead, and after much splashing and stumbling through the shallow stream, we made it to a position close to the house and the attached keep. I could see our scouts ahead creeping forward through the tall grass. Still no signs of life, even after all the noise we made in the stream. And the livestock were gone. It was too quiet and making me anxious.

Eventually, the scouts returned. "Someone in the house," one of them said. "Heard him cry out for help."

"Then we will advance," the laird said to the men closest to him. "Spread out, stay low. Take the doors and windows…all sides. Let the rest know. Forward on my signal. He waited for the murmuring to subside then glanced back at me. "Ready?"

I nodded. The next minutes were often the worst, those before engaging the enemy after the order to advance has been give. Some men pray, others involuntarily urinate. But there was no going back, or risk being killed as a coward. It was time to be a real soldier. We rose to go. But nothing happened as we moved forward. No cries, no shots, just the muffled grunts and sighs of men moving through the vegetation.

The laird took position with two men at the main door. He mostly had recovered from his injuries, but I knew his health was too fragile for this and I needed to stay close. A curt nod from him and one of his men kicked the door in. The laird entered first, his favourite claymore at the ready. I could hear others entering through the back door. There were female screams and some crashing, but no other sounds of conflict. We met in the middle of the house. "Just two women tied in the kitchen," a well-scarred warrior said.

"The stairs to the keep should be over there," the laird pointed. "Just wide enough for single file."

"We need a volunteer to go first," said I, just in case our foolhardy laird felt the need.

Most men said, "Aye." One stepped forward. Short and slim, he wore a damaged eye and matching ear.

The short man must have noticed me inspecting him because he said, "Me eyes work well enough and I'm a lefty. Ah can manage 'em stairs better 'n most."

The laird clapped him on the shoulder and thanked him. If there were traps or stiff opposition this could be the end of him, and he knew it. "Got yer back Charlie," another man said to him.

The keep was three stories, two above us with the dungeon on the top floor below a crenellated battlement. The stair wind in most castles was clockwise, giving advantage to right-handed defenders who would be stationed on the landing at each floor. We could not use torches lest they provide easy targets, making the climb even more dangerous, as around every corner there could be an unseen tripwire or enemies waiting to strike. Within minutes our eyes had adjusted to the dark as well as can be. We stood back as the two men started up. Did not want a crowd going up behind them in case they had to make a quick retreat. They were experienced, went up cautiously, stopping every few steps to listen for sounds from above. Moments later, the warrior who was following Charlie came back and told us there were muffled sounds from above, but the first floor was clear.

The laird ordered four men to follow him back up to secure the floor. One came back and reported it done. The laird and I went next. It was a cramped space with shoulders almost touching both sides. I smiled and thought it must have been designed to keep out giants like Cawdie. On the second floor were two rooms set up as a makeshift barracks. One of our men lit a torch. I stumbled through the rooms, counting. Twenty-eight bedrolls in total and they looked freshly used. That number was worrying.

"Damn," Norman whispered having observed the same scene. "I can hear the sounds above. Let's find out who they left in the dungeon, shall we?" He told Charlie and the other man to continue. They started the climb. Norman motioned with his hand for us to gather, "Looks like the main body is gone. Don't know what is up there but we need to keep our wits alert. They might've set some traps."

The man who followed Charlie shouted down that all was clear. There was nothing on the top floor, but an old man gagged with a piece of cloth and tied to a ring on the dungeon wall. "It is old Willis, the Talisker caretaker," the laird said. "His daughter the one who told us that Elspeth was held captive." Norman knelt beside him, cut his hands and gag free, and offered him water. Willis pushed it away and started speaking so fast he was tripping on his words. "They await. 'Tis a trap!" he said in a rush.

"Explain, old friend. We are here and your daughter is safe. Tell us all."

He did. And it was a frightening prospect. Niall and Ranuff were here with their men, around thirty or so of them. "And…and there is that crazy MacDonald woman and her cutthroats—"

"What!" I cried. "What MacDonald woman?"

Willis's head twisted up to see me. "The one from up north…said she's heading south. Be careful of them, a murderous lot, they are."

I sensed my blood pressure rise. "So, we have over thirty warriors ranged against our twenty," I mused aloud.

"And don't forget them witches," Willis added. "Here help me up."

Norman gave him a hand up, and I said, "Describe the witches."

"Don't have to. Know them well enough. 'Twas Una and Doideag…that bitch from Mull with her ugly dwarf and fairy dog. They were the ones who formed the plan. Heard plain enough. When they left, I suppose they forgot to kill me."

"What plan?" I asked.

"They are up the glen about four miles where it pinches down. They intend to ambush your lads, then march on to Dunvegan and announce they have destroyed you."

The laird nodded as he listened, no doubt remembering Murdoch's objections to spitting our forces. He had advised overwhelming force to crush the enemy. The laird, bless his kind heart, wanted a surprise assault with minimal bloodshed. Hence the subterfuge.

I touched Norman's arm. "We knew the risks and took the gentler road. We just have to deal with it."

"Get all men out of here!" the laird commanded. "Assemble outside. Ready the cannon for transport."

* * *

Night black was becoming morning grey as we made our way slowly up the trail away from Talisker. It was tough going dragging that cannon, the men taking turns on the ropes. We were approaching the narrowing of the glen where the old man had said the ambush lay, when we heard the first of the musket shots ahead.

"Scouts move up," the laird ordered. "The rest, load muskets and be ready."

"Careful, Norman. This could be a trap. The narrowing will be a dangerous bottleneck if we have to retreat," I whispered to him.

"And Murdoch's lads could be suffering too. They could be outnumbered. We'll just have to take that chance."

The scouts already were out of sight when we set off. Five men were left behind to drag the cannon. That left eleven veterans, the cannon having been more a burden than help, so far. We heard first contact twenty minutes later as the firing increased sharply. "I need some good runners to support them," the laird shouted back at us.

One of the younger veterans volunteered, a rangy fellow with a gleam of adventure in his eye. "I'll go as well. Some may be injured," I said. No one objected so we were off, running through the morning mist, leaping over rocks, and avoiding the muck as best we could. It was great fun after that tedious slog up the glen. We found the scouts crouched behind a boulder taking tremendous fire from the enemy. Thankfully, no one was injured but they could not load and fire fast enough and it was only a matter of time before the opposition made a foray.

The rangy warrior settled behind a hummock to the left. I took the right, dropped my medical pack, and readied my pistol. We just had to keep up a steady rate of fire and wait for our main group to arrive. We had adequate cover. The enemy did too, but they had to traverse an open area to get to us. I prayed they would be cautious and wait. But they were fighting on two fronts now, and that can panic the best of us. The battlefield was not stable, despite appearances. We traded volleys. Then after several, they stopped firing. Something was up. A massive volley came next, the smoke obscuring the field before us. I saw shapes moving through the smoke, then heard their screams. "They're coming," I shouted. "Retreat! Retreat!"

We four turned and ran back down the trail, musket balls seeking our backs. I heard a cry, glanced back, and saw one of our men fall. "Faster," I gasped. Our enemies were stopping to reload. That gave us time and soon we were too far ahead and obscured by the thickening mist. But we could not stop. The rangy fellow flew past, fear giving wings to his feet. I stopped to help the remaining scout, an old warrior with fair hair and crazed grimace. "Can't make it," he said between coughs. "You go ahead. I'll cover."

He was right, of course. That is what they were taught to do on retreat. Those too slow sacrificed for their comrades. I should have agreed. "Fire, pull back, reload, repeat." I told him.

He gave me the sweetest toothless smile. "Aye, sir," he wheezed.

And that is what we did. Amazingly it worked, helped immensely by the concealing mist, and soon my tall friend returned with news that the main body was close and we should stay put. Mercifully, they arrived minutes later.

It was not so much a well-organized assault as a collision in the fog and smoke. Our backs were to the narrowing of the glen. We had to push forward or die. I tried to stay close to the laird but could not see beyond several feet, and the deafening tumult added to the disorientation. And we were past the gunfire stage now. It was down to steel.

I engaged an enemy with my cutlass. He was wearing MacDonald tartan. "You again!" he growled on recognizing me. He lunged, hacking with his claymore. I stepped aside and sliced his thigh. "Forrester is here!" he yelled, then swore an oath to kill me. But I had done enough damage to stop him moving well and the claymore was slow to wield, so I waited for him to wind up for another swing. That would be my chance to finish him. But suddenly at his side appeared another man, young, with dark curly hair and dressed in Lowlander clothes. He had a longbow, and his arrow was pointed at my chest. I panicked and rolled sideways in time to miss the claymore and arrow, both. The young man seemed familiar, but I did not have time to think about anything beyond survival. I rolled again, this time toward the MacDonald man. I was close enough now to strike and did but missed as he stepped back. Meanwhile the young man had nocked another arrow and was starting to pull the bow string. I thought I was done, caught on the ground between an arrow and a claymore. I could not get away in time. But I had to do something, didn't I? Better to try anything than go down without a fight. So, I pulled the dagger out of my boot and flung it at the bowman, then turned and rose to one knee to ward-off the sword strike with my cutlass. The young Lowlander's arrow found home, but in the belly of the MacDonald warrior. Between that and my cutlass slash, he fell in a heap, the final curse of his unfortunate life spewing from his grizzled maw.

Now I had advantage. The Lowlander was trying to nock another arrow, but it takes several seconds, and he did not have that much time with me but feet away, rage powering my muscles. Two short steps and I ran over him shoulder first, knocking his wind out. I leapt on him, cutlass at his throat. "Wait, wait!" he cried. "I'm Robert, Lady Myreton's son. This is all a mistake. I'm on your side. Remember me?" And I did remember Elspeth had been adamant that Robert participated in the murder of Cawdie, and later Lady Myreton had identified his fletch found in the body. I looked in his frightened eyes. It would take but a quick slice, a second, no more. But he lay helpless, yielding, and I relented, a trace of pity yet in my heart. *Kill him now, ye fool,* the voice of Captain Forrester in my overwrought mind commanded. I cursed, readying the stroke. Robert's eyes widened. Then a cry for help pierced the din. It was Norman's voice. I looked up and told the warrior near me to bind and him. I left them, the warrior with his musket to Robert's head, ordering him to roll over to be secured, and Robert clutching his throat and weeping.

I found the laird in time to stay his hand. He looked like an avenging angel, standing over Niall like that amid the fray. Niall's arm was dripping blood, his sword on the ground beside him. "Let's end this, but not in slaughter," I said.

Norman glanced at me. "Then tie him," Norman barked.

The battle ended soon after when the cannon arrived. One blast was enough to convince the enemy. They scrambled up the surrounding hills, leaving their dead and injured. The smoke and mist cleared and around us were appalling scenes of suffering. Men were moaning, others crying for help. And among those many voices, one cut through. I heard Elspeth sobbing. "Where are you?" I yelled, my eyes searching the chaos.

"Over here," Murdoch yelled back.

She was sitting on the ground holding someone's hand, her dark cloak sullied with blood. "Elspeth?" I said when she looked up.

"I…I killed him!" she sobbed.

I looked at the body beside her. It was Ranuff, and near him a blooded dagger. Tears were streaming down her cheeks. I knelt. My arms went around her shoulders. I let her cry it out.

Murdoch had been tending one of his wounded and shouted to me that he could use some help. But I could not leave Elspeth like that, not till I knew she would be all right. But she too heard her father's words and replied, "Give me a minute, Father."

Her sobs subsided as she gathered her will. She dropped Ranuff's hand and took mine, then found Fortuna on my ring and mumbled something. "I will be fine, Malcolm. Many need us." She weakly smiled then rose to her knees and shouted to her father, "I need to find my medical bag."

I left them like that. I too needed to help the injured, and there were many for such a brief battle.

* * *

We buried the dead and moved the injured and prisoners back to Talisker. The laird sent for wagons to transport them to Dunvegan. We had captured Niall Morrison and the MacDonald woman. Ranuff was dead and the witches missing. Gone too was Lady Myreton's stepson Robert, the body of a throat-slit warrior lay where I'd left him.

In time, most of enemy warriors returned and surrendered. They begged forgiveness and said it was Ranuff's lies and threats that had turned their heads. In truth, they had nowhere else to go. Living as an outcast in this harsh land being the worst of choices. And they likely believed that kind-hearted Norman would not kill them. But he did put on a good show and scared them stupid, to our amusement, I am ashamed to admit.

* * *

Next day Elspeth and I were on our rounds of the injured. She was doing an outstanding job of keeping her demons bottled, but I expect Ranuff was the first she had killed, and he a former friend and romantic interest. I smelled a whiff of tobacco then heard a cough. "What is it Murdoch?" I said, wrapping a lad's bandage.

"A word," he whispered.

"Can it not wait?"

"Heard you will be leaving tomorrow."

"Aye."

"Then it can't"

"Outside in five minutes," I muttered.

* * *

Murdoch and I had come through this battle relatively unscathed. I had Fortuna to thank, according to Elspeth, and he the experience to know when to attack and when to retreat. For retreat is what he had done when ambushed by Ranuff's men. "We waited. Held them off and when we heard your men attack, we did as well," was all he said in explanation.

He was leaning on the side of the house searching his pouch. By the light of day, he looked tired, that worn look that grows on men's faces who have endured too much. "Lost my flint," he said.

"What is it, Murdoch, we're up to our—"

"'Tis my Elspeth," he said, locking eyes on mine.

"She's had a trauma…not easy killing a man," I said.

Murdoch shook his head. "She didn't."

"What do you mean?"

"I gutted him…for what he did to my kin and Cawdie."

"You?"

"Aye, and she saw me do it. That was my dagger beside him."

* * *

"I should just kill you and be done with it," the laird said to Lady MacDonald. "I doubt you'd be missed by your laird."

She sat on the floor of the storeroom saying nothing, jaw clamped, eyes defiant. Then she spat on his boots. I fully expected an angry response, but the Norman held his temper. "Then 'tis settled. I was considering mercy, but—"

"'Twas *his* father to blame," she said pointing her chin accusingly at me. "Those men in Edinburgh who call themselves our lords murdered my dear husband at Glencoe and left me with wee Rory and no hope."

Norman looked over at me, a questioning look on his fair face.

"The Glencoe massacre?" I asked, unsure of what she meant.

"Aye," she sneered. "You lot murdered more than twenty of our men, then Malcolm Forrester, son of the lord responsible, washes up on our land and murders me Rory."

"But my father had nothing to do with that—"

She scoffed.

"*You* attacked us when we wrecked," I spat out the words.

"All we wanted was enough to live," she muttered. "We would have helped had you bargained properly."

"I doubt that. Had it been so you could have said it at the time instead of replying with threats and bullets. And then we met on the road to Portree, and it were more of the same."

She turned her head away. "Them witches were the only ones willing to help us. Kill me if you wish. I have nothing left and our laird be deaf to my plight."

Norman cursed then turned quickly to leave. "This is a MacDonald matter. They need to deal with her. Release and banish them with sufficient food and drink to get them off our land. Be off woman before I change my mind!"

* * *

The wagons arrived to transport the injured to Dunvegan. The laird and Murdoch would march the captives through the village as warning, and word of the laird's victory would spread quickly. What would happen to the prisoners remained unclear. Murdoch urged caution. "Wait till tempers have been soothed by ale and women," he counselled. I fully agreed. The clan needed a solution that did not include more revenge. And then there was the problem of Niall Morrison, already banished for fraud and treachery and now a leader of the traitors. I suggested a public trial. Some wanted steel justice. No one suggested clemency. Elspeth was silent on the subject.

"The leaders of this conspiracy will be punished," was all the laird said about it at the time.

* * *

It took a few days to decide and prepare. Wud and his son Jimmy stayed at Talisker with the birlinn. Many of us took a rope and pulled the ship onto the beach at high tide. There would be a few men garrisoned there as well, in case someone tried to retake the house and keep. The rest of us would return to Dunvegan to regroup and recover before we made our way back to Talisker and thence south to the shipyard at Loch na h-Airde on the Rubh' an Dùnain peninsula, several miles south of Talisker along the coast of Skye. We would there try to find that old man who could read those strange inscriptions on Elspeth's stone triskele balls and on the ring, we found at Rodel.

"I want my father with us when we sail south, in case we run into trouble. He knows the MacAskill men from the old days." Elspeth said after we finished our inspection of the injured loaded on the wagons.

"He'll be a welcome addition, but it's the laird's decision. He wants his victory parade and who knows what will greet him when he arrives."

"If you mean Sir Ross Campbell and Gregor. I know you don't trust them, but I do."

I was about to say something sarcastic but thought the better of it. "Then it will be you, me, and Murdoch, with the laird's permission."

"Several have reported they saw the witches heading south. And some of our prisoners told us they may be going to Mull."

"And we don't know how much they know about the MacLeod treasure, do we?"

"Let's hope they know less than us."

"We know little," Elspeth chuckled, "If that is so, they know almost nothing.

I laughed. "I still think it a quest for fools."

"Then we are perfect for it, aren't we?'

"Well at least we still have your balls."

"We do indeed...disguised as jars of medicine." Elspeth nodded in the direction of her medicine bag on the floor by her foot.

"Shh! Witches have large ears." I grinned at her.

"Let them hear. I am as sick of black witches as you must be. We need this over and done. Now let's see what is left in the kitchen to eat before we go."

* * *

Our greeting when we arrived back at Dunvegan was not as expected. Instead of adulation, there was horror. Replacing cheering and laughter were sobs and sorrow as families re-united with their damaged sons. It was sight I shall never forget, and I prayed the young laird felt the same. We witnessed the truth of war. Decisions can lead to injury and loss of life. We dismounted and walked silently to respect the bereaved. "I think many will want to go to Talisker to visit the graves of the dead," Elspeth whispered to me as we reached the castle stables.

"That's natural and I'm sure the laird will help," I said. "But he has more immediate problems, such as housing the prisoners and tending the injured."

"And we need to find that treasure before Una and her friends do."

"I don't believe anyone knows for certain where it is, not us, not them," I told her.

"Mayhap, not yet."

"Our opponents are fleeing to safety. We must use our time effectively. The birlinn is ready at Talisker. We need to replace the lost and injured crew and restock supplies."

"But first there is much to do here," Elspeth said as we made our way through the sea gate. She was looking haggard, and I wondered how much more of this she could take. I for one wanted to be home at Torrport where I could have my boy Jocki fetch me a steaming coffee and fresh bread and jam. It was a grand life and I promised myself I would leave this strife-ridden rock pile and return home on Captain Wilson's birlinn as soon as could be.

And just as I was thinking of Wilson, lo he appeared, as bright and jolly as the last time we met. He was standing in the castle bailey along with Sir Ross and some of the men of the castle guard. "Good tidings?" Wilson asked.

"We won, but at great cost, and the witches escaped," I said to them.

Sir Ross's face sank, "They escaped? All of them?"

"Fraid so, but at least Ranuff is dead. We believe the witches are headed south."

Sir Ross looked especially troubled. His face reddened, his head shook. He seemed about to curse, which would have been a first for him, so I said, "We'll find them. They'll be brought to justice, and—"

I was about to explain further, when he turned and strode away uttering a string of oaths that shocked Elspeth who unfortunately was within hearing. My gaze went from Sir Ross's back to Captain Wilson. He looked at me and grimaced. "And what of you, good captain. Do my tidings displease you as well?"

"'Tis good to see you have returned without injury," he said, then leaned closer and in a whisper said, "This may be a good opportunity to leave this luckless isle. I be ready to sail when you are, sir."

I heard him well. It was the most tempting offer I had had in a long while. I reached into my coin pouch and filled his palm then whispered back, "Wait for me. My work is not done. I will make it doubly worth your while to continue in my service."

Captain Wilson nodded then said to those nearby, "I have coin to buy your best wares for the market at Glasgow. Put the word about. I will be at the inn for commerce."

Elspeth must have understood what had happened. I had agreed to stay when offered an effortless way home. She came close, touched my hand, and silently mouthed a thank you. I smiled at her in return. But it was a smile not matched by inner turmoil. Just then, Lady Anne burst out into the castle bailey and ran to her husband. I was expecting a heartwarming family greeting, but out of Lady Anne's mouth came something else, "She's gone! Gormal is gone!"

Chapter 21: Elspeth

Gormal had escaped? I stared at Lady Anne in shock. Only another witch could have freed her. Someone with the knowledge and power to counter a spell. There were only four people in Dunvegan who might have managed it. Me, Aunt Mairi, Lady Myreton and Ysabell. I looked behind Lady Anne and saw Ysabell. Without thought I stepped around Anne and slapped Ysabell with all the emotion that had been trapped inside me for weeks. Her neck snapped back, and she stumbled and gaped at me. Verily, it was a miracle I did not kill her. "It had to be you." I heard my voice icing the air. "Now what have you done you brazen faced traitor? And the rest of your worthless coven? Where are they now? You have endangered us yet again. 'Twas you who conspired to murder Cawdie, and you who brought death and injury to those who went to Talisker."

My worst self longed to strike her again. My hand stilled. Gregor had appeared behind Ysabell; his presence prevented me from moving. Caught in my emotions like an insect on a spider web and ashamed he had seen the ugliness within me. For ugly it was. "You know what she did?" I excused myself to him knowing full well there was none.

"She waits to hear word from Talisker." His voice was low, uninflected and unjudgmental. I stood humiliated before everyone in the bailey.

Ysabell's creamy cheek bloomed dark red from my blow, the color repeated in the sluggish track of carmine that crawled from swelling lips. She disturbed the bloody pattern with her tongue, "Please, Elspeth, please. Niall...tell me about Niall? Is he alive...wounded?" Fear slicked her words.

"Please...I must see him."

I ignored Ysabell's pleading and turned next to Lady Myreton who had been watching silently. "The arrows. You saw them. Robert made them. They were bespelled. You know that. I saw you touch them. He was there at Talisker. We need to know all now."

Lady Myreton touched my arm and whispered, "Not here. We have much to discuss. Once the wounded are settled, meet me in my room. And bring Malcolm."

* * *

She was pacing when we arrived, her room a collection of bright clothing, draped and hung, as though in a boudoir. Malcolm pushed aside a fine dress and sat. I planned to confront her. We needed truth and retribution. Was she friend or foe?

"Yes, I felt the spell when I touched them at the cottage. It was my fault. I do not deny that. I knew Robert was evil, but never thought he would kill anyone. He must have hated me terribly." She paused then explained, "Robert's mother died, and a year later, my father. I was left without fortune; my father having been an impecunious scholar. He and Lord Myreton had been childhood friends and were working together on a Treatise on Sports, Games and Pastimes. In this endeavour, I was my father's scribe and knew Lord Myreton well." *A weak smile turned her lips. "He felt an obligation and* desired my youth. I was grateful and readily accepted his proposal of marriage." She stiffened and looked to Malcolm who seemed disinterested. She continued, "I am perfectly aware I was a sop to his old age but be certain he never regretted wedding me. And in time I came to love him dearly."

"And what of Robert?" Malcolm demanded.

"Patience Malcolm. Robert was Lord Myreton's only child by his first lady wife. He had been well-loved and indulged by his parents and was studying at the university or pretending to do so. And he often brought his friends home, away from the strict tutors, and when his father was gone on business. One of Robert's friends was Ranuff Talisker, a handsome but gloomy lad who enjoyed hunting with bow and dagger. It was through him that I first met a lady from Skye, his mother Una. She was visiting Ranuff at university, when I brought Robert some fresh baking on the way to purchase linens for the dining room. Una was a curious woman, rustic, in her MacLeod arisaid. And I was intrigued by the strange silver clasp at her shoulder. It is a triskele, she told me, a clan symbol. We conversed well as the boys joked and jostled. Eventually Ranuff reminded his mother that she had best go, the last coach to Leith soon would depart and she could not stay in Edinburgh. I inquired and Una explained that the inexpensive inns were full, and she had little coin to spare after filling her son's purse. Of course, I invited her home. It was but a few miles to Corstorphine and she could have the use of a carriage to visit her son. Una clapped her hands in joy and thanked me well. It was all smiles as we departed. Even Robert seemed pleased with me, a rare occurrence.

Una stayed a few days and we discovered we had common interests, including study of the occult. As we parted, she invited me to visit Skye, perhaps in late summer after the midges have had their fill of blood. Surprising myself, I accepted her kind offer and next summer met the other lady adepts at Dunvegan, this while Elspeth was away at university in Italy."

I nodded, "Aye, Aunt Mairi said you are particularly gifted and gradually became part of the circle at Dunvegan."

"If I have any talent, it is because of others. Let me continue, please. The relationships will soon be clear." A questioning glance was offered to Malcolm, and when he nodded, she said, "When his father died Robert barely grieved. He inherited the title, a home in Edinburgh, and a goodly amount of gold. It was a fortune but less than expected. Lord Myreton had not been completely blind to Robert's character, and had made certain provisions for me, a settlement that included Corstorphine and income from some private investments." She hesitated. "But all entailed to Robert should I die."

"Ahh," said Malcolm. "That illuminates much."

"Aye," said she, with an expression of calm acceptance. "Before long Robert gambled away much of his fortune. His Edinburgh home fell in a casual game of cards. So, he came back to Corstorphine. I received him, paid his debts, and gave him an allowance which for him never seemed enough. He was soon in debt once more and taking objects from my home to the nearest moneylender."

"Is that how my mother's side table of the boar hunt ended up at Dunvegan?" asked Malcolm.

"Indeed, and I offered to buy it back for you, but Norman declined, instead offering it as a gift. He said he would have it shipped to you in spring."

Malcolm smiled and reached out to touch her hand. She touched his finger briefly, then withdrew, "Malcolm, there were many other objects stolen, and crimes committed. And regrettably, I cannot put it all aright." She stopped, suppressing a sniffle, then went on. "I once heard him tell Ranuff that his sire had left everything to a cunning whore who had stolen his birthright. And Robert made much over trying to get me into his bed, believing I would be flattered by the offer of a youthful lover." She smiled tiredly. "I was becoming frightened of him, and his antics. It was more than I would bear. So, I threatened to shrivel his yard and bullocks with a spell should he fail to desist. By then he knew of my...emm...skills. It was a ruse, I would never harm him, but the intimidation worked for a time."

Lady Myreton looked directly at me. "Ranuff and Robert must have made an unholy bargain back then. I have thought of little else, Elspeth. Una had access and the ability to bespell arrows that insured they fly true to the person for whom they are intended."

"And Una would have known from Rhona or Mairi that Elspeth was expected to be traveling to Glasgow as well," noted Malcolm.

"Aye. That would explain much of it," I said. "But what advantage to Robert?"

"My death, obviously," said Lady Myreton. "He will get all when I die, for I had no children by my husband. And he knew I would likely be called by the circle, should the laird and his family be threatened."

"You could have warned us," said Malcolm, bitterly.

Lady Myreton eye's flashed in anger, "I knew not till I saw the Myreton fletch from the arrows in Cawdie's body, and I informed Mairi at once. I left Robert at Corstorphine. I swear."

Malcolm rose, he too flushed with anger, but before he left, he turned to us and said, "I have been weak and failed to stop him when I could. For that, I apologize."

* * *

Aunt Mairi requested a gathering of the circle that night to deal with Una, who was implicated in the death of Cawdie and the poisoning of the laird. Aunt Mairi wanted the circle to withdraw the powers Una had been granted as a member. Three or more members can call gatherings, and four are required for assembly of the elements. I knew the three: Aunt Mairi, Lady Myreton, and me, and was not surprised to find that Gregor had been invited to make the fourth. We now had air, fire, earth, and water, the four elements. We could gather. But first I had to address the bees.

We learned as children that the bee is the wisest and cleverest of all living things, surpassed only by man. It is a fastidious creature, never settling on unclean things like blood or flesh, but only those of sweetness. Janet had plaited two hives for her cottage after we arrived. And Cawdie had placed these in a protected place in the back garden and hired a beekeeper to introduce a swarm.

It was traditional to tell the bees all things that happen within the owner's family. Should you not do so, it was believed the canny creatures would become sad and either sicken or produce less honey. But now it was cold and the hive dormant. I put an ear close and could hear the faint hum and motioned for Janet and Solas to come close. In our own way, we told the bees of Cawdie's death, and tied the traditional strip of black cloth on the handles of both hives. Janet threw down a blanket on the autumn grass and we sat, holding each other close under warm cloaks and a shroud of grief, and cried for Cawdie and ourselves. We were alone once more, without our protector. The bees understood and hummed louder. And in my mind the bees sung of spring, gay flowers, warming light, and the gentle touch of fresh breezes. "All will be well," said they. "Cawdie is waiting for spring and his beloved. Neither tarry nor haste, for Cawdie is patiently waiting."

Janet nudged my arm, sending the reverie back to the bees. She whispered, "We should get back before we chill, and you should sleep as you will not tonight."

* * *

It was the hour of witching, the darkness punctuated by our rush torches. All was quiet in the ancient copse behind the kirk. There stood a circle of stones adjacent to the stone slab used as an altar. It was the place they had sacrificed Cawdie to the Evil One, and it brought forth chills and tears. A fire was lit in the middle, and a white line of salt poured, making a circle, and squares drawn within. The points of the outer square were aligned with the four cardinal directions. And within the outer square was a smaller version, rotated to the right, forming four triangles, with each triangle symbolizing an element.

Each of us four took a triangle on which to stand. Four elements represented by four people. We were created from varying amounts of these four things. The proportion of air, water, earth, and fire in us make us who we are. And when the proportions are balanced, all is well. When they are not…

Aunt Mairi was strongly Earth, the beginning of winter, her season, so she was immensely powerful. She balanced patience and arduous work, with the wisdom of age, and cold and dry to cool youth. Her robe was earth black and her humor melancholic. She was on the west triangle.

I smoothed my red wool robe. I stood as blood, red, hot, and moist. My element was air and I belonged to Jupiter who governs healing, religion, and miracles. The god had been good to me, lending me his gifts for travel. higher education, and law, although I have seen little of the wealth, he was touted for bringing. I represented the young and most powerful in spring.

I was positioned in the south triangle.

Gregor held fire. His nature difficult for me to understand although considered the most trustworthy and secure of all. It was choleric, hot, and dry as was his humor, and ruled by Mars. Disconcertingly, Gregor was dressed in a red robe almost the color of mine but brighter. His place was the east.

Lady Myreton served the Moon in shimmering silver. Her element was water, thus cold and moist, her organ the brain, and her season autumn. Her humor was phlegmatic. She was exquisite to behold in the north triangle. I reminded myself that the cosmos permeates everything, linking all with a common thread. And our purpose was to maintain the pattern. If we cannot, our fates could be changed.

Aunt Mairi whispered that it was time to begin. She raised her arms to the sky, and the world stopped. Nary a sound nor movement escaped the boundaries of the copse. She began the calling with an invocation to the gods. We echoed her words and strengthened them chanting the old responses, our hearts and minds uniting as one. The air hummed with power. Suddenly the ground beneath shivered, gave a convulsive tremor, and quieted. Wind soughed through the bare-branched trees, setting them talking among themselves once more. Flames wind-danced in the center square, and mist crept at our feet. From somewhere came the cries of sea gulls in the darkness. Then they too faded.

Aunt Mairi's voice lifted alone in the wind. "Una Talisker, I conjure thee who was one of us by these powerful words proceeding from my mouth. You have caused much suffering and shown contempt for the gods. Therefore, by the power and authority given to me by your peers, I pronounce you cut from us, accursed, and deprived of your talents. And I cast you into the darkness of your own making without redemption."

A twisting column coalesced before us into the shade of Una. Her shriek tore from it. "You cannot do that! Mairi! You have no right to strip me of my life. 'Twas done by my own work, my own skill, my own blood. And I have served well." Her shrill plea melded into the rising whistle of the wind.

Mairi answered, "You cannot have both. Choose! You have allied yourself to those who would destroy us. Tell us who they are and where they are at this moment. Redeem yourself!"

Una's shade rotated into itself. "Too late, too late. You cannot stop us now. The old wrongs will be righted. Blood will free blood. I spit on you, Mairi, and those of your kin. We have allies now, more powerful than you. And we have called the dark ones and they have heeded us. They walk with us now! We will join in battle before you can prepare, and the treasure will be ours!"

A slender frond from the spinning column snaked out toward Aunt Mairi who held out her hand toward it. But it seemingly encountered an unseen barrier that flung it back threefold like a leaf in the wind. The shade vanished into guttering flames which soon dispersed.

Aunt Mairi exhaled "Enough. We can do no more. Tomorrow will come, and we will do as we must. I thank thee all. Her place with us is no more. But she will be a formidable foe, and I am deeply saddened by her loss."

My body crumpled. I sobbed. It was over. We had lost her. We gradually regained strength and removed all traces of our presence in the copse and left.

* * *

"Wake up Elspeth. It's dawn and we must prepare."

I rose, unsteady and nauseous, opening the door to find Malcolm grinning and eager. "What?" I said, forcing my eyes open.

"My God, Elspeth, you're a sight. Spend all night drinking? Come, get dressed, the laird is up with news, and we must prepare to leave." I wanted to slam the door in his cheerful face and return to bed, but he was right, I had much to do.

I reached for the dish of baked lamb cut in small pieces with peppers and cucumbers. The whole seasoned with equal parts of vinegar and pickled cucumber juice and eaten cold. Gregor had arisen early and made the curative concoction for us. I was still nauseous, but picked at it, as did Aunt Mari and Lady Myreton. It helped, but it was no cure, for my emotions had been drained, and there was no remedy but time. Malcolm and my father availed themselves of small portions, ate without comment, then dug into the heaping bowl of honey-sweetened oatmeal.

The laird banged his mug on the table and announced we would be leaving for Talisker on the morrow then onward next day by sail to the shipyard at Loch na h-Airde. He told us the traitor Niall Morrison would await judgement while he healed, assisted by Ysabell Talisker. And neither would be allowed to leave their room of confinement. He also announced that all other prisoners would be released and forgiven if they publicly swore their allegiance to the laird on pain of death should they betray the clan again. But I was uneasy. Could men who forfeit honor be trusted again? But I knew the laird had not the ability to care for so many. They would have to be killed, banished, or put to beneficial use. The laird chose the later. They would be used to labour unarmed. I prayed they would not betray the laird's kind heart once more.

* * *

I spent the day in final preparations and reviewing what we knew about our quest. The stone balls went into the bottom of a bag of oats. The ring remained secure on the chain that Gregor had given me. Everything foreseeable had been planned for and was ready for our departure. The remainder of the day was restless. Aunt Mairi, Lady Myreton, and Gregor were included in our number. We needed their abilities to defeat the witches. Once packed, we visited Janet. She served us morning tea and sweetcakes as Solas pattered quietly about, listening to scraps of conversation. Afternoon was spent visiting patients with Doctor Bethune. I gave him my notes and more advice than necessary, but it took my thoughts away from our difficulties and proved therapeutic since by late afternoon I was once more cheerful.

Back at the castle, they were loading carts with all manner of provisions for a long voyage. Sir Ross Campbell, who would remain to oversee the castle and command the guards, was efficiently directing the men. I greeted him and was told to bring my bags forthwith. For some reason that reactivated my nausea, perhaps it was his cold tone or the sudden realization of what was soon to come, but I entered the sea gate unsettled. The bailey was filled with men hustling about, packing their kits, cleaning, and oiling weapons, and lowering all down the wall to the waiting carts. And among the men were many women, mothers, sisters, and lovers, admonishing, hugging, and kissing. But this time the tenor was more worried and frantic than last. I watched them a moment, until familiar faces caught my eye. It was Malcolm and Teresa, off to the side near the row of privies. They were holding hands, gazing lovingly into each other's eyes. Malcolm was smiling and speaking. Teresa nodded, tears wetting her pink face. Malcolm bent and kissed her forehead, then strode away purposefully. I wondered if it were more between them than convenient passion. No, Teresa would never leave Dunvegan and her inn, and Malcolm would make a terrible husband. It could not happen. They were too sensible. I watched as Teresa wiped away her tears and picked up the basket of breads and pies, she had brought for us. I smiled and wished her well.

Next morning the dark fall dawn wrapped us in thick misty grey, blessedly without rain as we readied for the march to Talisker. Then a cry came down the line. As we set off, I glanced at Malcolm on one side and Gregor on the other. They could not be more different. *My sword and my shield,* I said to myself, my heart thankful.

Crunching boots on gravel along with snorting horses and squeaking carts announced our departure. A line of sombre villagers watched us go, some praying and others merely standing with their thoughts. And I saw Janet and Solas waiting near the cottage. I went to them and gave each a hug, promising to return. I left the village uneasy, their love drawing me back.

Chapter 22: Malcolm

"I am glad you enjoyed the goose," Elspeth teased.

"Indeed. 'Twas I and the goose both, stuffed," I answered. "That was quite a meal, to be sure. We won't have to eat for the rest of the week."

"I was not so imprudent, but I did bring some additional supplies to satisfy your appetite." She patted the linen bag set between her feet. That was about all the space she had left after the birlinn had been loaded with men and supplies. We had set sail from Talisker at first light, looking more like a war party than an expedition. That was the laird's doing. He wanted no further unfortunate surprises, so the oars were manned by his toughest most experienced men, including Murdoch, who brought enough guns, shot and powder for another small war. This time we would do it Murdoch's way if there was trouble.

Elspeth, Lady Myreton, Aunt Mairi and I were huddled in the covered part of the birlinn aft of the mast. The shelter not much more than a small tent made by Wud and his son out of saplings and canvas. And we shared this with a great many barrels, sacks, and crates, brought from Dunvegan. Protecting our goods was the real reason it had been built. Our comfort being but an accidental result.

Elspeth nudged me. "I have a letter from Janet. She gave it to me before we left and said I must wait till we set sail before reading it."

"I trust she is well." I smiled.

Elspeth shifted to retrieve the letter from her cloak, waking Mairi who was curled beside her. The letter was folded and sealed with wax. "Funny how formal she can be at times," Elspeth muttered. "She could have just told me."

Lady Myreton was huddled beside me. She had insisted on coming because of her stepson Robert. I tried my best to dissuade her. This was no place for a lady, I had said, to no avail. Aunt Mairi and Elspeth had sided with Lady Myreton. They all agreed we needed all the help we could get if we were to confront Una, Doideag and Gormal. It was my turn to scoff. But it was the laird who decided who would come or be left behind, and we ended up with a birlinn filled with women and their abundant paraphernalia.

Elspeth carefully broke the wax seal then unfolded the letter. I watched her face as she read. She went from frown to smile to tears within seconds. I handed her a rag to blow her nose. "Let me guess, she wants to run away with the ratcatcher," I said to stem her tears.

"Not quite," Elspeth grinned between wipes. "It…it is a female thing. She sends her love, and that whatever may be, she will stay with me and Solas."

"Is that all?" I laughed.

"Not quite. She sends her regards to you as well."

"And?"

"You mustn't be greedy. Regards is a good start. You made her laugh… for the first time since—"

"I know. That was my intent. I miss Cawdie too."

"You are a good friend."

"Till I'm not, it seems."

"I trust that day will never come for us."

I reached across and took her hand. "Let's finish this business so we can have our old lives back."

Elspeth smiled and wiped her nose again. Aunt Mairi and Lady Myreton were smiling while pretending to sleep.

* * *

Loch na h-Airde was not a picture of a pretty harbour. It is south of Talisker on the west coast of Skye, on a rocky, barren peninsula. At first one might wonder why anyone would situate a shipyard in such a place. Then it became apparent as we sailed closer. It was the entrance, a narrow channel from the sea to the loch, cut into the rock and barely wide enough for a Viking long ship or its descendant, the birlinn. But that was not all. The channel was shallow and could only be navigated at high tide and with permission of the gatekeeper who manned the chain and wooden gate that closed it. "High tide is in two hours. We must wait at sea. I have signalled our intent to enter," was all the captain said, when he poked his head in to inform us.

"That gives us time to prepare," Aunt Mairi said to us, including Lady Myreton who had the rare ability to sleep peacefully at sea. Elspeth yawned then rummaged through her bag, packed with food, medicines and of course the items we needed translating. There were the four stone balls of roughly the same size but with various numbers of bumps or protrusions on them. Each ball also had the triskele symbol and lines some believed were Norse runes. Of course, I had seen them before, and it did not matter how many times we studied them; they remained a mystery. What was their use if anything? We knew the triskele symbol was ancient and found in many cultures, but did it have meaning beyond decoration? And then there were the runes. Each ball had different ones. Were the symbols nothing more than signatures, as Lady Myreton had suggested? Did they simply mean this ball belongs to Olaf, or Leif?

"Here they are," Elspeth said, passing them around. "Any last-minute ideas or suggestions before we land?"

"I have one," I said.

"Of course," Elspeth replied with a smirk.

"Well, we haven't seriously discussed what to do if this leads nowhere."

The three women stared at me as though I said something impossible. Elspeth reached into her bag again ignoring my comment. "Here is the ring," said she, holding it up for us to see. "It has runes too."

"Or scratches from ill-use," I countered, my opinion falling on deaf ears. The women looked away. "All I'm saying is that we need to know when enough is enough. Maybe the clan traditions are myths accreted over time. Perhaps the balls are ancient children's toys woven into myth. Do any of you know for certain?" I asked in a voice laced with exasperation.

"Our laird decided we would follow the signs wherever they lead, and that is precisely why he ordered this ship well provisioned," Elspeth explained gratuitously, since we were all there when that decision had been made.

"It was done with an abundance of caution and at the insistence of your father, Elspeth. The decision was not meant to be an endorsement of clan fables." I sensed the three women bristle at my last comment.

Then Aunt Mairi spoke, "I promise we will not keep you here any longer than necessary, Malcolm. Then you may return to your life of lust and leisure." I guffawed, but I was glad one of them had the backbone to argue.

Elspeth smiled at Aunt Mairi, "We know what we know. Clan traditions are *not* lies *nor* children's tales!" We left it like that, in disagreement.

* * *

We poled ourselves into position using oars and a profusion of profanities, as our birlinn slowly entered the channel on high tide. Groans and grinding noises greeted us as we briefly touched sides and bottom. It was a tight fit, as intended. No one could enter without difficulty, and it had been an arduous task holding position off the coast while we waited. It was the perfect place for a defensible harbour where men could work safely in the calm of the loch and surrounding lands.

"Aye!" Wud answered the man lifting the channel gate, then he leapt off the birlinn. The two men embraced, pounding each other's backs.

"His brother, I think," Murdoch said. "But it's been a while and people change." The birlinn shuddered to a halt part way through the gate. "This is where they have you if you try to enter unbidden. It takes a pull now to get through. Look to the right at that old dun fort. Men could be up there firing down on us while we are stuck. And on the other side…those are not just village huts. They are fortified…thick stone walls and firing slits.

Welcome to the friendly home of the MacAskill family." Murdoch barked out a laugh then said, "Give a hand with the ropes, lads."

All the men but the captain and mate disembarked, and ropes were attached on both sides to pull her through the gate. It was easy but the logic of the trap was stunning. Either get off and tow and expose yourself to fire from both sides, or stay onboard stuck at high tide, or yet worse, try to back her out and flee. I was beginning to understand the MacAskills. Once we were through, we were pulled to the nearest jetty made like nearly everything else here of dark stone. He was waiting for us with three men, fully armed. "My laird, a pleasure to see you," the best dressed of the three stepped forward and offered his hand to Norman.

"Haven't seen you since college," Norman grinned.

"Och, those days! Drank our way through Edinburgh, didn't we?"

"Hush now! Ladies present," Norman answered.

"We were surprised to see your colours at sea this late in the season," the MacAskill man said then turned his head to our ship's captain. "Should've consulted your charts, Willie. Left your laird out there bobbing for hours waiting for the tides, didn't you?" I could see our young captain wither under the criticism, but he said nothing in defense. We all knew it was the laird who had ordered him to sail early. The rest of the introductions followed, then we were taken on a path following the outline of the loch toward his house.

"Business is good, I see," Norman said.

"Aye...many ordered for next spring...coastal traders mainly. Just got a shipment of wood from the Norwegians."

"Mine was crap, green as hell," Wud interjected.

"Too much demand these days because of the war on the continent. But we are dealing with it. Set up a peat-fired kiln for the wood. Slows us down but we have no choice, do we?" the MacAskill said.

The port was alive with a surprising amount of activity. There appeared to be four cradles in use with ships in various stages of construction. Behind the shipbuilding area was a scattering of stone huts topped with fresh thatch, looking well-tended. I noticed that Elspeth was not paying attention to the discussion on shipbuilding, so I hung back. "Been here before?" I asked.

"Aye and heard stories."

"Of?"

"Of those here before the MacAskills. That dun for example, built long before we came, as was the channel itself. Appears to be an unpromising place to live, until one imagines the possibilities."

"Indeed, but for the lack of shipbuilding supplies, 'tis perfect," I teased, and Elspeth laughed. "Let's find that old man. Not interested in another MacLeod Clan gathering."

"We must observe the traditions of hospitality. Be patient. We need their help."

The loch is about a half mile in diameter and this day dotted with ships of various sorts and sizes, some bringing wood and supplies, others recently freed from their birthing cradles to be fitted and finished in the sheltered calm.

"As long as there is trade, there will be a need for ships, and ours are the best…generations of skills passed down," the MacAskill said to the laird, who in turn uttered the customary congratulations. "Come meet the family," the MacAskill said, beckoning us.

On the far end of the loch stood a long stone building which looked like a round hut that had been cut in two and a section added in the middle. It was surrounded by a stone wall with an iron gate. It was the home of the MacAskill, the head of the family who had met us at the jetty. Elspeth whispered to me that his name was Murdo. Our little gaggle finally made it to the courtyard shared by many chickens, geese, and a mule who gave us a curious look before returning to work on what little dead grass there was left to eat.

Muddy boots off and cloaks doffed in the entry way, we found ourselves happily accosted by several wee children and two dogs vying for attention and smells. They were shooed by a plump woman who introduced herself as Margaret, Murdo's wife. All good, so far. No threats nor tears and we were in a warm, dry home which smelled of fresh baked bread and steaming coffee.

"I think I want to stay awhile," I whispered to Elspeth.

She laughed, "I thought you wanted to leave as soon as."

"That was before the enticement of bread, coffee and a warm home."

Margaret led us to the gathering room, as she called it. It was the far end of the building. One side of the room had round stone walls with a massive fireplace, and the other, straight walls with small, shuttered windows. There was a narrow wooden staircase up the middle to the sleeping area above. And seated on the far end, nearest the fireplace and huddled under a blanket, was the oldest looking man I had ever seen.

Norman went over and knelt before him then took his shrivelled hand and whispered something. The old man's eyes opened, and he said in a voice stronger than expected, "Thank God you have finally come. I have been waiting."

* * *

While we filled our bellies, and the coffee sharpened our senses, he told us the history of the MacAskills, and that this house had been built on the ruins of buildings as old as the dun fort that guarded the entrance to the loch. "It was the ancient ones who built this before the Christians, and long before the first MacLeod brought us here."

As he spoke, I noticed that the left side of his face drooped and his words slurred, a sign of apoplexy. A little girl with freckles and dark hair made her way easily onto Elspeth's lap. I thought of life and family, the wee girl contrasting with the old man, with Elspeth between. It was all there, past, present, and future. My thoughts were broken when Norman interrupted, "We have inscriptions. We think they are the old language…runes. Can you read them for us?"

The old man frowned. "Mayhap. They have many meanings, and such are lost. I can have a go. Show them."

Elspeth already had them ready. She knelt at his feet and handed him the first stone ball. He turned it over several times in his hands, his eyes closed searching the surface of the ball as if he could read it. His palm sensed the knobs, the index finger of his right hand slid through the grooves of the triskele, and finally he found the runes. His hand and breathing stopped. He sat motionless. We waited. Then he said, "How many more of these do ye have?"

"Three," Elspeth replied.

"There be one missing, then," he said, "but I know where they go." There was silence as we wondered of his meaning. Then he asked, "Is Mairi MacLeod among us?"

"Aye, Roderick, I am here."

"Come to me lass," he beckoned.

She knelt before him, took his hand, and kissed it. Half his face smiled. Then he bent toward her and asked, "Did Una betray?"

I could see Aunt Mairi's eyes glisten then she whispered, "Aye."

Roderick nodded, then lifted his head and said in a commanding voice, "Take me to the cairn. We have much to do!"

* * *

It was a large mound, more than twenty feet wide and half that high, covered in grass and rocks. It was unremarkable but for the stone entrance. Roderick had ordered torches, a broom, and a cross-eyed lad called Kenneth to help him walk. We settled on the grass before the entrance as Kenneth crawled in to burn the spider webs and sweep the floor. The ladies were appreciative, but it was not done for their benefit. "Do you not wish to see the other balls, Roderick?" Elspeth asked as we waited.

"Nay girl, ah ken see with me fingers better than you with yer eyes and they work in the dark too," he told her.

"I understand," she said. "I have a niece with your gift."

"'Tis nae a gift, but necessity," he said as Kenneth poked his head out of the entrance and bade us come.

The interior of the cairn was divided into five chambers with four small ones on either side of the narrow central corridor and the fifth at the end.

The side chambers were empty but for the rubble which had fallen from the roof. The structure was made of grey stone, except the floor, which was black, the same as the Dunvegan dungeon. The memory of it made me shudder. Kenneth led the way with his torch, Roderick behind steadying himself on Kenneth's broad shoulder. The rest of us followed in single file, the remaining spider webs tickling our cheeks. The tomb smelled of dank death and as we progressed the feelings of tight dread increased, made worse by the choking smoke from our torches.

We reached the furthest and largest chamber which assumed about one third of the tomb. "Spread out and get on your knees, all of ye," Roderick said.

"We can dispense with the prayers," Norman said from across the room, then coughed. This was making him nervous. We needed this over before one of us panicked. It was that kind of place.

Roderick tried to laugh but it came out as a chilling cackle. "Kneel to see, nae pray. Look at the floor. Feel it."

We did. It was flat, as though made so, but also there were lines and holes in various places. We were crawling about silenced in amazement. Aunt Mairi spoke up. "'Tis a map. Feel the grooves. They always said there was a map."

"Aye, but of what?" Roderick responded. "Girl put yer balls in the middle here. 'Tis time."

We watched as Elspeth placed the four stone balls.

"Now listen carefully and think. There are five holes in the floor of the identical size as the balls. But the holes are nae identical. Each has a different number of indentations. Ah haven't felt all the balls, but ah'm guessing there is a ball with two knobs, one with three, one with five, one with seven, and one with eleven."

"I have noted that as well, Roderick. We have the first four," said Elspeth.

"The one with eleven must be with Una," I heard Aunt Mairi whisper.

"Indeed, let us hope it yet exists," Roderick replied. "Now girl...is it Elspeth?"

"Aye."

"Elspeth, take the balls and discover the one hole where each fits."

There was much scrambling and apologies but eventually it was done. "Those are quadrants," said I. "The floor divided into equal spaces," remembering my geometry.

"Or the points of a compass," Norman added.

"That was the easy part," Roderick said. "Now ah must read the runes for each ball."

We waited as Roderick crept across the floor to the first hole, Elspeth guiding him.

"The one you showed me before said *Vestur* in old Norse. That means west. My heart flew to the sky. Ah knew then we had solved it." His fingers caressed the ball. We could hear him muttering and laughing. Several minutes later, he and Elspeth returned to the middle of the floor. He announced, "Each ball has the triskele symbol adopted by Clan MacLeod as part of our standard. Each ball has a different number of knobs, so they only fit properly in one of the holes. And each ball has runes that translate to one of the four cardinal directions, west, east, north and south." He stopped.

"And the fifth hole over here by me?" Norman asked.

"That be your destination, and the ball held by Una," Roderick answered him.

* * *

The stone balls seemed to be glowing hot in the torchlight as they set in the black floor. It was an eerie sight. They seemed to have regained their power, together but for one, and doing what was intended, providing orientation to the lines cut into the basalt of the floor. We were on hands and knees following the lines with our fingers, but it was hopeless. Even with the balls to orient us, the shape of the map was an undefined black on black.

"We need something to fill the grooves," I muttered.

"Shipyard lime?" young Kenneth said in response.

"Brilliant lad!" Norman exclaimed. "Fetch it."

He was back minutes later and we each took a quadrant and started filling the grooves. It was a messy job but put right when Kenneth suggested he sweep the whole map to remove the excess. We stood and watched. Out of the chaos of white on black, it emerged as he swept: a crude map of the Isles off the west coast of Scotland. There was butterfly shaped Skye, the Isles of Canna, Rum and Eigg south of Skye, with the Isle of Muck like a punctuation mark below them. Further south yet were Coll and Tiree like a finger at sea and finally there was the Isle of Mull, shaped like an old boot. We stood in awe. The limestone clearly outlined a map of the Western Isles, but there was more.

"The fifth hole must be Iona, based on where it is positioned at the tip of Mull," said I.

"And it is different," Norman, who was standing closest to it, said. "It has wee lines radiating from it, like the rays of the sun."

"And the old name for Iona is the Place of the Yew," Elspeth mused. "That reminds me—"

"I saw the fifth ball when Una and I were young. It has one rune symbol on it that looks like a zig-zag," Aunt Mairi explained, "and it did have many knobs, but I know not how many."

Roderick had been sitting as we spoke. He scattered some lime before him and drew a symbol in the dust. "Is this what you saw?" he said to Mairi.

She came close and bent down to look, "I think so."

"That is called *Eiwaz,* the rune for the Yew tree."

"It was in the knot garden plan too," Elspeth exclaimed.

"I hope Una doesn't know this," Norman uttered what I am sure we all were thinking.

* * *

We left the dark of the cairn and returned to the MacAskill house to discuss what must be done. Most believed the treasure lay at Iona but where exactly and why? Regardless, it was decided. We would go to Iona. "'Tis a long voyage," our young captain said, we can hug the coast for most of it…safer but much longer, or sail on a straight course."

"If Una has figured out the treasure is there, they likely will ride south to Sleat and try to get a ship to Mull," Norman added then paused. "Although we don't know where they are for certain, we should assume the worst, and that means taking the fastest route to Iona."

We all nodded, but I for one worried about being on the open sea in a small boat this time of the year with an inexperienced captain. We would be out of sight of land for much of it without a nearby shore to seek for safety. It was a recipe for complete disaster. But I said nothing. It was Norman's role to decide.

Elspeth sat grim faced fiddling with something in her hand. I could tell by her stare that her mind was fully engaged. "What is it?" I asked her.

"I was thinking of the signs. Assuming we get to Iona, then what? And then I remembered this." She held up the ring, the one we removed from the finger of Alisdair Crotach at St. Clements, that day which seemed years ago now.

"We need it translated," Elspeth continued. "Roderick, can you do it?"

The old man was on a stool nearest the fire, half-asleep, wrapped in his plaid. One eye fluttered. "What ring?"

"The one from St. Clements," Elspeth answered. "Can you read it?"

She offered the ring to him. He waved his hand away. "Dinnae have too. Seen it afore. 'Tis the ring of Leod. It says, 'Ah belong to Leod, or some such." We looked at each other in wonderment. I needed confirmation. This was important, so I asked, "How do you know what it says?"

He gave one of his cackling chuckles and proceeded to tell us of when he went to Rodel with some of his hell-bound friends. He admitted they went to loot, but when they arrived, they soon realized many others had been there before. The tombs were empty but for the one of Alisdair Crotach. And when they found the ring and read it, they became afraid. Roderick said that one in his party believed that the ring of Leod must be a powerful talisman since he was the first of our line. Another said that whoever takes it would either be cursed or blessed. He said they laughed and dared but, in the end, none wanted to risk it.

"It has remained there till ye took it. Should have left it," Roderick nodded then pulled the plaid around his shoulders more closely.

"Clan tradition has the tomb of Leod at Iona. That is what we were told," Norman interjected.

"Surely it has been looted long ago," Elspeth mused.

Norman shrugged. "His tomb is said to be in the floor of the choir."

"I agree with Elspeth. This could be a futile effort," I said

"We must try. We are as ready as ever for it," Norman countered.

I nodded but knew it would not be easy notwithstanding our preparations.

"Leod was our first chieftain. They say he lived in the 13th century and was a son of Olaf the Black, King of the Isle of Mann, and the Hebrides. Olaf was a descendant of Godred Crovan King of Dublin and the Isles. They were of Viking and Celtic descent. Funny that I remember that. I was a boy playing on the floor when I heard my father tutoring my older brother Ruairidh Og, who became chieftain when father died. He got consumption and passed six years later, leaving the unwanted burden to me." Norman looked away and sighed. Then I noticed he pulled his body straight like a soldier, turned to us and said, "Prepare the ship. We leave for Iona on the tide. Send word of our destination to Sir Ross Campbell at Dunvegan."

* * *

A sky of mare's tails and mackerel scales met us in the morning. "We must leave now before the storm is upon us," our captain said. His mate suggested we stay and let it pass, that the skies foretold a major storm.

"We must not tarry," Lady Myreton commanded. "Mairi, can you not feel the dark forces gathering to the south?"

"More than dark… 'tis evil itself."

Norman had been listening to this, then said, "Waiting for the storm to pass could mean a delay of several days. 'Tis high tide, so we will leave and depend on God's grace. Any objections, speak now."

Murdoch cleared his throat.

"Aye, what is it?" Norman looked at him.

"We have two of our crew unwell. I want to leave them here and take four of their best shipbuilders and fighters…just in case."

"Done!" Norman barked.

"And a cask of their finest whisky," Wud said, making us laugh.

We had no time for a proper breakfast, so we filled our pockets with bread, cheese, and oat cakes, scrambled aboard ship and poled our way through the channel and out to sea. The captain turned our birlinn south, had the sail raised high and yelled, "Let us fly on the wings of angels to Iona, lads!"

* * *

The Westerns Isles of Scotland are windswept on the best of days, and late fall storms can bring every form of rain, ice, and snow in abundance. We had crossed the open sea south of Skye approaching the Isle of Eigg to starboard. The prevailing winds had been favourable but now they were veering from westerly to southwest, the hard rain whipping us, the waves piling up before us. Small boats in large seas are seldom a favourable match and we were rising and falling with stomach lurching regularity. The captain had lowered the sail to half to cope with the winds and we were having to row to keep her strait. A moments inattention could have us broadside to a twenty-foot roller and that would be the end. But at least our wee birlinn was holding together but for the few frightening groans as wood forced on wood.

The women were bailing frantically as we men pulled our guts out on those oars. *We are not going to make it,* I thought. But we kept on, every stroke an agony with no respite, as it was too dangerous to leave our seats. I was cursing my bad luck when a glint of sunlight broke through the clouds and Fortuna gleamed hot as she reached through the oar stroke.

I laughed and cried out through the gale's roar. "Fortuna, we need you! Guide our ship to safe shores!"

Elspeth looked up from bailing, her hair soaked and stuck to her face. She loudly repeated my prayer, then the men nearest joined in, till we were shouting as one. At least it made us feel somewhat better if nothing else, and maybe some divine being who cares about a boatload of wretched ones had heard.

It seemed like many hours later and we had been making slow progress rowing since the winds now were in our face and our sail fully down. The man in front of me pointed to port side and said he thought the dark smudge on the horizon was the mainland and we should be crossing the Sound of Mull next. The bands of rain and wind had merged, and we were beginning to feel the storm's full fury. *We aren't going to make it to Iona,* I said to myself again.

Then I could feel the birlinn turning to port into the Sound of Mull. I looked over my shoulder and could see the captain and first mate pushing hard on the rudder turning her. Then the man behind me shouted in my ear, "We are running up the sound for safe harbour. Pass it on."

As we turned, the sail lifted and caught some wind. "Haul her up," the captain ordered. The flapping subsiding as it filled and billowed. We slumped over our oars for a brief rest. I was relieved but for the niggling feeling that something worse than the storm may be our fate. I wanted to shout at the captain to take our chances on the unforgiving sea. We flew onward to our fate, but I feared not on the wings of angels.

* * *

We were headed for Tobermory, the only decent harbour on Mull's north coast. My heart chilled when I heard. *Surely not,* I complained to myself. How is it possible we would end up at the very location of Captain Forrester's defeat at the hands of the witches those many years ago? Still, the prospect of dry land strengthened our arms as we fought our way into the shelter of the harbour I recognized at once from my drug induced dream. It was in the shape of a gentle arc guarded by a headland to starboard and what appeared to be a peninsula rising to port out of the sea spray. The entrance to the harbour looked to be about eight hundred yards in width. It was enough and our captain shouted for us to pull for all we were worth to keep her near the middle of the channel and away from the jagged rocks on one side and the shoals on the other. It took us some time and more effort but eventually we succeeded. The waves subsided by half. A good thing too because we were spent.

As we rested on our oars and let our hearts and muscles recover, I looked about. Tobermory Bay appeared to be a mile or two in length and half that in width. A bonny harbour but for the rotting prow of a large ship that thrust out of the water near the middle of it. My eyes were drawn to that ship. *My ship,* I thought. *My beautiful Florencia, the ship crushed by the mighty quern-stone, the day we died.* I shook my head. *Damned witches!*

We had no time for admiring the view because we had to approach the dock carefully or risk crashing. And it was not easy with the waves and gusts, but we did it with port oars out to protect her from the wooden dock pilings. We splintered a few oars, a small price to be yet alive and on firm land. There we found a collection of dark stone cottages built along the curve of the bay. One building was larger and appeared to be an inn. The crew stayed aboard as a few of us tried to secure respite. Surprisingly, it was easily done.

"Your rooms are ready captain, and a cauldron of stew is simmering," the ruddy innkeeper said to me in what appeared to be a genuinely friendly manner.

"I am not the captain. He stays with the ship and his men."

"Nay," the innkeeper replied. "You fit the description."

And then I understood. "Who told you we were coming?"

"An old friend...Doideag said you were coming. She paid for your rooms in advance. If you are wanting a dry place for your crew, we have a shed out back. Best I can do," he said.

After hearing that, I was not sure I wanted to stay in this inn. It was not much, with its sagging walls and soot-stained ceiling. One of those places that made you itch and sneeze, and then there would be the suspect food and drink that could be poisoned by witches.

I was considering our lack of options when Norman asked him, "Who was with this Doideag?"

"'Twas only her...although, she bought food and ale for more."

I asked him, "And where do they stay?"

"I know not, but it must be close by since she carried her food away without transport."

"Then if you see her, tell her that her friends have arrived and wish to meet."

Murdoch must've thought I was being too diplomatic because he stepped forward and said in a threatening tone, "We come in peace, but prepared for war. Anyone who stands against us will fall under our swords."

Norman reached out to stay Murdoch's fire.

"Emm," the innkeeper took a step back. "I assume by your dress you are from Skye. We are allies of Clan MacLeod going back many a year. You will not find enemies here, I assure you."

"Innkeeper I am Norman MacLeod of MacLeod and bring greetings to my good friend John MacLean, Chieftain of Clan MacLean."

The innkeeper's face brightened, "'Tis an honour to have you among us Sir Norman. I...I...we must find you more suitable accommodations."

Norman smiled, "Your inn will be sufficient, so long as the witches have not tampered."

"Oh no...never. We are an honourable family and will serve you well. But I must tell you that our chieftain is not here, nor anywhere on Mull—"

"I know, when he lost Castle Duart to the Campbell's, he left Mull."

"And our great Castle Duart was put to ruin by those Campbells," the innkeeper said, sadness overtaking his face.

"I will tell your chieftain of your kind service, or treachery, and we will pay twice what you received from those witches for our accommodations and victuals." The laird threw a small pouch of coins on a nearby table. "Take what you deserve, good fellow."

As the innkeeper was counting out his coins, Elspeth arrived, her cloak dripping water, an angry look on her face. "Have you men forgotten you left us standing out there in a storm?"

I grinned at her. "Good news!" said I. "We have dry accommodations for everyone."

I could see by the scowl yet on her face that my news was not enough, so I added, "Even better, the ladies will share the stables with the warriors."

She swatted my arm, her scowl lifting as she turned away and laughed into her sleeve. Then loudly over her shoulder said, "We will take the best rooms, innkeeper. The men can sleep in the stables." Of course, that is what we already planned, but it was entertaining teasing her.

Our young laird secured an inn room because of poor health. He shared it with Murdoch and another old man who was doing poorly having had his head banged by an errant rope. The rest of us bedded down in the straw we shared with an ancient horse who did not much like us and some poultry who did. Notwithstanding the rustic accommodations, it was a relief to be in a place dry and out of the wind. We undressed and wrung out our clothing before spreading them out to dry. But we had no fire, so the best we could hope for was damp instead of soaking wet by morning.

The storm lessened through the night, the banging of the slate shingles having kept us awake through most of it, tucked as we were under mounds of straw which smelled of summer and dung. The stable door opened before it was light and he yelled, "Doctor Forrester?"

I knew it was Murdoch and answered, "Over here, under a chicken."

"We need to meet with the laird. The rest of you, rise and ready yourselves. There is a water trough outside and a privy behind the inn. You can't miss it. Follow the smell." Murdoch kicked a pile of straw nearest him and said," You too Wud." Some men sniggered because of Wud's fondness for sleep. "Breakfast will be served in the dining room in an hour," Murdoch added as he left, launching yet more sniggering and jokes.

* * *

The tiny room at the inn was full. It was our war council. Everyone of import was there. Being last to arrive, I sat on the floor, my back propped against the door jam. And thankfully it was warm, so I removed my cloak for additional drying on a peg set in the wall. The room itself looked like it had not been thoroughly cleaned since the previous century, but for the floor which had been swept using the straw broom leaning by the door. I gazed about as everyone chatted. For the most part, we had survived yesterday's awful experience. Stomachs had settled, bowels flushed, and fresh bread, meat, and ale had allayed our hunger. The basics of life met; it was time to talk. The laird sat on one of the beds between Aunt Mairi and Murdoch. He looked hale, his cheeks pink, a sparkle in his eyes. *Damn him, he is enjoying himself!* I chuckled to myself.

The laird started with a joke, "There are two things in life we cannot change...weather and men." We all laughed. It was an old observation on the nature of existence. But for us, stuck at Tobermory, it was more than apt. He held up his hand. "Some may tell you that witches can control the weather, and others claim that evildoers can suddenly become saints. I will not debate the issue. I mention this because I fear opinions will divide us at the most in-opportune time. And if that should happen, I insist that *my* opinion and commands must prevail." Silence prevailed as smiles faded and purpose emerged. Norman looked at each of us. "If any of you disagree, I want you to withdraw now. There will be no reprisals. I need to know who is with me." No one spoke or left. We were in this together, united under his firm leadership. It was comforting. At least we have each other. Our laird smiled then turned to Murdoch, "What is our situation?"

Murdoch had been fiddling with his tomahawk pipe again, itching to use it. "The village is an arc fronting the bay with a trail exiting on both ends. Behind us is a steep hill. Our scouts have located three trails winding up that hill. 'Tis largely forested but with a few open areas with crofts. No search for witches was made. But our men out there are encamped in a death trap. The stables are stone-made with timber beams and straw on the dirt floor. There is one entrance, the double door. If that door were blocked with our men inside, the straw could be lit, and all would perish within minutes. Meanwhile, our leaders are separated from them, here in an unfamiliar building, trusting our threats and bribes will protect us."

"Yet the storm continues unabated. We have no where else to go," I added for clarity.

Murdoch smiled. "We could take people's homes at gunpoint, or we could stay on our birlinn, or setup camp in the open." I noticed a few shaking their heads, others looking grim-faced. It was obvious, we had few practical options because of the storm.

"The forest on the hillside could offer some protection and perhaps the storm will pass sooner than expected," I said, trying to explore more ideas.

"And we don't know where our enemy is located, nor if they have allies hereabouts." Murdoch countered.

Norman spoke next, "They have no laird to lead them. Mull is reputed to be a lawless place. We must make it lawful and set a good example. We cannot resort to violence unless attacked, and never abuse the locals unless we are betrayed. I don't know Chieftain John MacLean well, but our clans are longstanding allies, and I will be pleased to tell him we have restored order in his name."

Aunt Mairi banged her staff on the floor. "My laird, we need a decision. Do we stay or leave?"

"Thank you for your patience, Mairi," the young laird chided. "Murdoch and I have a plan. Listen well."

* * *

We were ready. Our laird wrote a friendly letter to Doideag requesting a parley and gave it to the innkeeper instructing him to relay it to her. He pretended he knew not of her whereabouts. It only took the suggestion of being scalped with Murdoch's tomahawk to change his mind. *Poor sod,* I thought. *Who'd want to be caught in this mess?*

Night had fallen. We were packed in the stables, all of us this time. The women had taken a corner and performed a magical ceremony while sitting in a circle, hands clasped with a candle between them. Elspeth came to us afterward. She held out three dark green threads. Three laurel leaves were woven into each, with faint traces of writing on every leaf. "These will prevent enemies overcoming us. Hang one thread six inches above the ground along the trails they might use. The way will be blocked to witches until they are removed by those who placed them."

I lifted one. It had three names written on it, Michael, Gabriel, and Raphael. "This is your protection?" I asked her incredulously.

Elspeth did not answer, rather she handed me a flat stone with a downward pointed crescent and a large V shape carved on it. "Paint three of these designs at eye level on trees along the trail as well. We have protected the stable. You may use these now."

Murdoch assigned a few men the task of setting out the strange threads and making the protective symbols. The rest of us settled as best we could, listening to the storm in its relentless ferocity. Later that evening, Murdoch reported that the talismans had been placed and scouts positioned. Some old warriors had volunteered, joking that they would rather be out in the storm than enduring their neighbours' farts, snoring, and bad jokes. Such are men. The best of them mock privation, so the rest of us may sleep.

Next, Murdoch set to work with two men. The double doors could be quickly barred from without, and we would be trapped. So, they replaced the iron hinge pins with twigs that could be broken easily by a few men. That was how Murdoch imagined it, anyway. He also ordered our boat to be moored far enough away from the dock to protect it from easy mischief. I for one, hoped it was still there in the morning.

"We are ready," Murdoch grunted as he set himself down beside Norman, dozing beside me. "If Highlanders accompany the witches, we will face them on the road. 'Tis is the only way they can bring a lot of men here swiftly. The trails are steep and treacherous, and in this rain and mud..." Murdoch stopped to think.

"False assumptions—"

"I know, I know...the natives in America prefer surprise attacks. Nothing will stop them, not terrain or weather...except...hmm."

"Except religion and superstition," the laird muttered from his somnolence.

"Precisely!" Murdoch said loudly. "Let us hope the locals are superstitious."

"Fine idea, but odds are we will face Highlander forces on the road or witch treachery here in the village," said I.

"Or both," Murdoch mused. "It is too dangerous to get our cannon off the birlinn, yet we have considerable firepower the locals cannot match." A moment of pondering, then, "A battle with local Highlanders is not so likely as the threat from the witches themselves. But it is best to be ready for any eventuality."

"But there is another alternative...at least one," I said. Sleepy heads turned to me. "Our approach to Tobermory Bay was slow, because of the storm. That could have given the witches time to prepare once they spotted our flag. It could have been merely a fortuitous occurrence they are exploiting. What if they want us here for as long as possible while they ride south to Iona?"

"That had occurred to the laird and me as well. But we cannot leave till this storm abates anyway. We decided that if we have no meaningful contact with the witches by then, we will leave justice for another day, and sail," Murdoch answered in his measured way.

"Or perhaps they will do both. Leave someone here to negotiate and harass us while others ride to Iona," Elspeth mused.

"We have established how little we know. Our scouts have been positioned, bellies filled, spells cast, now it is time to rest as one storm diminishes and perhaps another kind grows." I slapped my thigh and rolled to my knees to make a fresh nest in the straw.

* * *

The storm raged another two days and two nights. Our innkeeper kept us well-filled and content, and there were no signs of witches nor any threats to our security. It was just boring and calm, nestled as we were in the straw. Some of the men brought cards and dice, others a favourite book or Bible wrapped in oilskin. The ladies busied themselves mending worn garments and trading recipes. As for me, my pistol needed oiling, and a sharp edge ground on my cutlass. But mostly I worried about that ship sunk in the harbour and what it meant for our future.

The morning of the third day dawned bright. The winds had abated, replaced with fresh cold and a cloud-mottled blue sky. It was a radical change and raised our spirits when we emerged from our smelly stable. Sore muscles had healed and by the looks on everyone's eager faces, we were ready for more adventure.

Tobermory was visible clearly now as a pretty arc of stone cottages and upturned fishing boats with fish drying racks between. There was a nice wide road of stone and packed dirt fronting the cottages with a few boat launch ramps scattered along the length. All appeared well till one listened. There were no sounds but for the lapping waves.

"No one about. Even the dogs and birds have fled," Murdoch chuckled nervously.

"What did your scouts report?" I asked.

"Nothing," he answered.

"That means there is another way in and out of here. One we missed." I looked at him.

Worry creased his face. "Or they could have rowed away before we woke. Was there not a boat pulled up on that slip near the inn when we arrived? There seems to be a few other boats missing as well."

"I don't remember. We had other desires than counting boats that day. Is the innkeeper here?" I asked, hoping for some good news.

Murdoch shook his head. "Everyone is gone."

"And the food and ale?"

"Enough for now."

"They want us gone. The witches must have frightened them with tales before we arrived."

In front of the stables, a group of us men gathered. Murdoch wanted a house-to-house search, the laird an exploration of the heights. I watched as the ladies joined us, wrapped for the cold.

Aunt Mairi spoke, "The tales of Captain Forrester are thought to be true hereabouts. Not as mere fables, but history. The innkeeper's girl told me. She was a nervous lass having us here. Her hands were shaking as she poured."

"Malcolm, you must stay out of sight. We fear you are the target," Elspeth said, with a sincere look of concern.

I laughed. "Do you expect me to hide?"

"Nay, but Robert may be about, and he is an expert with his bow, and his arrows are—"

"But I have Fortuna to deflect his magic arrows, don't I?" I could not help teasing.

I was expecting a rebuke but instead she said, "I pray so…but please be careful. We know not what they have planned. And…and we all feel something evil nearby…not here…but that way, back out to sea." She tilted her chin in the direction of the harbour mouth. I looked in that direction, my eyes studying the entrance. There was something odd about it, fog, or smoke drifting across. I was about to mention it when our captain hailed us from beyond the inn. He was frenetically waving his glass and clutching what appeared to be a nautical chart while pointing in the direction of the peninsula. We beckoned him join us.

"That isn't a peninsula. See here," he pointed on his chart. "It's an island with a narrow channel between us and it." He stopped speaking while we looked.

"We need to reconnoitre that area. 'Tis close enough to concern," Murdoch said.

Norman nodded to him. "I agree. Send some scouts at once. William, what is the width of that channel, and can we navigate it with our birlinn?"

Our captain had another look at the chart. "Seems to be about one hundred yards across. No indication of depth, and there may a narrowing or some obstructions."

"We need to find out. Send your scouts, Murdoch," Norman ordered.

"Aye, my laird," Murdoch said, then turned to leave.

"Wait! There is more," Captain MacAskill exclaimed.

All eyes went to him. He pointed again, this time across the harbour to the tip of the peninsula, or rather the island at the entrance to the harbour. We saw it at once. Smoke, not fog. "Someone is there!" the captain said.

The ladies nodded grimly.

* * *

We did not know where everyone from the village went, nor did we know who or what was the source of the smoke on what our captain's chart identified as Calve Island. We needed to sort that and soon before we blundered further. Our suspicion was that they intended to trap us in the harbour, sink our birlinn then slaughter us, a repeat of what had happened to Captain Forester long ago. So, Murdoch sent two men west along the road, past our guard post to the harbour entrance across from Calve Island. Another two men he sent in the opposite direction to scout the channel between us and the island.

We plotted that morning, waiting for the scouts to return. Meanwhile, all the cottages were searched. No one had been left behind but for the village cats who seemed not to care. This was serious business, and worse yet, it seemed well-planned.

Before noon, the scouts had returned. Those who had gone east reported that Calve Island had two rocky arms of land facing the harbour entrance. Between the arms was a shallow bay; and beached on the shore of that bay were several fishing boats. They saw what appeared to be two camps, one on each arm of the bay, with many people milling about. More worrisome, there seemed to be cannons set in embankments at each camp and aimed at the harbour entrance.

"Where could they have obtained cannon?" Murdoch wondered aloud.

"Traders would not risk selling them. Too hard to hide. They would be caught and hung," Norman answered.

"Or they salvaged them," said I, nodding toward the prow of the *Florencia* in the middle of tha harbour.

Norman's face flushed. "Oh God!" he said repeatedly until Murdoch suggested they might not work properly anyway. It was faint hope, but we held on to it since it was all we had for purchase.

"The scouts who had gone east found that the channel was navigable, deep enough, but with little room to manoeuvre in a fight. It would be suicidal to try to get out that way with enemy on the banks of the island," Murdoch said.

My mind exploded with questions. "Then before we act, we must confirm what our scouts saw. Are those cannons serviceable? Do they have shot and kegs of powder? How many men do we face? What other surprises might they have in store?"

"The only way is to go there and see. We could sneak over at night. But in the dark...hmm," Murdoch mused.

"Then let's observe them during the day," Norman said. We knew what he meant. This could be great fun.

* * *

If they were watching, we wanted them to think we were preparing to leave. Their eyes would be on our birlinn and the harbour entrance. To that end, we brought the birlinn to the dock. Wud and Jimmy pretended to do some repairs as our men packed up and moved supplies out of the stables. Then in the dark of night, we would row one of the fishing boats they left behind across to the island and wait for dawn to reveal all. That was the plan. But none of us wanted to consider the possibility of failing to return healthy enough to report what we had found. And I mean "we" because our scouting party would be me, Murdoch, and one of his best warriors. Of course, Norman had insisted he go but was vociferously voted down by a chorus of female voices. There was no such outcry when my name was offered in his stead.

Murdoch nudged my arm, "Time to go," he whispered.

We had slept fully dressed, our weapons by our side. No time but for a quick pee before we ran to the boat readied for us. The warrior and I took to the oars while Murdoch managed the steering rudder. The night air was bitterly cold and silent. We would have to be careful to avoid slapping the water with our oars. We rowed up the channel before crossing over to the island at a spot recommended by our scouts. The location, a mud flat surrounded by bushes, was a good place to land and hide our boat.

We landed without incident, slogged through the muck, and tied our boat to a bush. It was dark but for the sliver of moon showing through the passing clouds. Murdoch whispered that he thought it was about seven o'clock in the morning. We followed a trail which headed toward their camps. Murdoch in the lead, we moved through the brush, his experience demonstrated in silence. The middle of the island was flat, the grass well-clipped by the summer's cattle. The lack of good cover forced us back to the marge where the land sloped to the sea. It was rocky and rough going. "Ahead and to the right," Murdoch whispered, crouching behind a clump of shrubs.

There appeared to be a few men siting near the remnants of a fire. We were close now and decided to stay put till dawn. Most men hate waiting for anything and the next hour was the worst. I was cramping from the cold ground and tense from having to practise the perfect quiet that would keep us safe. But I had to stay that way, or our mission was blown to hell. Cawdie's advice came to mind. He was superb at resting in place in almost any condition. He said, "Make yourself small. Imagine you are a squirrel curled up with your bushy tail wrapped around you. Then take long slow breaths and think of your beloved." Most of that worked and soon Murdoch prodded us back to alert consciousness.

Murdoch tugged us close, our heads almost touching. "We need to get closer to the headland. That is where the cannon should be. Stay low, crawl if you must." He once again took the lead, like a bear on all fours. We veered left to skirt the camp, following what seemed to be an animal trail. It was slow nervous work, and the weather was not concealing, the dawn's sun having already broken clear over the horizon. There was hardly a breath of wind, the bay on our left lay glassy smooth, and the late fall plants protested loudly as we touched them. It was a wonder no one in the camp heard our approach.

We came abreast of a low cluster of makeshift tents arranged around a smouldering firepit. I stopped and pulled aside some branches for a better view. And there she was, stirring the firepit embers with a stick. Gormal. My heart raced. They are here. Our women were right. There was evil across the bay. Murdoch saw me pointing at Gormal and nodded. We watched as a few others came out of the tents to relieve themselves. We had to be quick now, not wanting to be here much longer. Murdoch crawled the few feet back to us and whispered, "You two start heading back. I'll reconnoitre the cannon placements and meet you at the boat." We both readily agreed. He was much better at this than we.

Half-way back I found a good defensive position near the water with rocks on three sides. "I'll stay here in case he needs help. You go ahead and make sure the boat is ready," I said to the warrior. He grunted in agreement. I crouched behind the rocks. There were no sounds but for a few gulls who had started their morning search for food. I waited. Too much time elapsed. I imagined poor Murdoch captured and being tormented by witches. Shocking what one thinks when the mind is not occupied. But reality resumed suddenly with the sound of gunfire coming from the camp. *Oh damn! They've found him.*

Moments later Murdoch flew by my position on full run, his blood-stained tomahawk at hand. "Come-on Malcolm!" he shouted at me. I did not linger. We made it to our boat as the warrior was pushing off from shore. This was going to be the dodgy part since we were easy targets for anyone with good aim. I was facing backward, rowing, the warrior heaving mightily at my side. The opposition emerged moments later from the brush. There was nothing we could do but keep rowing. Murdoch was at the tiller, his back to them, a big target in buckskin and red serge. "Get down Murdoch, they're going to fire!" I yelled at him. But he did not move.

Instead of doing the sensible thing, he said, "Tell me when."

I watched them ready their muskets and begin to raise them to their shoulders. "Now!" I cried, hoping he had time to duck.

Immediately, Murdoch turned the rudder full right. We turned abruptly left and heard the volley of shot whiz by. One ball must have caught Murdoch on the back of his arm, because he lurched sideways. We kept going like that, turning as needed till we reached shore. The warrior and I were done in. Murdoch looked at his arm. "Damn," he said. "They've ruined my jacket."

* * *

"They have us trapped in the bay," Aunt Mairi said.

"Nay Mairi, we have them trapped on the island," Murdoch argued.

We were meeting again at the inn. The local ale and food had been consumed and we were down to the supplies we had brought, since Norman had decided not to loot the village, at least not yet.

"And you said they outnumber us considerably?" Mairi asked once more.

"Two to one at least, but our men are better trained, and they have their women and children. There must be a hundred of them camped out there," Murdoch explained.

"We must protect their children," Elspeth muttered. We were all thinking the same. This could be a horrific bloodbath if not managed well.

"Will they stand and fight?" I asked Norman.

"We are supposed to be allies. I'll encourage peace, of course," Norman responded.

"We don't know how much hold the witches have on them. But remember they were able to corrupt the minds of some of our own at Dunvegan," Mairi stated plainly.

We sat a moment considering the grim possibilities. We could try to escape but the harbour mouth was guarded by two cannons and several fishing boats. Murdoch reported that the cannons looked serviceable. They had barrels of powder positioned and many flame arrows stacked by the fire. We would be risking hell raining down on us if we tried to leave that way. And sneaking out the narrows on the other side would be no better. Our only viable choice was to attack without risking the birlinn.

Murdoch broke the silence. "My laird, do you agree that an attack provides our only chance of success?"

The laird sighed, "Sadly, it seems so. Murdoch, you are our war leader. Tell us what must be done."

Murdoch rose and pointed to the chart flattened on the table between us. "We will remove our cannon and supplies from the birlinn and haul it using the horse to this point across from their cannon positions here." He tapped each place with his finger. "Meanwhile, several men will take our fishing boat back across the narrows to the cove we used earlier. They must secure the landing area. The rest of us will follow in the birlinn. Around one o'clock and when our gunner is ready, he will fire two shots from our cannon then wait fifteen minutes before resuming firing. Meanwhile, we will form up in the middle of the island where the grass is low and there are few obstructions. Once we hear the first two cannon shots, we march on their camp."

"We will have sixteen men, no more." I reminded everyone.

"Aye, there will be two men on our cannon, and two left on the birlinn—Captain MacAskill and his first mate," Murdoch said.

"And what of us?" Elspeth asked.

Murdoch's expression was stern when he faced the women. "You will stay here...and pray...or whatever."

Elspeth's face reddened. "We are needed and—"

"Nay Elspeth! You will stay. I cannot risk everyone." Norman MacLeod rose to full height and said in a commanding voice, "'Tis settled. Murdoch begin your preparations."

I looked around the table. We all knew this likely would be suicidal. Our sixteen against forty or more, and we did not know what traps the witches had laid. Nonetheless, the women held their tongues and we set to work.

* * *

We had pulled our cannon into place across the harbour entrance from Calve Island when I saw Murdoch next. It had been warm work carrying cannon balls and kegs of powder, but it felt good giving muscles something to do after days of rest. As we prepared, they watched us, the men over there. That was part of our plan. We wanted them to know they were in for a pounding.

But Murdoch and I had unfinished business. "Enjoying men's work," he teased.

"Indeed, you could try giving a hand," I fired back. In truth I love manual work like this, up to a point. But then I could always walk away when tired or bored, whereas the other men could not. "A word, sir," I said to him.

"I left things out, didn't I?" he said, once we were out of earshot.

I nodded. "You saw two cannons placed at the headland."

"Aye, they looked Spanish, about six feet long. Seen many like them in America."

"Were there balls?"

"None that I saw. Just piles of beach stones beside the firepit."

"But if they have two cannons there may be more. The *Florencia* had many. And you didn't get to the other side of the island."

"We will find out when we attack, won't we?"

I grabbed his sleeve, the buckskin soft and yielding, unlike the man who wore it. "You don't want the men to know, do you?"

"I selected these men because they will not flee in the face of adversity. Risk is part of war, and they know it."

"Granted, but our priority is the protection of the laird, and he seems to fancy reckless attacks." I chuckled, but more out of worry than glee.

"I will do my best, Malcolm. Please do yours. We must let him lead from the front as a proper Highland chieftain."

"This could go very badly. I expect you to manage a strategic escape, if need be," said I.

He seemed to not like my tone and shook my hand free of his sleeve. "Very well. When I sound the first retreat, the men and I will stay and fight. That will be your opportunity to leave. But seriously, Malcolm, I doubt Norman will agree to go with you. He knows who he is, I hope you do as well."

I swore under my breath. There is no dealing with some men. My brother George was the same. With them honour bests prudence every time. I was annoyed with him and everything, the situation we found ourselves in, the stupidity of it all. We could die at the hands of some old women. It was disgraceful.

Murdoch must have sensed my frustration because he said, "You know this is not solely because of the laird and that damned treasure." I looked at him. He turned his head in the direction of the enemy camp. "This is personal. It is also about me and—"

A warrior who'd been helping position the cannon suddenly cried out, "Ho! Sail!"

* * *

I laughed aloud when I recognized the patchwork sail of Captain Wilson's birlinn. We ran to the shore waving our arms. They altered course toward us. We were surprised not so much by the boat, since it often plied these waters, but by what she was carrying: Sir Ross Campbell and a load of young warriors. We were ecstatic.

"Welcome to the Hell of Mull," I said taking Sir Ross's handshake once he splashed ashore.

"We got your message and thought you might appreciate a wee visit." Sir Ross grinned then looked around. "Och 'tis a bonny place, Malcolm. And how are the laird and ladies?"

"Nervous, I should think. They are in the village preparing for an assault on the island," I tilted my head in their direction. "The witches and their followers are encamped there with two or more cannons and have us trapped in the bay."

I was about to explain more but Ross waved his hand and said, "I know that island well. Gregor bring my glass."

My curious look brought further explanation, "These are my lands, you know. Legally anyway, although they provide no coin." Ross smiled and took my arm, "Oft times I am surprised how little you know…considering your father. You do know Clan Campbell conquered Mull a generation ago?"

"Of course," I said.

"Well, I am the younger brother of the Earl of Argyll, Chief of Clan Campbell, and as I said, this is *my* land."

I was stunned. "I never imagined—"

"Indeed. Your esteemed father is superb at keeping our secrets," Sir Ross grinned. "But did he not advise you to trust me?"

"I, ahh—"

"Of course, he did. But you couldn't because of pretty Elspeth. We are both fond of her Malcolm, but I assure you it cannot be more than that on my part. And you likely assumed I came to Dunvegan for her, didn't you?" Ross was enjoying this too much. He could be infuriating but then so could I.

"Then why did you come to Dunvegan, if not for courtship?"

"For the same reason you did," he answered, revealing little.

"To do Elspeth a favour?"

Ross snorted. "You would not have come just for her. We arrived at almost the same time because our Queen and her government commanded it."

He had me there. My father had asked me to come and that request undoubtedly had originated from Queen Anne's government. I stopped to think, watching the men disembark. "There is more isn't there? The witches are originally from Mull...your land, as you insist."

"Aye, they are a constant irritation. Despite my efforts to increase their wealth by securing markets for their goods, the locals remain loyal to these witches. That is why I cannot live among them. And when I heard that some witches had moved to Skye, I was alarmed their poison might spread, so I had two good reasons to come."

"Then we have common cause," said I.

"We always have, Malcolm. We always have."

The young warriors were given the chance to relieve themselves and stretch their legs. I nodded to a few I had treated at Dunvegan. It was good to see them again. Captain Wilson jumped ashore, a happy smile on his weathered face. "We meet again," said he, shaking my hand. "Those clouds yonder are threatening. They came out of nowhere as we entered the Sound of Mull. Strange to have another storm so soon after the last. We cannot stay beached here though...no shelter."

Sir Ross had been conversing with his manservant Gregor but must've heard the last part because he said, "There is anchorage on the other side of the island. Not as good as Tobermory Bay, but if you secure your boat well, she will survive."

"Ross, our forces are gathering in the village and within the hour we'll cross over to the island. Once in position, we'll signal, and the cannon here will begin firing. Bring you men as quickly as you can to join us."

"If only an hour, we must leave at once," Wilson said.

"And captain, if you can come back to guard the entrance to the harbour, it will be helpful. But do what you think best."

"We brought a small cannon too. Fits on the gunwale pivot." Wilson pointed.

"Brilliant, but I hope there is no need," said I.

"Time is the essence gentlemen. All men back onboard!" Sir Ross shouted. There were a few grumbles and more shouts of hooray. "Gregor you stay with the birlinn. I'll command the men," was the last I heard Ross order as he vaulted aboard with the others.

The gunner assured me our cannon was ready. I ran back to the village.

* * *

I joined the main party, those of us on the birlinn. Murdoch and I would stay close to the laird and defend him. It was noonday and the advance party was readying their fishing boat in plain view of anyone watching from the other side. Their task to secure the small cove so we could land the main force with the birlinn. And on the birlinn I discovered that some of the laird's orders had been overturned by higher authority. The women would be "escorting" our main force. Their term, not ours. They were in the back, under the canopy. Elspeth was in her woolen cape, now belted on the outside, dagger in full view. Then there was Aunt Mairi who had attached a wicked looking metal spike to the tip of her staff. And stolid-faced Lady Myreton wearing an adaptation of a belted plaid with a bow and quiver stuffed with arrows on her back. They wisely had decided not to rely solely on witchcraft.

The advance party pushed off from shore, turned to starboard and headed to the narrow channel where they would cross. They were about twenty-five yards away from us when we heard the first sounds of musket fire. "Poor sods," I muttered. "They have no cover in that boat."

"Row laddies!" we heard the steersman yell over the din. He did not have to say it twice. We saw the prow lifting as they accelerated to the landing area. All leapt into the water and crouched low as they made their way behind obscuring plants and rocks. We waited in nervous anticipation, watching. There was sporadic gunfire, chilling shouts, then all went silent. A few minutes passed then one of our warriors emerged and waved the patch of MacLeod tartan he had been give to signal.

"They have secured the cove. Take us there, captain, before our lads are overwhelmed," Murdoch ordered.

Our men needed no encouragement. They were rested, eager, and pulled strong. I was at the prow with Murdoch and the laird, our eyes on the island, searching for any sign of movement. It was then that the first gust hit us. Low grey clouds had arrived, accompanied by gulls, many of them circling and crying as though warning us of what might come should we continue. But nothing would stop us now. I looked over my shoulder. Our birlinn was crammed with men and weapons, muskets, pikes, and swords spiking out like a hedgehog of death.

"Spread out when we disembark. The first off find our men and form a perimeter," Murdoch yelled. But they already knew what to do. These were his men, his old comrades. I looked at their faces as they strained on the oars. They stared straight ahead. No one spoke. I wondered what they were thinking. Was it of their loved ones, or perhaps imagining what they would do when they got home? Or maybe like me relishing the prospect of conflict and victory. My musings ended when Murdoch shouted to brace for grounding. It came moments later, a grinding crunch as hull met bottom. Norman was the first off, then Murdoch and me. Murdoch immediately took the lead, as much to shield the laird as anything.

The warrior who signalled us came forward and said, "There are enemy about but not many."

"They must've seen Sir Ross and the lads on the other side of the island. If the enemy attacks us here, they risk being taken from behind. The advantage is ours," Murdoch said as we gathered around.

"Then let us gain the high ground as soon as we can," Norman said.

"Aye, sir."

There followed the well-practised chaos of disembarking and forming men into groups. We pushed our way up the embankment through the brush and toward the center of the island. There was no opposition, yet we sensed eyes tracking our every move. The island was not wide, and it took little time to reach the flat area in the middle. The first of the rain showers met us accompanied by sharp gusts. Toward their encampment we could see a black line along a low ridge. Behind the line, smoke.

Murdoch checked the time. "We are early. Now we wait. It will gnaw at their nerves," he smirked.

* * *

Our men had settled in the grass for a rest and drink. Within minutes we saw the first of Sir Ross's contingent arrive on the plateau. Some men jeered but I am sure all of us were relieved to see them. We were more than a match now, or so we hoped.

Murdoch leapt up and called one of the warriors to us. It was my fleet footed friend from our battle at Talisker. We returned greetings. "Run to Sir Ross and tell him to hold his men on our right flank. We will advance up the middle. Wait for us to move first. Understand?" Murdoch told him.

He said, "Aye!" and was immediately on the run. The first of the cannon volleys came next, followed by the second. Murdoch glanced over at Sir Ross listening to our runner. Ross raised his musket in acknowledgement.

"Form up!" Murdoch barked. "We have fifteen minutes to get in position before the cannonade begins. We will advance on them but not too close. The cannonade should push them toward us." The laird led us forward, his standard bearer beside him, then Murdoch and me behind. This was the nerve-wracking part. We did not know what or who lay ahead, and the laird was an easy target in his yellow and black battle plaid. We even had a piper. No MacCrimmon, but the pipe's wail warmed our blood. We advanced slowly to the beat and watched as a dark line of humanity emerged in front of us. To our right, Sir Ross and his men had begun their advance as well, coming toward the enemy at an oblique angle. I smiled. It was perfect. The enemy would have our cannon at their backs, our veterans in their teeth and our young men attacking from their side. They were doomed. And I did not believe for a second that their witches could save them.

The cannonade boomed its start. Murdoch called a halt. Sir Ross did the same. We waited to see the enemy's response. The weather worsened. Gusty winds hurried grey clouds; the unsettled day matched our moods. And even more disturbing were the birds. Instead of finding shelter from the storm, they were circling and diving above us, screeching bloody murder. I heard one of our men say, "'Tis an evil omen, those gulls."

Another warrior agreed and said, "They wait for the coming slaughter. Seen it before. Soon they will be feasting on eyes and guts."

I noticed Elspeth watching the gulls as well and I could see her lips moving imperceptibly. *Make them go away,* I thought to her.

I looked away from the gulls past the rusting fall grass to the enemy line. Individuals began to resolve in sight. "Oh shit!" I blurted. I took the laird's elbow and yelled, "We can't do this!"

I grabbed Murdoch's glass and searched up and down their line. "They intend to fight us with women and children. See for yourself."

Norman and Murdoch took turns looking through the glass. No one said a word, it was so appalling.

"It'll be a slaughter and your name will go down in infamy," I said to the laird in case he missed the implication.

Norman MacLeod of MacLeod smiled. "This is my time," said he, then turned to the standard bearer beside him and commanded, "Raise the flag!"

The standard was quickly replaced by something that looked like a scrap of stained yellow cloth. Our women had come forward to hear and see better, with Elspeth at my elbow. "What in hell is that?" I asked her.

"By the gods, 'tis the Fairy Flag! He really does intend to fight." Her oval face turned white. She stood motionless; her breathing forced.

"What does it mean?" I asked her.

She grasped my arm and said, "It is used only in battle, and we have never lost with the Fairy Flag."

I was about to ask more when the laird commanded, "Advance! Malcolm and Murdoch with me."

The laird set off at a quick walk with his standard-bearer holding the Fairy Flag high. Then he stopped and held up his hand to Sir Ross in a gesture to stay put. We were but a quarter mile from the enemy line when I heard Elspeth shout. She had trailed us and was holding up a dead fish and pointing to the gulls. I laughed. Of course, our eyes would be on the enemy line, and no one would be looking down to see that the battlefield had been sown with fish to attract the gulls. I looked about and there were many more among us. I picked up a rotting fish by the tail and said to Murdoch and the laird, "Not magic but trickery!" A few men sniggered, but no one dared mock the witches or the fates they claimed to control.

We drew closer to the enemy line. I threw my fish at them and yelled that we would not be deterred by gulls or storms. I doubt the enemy heard but our men most certainly did. That was the point. Yet there were no signs of witches, or even worse, Robert and his deadly bow. And the laird would not let us shield him. Undaunted, the young laird walked confidently forward.

Instead of cries of anger, from the other side came shouts of fear. And instead of banging of weapons, many were pointing up at the Fairy Flag. Despite efforts to control their line it began to crumble as we approached. Women screamed, boys looked fearful, and on their men, the faces of those confronting imminent death. Then we heard a cannonade land.

The ground shook. Smoke and dirt scattered behind the enemy. Many screamed as they surged in panic toward us.

"Halt!" Norman shouted and turned toward us. "'Tis time we spoke with our friends. Murdoch, Malcolm, and Mairi come with me. Elspeth and Lady Myreton follow close and pray. I will offer peace before war."

We knew now what he intended. It was a risky move. He would expose himself to win. It was worth a try, and better than the inevitable slaughter. I heard the women starting to pray behind us and found myself joining them. *Please God, stop this before it is too late.*

We walked slowly toward the enemy. Our men in line behind us, muskets at the ready. Sir Ross had joined us; his bonnet pulled low, cloak hitched high, almost obscuring his wind-reddened face. He greeted the laird and said in a matter-of-fact voice that this was his land and people, and he was responsible. The laird smiled and thanked him. The enemy moved closer to us as more cannon balls struck behind them. They were trapped. We were but twenty yards apart now and no sign of Una and the others. It was unsettling in the extreme. It would only take a fright or fit of anger and the maelstrom of war would be upon us. We stayed close to the laird, with Murdoch constantly watching their line for threats, and me at the ready to defend.

The laird stopped and held his hand up high. In a very loud voice he said, "We come in peace. You are friends and allies. We only want justice. We just want the witches who have harmed us."

We could see the emotions playing on their faces, but the predominant one seemed to be anger. "The witches said Captain Forrester was coming to take our women!" the innkeeper who seemed to be one of the leaders shouted.

Surprisingly, in response it was Sir Ross who took a step forward. Not to be outdone, Norman and the rest of us followed. Sir Ross exposed his ruddy face. Instantly there were gasps from the crowd and the innkeeper's eyes went wide. He went to his knees, "My laird! 'Tis you! What—?"

"What am I doing here? It is as Laird MacLeod said. We are here for the witches who continue to curse this isle. Bring them to me forthwith and there will be no bloodshed."

"But...but..." the innkeeper sputtered, his eyes looking about as if to find an answer in his compatriots faces.

A man stepped forward, brawny, older, with the large, scarred hands and weather-creased face of a fisherman, "I am Joshua, my laird. Be assured we stand not against Clan Campbell nor MacLeod. But we will protect our women as we did long ago when we and the witches crushed that evil Captain Forrester beneath the waves. And if he comes again to harm us, we will do it again, allegiance or no." Shouts and claps of support followed.

"Then hand over the black witches and we will depart with well-wishes," Laird MacLeod said with authority.

"But there be Captain Forrester. I have seen him and heard his voice," The innkeeper exclaimed, pointing at me.

My blood boiled at the repeated lies. I could be silent no longer. "I am *not* Captain Forrester! We share a last name is all. I am a physician from Edinburgh who has come to help Laird MacLeod and his family. In the Name of all that is Holy, stop this nonsense! The witches have poisoned your minds."

With that outburst on my part, the crowd erupted. Some took my side, most disagreed. It was then that a commotion began behind them and the crowd slowly parted revealing Una leading Doideag and Gormal. Everyone went silent but me. "We meet again, witches!" said I, trying my best to control my anger.

Una walked up to Murdoch and spat in his face. "You foul deceiver," she hissed. "You come to me wanting peace after leaving me with a swollen belly."

I for one was stunned. Murdoch raised his hand to touch her scornful face. "That was long ago and...and I didn't know—"

"Did you not know Ranuff was yours? I don't believe you! I told you as much, but you had eyes for that whore who birthed your daughters. And you ruined everything, didn't you? Our son should have been laird, not this weakling who stands before us. And look what you did to our Ranuff. You murdered him! And I shall bring revenge on you as I did afore!" Una's fearsome glance struck us like a slap. She returned to Doideag and Gormal, all the while glaring hatred at Murdoch.

My mind was reeling. I looked back at Elspeth. She seemed in shock; tears were forming at the corners of her eyes. Was it her half-brother who killed Cawdie? I watched as Elspeth tried to hold back sobs. My heart was touched beyond words. The poor girl.

"This is a family affair and I promise we will make things right, Aunt Una," Norman said, emotions affecting his speech.

Then I noticed a wee smile on Doideag's face. Was this all a ruse? Was any of it true? A quote from college came to mind. Something about words, be they true or false, being more powerful than the strongest armies. And then I thought of Robert and the dwarf. They were nowhere to be seen. I touched Norman's sleeve and whispered, "Be careful. Their words weaken you."

He grumbled in return, and said, "Our fate is in God's mighty hands." It was true, but not what I wanted to hear from him.

Murdoch stood silent and shaken, his eyes downcast, his face saddened. *He must have slept with her,* I thought. *As for the rest?*

There was a momentary silence. Even the wind and gulls seemed to pause. Everything depended on what we did next. I decided to force the issue. "And what of you? Where is your little friend with his pistol and evil dog? Is he here to kill the laird while our hearts are distracted?"

Doideag, her gaunt body and face framed under a dark cloak had been mumbling to herself. My remark must've caught her off-guard because her head snapped to me. She snarled, "Your time has not yet come, captain... but soon. You are next. Be patient."

"You speak nonsense. You have no power over anything or anyone unless they so choose," I said calmly, although nerves felt otherwise.

Doideag laughed in that condescending way women do. "My sisters and I brought you here, didn't we? Of all the places to land in that storm, it was our home, in the trap we carefully set, the very place we defeated you afore."

I laughed in derision. "Nay, Doideag!" I raised my voice so all could here. "It was God and His Holy Vengeance who led us here to bring peace and justice to this land. And it is you and the other black witches who arrogantly stood against Him. And I include you, Gormal. What do you say? Are you on the side of darkness or will you choose the side of God?"

Gormal's formless face was blank. She averted her eyes and did not respond. I turned my head to Sir Ross who had remained silent through all this. "Arrest these witches, Laird Campbell. Bring them their justice!"

Sir Ross opened his mouth to speak, but suddenly Lady Myreton screamed, "Nay! Robert, stop!"

Her cry must have awoken Murdoch from his reflections because he launched himself in front of Norman in time to catch an arrow on his outstretch sleeve. Murdoch fell to the ground face-first. Doideag laughed, raised her arm, and shrieked. Instantly there was a gunshot, then a powerful explosion from behind our enemy near their cannon. *Their powder kegs!* I thought, as smoke, dust and debris filled the air. More kegs exploded; people fled to escape. Elspeth rushed to help her father. Norman knelt beside her while Lady Myreton stood above them, her bow drawn. Mairi shouted to me that the witches had escaped. She pointed with her staff in the direction of the explosions. It had all been a distraction!

I drew my cutlass and went after them. But not more than ten feet away was Gormal, huddled on the ground weeping. I almost tripped over her. In no mood for more trickery, I roughly grabbed her cloak and was about to yell in her face when she looked in my eyes and said, "I can…I cannae do this anymore."

"No riddles or deceptions, woman. You have seconds to live. Tell me now! Where have they gone?"

She pointed behind her, "They have a boat—in the rushes. You must stop them! They intend to kill Lady Anne and the babies! Hurry!"

Oh God no! I thought, leaving her sobbing the name of Jesus and begging forgiveness. But I had no time for consolation. I ran through the enemy camp, stumbling through ropes, pots, and bedding on my way to the marsh I had spotted from across the harbour entrance. It was to my left, slanting down from their cannon and the burning powder kegs. I prayed I would get there in time to stop them leaving. Sliding down the rock-strewn embankment, I pushed through the willows on the edge. They were in plain sight twenty feet away and poling their fishing boat into the bay. Una was at the rudder with Doideag on one oar and the dwarf on the other while Robert struggled to raise the sail. The black dog spotted me and barked. I reached for my pistol. It was gone. Una looked back and laughed. I was too late and had nothing to fire at them.

In frustration I bent to pick up a rock to throw. It was then that I spotted Captain Wilson's birlinn turning into the harbour mouth. He saw them! I must do something, anything, to slow them. They were poor oarsmen, but I couldn't rely on that. Captain Wilson was hundreds of yards away. I must hinder them before Robert raised their sail and chanced an escape though the narrow channel on the opposite side of the bay. And I had only one option.

My weapons dropped and cloak slid off, I unbuckled and unpinned my belted plaid, pulled my shirt over my head, and removed my socks and shoes. I was naked in the frigid wind, already regretting my decision. I waded through the reeds and muck. It deepened quickly. I had to do it now. "Oh God," I gasped. "I hate freezing water!" I dove in then emerged, my body in cold shock. I had to swim fast. At first it was more of an uncoordinated flail then as muscles loosened, smoother and faster I went.

Spotting Wilson's birlinn, they had turned toward the shipwreck in the middle of the bay, the shortest way to the channel beyond. I was gaining on them, not so much because of my swimming prowess as their rowing ineptitude. And Robert had tangled the ropes, and was rocking the boat, scrambling about trying to sort things. Meanwhile it must have become apparent to Una that I would soon catch them because she ordered the dwarf to shoot me. He obediently stopped rowing to find the tiny pistol he had hidden under his jacket. With Doideag yet rowing, it had the effect of suddenly skewing the boat to one side which almost tumbled Robert overboard. I would have laughed had I not been spitting seawater.

I got close enough to grab the rudder. Una shook the tiller violently, dislodging my hand. "Stop, before it's too late!" I warned her. She screeched an obscenity. Further entreaties were pointless. Action was all now.

In a few strong strokes I was in touch again. This time with the transom. I grabbed on. Una banged my hand with her shoe. I grimaced in pain but didn't let go. We locked eyes. She must have known then it was over. I grabbed on with the other hand and pulled myself up, butting my head into her face. She sputtered and cried. I shoved her aside. It was Robert I was after. He obviously knew it too and had dropped his ropes and was reaching for his bow. I had to get to him quickly. Clambering forward, I bashed my half-frozen legs on the wooden seats. But my fixation on Robert was interrupted by the sight of the dwarf unsteadily raising his pistol with his dog ready to tear at me. I charged them both, knocking the dwarf overboard while receiving a bite on my arm in retribution. The dog and I faced-off, he snarling and me in savage fury born of pain. Fortunately, the dog thought better of it, whined, and jumped over the gunwale to join his master who was pleading for someone to save him.

That left me with Robert. He stood sneering, his bow at shoulder height, a lethal arrow pointed at my chest. At this distance he could not possibly miss. I took a deep breath and glanced back at Una and Doideag. They seemed transfixed at the scene. It was the time of my death, or second death as they would have everyone believe. Una's nose was bleeding, her cheek reddened. Her gruesome expression revealed her intent. She ordered, "Kill him. Kill Captain Forrester!"

Robert drew the bow string further back. I was getting ready to jump sideways in the hope he would miss my heart. Then I saw Robert's eyes flick away, and he dropped to one knee as the musket ball missed his head and imbed itself in the mast. I looked back. Gregor was standing on the prow of Wilson's birlinn, musket at his cheek, smoke drifting from the barrel. They were closing fast. I just had to delay till they caught us. But Robert was undeterred and rose again to fire at me. This was my chance and I leapt and sent him crashing backward, almost piercing myself with his arrow. It was down to wrestling now, and I had to avoid the dagger he had tucked in his boot.

He was stronger than I thought, and quick. He squirmed sideways and flipped me over. And in seconds he had my throat pinned against the base of the mast. My arms banged on his while he choked the life out of me. I knew I soon would be unconscious. I had to release his grip. Then a flash of gold came as a vision filling my sight. *Was this it? Am I dying? Are these to be my last thoughts?* I curled my first. *Not yet!* I yelled to myself. I struck upward with all the force I could muster and connected with something hard yet yielding. His grip lessened. My vision returned. He slumped on me, blood oozing on my chest. My left hand was smashed. I looked at it. Blood covered the ring. Fortuna had her blood sacrifice.

I pushed Robert off, got to my knees and took a breath, clearing my throat. The women cringed fearfully. I told them to stay put or die. The birlinn approached, Gregor was standing, dressed in black and looking like an evil pirate. Beside him, Captain Wilson's mate was manning the gunwale cannon. I waved to them. Thankfully, this would soon be over. Then something touched my senses. Gregor shouted. My head turned back to see Robert releasing the dagger. It spun slowly in mid-air. I tried to move but could not. Fortunately, the dagger deflected off one of Robert's errant ropes and embedded itself in Doideag's cloak, fixing her to the transom. To starboard, the prow of the *Florencia*, upright and proud, slid past. I was momentarily distracted by the sight of her and failed to notice Robert rise. He threw me down and punched me hard in the face then leaned over and grabbed a rope, meant for my neck. We were grappling with each other and the rope when I saw Doideag release Robert's dagger from the transom. With a look of hateful glee, she stabbed the dagger down toward my face. I let go of the rope to grab her wrist. She was weak but determined and spattered my face with spittle as she cursed my existence. But dealing with Doideag meant I had but one hand to deal with Robert. It was in a desperate situation. My strength was ebbing. It was only a matter of seconds before they had me.

I tilted my head back. Upside-down I saw the birlinn. It was close enough for a shot. I yelled as loudly as I could, "Fire that damn thing!" It came out like a gurgled scream. But they must have heard and the blast that soon followed ripped through Robert and the hull of the boat. Women were screaming. Robert went slack. His body dropped to my chest, pinning me. The boat sank so quickly we had no time to escape. We went down together with me observing the surprise on Doideag's face.

Underwater, Robert floated free enough for me to kick myself away. I struggled to the surface, my arms grasping, my lungs crying for breath. And then my right arm bashed something solid. I grabbed it and pulled, thinking it a piece of the boat. My head surfaced. I coughed and coughed again, holding the wood tight and leaning back to breath more easily. When my eyes cleared, I saw the prow of the *Florencia* above. I had been holding one of her ribs. The gulls were whirling and screeching against a background of slate-coloured clouds. One gull stared down; our eyes connected. He angrily shrieked my name, or so I thought.

My body was numb from the cold, my mind losing focus. I thought I said to the gull that I would like to join him in the sky. I heard him cry again as he whirled away. My arms were weakening, my body sinking lower, my hold on dear *Florencia* almost gone. I tried to take a deep breath before I submerged but nothing happened. The ice-cold water touched the back of my throat.

Chapter 23: Elspeth

"Hold fire! Let them pass! Everyone down!" the laird cried in rapid succession. Smoke and debris from the explosions had filled the air along with the panicked screaming and shouts of the villagers who fled toward us and away from the blasts. I crouched and covered my face, making myself as small as possible. It was a frightening experience, and I prayed there would not be wanton slaughter. Thankfully, there were only a few shots heard and the sounds were not of violence but fear, intermingled with the repeated commands by Laird MacLeod and Sir Ross to cease fire and remain calm. Long moments later, when the tumult subsided and the smoke cleared, we found ourselves amid a disorientated, frightened mob interspersed with grim-faced warriors, kneeling and ready to fire. I exhaled in relief, then reached to Aunt Mairi who knelt beside me and squeezed her hand, letting her know I was yet with the living.

I could hear children crying and women sobbing, so I stood to see better, shaking the dust from my cloak then helping Aunt Mairi to her feet. I turned around and beheld a field held in the grip of chaos, but for the warriors who had lowered their weapons and waiting for further orders. I grabbed my medical bag and went immediately to Norman asking of his health. But he ignored my question, instead beckoning Sir Ross for a consultation. Us women joined them but interfered not. This was men's work. But I did study each closely, looking for injuries. Thankfully, there were none of any consequence.

Decisions were made expeditiously. A group of veterans under the command of Murdoch would push forward through the camp toward the cannons and route out any remaining opposition. Another contingent lead by Norman would return to his birlinn to secure it and the harbour. The remainder, under the command of Sir Ross, would protect the rear and assist the wounded to evacuate the island. "And what of Sir Malcolm?" said I.

"We will find him, fear not Elspeth. Now please help the injured while we stabilize the battlefield.

Methodically, we went through the crowd, Lady Myreton in the lead, assuring everyone that all will be well while seeking out the injured for us to treat. Surprisingly, there were few with serious injuries and but two deaths. One, a man who had been shot, and tragically, a bairn who had been trampled. Within the space of an hour, we'd finished, and my mind returned to Malcolm and the missing witches as I watched the villagers return to the fishing boats to leave.

"Let us find Murdoch," Aunt Mairi said. "He will know what happened."

"Of course," I smiled wearily up at her. But before I could get up and collect my bag, my father appeared, heading with his men toward Sir Ross. I ran to him and disrespectfully interjected, "Did you find Malcolm? And what of the witches and Robert?"

He turned to me but did not reply till Aunt Mairi and Lady Myreton had joined us. "It seems your Malcolm is alive. Gregor has him on Wilson's birlinn. They intend to take him to the village. As for the others…emm. My sympathies Lady Myreton. It seems Robert has been killed." He briefly bowed his head to her. But she said nothing in return, seeming stunned by the report.

"And the rest?" I prodded.

"Ahh, dunno. The witches may have drowned. Gregor had them not. I know little more. We were active, you see."

Sir Ross had been listening, and when it appeared I had no further questions, told us that the island was to be evacuated immediately, since it was not safe to have our forces divided. Then he instructed us to head to the laird's birlinn at the landing point where we would be taken back to the mainland.

And so, it ended. It could have been much worse, with the witches having shown no powers beyond simple tricks to enable their escape, while leaving the villagers at the mercy of our enraged men.

* * *

On landing, Gregor greeted us and said, "He is in the tavern, alive but badly used." I mumbled my thanks, wanting to run to him, but there were others to assist first. The men carried the adult patients, and we helped the children, ferrying everyone and placing them as quickly as we could. In medicine, rapidity of treatment is paramount. I spotted Malcolm. He was conscious and babbling incoherently, his abused body yet ridding itself of seawater. Gregor had wrapped him in a blanket and placed him by the newly stoked fire. He seemed stable for now. I would return once the others were settled.

We set about organizing the tavern. Water was put on the fire to boil, tavern tables became beds, chairs a place to hang litters, and the kitchen looted for pots, bowls, linens, and cutlery to treat the wounded. Mairi and I made the rounds inspecting and treating as best we could. They came in waves as the boats gradually emptied the island, and soon the tavern was full, with more injured than anticipated. But none were seriously wounded. No amputations, no arrows, nor bullets to remove. Yet it was rough and swift work, no time for the subtleties of proper medicine.

It was a good hour or more before I could return to Malcolm, who had lapsed into unconsciousness, interrupted by cries, and shaking spasms. I brought a basin of heated water and sponged his face clean of the vomit and pink froth oozing from his mouth. I washed his salt patched torso, noticing the redness and broken skin at his throat and the many welts on his arms. *He has been in a horrible fight, as well as almost drowning,* I noted to myself. *I wonder if was with Robert?* But it wasn't till much later that I learned the gruesome details of their struggle and Robert's death, from Captain Wilson's first mate, the man who killed him.

Once I had finished cleaning, I leaned over Malcolm and whispered into his ear. "Malcolm Forrester, we have unfinished business. Wake up, I need you here." I smoothed back the dark damp hair, plucking a wee frond of seaweed from a tangled strand, willing him to survive.

For the next few hours, I applied heated blankets to his body, and Aunt Mairi provided a continuous supply of hot stones wrapped in cloths for his feet. Eventually, his body calmed, and he was sleeping naturally. My head dropped to his chest where the strong thump of his heart pulsed through the blanket. My tears leaked onto the rough wool as I thanked the gods. Aunt Mairi touched my shoulder and said, "There are others."

With a sigh, I rose, and together we once more made the rounds, assuring ourselves of the welfare of our charges. But throughout the day and when I needed respite, I took a cup of water and sat by Malcolm and holding his hand I watched his face for some sign of returning awareness. What would I do if I lost him too? I concentrated, trying to reach him, infuse him with small tendrils of my strength, a process I was re-learning painfully and belatedly.

Then Malcolm coughed. And without warning his eyes snapped open and he pinioned me with a menacing glare leavened with an unexpected flash of dark humor. He sneered with Malcolm's mouth. "Greetings, lass." His rumbling voice carried shades of yesterday.

I stiffened, then sat back and took a deep breath. "Greetings, Captain Forrester."

He grunted, surprised. "Clever wench be ye?" he rasped, with obvious effort. "Yer fancy friend near kilt us. Ah barely got him back afore 'twas too late." He pulled in several labored breaths.

"Thank you for saving him," I replied calmly, but fearful of what might come next.

I could hear the squirm in his gravely speech as he sloughed off my words. "He is nay like me, lassie, good to look on, but…" He choked on a chortle and hawked up a gob of something unsavory. "Ah be seeing ye again, lass. Bound to, eh?" Malcolm closed his eyes and sighed.

Moments later, his eyes opened once more, looked at me, and managed a mangled "Hullo."

"Good to have you back, my friend," I whispered to him.

Aunt Mairi, who had been boiling clothes nearby, laughed and said, "You needn't have worried lass. They kill not easily."

By evening, most of our patients had returned to their homes, leaving the unwanted and those few in our company to spend the night. Aunt Mairi and Lady Myreton found an empty room at the inn, But I preferred to stay with the few remaining patients and awoke at dawn beside an alive Malcolm and a dead fire.

* * *

The next day brought warm sunlight and healing, the gusty winds having passed overnight. We spent the morning dealing with the last of our patients and returning the tavern to a useful state for serving food and drink. And later, we learnt that Sir Ross had visited many families in the village handing out coins to the elders, and promises of more support in future, provided the black witches were no longer honored. We hoped it were enough. Then our laird returned and reported that after a thorough search, Una and Doideag were presumed drowned. I was not so certain of that. As well, the dwarf and his dog had somehow escaped, after having been rescued by Captain Wilson. Listening to this, Malcolm, revived but irrational, insisted that Gregor had spirited them all away. I told him it was nonsense born of illness. He sulked but said no more on the subject.

As we rested Murdoch tried his best to raise our spirits, telling of the bravery of our men, the calm courage of our laird, and the excellent outcome that resulted. The laird laughed and the men traded insults, then my father came to us ladies. He kissed each of our hands in turn and thanked us overly well. I was last and he faced me after a kiss, an open smile gracing his rugged face. But my mind was not on happy victory. Rather it was considering Una's words and her claim that Ranuff was his seed and my half-brother. That would have to come surface later when I was not so tired, and we were alone. Had Una played a part in my mother's death? I hoped my ears had deceived me, or Una's words were born of envy or imagination. But I dared not put it to the test. Not yet.

"We must gather our supplies, load the birlinn, and do whatever else needs doing before we leave on the morrow," the laird said to us.

And so, we set to work, but for me there was little to do, beyond repacking and helping prepare a mid-afternoon meal. However, others, including Lady Myreton, had more onerous duties, for Robert's mangled body yet lay in the stable, along with two villagers, the latter mourned by many. Lady Myreton made arrangements to have Robert interred with the others in the Tobermory cemetery, at her expense. I watched her carefully as she spoke with the village elders in the tavern, showing no signs of grief or remorse for the loss of Robert. But genuine sympathy was expressed to the mother of the wee bairn. Afterward, she went to Malcolm who was sat swallowing his oatmeal with difficulty. She kissed his ear and said something that made him look up at her in deranged shock. And I wondered if he had inadvertently provided her a boon that had cost his sanity. Moments later, she came to us and said, "I must now see this fine village before we go, for I shall not ever return." She hiked up her arisaid and left with a song on her tongue.

* * *

That evening, the Laird MacLeod called us together for a final discussion about our ultimate destination, Iona. The fact that two of the witches could not be accounted for was worrying especially since their plan to harm Anne and the children was known. And there was no way of telling how widely their coven had spread nor how many had shared information and speculation about a treasure. But the men assured us, that even if alive, they could not out-pace us with our birlinns. "Unless they can fly," quipped Malcom, I assume to annoy me. In addition, Murdoch judged that they could not out-fight us, as proven on the island, and we had experienced no deaths and were yet well-stocked. So, it was concluded that it was prudent to finish our quest, with our group lead by Laird MacLeod setting out for Iona, and Sir Ross with his cadre returning to Dunvegan. Captain

Wilson would then return from Dunvegan to gather Malcolm at Iona for the voyage to Glasgow, and thence home.

* * *

Oddly, it was a relief to be back at sea and away from a place beset with troubling memories and lingering magic. All were cheered by the sun and fresh winds, all but Malcolm that is, who sat morose, clutching the gunwale. And while the other men sang, he grumbled of the cold and evil witches. But who could blame him, I suppose?

We slid down the coast of Mull that day, and for safety, weaving in and out of the many bays and inlets, with favourable winds doing most of the work. And having stopped twice for relief and nourishment, we landed at Iona as the sun was setting. No one greeted or opposed us, so we unloaded and made camp near the sand and rock beach, with the ruined abbey half a mile or so to the north and set back part way up one of the hills which made up the small island. Once encamped, there was little we could accomplish till morning, so we settled in, our heads full of speculations about what might be found on the morrow.

* * *

A glitter of silver blue lay on the path before me, a piece of sky caught in a small puddle left by the rain. Each of us broke our fast with whatever we had managed to carry. Mine was an oatcake and a small onion, which I ate as we walked the path toward the abbey. Its grey ruins reared before us, pocked with the curiously elaborate remains of doors and windows. The scene before us came alive, imagined from oral reports of those who had visited and returned to Dunvegan with a wealth of vivid tales.

Gregor stayed behind with the men while the laird directed, sending my father ahead to reconnoitre, starting with the seemingly empty ground between a small chapel and the old gardens. Beneath the wild grasses lay the unmarked graves of those who had not received a Christian burial, their souls eternally denied passage into the next world. Murderers slept beside the unshriven or those refused hallowed ground for other reasons. It was where they buried witches.

A small cell lay near the west end of the chapel was reputed to be the final resting place of St. Columba himself. My knowledge of this saint was learned at church, but Malcolm had enjoyed adding one diverting comment to my education. It seems the holy man did not want women on his isle and thus banned cows, claiming that where there were cows there were women, and where there were women there was mischief. As a result, workmen who built the abbey were made to leave their wives and daughters nearby on Eilean nam Ban or Woman's Island.

We each bowed our heads as we passed St Martin's Cross in front of the abbey, and I ran my fingertips across its carved surface. Then my father was dispatched to search the area for signs of other people, while the laird and Malcolm entered the main door to the church nave. I hung back to circle the building, searching for something that might help us in our hunt. The abbey walls showed more damage than I imagined, there were no rooves intact and many columns and wall sections had collapsed. Yet there was a comforting connection that flowed between the abbey and the church at Rodel. I stopped when I came around to the door to the church once again, then conquered my cowardice and entered the crumbling confines of the building.

The ceiling was open to the sky. I turned toward the altar and walked past the transept, topped in the center with its massive tower, then into the choir. At the altar, stone abbots still lay guardian on either side of the dais. John MacKinnon, last abbot of the Holy Isle guarded on the right. His tomb as impressive, as the man was in life. A sculpted likeness, clad in episcopal habit, complete with crosier and ring edged the breast of the black marble effigy. A second slab tomb on the opposite side protected Abbot Dominic. Between the tombs of the abbots and embedded in the floor was one of the largest pieces of marble I have ever seen. And portrayed upon it was the figure of a huge warrior holding a staff. It was the tomb of Leod.

I sensed a touch of heat on my skin coming from the ring we had taken from St. Clements. I wore it on a woven cord around my neck, with the necklace Gregor had given me. I pulled the warm ring from beneath my shift and looked at the runes once more, remembering their simple meaning that the ring had belonged to Leod. Now the ring had returned to its owner. I looked to the others and said, "It is here. The tomb of Leod is here under the floor."

I walked into the light streaming over the altar in front of me. A three seated sedilia had been constructed in the south wall to seat celebrants during church rituals. It was beautifully carved with intricate details. Three arches separated by two columns separated the seats. Partitions had been placed but kept low so those seated could speak. A piscina bowl carved with oak leaves, used to dispose of ritual water stood just beyond them. I wondered if the liquids that had drained directly into the earth beneath for so many centuries had rendered it holy? I stepped back to the stone floor bearing the two abbot's tombs and the third of Leod between and noticed that portions of the floor had long since been taken by those in need of building material. Some attempt to clear the uneven pavement of broken rocks and debris had been made, perhaps mute evidence of some continuing reverence for what had once been.

Movement caught my eye. The men had come. I cleared my throat and pointed to the three tombs. "Mayhap the one in the middle is that of Leod." I surprised myself by laughing. They followed my glance and looked down, the huge marble slab at their feet. We knelt and ran our hands around the edges of it. Nothing looked disturbed except for many small gouges, evidence of prior efforts to open the tomb.

"It must be in here," said the laird. "It looks as though it hasn't been opened. But if others gave up. We won't." He felt the slab edges again. "This was from long ago." He ran his hand across the slab top almost reverently. "We need to get it open without causing further damage if we can. Murdoch, bring everyone from the boat but the captain and mate. Bring all our tools, ropes and wood." Murdoch left on a run. "What say you, Malcolm?"

He had been unusually quiet, and the few times he had spoken, his words were confused. We had ascribed it to his trials at Tobermory, but this day he made his good-mornings and bantered with the crew as we ate our early meal on the beach. I for one, hoped his good sense had returned, and the cruel Captain of old gone. "Before we start," said Malcolm, after a moment of consideration, "let us review our situation." He looked at Norman and I for approval to continue and when we nodded, said, "Clan traditions lead us to Rodel where we found a ring and some inscriptions, and your triskele balls clarified the map at the shipyard. All lead to where we stand now, at Iona. But…but, we have a missing piece, don't we, that could be essential and decisive…the missing triskele ball, once held by Una and perhaps lost." He let us consider it before he continued. "While it is logical to assume the so-called treasure lies in the tomb of Leod, it may not. Could the last triskele ball not point us from here to somewhere else?"

"I take your point, Malcolm, but your conjecture leads nowhere. Shall we quit when we have suffered so much to get here?" said I.

A wee smile returned to Malcolm's lips. "Nay, Elspeth, but we must consider the possibilities. What if the tomb is not what we assume? Does it hold a body or nothing? Perhaps underneath that massive lid, lies more rock. Perhaps it is a trap to harm or frustrate?"

"We won't know unless we try," said Norman.

"Ahh, but this tomb has held its secret secure for many hundreds of years. Where better to place a treasure? And if you did manage to find a treasure, where would you put it that is equal to here?"

Norman laughed and slapped Malcolm on the shoulder. "My friend, you could have said this earlier."

"Perhaps I was hoping the realization might come on its own. But now that we are here, let us proceed, but with abundant caution and a willingness to change course with circumstances."

I couldn't help but counter Malcolm's doubts. "You continue to suspect clan traditions. They may be oral, and based on enigmatic objects and symbols, but we believe them to be accurate and true. But I do agree, the lack of the last triskele ball puts us at disadvantage. Had we it, this would be a task clear of —"

Norman interjected, "But Elspeth, Malcolm is right. We need to consider other possibilities. Let us then agree on what we will do should here be no treasure, at least."

Malcolm smiled. "Here is my recommendation."

And so, within minutes, we three cobbled together a simple plan of action adapted from Malcolm's. "Here is the first load of supplies," Norman said turning from us. "And we will open that tomb if we can. Wud put the ropes over here."

I set myself on a block of stone out of the way of those carrying and placing. Aunt Mairi and Lady Myreton joined me. They had brought ale and bread for the men and arranged a table among the stones. Meanwhile I listened to the men plan. Wud was consulted and suggested a scaffold be built above the tomb. He had brought a few block and tackle winches from the shipyard, along with several steel pry bars and chisels. The idea, as he explained it, was to pry the lid up sufficiently to be able to pass ropes underneath that could be attached to the winches which would be used to lift the slab. It sounded a reasonable plan. But as I sat and thought, I wondered how my life had suddenly become so filled with tombs.

* * *

The men had been working for several hours, chipping carefully at the thin line of cement that secured the black slab to the floor. Chisels and hammers from the birlinn tapped and dug. And the pile of wood and rope brought from the birlinn had become a scaffold in the shape of a square about ten feet on each side with two winches dangling a few feet below sturdy beams set on the top.

Eventually the seal was broken enough for the pry bars to enter. It took ten of our strongest to shift it and a great cheer erupted from us onlookers when we saw it move for the first time. The men were told to stop and recover, and as we offered ale and bread, they were told by the laird that the next part would be most dangerous, and we must take care that injuries not happen. He then reviewed the next steps of prying, setting in wedges between the top and the base, and stringing through the ropes under the top so it could be lifted.

While we watched, curiosity was rampant. All of us were eager to see this "treasure" that had been bought with so much effort and blood. Men grunted and swore, the strongest and heaviest on the pry bars, the others banging in the wooden wedges, till at last the lid was a few inches above the base. The men rested once more. Malcolm came to me, appearing rather ghoulish, his face layered with dust stuck on with sweat. "It's going well," said he. "We could have the lid off by nightfall, with some luck."

He seemed fatigued as he sat beside me, Lady Myreton offering ale and a succouring smile. "How are you feeling?" I said, worried of his stamina.

"I cannot deny, this is arduous work, but all hands are needed," he replied, wiping the grit off his mouth before taking a swig.

"They will forgive you, if you rest," I said, noting he had avoided my question.

"I will, as required. You need not be concerned, and soon it will be finished." He patted my hand and swallowed the last of the ale before returning to the other men.

The laird gathered the men once more and told them what would be required next. But meanwhile as they were speaking, I noticed we had a few visitors and went to greet them. Crofters, they were, two men and a boy, come to see what was going on. The were tall and thin, dressed head to toe in skins and woolens. And by their form and countenance they appeared as though they were but different ages of the same being.

I smiled and bowed to them. "'Tis the MacLeod and his men, come to restore the ancient tomb of his ancestor," said I, dissembling, as we had expected snooping locals and prepared a story.

"Didnae know there was anything wrong with it. It looked weel enough lest time ah was here chasing me cattle," the older man said.

I chuckled and explained that each century there must be work done, otherwise the tomb would fall to ruin like the rest of the abbey.

The younger man scratched his beard and said, "Never heard of that afore."

I nodded, thinking how incompetent I was at lying, and ended the conversation with an offer of bread and ale which was politely declined by the crofters, who immediately bade me farewell.

I returned to the tomb and watched as ropes were guided under the great slab with the help of wooden rods. The ropes were then threaded through the block and tackles winches till all was ready with several men managing each rope. Wud and the laird inspected it all, moving all others out of the way, and declaring the slab safe to be raised. Prayers were said, fingers crossed, the slack tightened, then the laird cried, "One, two three, pull!" It moved little despite the effort exerted. So, all of us were called to help. The rope was long, and we ladies found spots in the middle to grip. "Just lean back and use your weight, every little bit helps," Malcolm said, grinning.

On our next pull, the stone slab moved a few inches higher and began to sway since it was free of the wooden wedges. Men jammed more wood under the slab with each pull till we had it up more than a foot off the base. The laird ordered a stop as they stabilized the weight with more supports. Then he sent for a torch and told the men to rest. I went back to sit on my stone block, feeling pain radiating from my right shoulder, praying it was not damaged.

"Let us see what is inside to encourage us to pull further," he said.

While the ceiling was open to the sky and the day fine and crisp, the inside of the tomb remained too dark to see. A lit torch brought, Norman, Malcolm and I gathered to discover what might be inside. Malcolm lowered the head of the torch through the opening. We held our breath and peered in, a hush surrounding us. Cupping my hands around my eyes, I let my vision adjust. Eventually, the interior resolved, my eyes searching every side and corner.

"Nothing," Malcolm whispered. "I can see nothing but a few scattered bones and much dust. How about you?"

My mind sighed.

"Alternate plan?" Malcolm whispered.

"Aye," replied Norman.

I merely acquiesced, my heart sinking into the empty tomb.

Norman addressed us all. “The tomb is empty but for the bones of Leod, our illustrious ancestor. There is no treasure within.” He waited for the groans and cursing to subside before he assured, “You will receive your bonus regardless and we will return to our families at the soonest. But first we must say our prayers for our ancestors before we leave. Murdoch take everyone outside for a stretch and relief. Mairi will you please conduct the ceremony?”

She blinked, then acquiesced, then once everyone had gone, we told her that we intended a thorough search before we left and could she please chant many prayers and invocations to cover our deception. She laughed heartily then began. So, in a veil of prayers we huddled near the alter.

“Where to begin,” said Norman. “This place is a massive ruin. A treasure could be anywhere.”

I muttered, “Think, think. We must have missed something.”

Malcolm chuckled, “Indeed, that something being the missing triskele ball. This might well be impossible.”

I slapped my cheeks repeatedly as though to shake loose the answer. Then Malcolm said, “Let’s go over the signs once again.”

So, we did, all of them, or so I thought. “You missed the engravings in Latin we found at Rodel,” Norman said.

“Aye, but they didn’t seem to mean much,” said I. “One was ‘Protector of the Word,’ if I recall, and the other…hmm—”

“Keep your faith in God above,” said Norman with a grin.

“Above?” said I, a shock of realization jolting me. I looked up and beyond, turning my gaze. But the ceilings were gone. There were only walls, but for one place where one could look up and yet see stone—the four massive arches holding up the tower at the transept. I ran to them and gazed above, and there was something, where the capstone should be on the arch facing the choir. It appeared round, the size of a triskele ball but embedded at the top of the arch. “What is this?” I cried. But it was too far above to see properly, and we had to find a way up.

“A ladder,” Malcolm said. “There is enough left-over rope and wood to make one."

Several minutes later, we had made one, albeit very crude, with few steps. We carried it to the arch and lifted it. But it was too short. "Norman and I can hold it while you climb with a torch. It may be nothing but a trick of light and shadows, after all."

Malcolm grabbed the torch and re-lit it with flint and steel, while Norman and I placed the ladder. I motioned for Aunt Mairi to come close enough to set her feet at the base. She wisely increased the volume of her chanting to cover our noises. I took the first step, then the next. The ladder was shaky, despite the men holding it aloft. I reached the third step and asked for the torch. I was a few feet from the top of the ladder and several feet away from my goal. I uttered a brief prayer, took a breath then held the torch high.

Half covered triskele legs appeared in view on the face of a ball set in mortar. My heart stopped. I gulped. "It is here." said I to those below. I looked more closely, straining my eyes for detail, but could see little. "I see no bumps or runes on it. But...but what appears to be a cross carved beside the triskele."

Then Norman said, "Come down, Elspeth. We need to consider what to do."

"I cannot reach it, even if I stood on the top rung of the ladder," said Elspeth, grunting as she held the torch high.

"That was obvious," Malcolm said. "And even if one of us men went up, we would fall short."

"We could call the workmen back and make a new scaffold," said Elspeth. "But that will entail having many in on our secret. Everyone thinks there is no treasure."

Malcolm steadied my hand as I came down. "And it is best that it remains so. Let us try to remove the ball and see what that reveals," said he. "Elspeth, you have a dagger that can be attached to the end of a pole. There is one lashed to the scaffold we can use. With your dagger on a pole, you could try prising the ball from the mortar."

"Agreed, worth a try," Norman said.

But I soon realized that I must dig while holding onto the pole with both hands, and with only my two tiny feet on the rung for purchase. It seemed impossible, but urged on by the men, I climbed the ladder once more, this time with the torch tied to the ladder side. My shaky hands gripping the offered pole and I looked up at the ball several feet above, then back down, the ladder shifting a bit as I moved. "Please keep it steady," said I, a quiver coming with my request.

I lifted the pole, my dagger striking the mortar beside the ball. "It is soft," I mumbled. Several strikes latter, my arm was aching with fatigue.

"It's coming. Try prying the sides of the ball," said Malcolm.

"Easy for you..." I mumbled and raised the pole once more. But this time the dagger caught a hole beside the ball. It seemed stuck and I wiggled it back and forth, till at once all gave way and the ball fell, bringing with it a flurry of bits and dust. I fell forward, banging my shoulder on the ladder. Immediately, one foot slipped, and I found myself hanging by the crook of my arm from the ladder rung above.

"Let her down! Let her down!" Norman yelled.

Seconds latter I was on the ground, well-shaken, but thankful it was no more than a sore arm. The triskele ball was nearby. I crawled over and touched it, rolling it to see all sides. Mairi stopped chanting to whisper, "What does it say, lass?"

"Emm, it seems unfinished with a cross crudely etched on one surface."

Malcolm had been pacing, his eyes searching. He went back to the tomb of Leod and looked back at us and up, then said, "Protector of the Word." Then returned and noted, "On his back in the tomb, he would be looking directly at the top of the arch and the triskele ball."

"Elspeth did you see anything else up there?" Norman asked.

"Nay, it happened so quickly."

Norman had been looking up, his hand shading his eyes. "There is a large hole behind where the triskele was set, but I can see little more from here,"

"Then we need to go up again," said Malcolm. "But Elspeth cannot be the one. If I take a side of the ladder and Aunt Mairi and Elspeth the other,

Norman could ascend and see what might be there."

It seemed unlikely, but we tried. At least our laird was not afraid of a fall or worse. And he was able to climb high enough to touch the hole easily with the dagger. He set about prodding and digging as we steadied the ladder, the pain in my arm increasing. "Hold fast, Elspeth," Aunt Mairi murmured. But with each strike of the dagger on the mortar, the ladder lurched further, till we had to stop to rest.

"I thought I glimpsed something shiny, then it vanished in the dust," Norman said.

"A mote in your eye?" Malcolm teased.

"Or an angel directing my hands," said Norman, chuckling.

Malcolm grinned, white teeth and pink lips animating his dust coated face. "One more time, then."

Before long, Norman looked down and whispered, "I have something on the tip of my dagger. I may be able to lever it out." It inched out gradually, till he said, "Seems to be a box. I may be able to grab it."

All were looking up, the dust floating down. I wiped my glistening eyes on my shoulder as Norman carefully descended holding what looked like a box covered in rotted fabric. We set the ladder down and Norman held it before us. Much of the fabric had powdered away revealing a low rectangular box with a peaked top, the whole larger than a large book. Glints of light illumined the bejeweled surface as I brushed at it lightly. The exquisite workmanship belonged to another time. Suddenly the truth of this object caused me to withdraw my hand quickly. I had been carelessly touching a *cumdach,* an elaborate coffer used as a reliquary to protect a sacred book or codex bound between two boards. I had seen such in Europe, but only from a distance, safely enshrined on altars or being carried in holy processions. The precious materials of this one glittered, and the golden skin of the case flashing beneath six large gems mounted on the impossibly pristine surface. I looked helplessly at Malcolm and the laird. "This is a cumdach, which shields a more precious thing. My laird, you must be the one to reveal its contents, for I am unworthy."

Norman stared at me a moment, clearly puzzled, then Aunt Mairi suggested we take it to the altar. Once there, I took off my shawl, shook it out and laid it on the surface. Norman followed, placed the box reverently on the fabric, and looked for the latch. He gently opened it. Inside was an elaborate jeweled book.

Norman lifted the contents and laid the parts on the cloth. It was not a complete book, but one cover and several folios that clung steadfastly to it. The surface of the cover was thickly clad with more intricate designs fashioned of costly gold and silver plates embedded with precious and semiprecious stones. The trappings of our "treasure" were valuable beyond price.

The laird's hands trembled as he unfolded one of the parchment folios. Swirling luminous figures and imaginary beasts were captured in vibrant interlacing patterns on the fine vellum leaves. Latin phrases bound in Christian ornamentation carried and preserved the holy words written so long ago. Colors and designs leapt with preternatural freshness from the pages. After a moment he closed the leaves and replaced the vandalized book inside the cumdach, concealing the whole completely within my shawl.

A collective exhale broke the silence when it was covered, as though we all awoke from enchantment. Aunt Mairi said to us in a faint voice, "This is terrible…much worse than we were told."

"What is it," Malcolm asked.

"According to legend, it was made by the monks here at Iona, long ago" Aunt Mairi explained. "And the rest of it is reputed to be in Ireland. But I assumed they meant a cumdach with a holy relic like a saint's finger…not this!"

"And how did it end up here?" Malcolm asked her.

"Plunder, possibly. And there were other pieces with it such as the ring of Fortuna," said Mairi.

"But they saw themselves as the 'Protector of the Word' so perhaps there was a more benign motive," said Malcolm.

"Och, we may never know, but it can never be destroyed, sold, nor given away, without risking divine disapprobation," said Aunt Mairi.

"Nor can it be allowed to fall into the hands of evildoers," I added.

Then Malcolm cleared his throat and smiled. "But it could be re-united with its other half."

"Aye," Norman said with a hard nod. "And that other half apparently lies in the land of the Catholics, and I as a Protestant laird—"

Then my father called from the nave door. "The men are impatient, my laird."

Norman replied to him that we have finished and would invite them back in a moment. "Elspeth, put it in your medical bag. Hurry!" he commanded. "We will decide on its future later." Then he coughed twice and spit, the blood-stained saliva staining the grey floor. "Damned dust," he muttered. Malcolm noticed it too, his eyes glistened with sorrow.

* * *

The laird ordered the tomb stone replaced and sealed, with all signs of the intrusion cleared. We would try to leave no evidence of our sacrilege for other seekers to find. But when the men lowered it, a rope slipped, and the great slab cracked as it tilted and slammed against the base. It was a great tragedy, but the laird made the best of it, saying the crack would deter others, seeing that the tomb already had been plundered. Thereafter we worked in silence, wondering if what we had done had met with approval by our ancestors. It was dark when we were done.

Chapter 24: Malcolm

It has been a ruin for hundreds of years, and before that a thriving community of monks. But why they had settled here was not obvious, Iona being a small island off the south-west coast of Mull. It was bleak, windswept, and immensely isolated. Perhaps that was the point. Who else would wish to live here but men who wanted to be free of the temptations presented by life?

Then came the Vikings and their lust for wealth. The undefended abbeys were an easy target, starting with Lindisfarne on Holy Island and eventually Iona, where repeated attacks left life impoverished and untenable. At which point the monks left and never returned. Most educated Scots knew the history and of how clans coalesced around those Viking sea-lords and Celtic chieftains. Clan MacLeod was one, and in a bizarre twist of fate or will, Iona became the graveyard of many of them, the very place their ancestors had desecrated.

The gentle slope on the island's lea side sheltered the abbey and ruins. Among them was the graveyard filled with tombstones, many with carved reliefs of chieftains' past. It was a forlorn place. Made to glorify God and now a place of silent mouldering death. But at least it was peaceful, till we came and disturbed the grave of the first among them, the ugly man, Leod.

I was sitting on a tombstone, introspective, watching the men load the birlinns. The laird's boat would return to Dunvegan, and Wilson's to Glasgow. I watched as two gulls fought over a piece of oatcake someone had discarded. "*We are worse and fight over the most insignificant of things*," I mused.

Elspeth was beside me. "You need a haircut," she teased.

"Not another from you, I should hope," I answered. She was smiling in that inquisitive way she has with her patients, her cloak mottled with grime and her wee hands stained with soot, muck, and dust. She had the look of a rogue.

"Your speech sounds better. How do you feel?"

"Umm. I still have bouts of the shivers and my neck is still quite sore."

"Let me look."

I lowered my blanket; the chilly wind immediately inducing another bout of the shivers.

"I can see. It is very bruised. Is it tender in front?"

"Aye."

"You are lucky he didn't crush your windpipe."

"Aye, I was lucky, wasn't I? Lucky to have been in that boat with a madman and some witches trying to kill me." I tried to laugh but it came out as a hoarse cough. I spit up more phlegm from having my lungs washed with frigid seawater. "It was fortunate Wilson showed up or I would be a feast for gulls."

"And don't forget Gregor. 'Twas he who pulled you out of the water."

"I will remember to distrust him slightly less." I grinned at her.

We sat for a moment. She, studying my face for more signs of illness, me wondering how this would end. "You will be well again soon Malcolm," she stated her verdict with absolute certainty.

"And you, dear friend. Will you be well soon?"

She shrugged and turned her head away so I would not see her eyes glisten. With a finger I turned her chin back to me. "You can cry with me," I whispered to her.

"Nay," she sniffled. "I will wait till we can mourn properly. You know how I am."

"I understand. Remember the smallpox epidemic?"

She nodded then looked up from her lap.

"At night when I was alone, I shed a few tears in my whisky. That also was a sad time."

"Especially Doctor Young," she said quietly.

"Aye, especially him...he was the best of us...as you will remember Rhona, Erika and Cawdie."

Elspeth leaned into me. Her arm went round my waist. "You know the worst of it was that we grew up with Una...and I never suspecting her feelings."

"She was indeed the worst of hags if anyone was, all those years driven by hatred and revenge. But I suppose Doideag and Gormal were not much better. Between them many were harmed, and for naught."

"Such suffering, such grief. But now 'tis done." Elspeth sat up straight, then said in a determined voice, "We look like drovers after a season on the trail. The women need a good cleaning, or no one will want to dance with us at tonight's ceilidh."

I chuckled hoarsely, again noticing the stains on her brown cloak and green arisaid. "The men are no better I assure you, and it's unlikely we will bathe before returning home. In my case, not before I'm certain the water will be steaming hot."

"All the women will be thrilled to dance with you Malcolm." Elspeth laughed.

We sat together quietly. It had been said and done. She sighed, made her apologies, and trotted off in the direction of Lady Myreton who was frantically pulling clothes from her travel bags.

* * *

The abbey ruins were even more lovely when lit by our driftwood fire set outside the main door arch among the broken Celtic crosses. Someone had the foresight to have stowed a barrel of whisky for our farewell party and all were enjoying liberal quantities quaffed from their favourite mug. Too, the whisky was required because our feast included a pot of gull stew which made my guts clench when I smelt it. *Must've included too many feathers and droppings*, I thought on hearing how the poor birds had been netted while roosting. The whisky also had been useful in dulling senses irritated by badly played bagpipes.

Despite my pensive mood and lack of appreciation of the local cuisine and music, I was determined to enjoy my final night in the Highlands. Lady Myreton was the first to accept my invitation to dance. She had replaced her practical hunter plaid with a gloriously tight, red silk dress with black slippers. Her face was accented with rouge and kohl, and scalp encased in a curly white wig which would have seemed extravagant in any royal court. When asked, she told me that it was the wig she had been searching for earlier, since wearing that dress without a proper wig would have been obscene, according to her. But she could have worn anything or nothing at all by the looks on the many lustful faces as they watched her dance with me.

"I am sorry about Robert," I said automatically as I took her delicate hands in mine.

"I should hope not," she replied. "He was here to kill us. Make no mistake, his heart was as dark as a lump of coal, and nothing could be done about it."

"There is always a path to redemption," said I, thinking of Father Hammett at Torrport.

"Perhaps...at least that is what they tell us. In his case, he had many opportunities to change but preferred the life of a brigand. You know I often saw blood on his clothing and wondered. When asked, he would laugh and say it was from a fowl he shot with his bow."

"But he knew Elspeth was coming to Skye."

"Aye. Their plan was to poison their sickly chieftain, dispatch Anne and the children, and replace them with Ranuff and his bride of choice. He fancied Elspeth's sister, and the treasure was to be a reward for efforts."

"And then we scotched it."

I held her impossibly narrow waist and gave her a twirl. Her dress flew up revealing well-turned ankles and calves. Some men clapped and hooted. She giggled. Once back in my arms she said, "You did indeed turn their plan on it's head."

"It was not intentional."

"You were called by the spirits at the right time. And don't roll your eyes at me!"

"I will refrain if you tell me how you and Robert became involved in this Highland tragedy."

"Oh, that part does not involve magic," she laughed lightly. "When Una started poisoning the laird after he returned from Torrport last summer, they worried Elspeth and especially Cawdie would return to Skye. So, they put out a contract on their lives and assumed they were doomed as soon as they bought those stagecoach tickets."

"Let me guess…heard this before…the ticket agent marked the carriage."

Lady Myreton nodded. "But I suspect it was chance that Robert was out hunting with his mates that day and saw an opportunity for loot. But then again, he knew Ranuff from school. I suppose we will never know how it came about."

"Good thing Robert was not a good shot on horseback."

"But Elspeth had Fortuna with her, didn't she?"

I gave her a mocking glare.

"Alright, I will stick with the facts. Mairi, and I were friends and she asked me to come to Dunvegan, I think right after Elspeth requested your help. I told Robert I was leaving, of course, and instead of staying at Corstorphine and playing the laird's good son, he decided to follow me and try his luck."

"And we know how that turned out."

"He chose his path, Malcolm, as do we each day."

I could feel her beginning to tire, her feet finding little purchase and requiring immediate rescue on my arm. Or perhaps that was intended. Women can be cunning. "We'll leave in the morning," I said after I steadied her once more.

She pressed close and whispered, "Will you escort me home to Corstorphine?"

"Aye, I'll drop you at your door."

She put on a pouty face. "Well, that is a start. Now leave me. I have other men who need a flirt."

I bowed and kissed her hand, then went to see the laird who was deep in discussion with Murdoch. They were parked on what was left of a wall that was once part of the abbey. "Don't know about you two but I've had my fill of desolate," I said with a grunt as the stone proved as uncomfortable as it looked.

"Och, you Lowlanders. Stay a while longer. 'Tis good for the constitution," Murdoch said, without sarcasm.

"Nay I must return home. My family needs me. Brother George heads back to the continent early in the new year and tradition requires we have a few more decent fights before he leaves."

"And your father wants a report on the doings of Clan MacLeod," Norman said with a relaxed smile.

"That too," I chuckled.

"Murdoch and I have been discussing it. You can tell your dear father that I am a man of my word and Clan MacLeod will stay out of any conflicts with the crown, and that our family will leave for Inverness in the spring to stay with Anne's parents. We need a break from Dunvegan, at least a temporary one."

"And Elspeth will go with them to see to their health," Murdoch added.

"Does she know?" I asked.

"Aye, she agreed today. Janet and Solas will accompany her too," Norman explained.

"Then it's settled," said I, hiding my disappointment.

"It is," Norman repeated and looked at me. "Only till we are settled, Malcolm. Then she is free to do as she pleases."

I bowed my head in acknowledgment.

"Meanwhile as soon as we get back to Dunvegan, a new factor must be hired to manage the estate. And Murdoch will finish training the men. We have much to do before spring."

I listened to them discuss the details. My eyes were on others. Mairi had consumed much whisky and was entertaining a cluster of the older men with ribald poems and tales of witchery. Everyone was smiling and laughing. It was good to see. Then Mairi noticed me watching. Her face froze in mid-laugh. She seemed to stop breathing, her arm levitated to point at something above me. I looked up but could see nothing but blackness. My eyes went back to Mairi. She wore a grimace of horror, then suddenly pulled her cloak over her head, and leaned closer to Elspeth who also was staring at a place above my head. I glanced up again but could see nothing. However, I did notice a feeling of lightness and my inner gloom dissipating. I wanted to laugh. So, I did. My head tilted up, mouth opened wide, and an astonishing string of cackles, hoots and screeches flowed forth as the others watched in amazement. It was over in seconds and when gaze met earth, it fell on Elspeth whose hands covered her face in a look of stunned shock. I smiled at her. She self-consciously dropped her hands and smiled back but I noticed her eyes look up a few times to that spot above my head.

Gregor's expression did not change but he moved closer to Elspeth, his eyes challenging mine in that gesture of protection and ownership men use. He was just doing his job, but I went from ecstatic to annoyed in an instant. I think I just did not like his presumption, but even more her apparent acceptance of it. I looked away. She could have at least been honest about her intentions. Proving myself a fool when it comes to women, I strode over to the pair and held out my hand to her. "We need to talk. It may be our last time," I commanded.

Gregor stared at me as though calculating his moves, his black eyes reflecting hot intelligence in the firelight. Elspeth took my hand and I lead her into the nave of the abbey, lit only by the fire outside. I was about to ask of her intentions when she blurted, "Malcolm, I saw him! We all did when you laughed as one mad."

"What do you mean? Saw whom?"

"A man, rising from you…from your head. He was a sea captain of old… like the paintings in Edinburgh. Methinks 'twas Captain Forrester."

I snorted. "You've been drinking too much."

"Nay. You know me better than that."

"Then it was an apparition made of firelight and mist."

She turned away, pulling her cape in. "Must you always land on science and reason. There are things beyond your ken."

"Agreed, but I did not bring you here to discuss your imaginings but our reality. Look at me, please." I said, taking her elbow and turning her gently, her green eyes black in the red firelight. A sudden irrational fear made me pull her closer. I whispered, "We part on the morrow. I may never see you again."

She loosened my grip, taking a step back. "Malcolm please, I beg you. Let us part as good friends. I have had too many decisions thrust on me, and worse, made for me recently."

"I see. Then it is settled."

"Nothing is settled. I will stay at Dunvegan till spring then accompany the laird and his family to Inverness. Once they are safe, I can go."

"To where?"

"I know not, but it will be with Janet and Solas. I must think of them as well."

I considered it a moment, the growing silence separating us the more. "And Gregor?" I asked, finally.

"He is a friend, like you."

"Nothing more?"

"Sir Ross loaned Gregor to us as protection when we travel."

"And hence his attitude?"

"Malcolm, sometimes your understanding of women fails you. Can you not see I have no room in my heart for anything but grief? And it will be so for a long while. I have lost my sister and my guardian...to evil...and...and I fear that you and others have been permanently harmed in this madness. So please do not push me to make decisions. None but those necessary or forced on me will be forthcoming."

The darkness concealed our feelings. We could only speak and listen. I thought I understood her frustration and perhaps inner anger, but then I am not adept at interpreting the noises of women, as she had reminded me often enough. "I owe you much money," was all I could think to say.

"I may need it, should we meet again," she replied, sounding weary of the night and perhaps of me as well.

"I will put it in a bank in Edinburgh for you."

Elspeth sighed. "More than coin, we need healing. I am so sorry for us Malcolm. We...I have abused you. Inviting you here was my mistake and I apologize."

"Nay, this was unfinished business, for us all."

"I suppose."

"I may look like a ruin, but strangely, I feel optimistic of the future."

"You do?" she said incredulously.

"Indeed, I do. You may not have noticed but I haven't killed anyone in a while."

Elspeth chuckled, "Now that *is* something!"

"It is. You know I hate and fear that part of myself. Now I think I may be able to control it."

"I am proud of you Malcolm. Now mayhap you will not only be a competent but a genuinely compassionate doctor."

I was not sure if she was teasing, but there was truth in what she said. "Thank you, my friend. Perhaps someday I will measure up to your exalted standards."

We both laughed.

"'Tis late, and we are exhausted," she said, tactfully trying to end our meeting.

"Then let me return you to Gregor, your new love."

"Stop it," she scolded.

I imagined her grinning in the dark as we left the kirk.

* * *

The morning was fresh and should have been cheerful but for our whisky clouded minds and sour stomachs that followed last evening's ceilidh which had ended with the predictable stumbling and retching. I decided to return to my spot by the fire, wrapped in cloak and blanket, nursing my fragile body.

"And what of the treasure?" I asked Norman as he dressed. "Any decision?"

"I will decide in time. Meanwhile 'tis under my protection."

"Hmm. Well, you know how I feel."

Norman chuckled. "I do indeed. At least now it is thought lost with only the four of us knowing the truth of it."

"Aye, but Mairi told me last night that she and Elspeth will put a spell of forgetfulness on me once they reach Dunvegan, so that leaves three."

"And Mairi is old, and I am dying," Norman whispered.

"So, that leaves Elspeth," I whispered back.

Norman looked at me, no more than that, his eyes connecting with mine when he said, "There could be worse fates. She is stronger than the lot of us."

I touched his elbow and sincerely wished him well. He reciprocated. And I knew I would never forget him. I said my goodbyes to the others. Aunt Mairi looking ready for another adventure and Murdoch who appeared heartier than warranted.

"Take care of the laird and Elspeth," I said, needlessly.

Murdoch grunted.

"And yourself, of course," I added. I still did not know what to make of him, even after all we had been through together. We stood awkwardly facing each other for a moment, then he leaned toward me and whispered, "Ah don't like that ugly Russian me foolish daughter fancies."

"Nor I. At least we have that in common."

Murdoch grunted again then strode off, grumbling under his breath toward Elspeth who was climbing the ramp to the birlinn, guided by that same ugly Russian. My eyes followed them. Emotions sunk in regret, and I realized I would miss her greatly. And as though she heard me thinking, she turned to look back. Her eyes met mine and she stuck out her tongue like a child on a frolic. I returned the rude salute. I waited for them to push off and turn the birlinn north to Skye before I took Lady Myreton's arm. "I will miss them too," she whispered.

Next day, Captain Wilson arrived. I took Lady Myreton to her seat under the canopy. Moments later we were loaded and the men ready at their oars, many speaking of returning home. I caught the captain's eye and said, "'Tis a fine day to sail. Let us pray it remains so." Then I laughed as I realized I had been touching Fortuna.

~The End~

Epilogue

Norman MacLeod of MacLeod, 20th Chief of Clan MacLeod died in 1706 and is buried in the Chapel Yard at Inverness. He was succeeded by his infant son, John, who died in October of that same year. Norman's youngest son Norman became chief, a position he held for sixty-six years. Lady Anne remarried in 1708.

As for Elspeth and Malcolm, that is a story for another day.

About the Author

Bettyanne Twigg (co-author)

Bettyanne Twigg was an objects curator conservator who has written and lectured internationally on historic preservation. Her alter ego "Elspeth" was a craft designer and miniaturist. She brought her love of research and history to her books. She and her husband, Homer, lived in the mountains of Maryland, with their dog, Pepper and sundry feral cats.

Albert Marsolais (co-author)

Albert is a retired scientist and businessman who worked in the field of genetics and biotechnology. He lives in Ontario, Canada with his wife Laurel.

You can connect with me on:

- https://marsolaistwigg.com
- https://www.facebook.com/marsolaistwigg

Also by Bettyanne Twigg & Albert Marsolais

The Convenient
"a most accomplished work in a league of its own."
-Reviewed by K.C. Finn for Readers' Favorite

An historical thriller of doctors, disease epidemics, murder, and political intrigue...

Malcolm Forrester a physician from Edinburgh, and Elspeth MacLeod, a healer from the Isle of Skye, were both educated in European universities, but only men are permitted to practice medicine in the Scotland of 1705. The two collide in Torrport, a small town near Edinburgh. Elspeth stubbornly seeking recognition as a physician, and Malcolm searching for a cure for smallpox amid the swirling vortex of war, politics, religion and disease. Poverty and misadventure are ever-present, and medicine a curious blend of old beliefs and new discoveries. Elspeth delivers a beautiful young woman of her bastard child and suspects she was poisoned. When the Laird's Second-in-Command is found dead, kneeling face-down in a tub at the laundry, the two find themselves entangled in murder, smuggling, and espionage, amid powerful opposition that resists change.

Manufactured by Amazon.ca
Bolton, ON